Collision

CARRIE LEIGHTON

sourcebooks
casablanca

This work has been translated with the contribution of the Centre
for Books and Reading of the Italian Ministry of Culture.

Originally published as *Better. Collisione*, © Adriano Salani Editore s.u.r.l. Milano,
Gruppo editoriale Mauri Spagnol, 2022. Translated from Italian by Nicole M. Taylor.

Published by Sourcebooks Casablanca, an imprint of Sourcebooks
P.O. Box 4410, Naperville, Illinois 60567–4410
(630) 961-3900
sourcebooks.com

Originally published as *Better. Collisione* in 2022 in Italy by Adriano Salani
Editore s.u.r.l. Milano, an imprint of Gruppo editoriale Mauri Spagnol.

Cataloging-in-Publication Data is on file with the Library of Congress.

Printed and bound in the United States of America.
VP 10 9 8 7 6 5 4 3 2 1

*I'm writing about a mistaken love. A pain you never
get over. The kind that changes you forever.*

*I'm writing about a love that fills you and drains you. A love that,
even in adversity, helps you to realize what you really deserve.*

*We all have unfinished business with the wounds of our
soul. This is how I healed mine: writing about them.*

Dear readers, our journey begins here.

Prologue

I COME FROM A REGULAR family.

My father was an honest worker, my mother a dissatisfied house-wife. As for me... To tell the truth, I never quite knew how to define myself.

Most of the time, I had a clear sense that life was passing me by; I was too busy looking at it to actually live it. I hid behind the printed page, daydreaming of love.

Romantic, I know, but "romantic" is practically my middle name.

I spent entire days reading, wondering when it would be my turn and what it would be like. I imagined love as harmonious as a symphony. Light as the flutter of a butterfly's wings. Gentle as a feather swaying in the wind.

That's how I pictured it: easy, pure, romantic. Because that's how it's supposed to be.

But I was wrong.

For me, love turned out to be none of that.

From the first time he touched me, it was the twang of an electric guitar. An onslaught like a hurricane.

A soul's fate sealed by its collision with another.

Because the truth is, nothing could have prepared me for this.

Because when you meet someone for the first time, you don't know it...

You don't know the impact they'll have on your life.

You don't know the power they'll have over you.

You don't know that every particle of your body will change, and that after, you'll never be the same.

PART ONE

One

CORVALLIS IN THE FALL HAS a special charm. With its little houses, parks, and dense forests all around, it looks like one of those enchanted snow globe landscapes that I used to collect when I was a little girl. The arrival of the first storms makes everything even more magical. Just like now, with the rain pounding violently on the asphalt, the rustling of the leaves in the wind, and the smell of the wet streets. There's no better awakening in the world, to me.

The peace doesn't last long, though, because the blaring sound of the alarm clock reminds me that today is the first day of my sophomore year at Oregon State University. Needless to say, I wish I could keep curled up under the covers a little longer, but after the third beep, Nirvana's "Breed" comes on at full blast, practically giving me a heart attack. I reach over to the nightstand next to the bed, groping for the phone, as Kurt Cobain's voice fills the room. When I finally get ahold of it, I turn off the alarm, pull up my green frog sleep mask, and force myself to open my eyes.

Clutching the phone in my hands, I give in to the urge to check for a message or call from Travis. Nothing. I should be used to it, but it's still a disappointment every time. That's how it always is with him: after every quarrel he goes off the radar for entire days, demonstrating time and time again how little he cares about salvaging our relationship, now on its last legs.

Is it possible to be exhausted before your day even begins?

Reluctantly, I pull myself out of bed and step into my fuzzy unicorn slippers. I gather my messy hair into a loose bun, throw on my fleece robe and inhale the intoxicating perfume of fresh laundry, and walk over to the window in front of the bed. I pull back the curtain, rest my head on the cold glass, and let my gaze wander over the garden path wet with rain.

Travis takes it for granted that I'll be the one to make the first move. But this time I have no intention of breaking the silence, not after what he did. Seeing an Instagram story with my own boyfriend falling-down drunk, dancing and grinding on a bar with two random girls, while I was at home all by myself in bed with the flu, is a kind of pain I wouldn't wish on anyone. When I called him furious and looking for an explanation, he dismissed me with his usual "Vanessa, you're overreacting," and wisely decided to hang up and not call back again. I spent the entire weekend holed up at home, depressed, drinking ginger tea to soothe my sore throat, reading and organizing books and notebooks to get ready for the first day back at college. But not even FaceTiming with Tiffany and Alex, my best friends in the world, was able to completely erase the memory of that video and the humiliation of being disrespected like that by Travis for the umpteenth time.

The situation has become so consuming that I don't even have the strength to cry anymore. Which is strange, because for as long as I can remember, the only thing I can manage to do when I'm overwhelmed by emotion is cry. In a burst of frustration, I hurl the phone on the bed, massage my face, and compel myself to think of something, anything else, because the alternative is giving me a headache. I'd better start getting ready, I have a long day ahead of me.

After a quick shower, I go back to my bedroom to get dressed, and even though I know it's stupid, I take another little peek at the phone. But once again, no calls and no messages. An unhealthy desire to call him and shower him with insults starts welling up inside of me.

"Nessy, are you up?" My mother's shrill voice snaps me out of those thoughts, along with the smell of hot coffee wafting through the house. It's a little like walking a tightrope between hell and heaven.

"Yeah, I'm up," I respond hoarsely, lifting a hand to my aching throat. The cold from the last few days totally wiped me out.

"Come down, breakfast is ready!"

I let out a big sigh, and still wrapped in my robe and with my hair wet, I head downstairs, hoping I'll be able to camouflage my awful mood. The last thing I need is to be subjected to one of Mom's never-ending lectures where she repeats that I've got to hold on to this one because he's from a good family. Who cares about his mistakes and my suffering—the love my mother harbors for Travis's family fortune is even bigger than the love she has for her daughter. When, two years ago, she found out that I was in a relationship with the scion of an oil company executive, to her it was like winning the lottery.

When I arrive in the kitchen, I find her already ready for the day: a perfectly arranged blond chignon, elegant white palazzo pants, a Tiffany blue button-down, and impeccable makeup, with mascara emphasizing her blue eyes and a light layer of red lipstick on her thin lips. Her innate class always manages to undermine my already scarce self-esteem.

Before I can even say "good morning," she comes at me with a barrage of unsolicited information.

"I left some bills and the checkbook on the entry table; it would be great if you could take care of them today." A little frenetic, she darts over to the coffee maker and pours two cups without interrupting my to-do list. "You have to pick up the dry cleaning, grab something for dinner, and, oh, before I forget," she says, handing me a mug—I listen to her go on, trusting in the coffee's increasing effect—"Mrs. Williams went out of town and asked me to take care of her chihuahua. I told her you would be happy to."

All these orders first thing in the morning put me even more on edge than I already am.

"Need me to do anything else? Maybe mow the lawn? Go see if any of the neighbors need help? Organize a get-together for the homeowners' association?" I look at her sideways, set my phone on the counter, and sit down at the table.

"You know Mrs. Williams doesn't have anyone else she can count on. I couldn't say no to her—how would that look?" She brought her mug to her lips, and after taking a sip, went on: "And I thought you'd be happy to take care of that little mutt. You love animals."

"Yeah, but that doesn't mean I have the time or desire to do it right now."

"Neither do I," she retorted, oblivious. "When I took this legal secretary job, I didn't know it was going to suck the life out of me. But someone's got to bring home the bacon."

I look at her, suddenly mortified. I'm well aware that since Dad left three years ago, Mom has had to cover all our expenses. I admire her for it, but she forgets that I have a life too and I can't live it as a division of hers.

"You're right, I'm sorry." I get up and take a box of granola cereal from the pantry and pour some into a bowl. "Taking care of Mrs. Williams's dog won't be a problem. I can take him on a walk before I leave for campus and when I get back. I'll take care of everything, don't worry," I reassure her conciliatorily.

"That's what I like to hear." She pats me on the shoulder, her fingernails perfectly manicured, pale pink. "And please, at least for the first day, try to look a little bit put together."

She drains her mug and waves goodbye unceremoniously with a promise to be back for dinner. I stay in the kitchen to have a little breakfast. I pour some milk over the granola and go sit at the table. After a moment, the phone lights up on the counter: a new message notification. Dropping my spoon into my bowl, I leap up like an idiot to see who it is, tripping on the kitchen mat with granola stuck to my lip.

I'm so pathetic I deserve to fall face down on the floor. Maybe a good knock on the head is just what I need.

When I realize that the sender is Tiffany, my best friend and my boyfriend's twin sister, I sink into disappointment once again.

I was really hoping to see Travis's name on the screen, but evidently the end of the world is a likelier event.

Hey nerd. Your life's purpose resumes today.

Yeah, I was so excited I didn't get a wink of sleep, I reply wryly.

I'm sure. Listen, I wanted to ask you, practice starts tonight, do you want to come with me?

My eyebrows furrow as I read and reread the message, not understanding. Since when does Tiffany care about sports? Her only interests are the latest trends in fashion and makeup, her weekly salon appointment, and her beloved true crime podcasts. She would never want to waste her time watching some dumb practice basketball game.

Then I realize it's not Tiffany asking me, but Travis, in a despicable attempt to extort information via his sister. What a coward! First, he falls off the face of the earth for two days, abandoning me to total self-pity without even claiming some far-fetched excuse that in all likelihood I would have bought or pretended to. Then he uses my best friend to get to me.

Annoyed, I reply: Tell your brother if he wants to ask me something, he'll have to make the effort to do it in person.

Her reply came immediately: He made me, I didn't want to. You know I'm on your side. I'm coming to get you; we can head to campus together. Be outside at 8. Love you.

I knew it was him. Infuriating! I throw the phone on the table. He made me lose my appetite. I rinse out my mug and bowl and go up to my room. I open my closet, and for a second, I entertain the idea of listening to my mother and wearing something cuter than my usual jeans and monochrome hoodie. I try on a white peasant top with lace trim. It's nice, but looking at myself in the mirror, I notice it reveals too much of my abundant chest. If I wear this, everyone's eyes will be on me, which is precisely what I try to avoid.

I hang the top back up in my closet, concluding that my usual anonymous look isn't so bad after all. I pull on dark blue jeans, slim fitting and high-waisted, and a white sweatshirt that hangs past my bottom—that's more like it. After drying my hair and putting it up in a high ponytail to tame the frizz, I grab my bag and slide in *Sense and Sensibility*, one of my favorite books; reading it between classes will help distract me.

Before leaving the house, however, I glance at myself in the mirror and instantly regret it. The image I see reflected is not pleasant: I'm pale, two violet bags weigh down my bloodshot gray eyes, and my raven black hair is begging for mercy. I let it down and smooth it a little, but the situation doesn't improve. I throw in the towel and, armed with my umbrella, go out before I lose my mind.

Two

AT EIGHT ON THE DOT, Tiffany pulls up in her fire-engine-red Mustang. I tell her to wait for a minute while I drop off Charlie, the neighbor's dog.

When I get in the car, the scent of fresh flowers crashes over me like a wave—my best friend's signature scent. With her wavy copper bob and hazel eyes framed by a thick coat of mascara, she stares at me warily in all her ethereal beauty.

"So…" she says, tapping her fingers on the steering wheel. "How are you? Are you over your cold?" she asks, testing the waters hesitantly. I know she's worried I'm mad at her for going along with Travis's little ruse. But she shouldn't. It's not her fault. He's her brother. In her place, I would've done the same thing.

"I could be better," I admit, clicking my seat belt into place. "I'm not totally over the flu, and I have a terrible headache."

"Did you take anything? I have Advil in my purse—do you want some?"

"No, don't worry about it. It'll get better," I reply, massaging my temples to alleviate the pain.

"Right, I forgot, your mother taught you to be scared of medicine. Well, if you change your mind, it's there." She points to the bag on the seat behind her, turns the key in the engine, and drives off. Once my little street is behind us, she decides to tackle the subject head-on.

"I wanted to tell you I'm sorry about this morning. I didn't mean to interfere. I shouldn't have, especially after what he did to you, but Travis was so insistent eventually I gave in!" she confesses, looking up toward the sky.

"Don't apologize. You didn't do anything wrong. He's an idiot," I reply, switching on the radio.

"That's for sure." My friend turns the music up. Without speaking, we zoom over to campus, passing by stately homes and neatly land-scaped gardens veiled by the gray mid-September mist. During the trip, despite her trying to be subtle, I can feel her eyes on me.

As we reach campus, the drizzle stops. She pulls into a spot in the student parking lot, but before I can reach for the door handle, Tiffany circles back: "Listen, you know I try not to come between you two, but as a friend, I have to ask: Are you sure this relationship is working? I mean, it's been over a year, and Travis walks all over you. He knows he can screw up because you never do anything. I don't know why you let him!"

"I know, Tiff, I know." I look down at my hands, folded in my lap, and shrug. "I know the best decision would be to end it. What can I say?" I look up at her, ashamed. "I can't…at least, not yet."

Tiffany shakes her head in resignation, moistens her full lips, and stares out through the windshield. "You're too much for my brother, and everyone sees it but you."

"You know what?" I ask, slapping my thighs, determined to defuse the tension and put an end to the discussion. "We're starting our soph-omore year, I'm really excited about my classes, and I have no intention of letting Travis ruin my day. So enough with the lecture." And with that, I jump out of the car before she can respond.

"Don't you realize that trying to avoid a situation you'll have to deal with sooner or later won't solve the problem?" she retorts, catch-ing up with me.

"Exactly. Sooner or later," I say, adjusting my bag on my shoulder.

Tiffany rolls her eyes at me but doesn't reply, and I silently thank her. Side by side, we walk toward the redbrick buildings, surrounded by shrubs and trees that in this season begin turning rich shades of orange and yellow.

"Gotta go, babe," she exclaims, after glancing at her thin wrist-watch. "I have an advising meeting in ten minutes. I'll catch up with you later, okay?"

"Sure, later." She gives me a big hug goodbye, and I watch her head into the sociology building.

Alone, I contentedly observe the scene, which is the same as every year: parents more enthusiastic than their kids, bags from Target with decor to liven up dorm rooms, seniors resigned to the confusion that recurs every fall because this one is their last.

Whereas for me, not so long ago I was an incoming freshman. I remember my mother cried like a baby that first day and took pictures of me in every corner of campus which she then sent to all her friends and relatives. This year, I had to forgo on-campus housing because we couldn't afford the extra fees, but it doesn't really bother me. Luckily, we live in town. And although Mom usually takes our only car, I always manage to find a ride.

I look around, a little anxious—in crowded places I always feel like everyone is looking at me, even though I know they're not.

I still remember the trauma of middle school, when on the first day, teachers would do icebreakers where we had to say something about ourselves. As my turn got closer, my panic grew. I would practice my lines in my head over and over: "Hi everyone. My name is Vanessa Clark. I live with my mom and dad. I hate nuts in cookies and pickles in hamburgers."

While that insecurity has lingered in the back of my mind, I over-came most of my shyness growing up. Partly out of pure survival instinct, partly due to my friend Alex.

Alex and I have known each other since elementary school. On the first day of first grade, I sat in the back, as close as I could get to the wall. I stared intently out the window to avoid talking to the other kids. My tactic was working until a boy with big eyes and brown curls took it upon himself to sit down beside me, waiting until I, timidly, turned to look at him. He offered me a piece of candy; I broke into a smile and took it without a word. That boy was Alexander Smith, and for thirteen years, he has patiently put up with all my obsessions, paranoias, and insecurities. He has been by my side for every important event in my life.

He was there when, at the age of nine, I had to get braces and refused to speak, smile, or laugh in front of anybody. He was there when, at thirteen, I dyed my hair green out of a desire to rebel and regretted it immediately. He was there when, in sophomore year of high school, I had a massive crush on Easton Hill. Oh, Easton... He was wild. Too bad he scammed me: he pretended to like me back just to make Amanda Jones, the prom queen, jealous.

It was a low blow, but Alex knew how to cheer me up: he came over to my house, ordered mountains of Chinese food, and we had a *Vampire Diaries* marathon. We repeated this routine for two more days, and on the third I was as good as new. Easton, Amanda, and the whole story were behind me.

Alex was there when my father left, but in that situation, he knew the best thing to do was say nothing.

He was there when Travis Baker burst into my life, bringing light where my father had taken it away. Alex and Travis were never tight, but in the early days they had a functional friendship. At least until Alex started pointing out all of Travis's failings.

Speak of the devil—I feel the phone vibrating in my pocket, and it's Alex, saying he's having car trouble and won't be able to make it in time for our usual 8:30 coffee. I tell him not to worry about it and head for the Memorial Union with a big smile stamped on my face, savoring the scent of wet grass, happy to be back in my favorite place in the world.

Once in the lounge, I sit down on a brown leather sofa and pull *Sense and Sensibility* out of my bag; I have some time before my first class. I love arriving early and spending a little time alone enjoying the atmosphere of new beginnings.

But I don't get the chance to read a single page. I look up, and there he is, standing in line for coffee. Travis, with his perfectly gelled auburn hair, open jean jacket, and olive-green messenger bag. I'm surprised because he's not usually on this part of campus. We go to the same school, but we have different majors, and he spends most of his time in the economics building or holed up in the gym. I, on the other hand, am usually in the liberal arts building or hunkering down in the library. The only time we cross paths is for lunch or at the end of the day.

The sight of him ties my stomach in knots. Instantaneously, the images of him hanging on those two girls pop into my head. Their bodies against each other, that feeling of betrayal and embarrassment. Angrily, I snap the book shut, sending a few strands of my long hair flying. I leap up and march straight for him. I plant myself right in front of him, arms folded, trying to ignore the barista's dismayed look. Enough nice-girl Vanessa; I feel the need to make a scene. I summon all my self-control, though, because we're in a public place. I shoot daggers at him with my gaze. His hazel eyes look back with astonishment and a dash of guilt. "Are you at least going to explain yourself?" I ask, sounding more upset than I wanted.

Travis looks around uncomfortably. "Not here, please."

"I don't hear from you for two days and then out of the blue this morning you ask me to come to practice! Oh, wait, actually, you have your sister do it for you! You owe me an explanation at the very least!" I growl through clenched teeth, surprised at myself.

Travis takes me by the arm and pulls me into a corner away from the curious onlookers starting to take notice of us.

"I know I messed up, but I was drunk…"

"Don't you dare. That's no excuse!" I break in, enraged.

"I didn't do anything more than what you saw," he says in self-defense.

"Is that supposed to make me feel better? Do you have any idea how that made me feel? You disrespected me, humiliated me in front of all your friends. You don't care about me at all!" I shout, my eyes starting to tingle.

"Don't say that. Look, we were just having fun. Maybe it got a little out of hand, but I didn't do anything. I would never do that to you, you know that." He reaches for me, but I dodge his hand, determined not to give in. I'm fed up. Fed up with his attitude, acting like nothing is a big deal, not even if it hurts me.

"I didn't hear from you for two days," I repeat, my voice heavy with disappointment. "Two whole days, and all that time you didn't think to check in on me even once."

His face fell. "I laid low because I thought it would give you time to calm down… I guess I was wrong. I'm sorry you saw that video, and I'm sorry I hurt you."

He seems sincere, but part of me knows it's just another excuse to pacify me. I look him in the eye and take a deep breath. "I've forgiven your mistakes too many times," I say in one breath, before I lose my courage. "And maybe that was my mistake. Forgive, forgive, forgive. Why should we even be together if all it takes for you to try hooking up with other girls is one drink too many?"

I can tell by his alarmed look that I've caught him off guard.

"Listen." He steps up to me and takes my face in his hands. "We might be in a rough patch, but we can get through it."

"What if I don't want to?" My heart is pounding in my chest, and there's a knot in my throat. "What if I don't want to get through it?"

A look of bewilderment flashes on his face, and for a moment I wish I could take back what I just said. Travis shakes his head. "Don't say that. You know that would be a mistake you would regret. We both would," he adds. "You're important to me, this relationship is important to me, and I'm ready to do whatever it takes to show you."

"Sometimes I think you just say that because you're trying to convince yourself it's true, but it's not really what you want."

I wonder if this isn't what really keeps us together—knowing that by ourselves we would feel lost. Do we stay together because we're too afraid to be alone? My God, how sad.

Travis rests his forehead on mine and brushes his nose across mine. "Give me a chance to prove you wrong," he pleads, and I realize I'm already letting his words shake my determination. He must have sensed my submission, because he cautiously presses his lips on mine, inviting me to reciprocate. I don't right away, but for some damn reason I eventually yield to his kiss.

That's how it always goes with us. But this time, even though I'm not ready to say it out loud, I can feel that something has changed inside me.

"You probably won't believe me, but I've missed you these last two days," he murmurs against my lips.

I let out a sardonic laugh. If he'd been missing me, he would've come looking for me. "You're right. I don't believe you," I reply bluntly.

"I mean it. In fact, I brought you a little surprise to make it up to you."

"What?" I ask skeptically.

"Guess who got you two tickets to the Harry Styles concert in Portland next Sunday?"

My face lights up, and it's all I can do to hold back my excitement; I don't want to let him off that easy.

"It's a nice gesture, really, but it takes more than concert tickets to make up for what you did."

"I know," he says, stroking my cheek and tucking a lock of hair behind my ear. "But I wanted to show you that I was thinking about you. Why don't we leave it at that and go enjoy the rest of the day? We shouldn't let this ruin our mood."

"You always get what you want." I give in to his request with a resigned sigh. Travis beams at me with the face of an angel, which doesn't suit him at all, and wraps his arm around my shoulder. We go back to the counter and order two coffees. The barista gives us a weird look, but I ignore it. Did she hear the whole thing? How embarrassing.

"So, you'll be there?" he asks, lifting the paper cup to his mouth.

"Where?"

"At practice. You know it's important to me for you to be there."

Practice bores me to death—I would rather climb Mount Everest with a pile of bricks on my back—but I can't bring myself to tell him no, even though he deserves it.

"All right," I reply, looking at the time on the phone. "I have my first class in ten minutes. You should get to Economics if you don't want to be late."

He smiles, kisses me, and pulls me close. "In front of the Dixon at five, okay?"

I nod without showing any enthusiasm, and we part.

Three

I'VE BEEN ONE OF THE first people to enter the classroom for as long as I can remember.

I let my gaze wander over the vacant chairs and opt for the first row. Maybe I'm a nerd, but I love listening to lectures without being disturbed.

Within a few minutes, the classroom fills up with students, and a guy comes over to me. It's not just any guy, it's Thomas Collins. I don't know him well, but I know that he moved to Corvallis last summer. He's a sophomore like me and plays on the basketball team with Travis. I've seen him several times at practice and during games. I have to admit, he really is talented, except he walks the university halls as if he owns the place. The guys respect him; no one openly dares to go against him. As for the girls, he loves to reap victims, fully aware of his powers of attraction.

There's bad blood between him and my boyfriend. Travis considers him a rank asshole—ironic coming from him—and more than once during the past academic year, he warned me about Thomas's reputation. Not that I needed his advice; on campus, I just take my classes and try to stay out of the spotlight. Despite the fact that I'm the girlfriend of the captain of the basketball team, no one bothers me. In any case, I don't need any more arrogant and conceited guys in my life, so I keep far away from Thomas.

But apparently that's going to be impossible today. Despite all the empty seats, Thomas decides to sit right next to me. But it's odd—last year he never even deigned to say hello, and he certainly doesn't seem like the front-row type.

For a moment I consider moving, but I have no intention of giving up this spot for anything in the world, least of all Thomas Collins.

With his trademark nonchalance, Thomas tosses a notepad and pencil on the desk, and sits down, or rather, sprawls out, drawing looks from some girls who pass by, winking. He reciprocates by sneaking a look at one of their bottoms. Wow, what a gentleman... Still, I can't help my curiosity, and I take advantage of his brief distraction to get a better look at him. Black, tousled locks hang over his brow, while the sides and back of his hair are shorter, almost shaved. His straight nose and sculpted jaw-line make him look tough and powerful, as do his muscular arms and his broad, athletic shoulders in his leather jacket, not to mention his tongue piercing and the tattoos on his hands and neck. At basketball practice even more of them are visible—he's covered from head to toe. Sure, some people might say that all this, combined with his amber-streaked emerald eyes, make him attractive, irresistible. But I am not one of them.

I look away before he notices me staring, and out of the corner of my eye, I see him take his phone out of the pocket of his dark jeans and plug in his earbuds, lifting them to his ears. I arch an eyebrow, upset. Is that what he's going to do? Listen to music during class? There is nothing more irritating than jocks who rest on their laurels just because of their athletic scholarships.

As if he read my mind, he turns to me with a bold look. He scans me from top to bottom, chewing on gum with his mouth half-open. I instinctively give him a dirty look to let him know that his pathetic, passé playboy tactics aren't going to work on me, and add snarkily, hoping to at least scratch the surface of his conceit: "Hasn't anyone ever told you that chewing with your mouth open in front of people is rude? Same way it's rude to listen to music during a lecture."

Thomas arrogantly arches an eyebrow. "Rude, huh? I get that a lot," he replies nonchalantly, going back to fiddling with his headphone cable. Only now do I notice a completely irrelevant detail: this is the first time I've heard his voice. It's low, scratchy—the kind of voice that many women consider sexy. "The point…" he continues, his irksome eyes latching onto mine, "is that I don't really give a shit."

Travis was right: he was a rank one. "You have a big head for someone who's all muscle and no brain," I say without thinking, falling prey to my unchecked anger. But if I thought those words would silence him, the smirk I see taking shape on his face a moment later tells me that I've miscalculated.

"I have a big something," he says, looking down at the fly of his pants and leaving me speechless. "You can see for yourself if you want," he adds smugly.

My cheeks burn in embarrassment. From the way he bites his lip to hold back a laugh, I can tell that was exactly what he wanted: to mortify me. I stare at him in dismay for a few seconds and then reply, "You're disgusting."

"I get that a lot too," he admits with a satisfied grin.

I stare at him, dumbfounded, about to come up with a snappy retort. But then I realize it's not worth it; I would just be playing his game. So I shake my head and turn away. I've already had enough bad mojo today. I have more important things to concentrate on.

I pull out my course materials, enthusiastic in spite of everything (and everyone), and meticulously arrange my workspace. I open the laptop directly in front of me on the desk and set a brand-new notebook next to it for taking notes, with my black pen on top. I place a pack of Kleenex in the upper left corner and a bottle of water in the right. My level of organization can be compulsive, I realize—another quirk I inherited from my mother. Out of the corner of my eye, I notice that Thomas has lifted the pencil from the paper where he's been doodling and is staring at me with a cocked eyebrow. And although I try to restrain myself from opening my mouth so as not to encourage him, I can't help myself.

"What are you looking at?" I blurt out, keeping my eyes on my orderly desk.

"The university provides mental health services, you know."

I'm struck speechless for the second time in two minutes.

"Excuse me?" I ask, hoping I misunderstood.

He nods toward the items arranged on my desk, and I sense that no, I didn't misunderstand.

"I just like to be organized. There's nothing wrong with that." I blink, dumbfounded, trying to keep my composure.

"That's not organized, that's sick, but hey,"—Thomas raises his hands—"no judgment. The first step is recognizing the problem. After that it's a breeze. Trust me, I know."

Okay, that's enough. Whatever problem this guy has with me, he has to get over it.

"My God, do you hear yourself? You really are unbelievable! What am I saying, you're worse than incredible, you're...you're..." I struggle to find the right term, a single word that would encapsulate a slew of insults sufficient to shut him up permanently, but I don't think it exists.

"I'm what?" he taunts, a mocking smile on his lips.

"Bigheaded!" I exclaim, feeling like an idiot for not being able to think of anything more offensive.

Thomas all but laughs in my face, again. This day is turning out to be a total nightmare.

"I've been called worse." He shakes his head, amused.

Oh, I bet he has.

"Let me tell you something: I don't know you, I don't know what problems you have, I don't know why you decided to sit here next to me, when clearly your only goal seems to be to annoy me. But my favorite class is about to begin, a class that's very important to me, a class I've been waiting for all summer, and if you dare—"

"Wait, wait, wait," he interrupts me, widening his eyes. "What did you say?"

I look at him without understanding, wondering if he'd heard a single word I'd said.

"That my favorite class is about to start."

"No, after that."

"That if you dare ruin it…"

"No, before that."

"That I've been waiting all summer for this class to start?" There it is again. That dumbfounded stare.

"Are you fucking serious? You spent the summer waiting"—he glances around incredulously—"for this?"

I lift my chin, proud. I will not allow this arrogant jerk to make me feel like something's wrong with me just because I love studying more than anything. "Judge all you want, I don't care. What I do care about is being able to follow the lecture in peace," I say flatly.

A few seconds later, the philosophy professor finally enters the classroom. He immediately notices Thomas's presence and rolls his eyes.

Same here, Professor. Same here.

"Mr. Collins, what an unpleasant surprise!" Professor Scott remarks sarcastically. "I've heard a lot about you at the faculty meetings. What brings you here today?"

"Nothing particular, just a requirement to keep my spot on the team," he replies coolly, tapping his pencil on the desk. "Though, to be fair, the girls taking it are pretty good motivation."

When I turn toward him furiously, I see that he was staring right at me. I feel my cheeks burn, and his smirk tells me that he wanted to humiliate me in front of everyone. The snickers coming from the back of the classroom were the icing on the cake. But why target me? I haven't done anything to him.

Professor Scott isn't at all bothered by the whole scene; he's resigned. "Find yourself something to do, Collins, and don't disturb the others," he says simply.

As if nothing had happened, Thomas straightens up in his chair and leans toward me, invading my personal space. I'm enveloped by the fresh scent of vetiver with pungent hints of tobacco. "Careful, you're blushing a little too much; someone might think you find me irresistible," he whispers.

I look at him incredulously, dumbstruck by his presumption. "The only irresistible thing about you is your ability to show yourself exactly for who you are."

"Oh, tell me, what am I?" he asks, as I see his eyes light up with curiosity.

"An asshole," I reply dryly.

The insult seems to catch him by surprise, and the corner of his mouth turns up insolently. I'm not in the habit of talking like that, but he really had it coming.

The professor clears his throat, hinting for us to quiet down.

"You may have skated by in previous classes by some kind of divine grace. But this year, Mr. Collins, in my class you'll have to work hard."

Thomas only replies with a slight nod signaling his assent.

"Meanwhile, for all of you who take this class seriously and intend to broaden your intellectual horizons, I am pleased to announce that today we will begin with Kant."

My eyes light up just hearing his name. I murmur gleefully as Thomas runs a hand over his face, muttering under his breath how stupid this whole class is.

Twenty minutes later, the arrogant tattoo-covered guy sitting next to me is calmly listening to music as if it were nothing.

I could disregard his disrespectfulness except for the obnoxious hum from his headphones preventing me from focusing on the lecture as fully as I'd like.

After lots of back-and-forth in my head, I turn to him and tap his shoulder. "You should turn that off, don't you think?" I say with a pointed glare at the phone resting on his thigh.

Staring at me as if I'd just told him we're not in a lecture hall but on a spaceship headed for Mars, he pulls out the left earbud and replies, "Why?"

"Because I want to follow the lecture, and you're distracting me," I reply calmly, trying to keep my composure. I don't want to argue with him again, I just want to take my favorite class in peace. Is that too much to ask?

Thomas puts his earbuds back in, turning up the volume in defiance of my request. To make matters worse, he resumes chewing his gum, and it smacks noisily between his white teeth. I have to summon all my self-control not to pull that gum out of his mouth and plant it in his hair.

I shoot him a withering look, the kind I usually give my mother when she finishes the box of cookies without telling me. Or Travis when I realize he's barely heard a word I've been saying.

"What's your problem now?" he asks, irritated.

"Oh, I'm the one with the problem? Really? I've been trying to listen to this lecture from the moment you sat your butt down in this stupid seat!"

"So listen, what's stopping you?"

"You are!" I exclaim, my eyes wide.

"Because of this?" he asks, pointing to his earbuds. "Jesus, you can't be serious."

"Ugh, you know what? Just forget it!"

I turn back to the slides and hold out for the last few minutes of class, looking forward to getting away from him.

"All right, class, that's all for today. See you Friday!" the professor declares twenty minutes later.

I've never been so happy to hear a teacher dismiss the class in my whole life. And all because of some jerk who sat next to me for the sole purpose of bothering me. Thomas wraps his earbuds around his phone, slips them into his back pocket, grabs his pencil and the notepad he has been doodling on the whole time, and walks off without a word.

I need coffee to calm my nerves. Today has been an awful day. I walk into the coffee shop and wait my turn. Looking through the windows, I notice that it has started raining even harder. The rain and I have always been in sync; it comes when I need it.

I start to step forward, but someone pulls me from behind. It's Alex, who wraps his arm around my shoulders. I hug him back, sinking my face into his sweatshirt with its citrusy scent.

I missed him so much last summer. My days without him were boring as hell. With Travis doing his own thing and blowing me off all the time, the only person I could count on was Tiffany. But she has a busy and exciting life—unlike me, always in my room studying, reading, or watching TV.

"Sorry I couldn't meet you earlier. How are you?" He musses my hair with one hand, while with the other he slips the Canon he's always carrying around his neck, ready to capture even the smallest detail and reveal its uniqueness.

"Next question."

His lips curl into a grimace. "What did Travis do now?"

Oh, this time it's not just Travis! Let's see, the list is long: the fight this morning, all my mother's orders, Thomas's arrogance, which I will likely be forced to endure for the entire term. Or maybe I'll get lucky and he'll drop the class or fail, and I'll never see him again.

"Nothing, it's just a bad day," I say simply, taking a step. I don't feel like burdening him with my stupid drama. It occurs to me that he doesn't know anything about my fight with Travis or the video on Instagram. Just as well. It would only be more proof that his concerns are valid.

"What about you? How's your first day going?" I ask, curious. "You have no idea how sad I am not to have you in philosophy." With that idiot today, he would've been a huge comfort.

"Aw, I'm sad too, but I had to do more art. And I joined the photography club," he tells me enthusiastically. All summer, he did nothing but bombard me with photos from Santa Barbara, where he and his family spend every summer vacation: beach clubs, boat trips, sunset bonfires. And while he'd had all that fun, I had nothing to show for my summer but the slew of books and shows I'd devoured in his absence, Travis's incredibly boring practices that I couldn't say no to, and all the draining arguments with my mother during which I tried to explain to her that I was no longer a child who could be controlled by her ridiculous rules. All wasted breath.

"Good for you!" I say, back in the present.

"You know, I feel I've found what I really want to do," he continues.

In the meantime, it's our turn to order. I ask for a cup of regular and a double cappuccino for him. "I'm sure you have. Your pictures are incredible. I'm jealous of your artistic talent!" I pay and a moment later collect the steaming drinks, but before I can turn around, he snaps a picture of me, leaving me momentarily stunned.

"Alex! Don't do that. You know I hate it." I blink repeatedly, dazed by the flash, and hand him his coffee.

"Sorry." He chuckles. "I couldn't resist. You're so photogenic," he says, looking proudly at the image on his ultra expensive camera.

I have no makeup on, my hair is frizzy from the damp, and I have a pair of eye bags that rival Uncle Fester's. I don't know exactly what he means by "photogenic," but I think we have very different parameters.

"Wanna see it?" he asks with a grin, his eyes glued to the screen.

"I'd really rather not, thank you." We sip our coffees and make our way down the hall to class. "So, how are things with Stella?"

Alex met Stella this summer in Santa Barbara and has been talking about her nonstop ever since. I met her on a few FaceTime calls, and she was really sweet, with soft and kind features. She seemed perfect for him. Unfortunately, she lives in Vancouver and now they have to deal with all the difficulties of a long-distance relationship.

"It's a new situation for both of us, we still have to figure out how to make it work, but she's planning on coming down here for the weekend."

I nod at his words distractedly, because my attention is drawn to a couple huddled together at the end of the hall. Immediately I recognize the bulging muscle of that idiot Thomas leaning over Shana Kennest: slender form, stunning figure, fiery red hair, and turquoise eyes. Compared to her, every girl ends up feeling like the ugly duckling, and she does everything she can to make sure they do. She's close with the basketball team—very close—and she seems to be proud of that. But it's clear to everyone that her interest in Thomas overshadows everyone else. Rumor has it that Thomas, though not granting her an exclusive relationship, prefers her over any other girl. In fact, he usually gets rid of the others without a thought once he's had his fun with them.

Thomas pins her against the wall, and my eyes run over his tattooed hands. Although Shana is tall, Thomas towers over her so much that she has to tilt her head to look him in the eye. He leans forward, and their lips almost touch as they talk as if they were alone in the hall. When I think of how rude he was to me in philosophy class, I'm surprised to see him being so friendly. Shana slips a hand in the pocket of his jeans to reach for his pack of cigarettes. She plants one between her teeth, but he takes it out and brings it to his lips. He wraps an arm around her shoulders, and before heading for the stairs down to the quad, our gazes meet for a split second. I wince in embarrassment at being caught looking at them. He, however, grins confidently and gives me a wink.

"Hey, are you listening? Who are you looking at?" Alex asks.

I immediately shift my gaze from that arrogant he-man and the redhead hanging on him and direct it back at my best friend before he notices.

"Nobody, sorry. You were saying?" I bite the edge of the paper coffee cup.

Alex looks around, but luckily the happy couple has already vanished.

"Stella is coming here this weekend. I was thinking that we could do dinner together, what do you think?" he resumes.

"Sure." I smile at him. "I've been waiting all summer to meet her in person."

"Perfect. She'll be excited."

We walk off toward the auditorium for our cinema studies class as I try to banish my feeling of annoyance at Thomas's self-satisfied smirk.

Four

THE HOURS SPENT WITH ALEX put me in a good mood; I've always thought he was serotonin in human form. I'm walking through hallways packed with students toward my next class when I hear my best friend's voice chirping behind me: "Carol's throwing a mega first semester kick-off party at her house, Friday after the game. We have to be there!"

"We have to?" I challenge, trying to remember who Carol is.

"Of course." Tiff moves her hand between me and herself. "We're mandatory." The sullen look I give her should be enough to indicate my lack of interest, but she runs around to block me anyway. "Nessy, you need to have some fun."

I snort a laugh. "You and I have very different understandings of the word 'fun.' Besides, I don't even know this Carol person."

Tiffany furrows her brow and crosses her arms over her chest. "You don't remember her? She's in Criminology with me, and she was a regular at all of Matthew's frat parties last year. Tall, blond, dresses kinda weird."

Carol. Tall, blond, weird. Not ringing any bells. Must be because I went to maybe three of those frat parties last year and never stayed very long. "I really don't know her, Tiff."

By now, we've almost made it to our sociology class, one of the few that Tiff and I have in common, and we climb the steps, dodging the other students coming up and down.

"So then it's time to get to know her!" Tiff enthuses.

I roll my eyes. "I can't just invite myself to a stranger's house."

We spot two empty seats in the third row and grab them. Once seated, Tiffany moves her hair behind her shoulders with a graceful gesture. "First of all, you're not inviting yourself anywhere, you're my plus-one. Secondly, who cares? Do you think I know all the people who are going?"

I consider her words, tracing small circles on the counter with my fingertip, lost in thought. "I don't know, Tiff, the semester just started. I don't want to fall behind."

"The semester just started today, Vanessa. We literally haven't covered enough material for you to fall behind."

"But by Friday we will have! And then Saturday morning I have the first meeting with my reading group. I don't want to miss that," I counter.

"Yes, and I'm sure by Friday you'll already be chapters ahead, like always. As for the reading group, you'll be fine. It's not like we're going to party until dawn. C'mon, live a little!" She wriggles in the chair, begging me with clasped hands. I mull it over for a few seconds, uncertain, but in the end I decide to go. It's what kids my age do, right? They go to parties, they have fun, they don't hole up in their rooms with only books, Netflix, and the occasional bestie for company.

"Okay, okay, I'll give it a shot." I grimace, as though I'm agreeing to try a particularly unappetizing food.

"Yay!" she screeches, clapping her hands. Here's the secret to keeping Tiffany Baker happy in one simple move: indulge her.

The rest of the day passes quickly between classes in English, creative writing, and French literature. On my lunch break, I decide to take some solo time and read in the student union. I have no desire to see Travis again, and I'm going to meet up with him at practice anyway. Thinking of practice, I check the clock, which reads four fifteen. I have forty-five minutes before I need to get to the gym, and I muse about what to do with that time. It occurs to me that Book Bin, a small new and used bookstore I love, is just ten minutes from campus. I text my friends immediately to see if they'd like to come. Alex has his photography class, but Tiffany agrees to meet me in front of the bookstore.

She rushes to the mystery section as soon as we arrive, while I walk slowly through the aisles, letting intuition guide me. As I wander through the old wooden shelves, I reach out and brush my fingers over the books, feeling for a little spark of something. I've always loved bookstores, with their stillness and the silence that hovers. It's probably my favorite music.

In the mood for something a little different, I browse the fantasy section until I find something that strikes me: it's about a clumsy girl who has the power to travel through mirrors and is given in marriage to a nobleman from a distant planet. Hmm, that doesn't sound bad at all; if I weren't so broke, I would buy it, which reminds me that I could really use a part-time job. I promise myself I'll print out some résumés and start canvassing the town. Or maybe I can find something suitable on campus.

After the bookstore, we head for the Dixon Recreation Center, which is already teeming with students in basketball or football uniforms. Before entering the gym, we sit down at the Dixon Café for a snack. Tiffany gets frozen yogurt, I go for the pistachio gelato with whipped cream and chocolate syrup, my go-to choice.

We chat as we devour our treats, and I tell her about the way Thomas delighted in ruining my first class of the year. Tiffany doesn't seem surprised; after all, his reputation precedes him. I sigh loudly when I look up at the clock to see that it is now five o'clock. We make our way toward the campus gym and I ask Tiff if she wants to come with me. Fingers crossed she'll say yes, but unfortunately, she declines.

"If I see another basketball, I'm gonna scream," she says. It's enough for her to have to listen to Travis's constant play-by-plays at home. It's only when we are at the gym's door, about to say goodbye, that I muster the courage to update her on my talk with her brother and our tentative new arrangement. The disappointment shows on her face.

"I just don't understand how you can forgive him so easily."

"It's...complicated." I shrug. There is a part of me, buried under layers of disappointment and resignation, that really hopes this time will be the last time. That Travis has realized his mistakes and will go back to being the sweet, sincere boy I fell for in the early days.

Tiff shakes her head. "You already know how I feel. He's my brother, but that doesn't mean I don't see him clearly. You have to make him understand that you deserve more respect and that he can't keep taking you for granted."

"I swear, this is the last chance he's going to get." I know as I'm saying it that she doesn't believe me, probably because I've said the same exact thing countless times before, but something about this time feels different. I feel like this really is the last one. I refuse to allow myself to keep being treated like garbage by someone who is supposed to love me. Heck, I'd be happy to receive half the care and consideration he lavishes upon his high school basketball trophies!

"Promise?" Tiff demands, extending her left pinky toward me. I entwine it with my own.

"Promise," I say.

"Oh!" she says, rummaging in her bag. "Before you go, I got a little present for you."

I don't believe it. It's the book I was leafing through in the bookstore. I turn it over in my hands, touched.

"I saw the way you were looking at it, and you deserve a little treat." She smiles, her face nothing but sweetness.

"Thank you, Tiff, but you didn't have to do that." I'm moved by her thoughtful gesture, and a little mortified as well. She must have realized I couldn't pay for the book, and that's not a great feeling.

"It's no big deal." She shrugs. "Now I gotta run. See you tomorrow, gorgeous." She gives me a big hug, and I reciprocate, squeezing her a little tighter than usual. I know she hates it, but I can't help bugging her just a bit.

The gym is still mostly empty, but in the corner opposite the entrance I can see a girl sitting on the floor, leaning back against the wall. She's intent on a small journal in her lap, scribbling something urgently. I cross the gym and sit down next to her; who knows, maybe we can be friends. I'm usually all alone at these practices.

When she notices my presence, the girl tears her gaze from the diary and gives me a shy smile.

"Do you think they'll give us an attendance award at the end of the year? We deserve it," I quip.

"I doubt it," she replies, rubbing the back of her head.

"Damn!" I snap my fingers in mock disappointment. "I was really hoping for that."

She laughs, covering her face with hands chock-full of rings. Most of them are thin steel ones, resting at different heights on her fingers. Her laugh is gentle, pleasant to listen to. Her black hair is cut to just above her shoulders, she wears purple lipstick and large earrings in the shape of rhombuses. But it's her eyes that really win me over: they're green and magnetic, and I could swear I've seen them somewhere before.

"I am Vanessa, but everyone calls me Nessy," I tell her, holding out my hand.

"Leila. Nice to meet you!"

"Are you new here? I've never seen you on campus."

"Yes, it's my first day of college. I'm in the Arts and Literature department," she answers, a little awkward.

"Oh, a freshman! And we're in the same department! How's it been?"

"Not bad, but it's only the first day."

"I'm sure you'll do well. The important thing is to meet the right people, and lucky for you, you have one right here," I say pointing at myself and laughing.

"And here I was preparing myself for complete social isolation, at least for the first semester." She gives me a wry grin. "Human relations are not my strong suit."

"Welcome to the club, sister! Speaking of clubs, have you already signed up for any extracurricular activities? It helps a lot with making connections."

"Actually, I was thinking about the French club, maybe the campus newspaper."

"The newspaper is really popular. Probably the most in-demand extracurricular after theater and choir. I'd advise you not to waste time if you really want to join, because space is limited. I was interested too, but right now I have too many courses. Maybe second semester I'll give it a try."

"Thanks for the advice. I still have to get my class schedule sorted out."

"Of course. But now tell me: Who is forcing you to come to these boring practices?" I ask her conspiratorially.

"No one, really. My brother plays on the team, and I... Well, let's just say I like to keep an eye on him." She smiles.

"What year is he in?" I bring my knees to my chest and wrap my arms around them.

"He's a sophomore. He took a long break after the accident, and he just started training again this summer. Since he insists on getting back on the team, I'm here to make sure he doesn't push himself too hard. He refuses to believe he has any limitations at all, and he needs someone to remind him."

"Oh, an accident? I hope it wasn't too bad."

"A motorcycle accident a few years ago. It was the worst time of my life." As she speaks, her voice cracks, and I regret my question immediately.

"I'm so sorry, I didn't mean to..."

Leila clears her throat. "It's okay, it's okay, I'm sorry I'm killing the mood with all my tragedies. When he healed from his injuries, we decided to leave Portland. I did my last year of high school at Riverside, and now I'm here." She hunches into herself, as if her entire life has been encapsulated in these few sentences, but the bitterness that lurks inside her eyes suggests to me that there is so much more to tell.

I stroke her arm, as if to give her some comfort and apologize once again. I want to slap myself for making her remember such a painful moment. Maybe my mother's right, and I *do* talk too much.

"You know, new beginnings are always the hardest. But I'm sure you'll be fine here," I encourage her.

"Baker and Collins, this is your last warning. I see that again, and you're benched." We wince as we hear the coach's voice thunder through the locker room door, followed by the rumble of heavy footsteps announcing the arrival of the boys. Leila and I exchange worried looks. When I turn toward the court, I see Travis heading to the side hoop with his head bowed, shoulders tense and breathing labored. Behind him is Thomas, his face dark with anger as he reaches the hoop on the opposite side of the court, his back to us. He runs a hand through his damp hair and from the insistent way he loosens the black bandana he keeps twisted around his wrist, I can tell that he's agitated. The fiery glares that Travis keeps sending Thomas's way can't be helping.

I really hope my boyfriend hasn't let Thomas provoke him. If the coach were to kick him off the team, his father would never forgive him. When he notices me, I smile sweetly at him, hoping to assuage some of his bad mood, but somehow that only seems to make him scowl harder. What's the problem now? He wanted me here, and here I am, and now he's mad? He's never happy.

Travis and Thomas are joined by their teammates, Matthew and Finn. Matthew is extremely tall, with brown hair shaved on the sides and eyes the color of dark chocolate. He's the only one of Travis's friends that I really like. Finn, on the other hand, is a womanizer convinced that he can win over anyone with his alleged charm. He has an eyebrow ring, very short bleached blond hair and greenish-blue eyes. He is a handsome boy, sure, but there's nothing else to him. Matt is famous for throwing crazy parties at his fraternity, Finn for being the one who makes them crazy.

The sound of the coach's whistle brings everyone back to attention, and under his direction, the boys begin practicing runs, dribbles, and counterattacks. After a botched pass, however, the ball rolls over to Leila, who retrieves it and passes it gently to that jerk Thomas. In response, he gives her a wink. I can't help but roll my eyes. My God, this guy really hits on everyone.

For a moment, I'm afraid I said that aloud, because Thomas inclines his head and allows his gaze to linger on me, lifting one corner of his mouth in a half smile. I answer with a scowl, hoping to snuff out that glint of amusement in his green eyes. But, in the end, I look away first.

"Collins! Move your ass! Back to your post!" the coach calls him back.

"What about you? Are you here of your own free will or did someone force you?" asks Leila, bringing me back to reality.

"My boyfriend plays basketball, ergo I am forced to come." I snort.

"Oh God, it's almost worse than having a brother on the team. I'm here for you." She pats my shoulder, and I give her small hand a theatrical squeeze. "And who's the lucky guy?"

"Travis. Travis Baker, number nineteen."

Leila immediately spots Travis and, for a moment, seems disoriented. She squints her eyes, as if trying to focus on a blurry image, and then something strange happens. Her expression changes and becomes inexplicably more somber, and her face pales.

"He-he's your boyfriend?" She points at him with the pen she was using earlier, blinking hard.

"Apparently," I answer with some hesitation.

"How long have you guys been together?" She asks, her voice much calmer.

"Two years, give or take. Do you know him?"

"No. Sorry, I didn't mean to get into your business." She tucks her hair nervously behind her ears, stretches her legs over the gym floor, and lays the diary on top of her thighs.

"It's okay, you didn't," I assure her.

Well, that was weird. Why did she react that way? Does she know him? Maybe.

Leila was at the party on Friday! She might have seen something more than "just a dance"? This is going to drive me crazy.

"So, who is your brother, then?" I ask, trying to dispel some of the strange awkwardness that has arisen between us.

"Number twelve," she replies dryly, staring at the diary on her knees.

Are you kidding me? "Thomas—your brother is Thomas?" I stammer incredulously.

"Do you know him?" She looks stunned. Apparently now the roles have been reversed.

"No, not really. We have a class together."

"Ah. Well, I feel sorry for you. My brother can be a real pain in the ass when he wants to be."

"Yes, I've noticed that."

"He's difficult, but he's not a bad person. He's just…"

"An asshole?" It escapes my lips before I can stop myself. She looks at me, and I can tell she's looking for a cute way to refute me, but then she gives up.

"Yeah, he's an asshole."

We laugh together, and as our laughter fades, I let my gaze wander to him. I had no idea that he had been forced to stop playing because of an accident. A bad one, apparently. In spite of myself, I feel a slight twinge of pity.

Five

I FOLLOW THE WORKOUTS AS if in a trancelike state, lost in a thousand conjectures. I get the impression that Leila is holding something back about Travis. What else could explain her sudden change in mood when I mentioned him? Then, as much as I hate to admit it, I couldn't help dwelling on Thomas's accident. He's lived in Corvallis for more than a year, we attend the same college, and I know of him, but I didn't know anything about his past. When the coach sends the players into the locker room, I realize that I have completely missed the practice, lost in my thoughts.

I say goodbye to Leila and wait for Travis in the parking lot.

"Are you okay?" he asks me as I climb into his dark blue pickup truck, which is brand-new and still shiny. I nod with half-closed eyes and curl up against the seat, seeking some comfort in the soft leather. The only thing I want now is to crawl into my own bed.

"Are you sure you're okay?" he insists with a twinge of worry in his voice.

"Yeah, I just have a really bad headache."

"Did you take anything?"

"No."

"Oh, that's right, I forgot…" he says, smiling.

"No one has ever died from a little headache, Travis," I reply, annoyed.

"I'll turn on the heat. It will make you feel better."

"Thank you." I lean my head against the window and watch the dark asphalt sliding under the car's wheels, illuminated only by the soft light of the streetlamps. Travis tries to engage me in some small talk, probably in an attempt to cheer me up after today's argument, but I have zero desire for chitchat. My mind is still lingering on what happened in the gym.

"Do you know her? That girl?" I ask, not turning to face him.

"Who?"

"Leila, the girl sitting next to me during practice." *Did you see any other girls there?* I want to ask him.

"She's Collins's sister," he says shortly.

I feel a jolt of fear run through me. "Yes. I know that. But how do you know that? Do you know her personally?"

"No, why should I?"

"I don't know, she just had a weird reaction when I said you're my boyfriend," I say with my gaze still fixed on the window.

"Maybe she doesn't like me? That wouldn't be a surprise."

"How can she dislike you if she doesn't know you?" I finally turn to look at him, skeptical.

"Why are you giving me this third degree?" Travis tightens his grip on the steering wheel. "I know they are brother and sister because they're together all the time. Maybe she saw me at a party and got the wrong idea. You know how people love to talk shit."

His answer only makes me more suspicious, but there's still one other mystery on my mind. "Why were you and Thomas fighting in the locker room?"

"It was nothing. We didn't agree on a game strategy, usual stuff," he replies and shifts gears abruptly. "Enough about that. I don't want to argue with you again." I can see from the clench of his jaw that he's beginning to lose his patience.

"Whatever," I conclude, unconvinced. I should probably keep pushing, dig down until I get the truth. But, as much as it pains me to admit it, I agree with Travis. I don't want to fight anymore today. So I put my own mind at ease: Leila must have seen him at the party, dancing with those two chicks, and thus was shocked to hear that Travis and I are together. Honestly, sometimes it shocks me too. As for him and Thomas… Well, they never have gotten along.

"But we're cool, right?"

"Yes. We've already talked about it, Travis," I reply.

"It's just that you seem strange. You're more distant. I haven't heard from you all day, and I can tell by the way you're shaking your foot that you're still angry."

"I'm not angry, I'm just stressed. The fight this morning, the start of classes, my mother…" I take his hand and squeeze it, trying to reassure him, though I know I'm not yet willing to forgive and forget.

"All right." He interlaces his fingers with mine and lifts our joined hands to his mouth for a kiss. For the rest of the way, I watch the road in silence, soaking in the heat given off by the air vent aimed right at me.

"Isn't your mom back yet?" he asks me as he pulls into the driveway, noting the absence of Mom's car and the darkened house.

"No, ever since she started dating Victor, I see her less and less. I mean, I'm happy for her and everything, but it's like she's never around these days and—" I open my eyes wide. "Crap! I was supposed to walk Charlie!"

"Who?" asks Travis, puzzled.

I rub my temples and sigh heavily. "Charlie, the neighbor's dog. Mrs. Williams is out of town and asked my mom if she knew anyone who could help. And Mom, naturally, volunteered me. I was also supposed to go to the dry cleaners, pay the bills, and get dinner," I say in a rush.

"Relax, I'm sure it's not that big a deal. You can pay your bills online, and you can order takeout for dinner. As for the dry cleaners, I can take you there right now," he says softly.

"No, don't worry about it, I can walk. It's stopped raining, and I would like to stretch my legs." I can read the disappointment in his face and immediately feel guilty. "But hey," I hasten to add, "why don't we have a night in tomorrow. Pizza and a movie?"

"Yeah, sure, no problem."

He smiles hesitantly at me. We kiss and say goodbye.

After taking Charlie for a walk, I return to the house. I hang up the clothes I picked up from the dry cleaners and take a minute to print some résumés. I'm so tired I don't even have the energy to get into the shower, so I collapse on the couch in the living room, exhausted. I flick through some TV channels, but I can't find anything interesting.

Giving in to my curiosity, I search for Leila Collins's socials. What I find fits with my general impression of the girl: photos of landscapes and mountains with long captions, a few shots of herself in which her face is entirely obscured except for her beautiful green eyes. I also look for her brother, but I can't find any profile with his name.

I scroll through my own socials and come across a memory from exactly one year ago. Travis and me at one of the big luncheons his family holds. The Bakers were celebrating his father's promotion, and while the adults were chatting with their guests, we were goofing off and taking silly selfies, like this one.

As I look at the picture, I can't help but wonder how we got to this point. We used to be great. Travis was loving and attentive with me. Perhaps that love had changed over time, until it disappeared almost completely. He has his own interests: basketball, friends, and parties. And I am no longer the same Vanessa who fell in love with him at seventeen, an intimidated little girl who hung on his every word.

I have thought of breaking up with him more than once, but, when the time came to actually do it, fear took over, paralyzing me. And he goes back to being the sunny, cheerful, caring Travis I fell in love with, and I wonder if I'm giving up too quickly. If I'm backing down without a fight. That's what my father did with Mom and me—he gave up without really trying, and I don't want to be anything like him.

Lulled by melancholy thoughts, I fall asleep curled on the sofa in the fetal position with my phone under my hip. An hour later, I awake to a vibration: a message from my mother. Were you able to run errands? I'm out to dinner with Victor, don't wait up for me.

Inevitably, a wave of sadness sweeps over me. She met Victor at the law firm where she works as a secretary. He's a successful lawyer, and on the rare occasions when I've met him in passing, he seems like a good guy. But since he has become part of our lives, I'm lucky if I see Mom long enough for a hi and goodbye. Not that I'm dying to spend time with Victor, but it would be nice if Mom wanted me to meet him, if she showed a little interest in me for once. I ignore the message, get up from the couch, and go to the kitchen to heat up the dinner I ordered. I eat it in front of the television while watching a few episodes of *The Vampire Diaries*, always the perfect cure for whatever ails me. If my mother saw me eating on the couch, she would go crazy—but she's not here right now, is she? So, my inner teenager agrees, I can do whatever I want.

———

Tuesday morning finds me singing at the top of my lungs in the shower. I seem to be over my cold, and I want to give Travis and his promises a fair shot. Mom still isn't back, but at least I won't have to put up with her orders today. I am lathering up with the moisturizing blueberry bodywash when my flawless singing performance is interrupted by the sound of three honks. I gasp—is Travis already here? No way!

I reach an arm over the cabinet next to the shower to check the time on my phone and realize that I have completely lost track of time. I bound out of the shower as though I were spring-loaded.

I have to be on campus in fifteen minutes, and I'm still dripping with bodywash! I run to my room to get dressed, but realize just as I am about to put on my jeans that I left my underpants on the bathroom sink. I run to the bathroom, slip into my panties and bra, run back to my room, and put on a pair of jeans and the first T-shirt I see. I fly once again to the bathroom to hastily blow-dry my hair before remembering I left the brush on the desk in my bedroom. This is what happens when a control freak loses control of the situation: she panics. Travis, through it all, keeps laying on the horn, fueling my frenzy.

"I'm coming!" I wave my hands and yell as though he can hear me through the walls. I take the stairs two steps at a time and almost face-plant but, fortunately, I'm able to grab the railing in time. I slip on my black leather boots, grab my bag from the couch, and hurl myself into Travis's truck. Once seated, I'm seized by doubt: Did I get everything? I look frantically through the bag even as I feel Travis's amused gaze on me. I glare at him and gesture for him to start driving.

"Nessy, um…did you…you have a…"

"What? What do I have, Travis?!" I growl.

I hate late people, and I hate being late even more! My hair is still damp, and that means I'll probably have a headache today too. I haven't eaten anything and haven't had a drop of coffee, dammit!

"Nothing, it's just that you're wearing your pajama shirt," he replies hesitantly.

"What?"

He points a timorous finger at me. I look down slowly, certain that he is joking, but when I see the obvious pink of my pajama shirt, I throw my head back and curse myself. Travis turns purple in an attempt to stifle his laughter.

Oh, so this is the day he's decided to die?

"It looks good on you, though, it goes with the color of your eyes," he snickers. "And the rabbit saying *I Need Some Bunny to Love* is a nice touch!" He laughs with delight, even clapping his hand against the steering wheel. When he notices my death stare, he immediately suppresses his laughter and swallows. "Do you wanna to go back inside and change?"

"No. That would make me even later. Just shut up and drive," I order, flaying him with my gaze.

I arrive on campus ten minutes late. I rush to my class in a blind panic, Travis trotting along beside me without a care in the world. "Come on, it's only ten minutes. No one will notice!" he cajoles, and I ignore him and continue toward my art history class. When we get to the door, Travis tries to say goodbye, and I shoo him away quickly.

By the time I cross the threshold, class has already begun. At the back of the room there is a large projector. In the center of the room, Professor Torres is introducing the film we will be watching, a documentary about Frida Kahlo, if I understand correctly. In one of the first rows I spot Alex, absorbed in Professor Torres's explanation. I really want to join him, but I'd rather not disturb the whole class by making my way down there. Instead, I'm forced to take a seat in the last row, right by the door.

The professor dims the lights, and the classroom plunges into darkness. On the projector, images of Frida Kahlo's work appear. I admire them, fascinated, when a low, raspy voice whispers to me: "I'm beginning to think that you're stalking me." What? I peer around to see where the voice is coming from. To my left, I spot the glint of two familiar green eyes, and my breath catches.

It is not possible, not again. Thomas Collins, with a pen between his teeth, still manages to give me his smug smile.

"Why would I be stalking you? You've wildly overestimated your importance to other people," I retort, turning my gaze back to the projector's screen.

"Really? Yesterday morning during Professor Scott's lecture, then in the gym, and now here. Seems like stalking to me. You know, if you want something from me, all you have to do is ask."

"You sat next to me in philosophy class! I came to practice for my boyfriend, and, just now, I sat down in the first free chair I could find," I snap, bewildered by his presumption.

"Purely coincidence, then?" he murmurs under his breath.

"That's right. Coincidence. And now, if you don't mind, I would like to pay attention to this class," I conclude dryly. After a few minutes, however, I realize I can still feel his eyes on me.

"You met my sister yesterday," he says when I glance quizzically back at him.

"Yeah. She seems nice."

"And what did you two talk about?" He lays down the pen he had been holding between his teeth and crosses his arms over his chest, giving me his full attention. Even in the dark, I notice that he has that same bandana twisted around his wrist, the one from practice yesterday.

"Why do you want to know?"

"Because I know my sister. She's got a big mouth."

"You're right to be concerned." I lean toward him, resting one hand on his shoulder, and I don't miss the way his body stiffens at my touch. "She told me all your darkest secrets," I whisper.

"She must not have told you much, then," he replies nonchalantly. "I have no secrets."

"Everybody has secrets, Thomas."

"You sure about that?" He narrows his eyes. "So, let's hear it then, what's your secret?"

"My basement is full of the mummified remains of cocky pricks who like to torment me," I answer immediately, coaxing a soft laugh from him. I'm getting the idea that the more belligerent I become the more he enjoys mocking me.

Now he's the one to draw closer, bringing his lips to my ear so I can feel his warm exhalation on me as he whispers, "It's a good thing there's none of those around here."

I am certain of just a few things in life. One of them is that I absolutely should not have gotten that strange swooping feeling in my belly at Thomas's low whisper. Disturbed, I clear my throat and try to compose myself, still very aware of how close his lips are to my skin.

"You can rest easy; your sister didn't tell me anything." I reestablish the proper distance between us and turn my attention back to the movie, ignoring my burning cheeks. Thank goodness he can't see my blush in the darkened classroom.

"Cute shirt, by the way," he murmurs mockingly.

And then I remember I'm wearing a pink pajama shirt with a winking bunny and a rabbit pun on it, and I pray that a chasm opens up in the floor and swallows me whole. Only after he is sure that I've been thoroughly embarrassed does Thomas avert his gaze. He ignores me for the rest of class. When we are dismissed and I'm about to say goodbye and leave, he's already on his feet. He heads for the door without giving me so much as a glance, leaving me, once again, stunned.

What the heck?

I'm trying to figure out what is more upsetting to me: that Thomas left without even saying goodbye or that it is bothering me so much, when

Alex catches up with me. We walk through the halls talking about the lives of Frida Kahlo and Diego Rivera. Then Alex tells me about his photography class and shows me some black-and-white shots from yesterday's session. I praise him for the pleasant melancholy they evoke. Having finished the morning's classes, we decide to get lunch in the cafeteria.

"I told Travis and Tiffany to meet us there," I tell Alex, taking my phone from my bag.

"Is that necessary? I mean, Tiff's great. But I'd rather have lunch without the risk of projectile vomiting. Which tends to happen when Travis is around."

"Come on, Alex, please make an effort? He's not going to be a jerk." Or at least that's what I'm hoping.

"Really?" he asks sarcastically. "I didn't think he knew how to be anything else."

"Please give him one more chance. If he gets out of line, I swear it will be the last time." I give him the doe eyes, my winning move.

Alex wraps his arm around my shoulders. "All right, all right, I guess I can just ignore him like always."

"Sounds like a good compromise to me!" I tell him with a big smile.

We find a free table in the crowded cafeteria, and, while waiting for the twins to arrive, we joke about our English Lit professor and his toupee, which jostled with every step he took and required constant adjustment.

"Tiffany knew right away that he was wearing a rug!" I say, opening my can of soda.

"At a certain age, you should just resign yourself to it," Alex says.

"I don't know, baldness is making a comeback! I read about it in one of Mom's *Vogues*."

Alex gives me a horrified look. "When has it ever been in fashion?"

"You're kidding, right? Most bald men are sexy as hell!"

"Come on," he says skeptically. "Name a few."

"Dwayne Johnson. Vin Diesel. Corey Stoll, not to mention Jason Statham! Oh, Alex, he's… Well, he's just a god among men," I exclaim dreamily.

"Okay, okay. Wipe the drool off." He dabs the corner of my mouth with a napkin teasingly. I'm elbowing him in the shoulder when, from a distance, we see the twins approaching. Travis gives me a kiss and takes a seat across from me. He says hello to Alex with a pat on the back, and my friend reciprocates without much enthusiasm. That's something, right? Basic civility? I don't have time to ask how they are doing, because Tiffany, bewildered, looks at my pajama sweatshirt and asks, "What are you wearing, gorgeous?"

"I was running late this morning and I didn't realize I had put on—" Tiffany raises a hand to shush me.

"Are you telling me that you walked around campus all day in your pajamas?"

I nod, resigned to my own carelessness.

"Oh God, what am I going to do with you?" She pinches the bridge of her nose, shaking her head.

"I know, I know," I admit with a guilty look and my hands raised in surrender. Travis struggles to hold back a laugh, and even Alex, who this morning had completely glossed over my unusual fashion choices, seems amused. "Okay, okay. Stop staring at me, and let's go line up for trays. I'm starving."

When I return to the table with the full tray, I catch sight of Leila sitting alone a few feet away from us. She senses my gaze, and we exchange smiles. I feel bad, seeing her alone; it is just the second day, and I guess she has yet to settle in. So I invite her to join us with a beckoning wave.

Leila smiles again but, as soon as she notices that Travis is also at the table, she turns gloomy and shakes her head "no." Another weird reaction to Travis. One—or both—of them are hiding something from me, but what is it?

"...right, Nessy? Nessy?" My boyfriend's calm voice brings me back to reality.

"What?" I ask, confused, when I realize I have everyone's eyes on me.

"Did you hear what we told you?" asks Tiffany.

"No, sorry, my mind was elsewhere," I attempt to justify myself, hoping no one will ask questions.

"What were you thinking about?" Alex, my dear old pal, asks innocently.

"Nothing, nothing important," I reply, forcing a chuckle.

Travis looks around suspiciously, as though trying to figure out what or who had distracted me, but he doesn't seem to spot anything.

"We were talking about Friday's party at Carol's house," Tiffany continues. "Trav will be there too."

Oh, the party.

"Alex, will you be there?" I ask, though it sounds more like a plea for help than a genuine question.

"I'm hanging out with Stella, remember?"

"Stella? Who's *Stella*?" asks Tiffany, intrigued.

"His girlfriend," I reply, giving Alex's shoulder a teasing squeeze.

"Wow, Smith finally found a girlfriend," Travis taunts him and earns himself a dirty look from me before wisely deciding to shut his mouth.

"Why have I never heard of this Stella?" urges Tiffany impishly as she strokes the rim of her glass with a finger.

"Because it just happened, and she's not from Corvallis. I met her this summer in Santa Barbara," Alex explains.

"Hey, why don't you bring Stella to the party?" I suggest, clinging to the last glimmer of hope.

"Let's just say, I have other plans," Alex replies with a smile that speaks volumes.

"Oh, I see. Are you planning to be lovebirds all weekend?"

"Don't use that silly word," he exclaims, embarrassed.

"What word?" I pretend not to understand. "Lovebirds?"

"Stop it," he begs, giving me his pleading face.

"Lovebirds, lovebirds."

He plugs his ears with his hands, squinting his eyes, while Tiffany and I laugh out loud. We keep teasing him through the rest of lunch.

A few hours later I'm waiting for Travis off campus with arms folded, shivering in the cold autumn air. I'm still wearing just my pajama shirt because I forgot my jacket this morning as well. How long does it take to get a car from a parking lot? It's already been ten minutes. Damn him.

I'm bouncing on my toes and rubbing my arms to warm them when someone lays a heavy leather jacket over my shoulders, making me wince. The next moment, I find Thomas beside me, sans his own familiar black leather jacket. I am so surprised by this thoughtful—too thoughtful?—gesture that I begin to immediately wonder what game he's playing.

"Thank you, but I don't need this." I shrug the jacket off and hand it back to him, but he ignores me. He lights a cigarette and slightly squints his eyes. When he exhales, the smoke creates a grayish cloud that envelops him.

"Keep it," he mumbles, as he fiddles with the small wheel of his lighter. "You're shaking," he adds after giving me a fleeting glance.

"To what do I owe this act of altruism?" I ask as I turn to face him.

He appears confused. "I wouldn't call it altruism. Pity, if anything."

What is that supposed to mean? He feels sorry for me? Like I'm some underfed stray dog running the streets? I shake my head, unnerved by his arrogance. "You know what? Take it back. I don't need your sympathy." I return his jacket roughly, hurling it at his chest. In response, Thomas lets out an amused grunt from deep in his throat.

"Touchy, touchy…"

"No, it's you. You rub people the wrong way," I retort, directing my gaze elsewhere. Thomas approaches and towers over me. I'm barely five-foot-six, and he looks like a giant next to me.

I swallow and try to pretend his sheer size doesn't intimidate me. I have to tilt my head to look him in the eyes, trying to read something of his intentions there. He, with the cigarette clamped between his lips, drapes the jacket over my shoulders again, this time making sure to wrap me tightly in it. He sucks in a puff from the cigarette and slowly blows the smoke into my face. Waving the cloud away, I give him a hate-filled look, which appears to just roll off his back.

"Expecting someone?"

"My boyfriend," I hiss, with my arms crossed over my chest. Then, it occurs to me: if Travis showed up right now and saw me here with Thomas, wearing his jacket, he would have a total meltdown.

"Solve a riddle for me." He takes another drag of his cigarette, closes his eyes, and blows the smoke out of his nostrils. "I've been wondering: Do you have a thing for assholes or is it daddy's boys you're into?"

I squint, bewildered.

"Travis isn't—" I rush to defend him, but the little voice in my head stops me. He isn't what? An asshole? He is, though. A daddy's boy? Yeah, he's that too. Thomas senses my wavering. He gives me the knowing smirk of someone who knows he's hit the bull's-eye. Okay, so give this round to Collins. That game is hardly over.

"And why are you here?" I ask to change the subject.

"I smoke and, you won't believe it, but the college frowns on people smoking indoors." He sucks in one last drag and tosses the butt a few feet away from us, never looking away from my face. "Crazy, right?"

"Well, you're done smoking now." I push the jacket into his arms, hoping to get rid of him before Travis arrives.

He slips it on and, instead of leaving, moves even closer to me. As he does, I get an intense wave of his vetiver scent. There's something else as well, a fresh, masculine fragrance, a little bit like the grass right after a downpour. Overwhelming. "What, trying to get rid of me?" He grins.

"No, not at all," I stammer, suddenly feeling my throat getting drier. "I'm just saying, you have no reason to be here anymore. Besides, Travis will be here any minute."

Thomas sinks his hands into the pockets of his leather jacket. He seems to want to feign indifference, but the hint of a smirk betrays him. "It's not too bad out here. There's an interesting view."

I look around, confused. What "interesting view" is he getting from a deserted parking lot, half-obscured by fog?

"I'd say there's definitely better," I mumble, tucking an errant strand of hair behind my ear as he stares intently at me for a handful of seconds.

"We should go out sometime."

I look at him without blinking. I make a huge effort not to laugh in his face.

"Excuse me?" I manage, finally.

"For a drink. Nothing too challenging," he says, completely confident.

"And why should we do that?"

He lifts one shoulder casually. "Does there have to be a reason?"

"I have no intention of going out with you. Besides, I've told you, I'm with someone."

"I asked you to go out, not to fuck," he retorts seriously. Meanwhile, I choke on my own saliva.

"Because I would never do that!" I say sternly, frowning.

"And I would never ask you. I have specific tastes." He lets his gaze run over my body, as if the mere idea of being with me disgusts him. "Different tastes..."

I clear my throat, trying to disguise the discomfort I feel. Without knowing it, he has hit a sore spot. "Yeah, well, the same goes for me."

"Sure?"

"More than sure." I lift my chin, hoping not to reveal any kind of emotion.

"Then we're good," he said glibly. "We can go out without you running the risk of falling in love with me, or any of that bullshit. Honestly, it'd save me a lot of trouble."

"Listen." I pinch the bridge of my nose, astounded at this level of presumption. "We are not friends, we don't hang out, we don't get drinks, we are practically strangers. And, frankly, I don't like the few things I do know about you," I stress. "So, the answer is 'no.' I will not go out with you. Not now, not ever."

Thomas stares at my parted lips, and I blush, wondering if they are visibly chapped. He pauses only a moment, then looks back into my eyes with a sly smile. He takes another step toward me until his chest is brushing against mine and, for some strange reason, I find myself holding my breath. "We'll see about that," he murmurs. I have the terrible feeling that I have just lit the fuse of something that's going to blow up in my face.

"There's nothing to see about," I babble nervously. "I would like you to leave now."

"Afraid your boyfriend might find me here with you?"

"Unlike you, I like to avoid trouble with Travis," I explain. Something in my words must have set him off. Suddenly his face hardens, and he instinctively clenches his jaw. If all it takes to trigger a sudden mood shift like that was one tiny mention of Travis, things between the two of them must be more serious than Travis would have me believe. Just then, I hear the sound of the pickup's engine. In a panic, I retreat back a few steps to get as far away from Thomas as possible. "If I say please, would you go away?"

For a moment, his eyes gleam strangely, and I'm willing to bet that he is thinking of staying right here just to wreak havoc. But then something seems to change his mind, perhaps my pleading expression, or perhaps his long-dormant conscience? He takes a step back, shaking his head slowly and raising his hands in surrender.

"See you around, stranger..." He gives me one last look, lingering on my shirt. I blush as he laughs smugly.

"Okay, you've had your fun. Better get going." I shoo him away, ignoring the heat in my cheeks and the nickname he's given me. He gives me a sly wink and slinks away, hands tucked into his jacket as he goes. I stand there for a moment, just watching him with the strangest feeling of confusion. I blame it on the adrenaline triggered by my fear that Travis would see us together.

I get into the truck, glad that I was able to get rid of Thomas in time.

"Sorry, Nessy, I found Finn in the parking lot and we got to talking," Travis tells me as I fasten my seat belt.

"It's okay, don't worry," I reassure him. The truth is I feel so dazed right now that I haven't paid the slightest bit of attention to anything he's saying.

"Are you all right?" he asks me worriedly.

"Yeah, just cold."

"Sorry I kept you waiting a long time."

"Not a problem." I smile at him. He turns on the heater and strokes my thigh. Then I see him sniffing the air with furrowed brows.

"Do you smell that? What is it?"

"Um, no, I don't smell anything."

"No, it smells like smoke and... What is it? Cologne? Mint? You really don't smell it?" he asks a little disgusted.

Oh God. Thomas's jacket must have imparted some smoke smell to me.

"No, nothing out of the ordinary," I lie, impassive. "Maybe you're still smelling Finn's cologne? You know he practically bathes in the stuff." I turn on the radio to distract him, and apparently it works.

I listen to him tell me about his day while letting my mind wander. Thomas's scent continues to invade my nose and my brain. What the hell just happened?

Six

"YOU KNOW, I'VE BEEN THINKING, ever since our fight yesterday morning, we haven't really had a chance to spend any time alone. So, what if I stayed over at your place tonight?" asks Travis hopefully, as he pulls into the driveway. I feel a twinge of guilt in my stomach. Just a few minutes ago, I was alone in a parking lot with a guy Travis detests. And I honestly can't say that being so close to Thomas has left me completely cold.

I take a deep breath before I respond, trying to come across as serene and unbothered. "Yeah, sure. That sounds great." I really need to get a grip on this situation and get back to being the Vanessa I've always been, the one who doesn't fall for the first halfway charming guy who comes along. The one who isn't a liar.

When we walk in, I find a note on the stand in the entranceway: *I'll be back late—I'm having dinner again with Victor and colleagues. Kisses.* I'm going to forget what my mother looks like if things keep going like this.

We quickly take off our shoes, and I turn on the heat. Barefoot, I walk across the Persian rugs that lie scattered between the hallway and the living room. Those rugs were the first major purchase my mom made when, twelve years ago, my father was hired as an accountant in a large multinational corporation, a job that was supposed to guarantee us a more affluent lifestyle. Twelve years of living, and these carpets look like they were just rolled out of the store yesterday.

Travis curls up in the recliner next to the sofa in the living room, while I go to the kitchen to see if there's anything to make for dinner, but the refrigerator is empty. What the heck! Thanks for the consideration, Mom!

"I guess we'll have to order in. There's nothing here," I shout to Travis from the kitchen.

"Okay, pizza or sushi?" he asks. If nothing else, he does know my tastes in takeout.

"They opened a Japanese restaurant nearby, and it looks like it's really delicious," I tell him, pulling the menu out from under a magnet on the refrigerator. I join him in the living room and sit on his lap.

"Japanese it is, then."

"Want something to drink? Soda, beer, something like that?" I ask after placing my order online.

"A beer would be good; I don't have to drive anymore today."

"Did you know my mother always keeps one for you in the fridge? We may run out of food in this house, but there will always be a beer for Travis."

"She loves me almost more than my own mother." He chuckles complacently.

"Don't kid yourself. It's only because you remind her of my dad in the good old days. Only better." I stick my tongue out at him and then go retrieve the bottle from the kitchen. I open it and hand it to him.

"Well, that's a low bar to clear," Travis adds, taking a drink.

It hurts a little, but he isn't wrong. For years I believed that my dad was the perfect man, my undisputed hero, my safe haven. No one else would ever measure up. By the time I was in high school, Mom and Dad were fighting more and more often. My mother had always been dissatisfied with her life—our life—but, by the time I was a teenager it seemed like she resented Dad so much that she couldn't even stand to hear the sound of his voice. I never really understood why. We weren't fabulously wealthy, but Dad made sure we didn't lack for anything. That wasn't how Mom saw it, though. In the years that followed, things just got worse: the fights, the accusations, the separation, the threats, and finally the divorce.

I found myself tossed around in this tempest, used as a buffer, a pawn, and a scapegoat. Dad finally had enough and walked out. He left us the house and a bit of money. And he left me, even though I'd always been on his side. Dad and I had always had a special relationship; things with Mom were...harder. Watching her yell at Dad made me sick, and I told him it wasn't his fault that she chose to be a stay-at-home mom rather than pursuing her career the way he had. But that was before I found out about Bethany.

Apparently, they had been together for years, in secret. She was younger than my mom and more accommodating. She was also well-established in her career. The only thing she was missing was a family, so I guess, she decided to take mine. Mom and Dad's last big blowout had been over Bethany. Specifically, over the fact that my mother had found out through mutual friends that Bethany was pregnant. Very pregnant. My parents had just separated, and Dad was about to become a father again.

It was a blow to both of us. I felt betrayed, abandoned, wounded to my core. It was like my heart had shattered into uncountable splinters. But I was not ready to give up on my father completely. So I tried my best to accept my father's new partner and their child. I stifled my pain and started visiting their house. Every time I walked through that door, my stomach would churn and toss, but that was something I was willing to tolerate if it meant I could still be with him. But I hadn't counted on Bethany taking an instant dislike to me. "I don't want her here," were her exact words as I eavesdropped on their whispered discussion in the kitchen on my fifteenth birthday. She was convinced that I wanted to reconcile my parents and take Dad away from her.

I knew at that point that it was only a matter of time. I was terrified by the thought that, sooner or later, my father would have to choose between us, and I knew he would not choose me. I was his daughter, but she was his lover and the mother of his infant child, and she was with him all the time, working steadily to wear down any resolve he had.

Slowly, my father had begun to show up less often, call less frequently, until, one day, without me even realizing it, I saw him for the last time. From that moment on, his new life without me had officially begun. My sixteenth birthday was the first that I spent without him. Without seeing his smiling face as I unwrapped my presents or blew out the candles, without hearing his off-key voice singing "Happy Birthday." I missed him terribly. I missed the atmosphere of warmth and family that only he could create. The special attention he gave me to make me feel cherished. I haven't heard from him since.

I spent the first year calling him every day and crying, blaming myself and hating myself because I had not been enough to keep him around. He didn't love me enough because I wasn't worth loving. But that phase of self-pity was followed swiftly by searing anger. I came to hate him completely. He had chosen another woman over my mother, another child over me, new memories over the home we had built together. He had stolen from me the chance to grow up with a loving father, all to indulge the whim of his mistress. The pain of it wore me down; I wasn't myself. I was angry with the world. I felt tossed aside and overlooked. Then one morning I had simply woken up and stopped. I had stopped crying, stopped blaming myself, stopped hoping for his change of heart. I even stopped hating him. Because I had realized that if he was capable of abandoning his daughter, then I, too, must be capable of learning to live without him.

I banish those bad memories and allow my thoughts to drift to Travis. Our story began just a year after I cut ties with my father. Travis was the twin brother of my best friend, Tiffany. Tiff and I met in high school, during the first semester of our freshman year when we had to write a paper together. We were so different that, at first, I hated the idea of studying with her. Yet, it was those very differences that wound up uniting us so deeply, eventually blossoming into a solid and loyal friendship that has now lasted for more than four years.

With Travis, however, everything was different. The first time I saw him was the day I went to their imposing mansion to work on the joint assignment I had with his sister. I was immediately thunderstruck by his curly red hair and dazzling smile. He didn't seem to notice me, though, and I was too shy to approach him, so I spent the next two years quietly fantasizing about my best friend's aloof brother. It took a lot of help from Tiff and an evening at the amusement park for Cupid to take his shot.

I was down in the dumps that night, and Travis was there for me. He bought me cotton candy and gave me a stuffed animal he won at a shooting booth. Over the next few days, he invited me to dinner, then to the movies and a few of his basketball games. Those first months were incredible. All the attention, love, and care that my father no longer lavished on me, I found in Travis. I don't know exactly when the magic ended, replaced by indifference and insensitivity, but I began to realize that having a girlfriend like me was more convenient for him than anything else. His parents liked me and he lived to please them, and I never made much trouble. No matter how much he neglected me or took me for granted, I hung in there. It's been a year now that I've been asking myself the same question: How much longer do I intend to just hang around?

When the takeout arrives, I put aside the past and gorge myself on sashimi, tempura, and soba while we watch TV. Almost halfway through the movie, Travis wraps his arm around my waist and pulls me onto his lap. So close to him, I allow myself to be guided along, as he positions me to his liking. And then he is kissing me, touching me, undressing me. I reciprocate, but my mind is elsewhere, lost in the memory of a pair of arrogant green eyes, a cocksure smile, the sound of a low, rough voice—no! I suddenly break away from Travis, who looks at me puzzled, his eyes clouded with desire.

"What's wrong?" he asks.

I bring two fingers to my lips and, incredulous and guilty, try to regulate my suddenly labored breathing. I have never experienced such a thing before. Thinking of another guy while making out with my boyfriend? That is not me, and I am not going to allow that tattooed jackass to get inside my head and ruin this moment.

"N-nothing. I-I thought I heard the sound of the keys in the lock." I spit out the first plausible excuse I can think of and start kissing him again to allay his suspicions. Travis wastes no time with foreplay. He gets up from the couch, taking me in his arms and carrying me upstairs to my room. We spend the rest of the night there, indulging in familiar, even mechanical sex that, I suddenly realize, stirs no particular feeling in me at all.

It is the smell of hot coffee and pancakes that wakes me the next morning. Beside me Travis is still sound asleep. I stare at him for a few seconds, and I let my fingers wander through his auburn curls, tousling them gently. I still feel a little guilty for having brief fantasies of another man, my mind playing tricks on me. Then I wake him up and persuade him to come downstairs to have breakfast.

As soon as we cross the threshold of the kitchen, I spot my mother, standing in front of the stove and beaming beatifically. "Welcome back, Mom," I say through clenched teeth, directing a glare at her. I haven't seen her since Monday morning, and now she's trying to play Susie Homemaker?

She greets us with a radiant smile. Hypocrite. I know she's longing to snap back at me, but she would never make a scene right in front of Travis. Not when it would reveal what a harpy she really is.

"Good morning, honey! And good morning to you, Travis. I made you guys coffee!" she chirps, pushing the steaming cup under my nose. She is trying to buy my good mood. I know her. I grab the cup and sit down at the table without sparing her a glance. Travis follows me, but, unlike me, he greets her warmly.

"And pancakes too!" she adds. She sets the plate down on the table and slides it toward me in one smooth movement. Apparently, she will make time for grocery shopping if it means she can give her dearest Travis the perfect breakfast. I look up at her but, before I can say anything, she's already reaching into the refrigerator and grabbing the whipped cream and maple syrup. She pours the syrup over the pancakes and makes two small mountains of cream on top of it. Fine. I surrender.

I give my mom a break, forking up a piece of pancake and dipping it in whipped cream.

"Travis, dear, did you sleep well? Are you going to eat anything? I know you don't like pancakes, but I can cook you some bacon if you'd prefer that. Or some eggs?"

I cannot suppress an eye roll.

"Thank you, Mrs. White, I will gladly have a cup of coffee," he replies.

"Oh, dear, how many times do I have to tell you? Call me Esther! Here's yours, no sugar." She hands it to him with a giggle and pats his shoulder.

"Call me Esther," I mimic under my breath. Travis stifles a laugh.

"So how are your parents? Your sister?"

"Dad is in Europe these days. Tiffany's okay, but I need Nessy to help me convince her not to keep majoring in sociology. She would do great at Dad's company with me someday, but she's dead set on becoming a criminologist."

"And what's wrong with that?" I ask. "Tiffany succeeds in everything she does. If she wants to become a criminologist, she's going to be the best criminologist in the country. You should be on her side, you know. You're her brother, her twin!"

"Don't listen to her, Travis," my mother interjects. "My daughter lives in la-la land sometimes. Tiffany should follow your example and carry on with your father's business." Mom draws closer and rests a hand on my shoulder. "My Nessy should also understand the importance of building a realistic future for herself that can guarantee her financial stability, rather than wasting time chasing fantasies. I've always told her that she should study law…"

Okay, that's enough. I get up from the table, furious. I haven't seen her in forty-eight hours, and now she's going to show up just to tell me how I should live my life? No way. "Thanks for breakfast, Mom, but no one asked for your advice." I storm up to my room to finish getting dressed. As I do, I listen with one ear to my mother and Travis, who continue chatting cheerfully in the kitchen.

"I can't believe you're trying to get Tiff to change her major," I blurt out as soon as we get into the pickup truck. Travis rolls his eyes, but I just keep going: "You do know that money and social prestige are not the only things of value in life, right? You and my mother are insufferable when you get together."

"You always blow everything out of proportion. Maybe your mother is right."

I huff and make to turn on the radio, but Travis intercepts my hand and squeezes it. "Hey, last night was good. Let's not ruin it."

I take a deep breath and, overwhelmed by a wave of guilt, I don't protest.

Arriving at campus, I immediately catch sight of Alex near the entrance of the liberal arts building. I run up to him as Travis moves to walk with some boys from the team.

I jump on Alex's back, and he gasps. "Nessy! I've been looking for you!" he grins, dropping me to the ground.

"Found you! Tell me everything."

"My mother came back from Italy today…"

"Wait, what? But you just got back from Santa Barbara a week ago!" I say, flabbergasted. Sometimes I forget how much his mother travels for work. She's seen so much of the world, I envy her. When we were thirteen, she took us with her to Washington, D.C., and we went on a guided tour of the city. It was a beautiful day, still one of my happiest memories with Alex.

"Yes, she had to organize an auction in a library in Florence. And she told me to give you this little souvenir. Here, I think you'll like it." He takes a paper bag out of his backpack and hands it to me. Inside, I find a package wrapped in tissue paper, and I tear it open like a little girl on Christmas Day. When I realize I'm holding a first edition of *Pride and Prejudice*, I almost faint with excitement.

"Alex! Is this a joke? Your mother got me a first edition of my favorite book?" I shout incredulously. "I…I…I can't accept this, it must have cost her a fortune, I don't…" I try to give it back to him, but he blocks me.

"Nessy, my mother doesn't want it back, she made me promise I would force you to keep it. Besides, you know her, unearthing goodies like this is her job. She likes to share them with people when she can."

"But it's too much! I mean, look, it's an actual first edition! I would have been happy with a little David magnet too." I continue to gaze in wonder at the novel, turning it over in my hands. "I just don't know what to say!"

"A 'thank you' will be more than enough," he replies, amused.

"Thank you! Thank you so much!" I hug him very tightly.

"Let's get coffee before class, shall we?"

I nod, contemplating the novel. It really is beautiful.

We sit across from each other at a vacant table and sip our drinks while chatting about nothing in particular. I tell him about the warm welcome I received from my mother this morning after days of absence and her conversation with Travis.

"So," he goes on, wiping away some grains of sugar that fell from his doughnut, "how are things with you and Travis?"

I put the coffee cup down and look at him. "Oh, let's call it... good."

"Let's call it?"

I stretch my legs under the table and sigh. "It's been a weird time, this summer. Travis has been gone a lot, and now we are trying to get back into the swing of things."

Alex nods, but he doesn't seem entirely convinced. "I don't know, Nessy. In these two years, I've never seen you as distant from him as you are now."

I shrug my shoulders, caught out. I don't have a chance to argue because I'm distracted by a group of boys. Among them is Thomas, with his phone in hand and Shana in tow. They sit on the high stools in front of the counter, and I notice that Thomas has his head bowed, peering at something on his phone. Shana reaches over him and flirtatiously whispers something in his ear, but he pays her no mind. Then she starts stroking the back of his head, but that's a bust too. Thomas just continues to look at the phone, dead to the outside world. Finally, the redhead is annoyed enough to turn away and talk to a blond-haired boy I don't think I've seen before.

"Who are you looking at?" asks Alex, bringing me to my senses.

"Um, nothing, I've just never seen that blond-haired guy there at the counter. Do you know him?" Yet another lie. What is happening to me? Alex turns and stretches his neck to look at the group of boys.

"I think he's an engineering major. Why?" he asks suspiciously.

"Curiosity." I redirect the conversation quickly to something that will distract Alex—my relationship with Travis. About ten minutes later, I see the guys walk toward the exit. I follow them with my eyes but I notice that one of them is missing. As they reach the threshold, I see Shana turn in my direction. The nasty look she gives me makes my skin crawl, even from a distance. I straighten up in my chair, confused and flustered. Since when does Shana know I exist?

"Hello, stranger." Thomas's deep voice is right next to me, and I can feel his warm breath on my ear, which causes a strange flickering sensation in my belly. I gasp as he slides into the chair beside me, with his legs splayed and one arm stretched across the back of my chair. Alex looks at us with wide eyes.

"Stop calling me that," I hiss, regaining lucidity.

"Calling you what?" he retorts, pretending not to understand.

I glare at him. "You know what. What the hell are you doing here anyway? You're not welcome."

"I'm greeting a friend. Isn't that what 'friends' do?"

"You and I are not friends. I already told you that."

Thomas chuckles, takes my hands, and crushes them against his chest, right where his heart would be.

"Are you telling me that last night was just a game to you?" he asks, seemingly hurt.

I look into his eyes, stunned, not daring to look at Alex and see his reaction. Then, Thomas bursts out laughing, and I realize that he is only mocking me. Again.

"I wanted to experience the thrill of saying that for once, rather than just hearing it yelled at me." He smiles at me with satisfaction.

"You're such an idiot." I lower my eyes to my coffee, uncomfortable. I hear Alex clear his throat. My God, what a mess.

"Am I gonna see you in any of my classes today?" Thomas needles.

"No, fortunately."

"Too bad, I'll miss seeing your pouty little face every time I turn around," he teases me.

"Well, I certainly won't miss having classes constantly interrupted so someone can feed his ego." I get up from the table, sling the book bag over my shoulder, and gesture for Alex to leave with me. Our first classes are going to start soon, and I have no desire to waste any more time with this bigheaded, tattooed prick.

"Okay, now explain to me what just happened. Do you know that guy?" Alex asks the moment we leave the cafeteria.

"No! Of course I don't! We just have a couple of classes together, and he's on the basketball team with Travis, you know that. He's just a blowhard who thinks he's God's gift to women, nothing more complex than that."

"We are talking about Thomas Collins, right? He never talks to a girl without ulterior motives."

"If by 'ulterior motives,' you mean 'irritating me at every available opportunity,' then you are quite right."

"You know what I mean, Nessy. Don't be naive."

I burst out laughing. "You're way off base, Alex."

He crosses his arms over his chest. "Then why are you blushing right now?"

"What? I'm not...I'm not blushing!"

"You are, though," he insists with a grimace that says "gotcha."

"Look, I don't know what you two are up to but—"

"We're not up to anything!" I interrupt.

"I'm just saying, you're better off not getting involved with him. You know I'm no Travis fan, but Thomas is somehow even worse. Besides, frankly speaking, I doubt he's pursuing you for your own sake. He hates Travis."

I know he's saying this for my benefit, and I even know he's got several good points. Yet, for some strange reason that I cannot fully grasp, his advice annoys me.

"So he couldn't possibly be attracted to me? Is that what you mean?"

"What?" he asks in amazement.

"I get it. Who could possibly be interested in a girl who spends her day reading or studying, a shut-in with no social life at all?" I look away from Alex, not wanting him to see my eyes get misty.

"What are you talking about?" Alex grabs my arm and pulls me back, forcing me to look at him before we enter the classroom. "Guys like Thomas don't love anyone. All they know how to do is use women. Don't fall into this trap," he explains to me calmly.

"I'm not falling for any trap. Travis has already warned me to keep my guard up. He doesn't even want me to talk to Thomas."

"I hate to admit it, but Travis may have actually gotten something right this time," says Alex.

"Well, I hate to admit this, but you are blowing things out of proportion," I retort, annoyed. All this scaremongering is getting old, and I hate being treated like some helpless child. I know exactly what kind of man Thomas Collins is. And I know full well that people like him ought to be kept at arm's length, if not farther away. "You should trust me," I grumble as we sit down. "I mean, yes, he is indisputably hot, with that bad boy appeal, but I'm not an idiot."

"That 'bad boy appeal'..." he repeats, incredulous. "So you are into him, then?"

"What? No! I didn't say that!" I sputter. Alex gives me a puzzled look, which manages to make me feel even more discombobulated. "And you seem to have forgotten the most important part of all this: I am in a relationship. I would never cheat on Travis. You know that about me."

It's true, what I'm saying. I am not a cheater. But why then do I feel like such a wreck whenever Thomas is around?

Seven

THE MORNING WENT BY WITHOUT any other problems. I didn't see Thomas again, and the tension with Alex dissipated. After spending most of the afternoon in the library to get ahead on my studying, I head to the gym for Travis's practice.

Before entering Dixon, I stop at the vending machine to get a bottle of water. The hallway is a little creepy at this time of evening. There's always an eerie silence. The walls are yellow ochre, the neon lights give off an annoying hum, and it's always cold. Shivering, I push a series of coins into the machine and type in the code, but just before the bottle drops, it gets stuck. The usual bad luck!

I try to shake the machine, but it's too heavy. I bang on the glass and the sides, but to no avail. I look around, hoping to find someone who can help me, and mercifully, I hear male voices heading in my direction.

Speaking of bad luck, mine seems to keep on haunting me. Up come Matthew, Finn, and Thomas, phones in hand, just like this morning at the coffee shop.

"Vanessa, what are you doing here?" asks Matt. "I would hug you, but I'm dripping with sweat."

I smile at him. "It's okay, let's just say you did."

"Are you coming back in with us? Travis has been looking for you all day. He says you disappeared."

Damn it, he's right. After greeting him at the entrance, I hadn't given my phone another glance.

"I got a little busy, but I was on my way. I stopped to get some water, but the bottle got stuck." My eyes land on Thomas. It's odd that he hasn't yet directed any of his sarcastic jokes at me. He's not even looking at me, focused as he is on his screen.

As if he'd read my mind, Thomas looks up at me. In the fluorescent light, his green eyes sparkle hypnotically. I feel an unusual tingle in my belly.

He takes a step toward me and I instinctively shrink back, but he was headed for the vending machine, not me. With a swing of his arm that doesn't cost him the slightest effort, he gets the bottle to drop down. He sets it on the adjacent table and gets a soda for himself.

"Oh, thanks a lot, very nice of you," I stammer, trying to smile. He has no reaction. He pulls a red pack of cigarettes out of his warm-up jacket and lifts one to his mouth. Before walking away, he shoots me a look that leaves me dumbstruck.

"What's with him?" I ask, confused.

Asking Travis's friends for information about Thomas isn't exactly the best move, but one of my biggest flaws is my curiosity. I can never keep it at bay.

"Who, Thomas?" Finn replies, nodding in the direction where he had headed.

"Yeah. He seems mad or something," I say hesitantly.

"He's pissed at his sister. He'll get over it. They've been on the phone arguing all morning," Matt replies.

I wonder what happened...

"Listen, Matt," I say after glancing at the clock. "Do me a favor. Tell Travis I really wanted to stay, but it's getting late, and I have to get home."

Bullshit, more and more bullshit.

"You won't come and watch? We finish in an hour, then he'll take you home."

"No, I'd rather walk." I take my jacket out of my bag and slip it on.

"Okay, your call. See you later." They head off with unconvincing smiles.

I say goodbye and head for the exit. I take my phone and find the texts Travis had sent throughout the day.

To placate him, I write him that I'm heading home and that I'll see him tomorrow. I put the phone away and scan the deserted area. Or almost deserted. Thomas is sitting on the lawn a little ways away from the main entrance to the gym, shrouded in a cloud of smoke. An instinct I can't control pushes me to go over there, hoping to figure out what is going on with him.

As I approach, I realize that I have no idea what to ask him. I begin to think that it was a bad idea to come out here. But I push my concerns aside. I'm going to be a mature person and just go up and ask how he's doing.

"You'll catch a cold sitting out here, you know?" Oh God. Of all the things I could say, how did I come up with something so ridiculous? Jeez, Vanessa, it's not like you're his mother.

"You just can't stay away from me, can you?" he asks me sarcastically, without even looking up.

"I had to pass by here on my way home, unfortunately," I lie.

"Then go home." He takes a drag from his cigarette and dismisses me, saying, "I don't want you bugging me."

I was ready to engage with Thomas's usual arrogant self, but the gruffness of his response catches me by surprise. I turn to face him, drop my bag on the ground, and bark at him, "All right, why are you being such an asshole to me? I haven't done anything to deserve it."

"I thought you were used to dealing with assholes. Or is your boyfriend the only one you can handle?" he asks with a presumptuous look that gets on my nerves.

"What's that supposed to mean?"

His head bowed, he runs a hand through his hair in a slow, tortured gesture. "Nothing. Weren't you leaving? What are you still doing here?"

He's right, what was I doing there? Did I expect we would be laughing and joking around like old pals? He's nice, then he's a jerk. And I'm just an idiot.

I shrug and without saying anything else I walk off briskly, leaving him and his bluster behind.

But before I turn the corner, I hear him call my name. It's the first time I've ever heard him say it. He says it again, louder, surprising me. My pride tells me not to turn around, but another part of me wants to give him the benefit of the doubt and see if he's sorry for the way he's treated me.

I turn around and go back to where he's sitting on the lawn. "I expect an apology," I say, standing there with my arms folded over my chest.

He scoffs. "That's not gonna happen."

"Then why the hell did you call me back here?"

"Because you're so out of it you forgot your bag." He picks it up off the ground and throws it at my feet. I grab it and can no longer hold back the wave of anger crashing over me.

"You've been a total jerk! You've been tormenting me for days, and now I'm trying to...to..." The words stick in my throat. The truth is that I don't know what I was trying to do. Nor what I was trying to achieve. "Ugh. You know what? Just go to hell!" I blurt out.

His only response is a snarky grimace. I know I should leave. I should for my dignity, at least. Yet I don't. I stay standing there, the soles of my shoes glued to the ground. There is something there...something in his dark, haunted eyes that makes me think he doesn't really want me to leave. But maybe it's only a foolish delusion.

"You like it, don't you, mocking me, teasing me all the time?" I ask.

Thomas rubs out his cigarette on the concrete, blowing the last mouthful of smoke upward. "You're an easy target."

"You know who likes easy targets? Bullies. Is that what you are?"

He lets out a long sigh and rubs his face with a weary gesture. "Are you done with your bullshit?"

"Are you done being insufferable?" I mirror his effrontery but I get no response. We simply challenge each other with our gazes, our eyes lingering on each other's for an interminable moment. And then Thomas breaks into a wry grin. "Now what have you got to smile about?" I ask, confused. Keeping up with his sudden mood swings is exhausting.

"You're funny when you try to act tough. You look like an angry kitten," he taunts. I shoot him a sideways look.

"Well, the angry kitten is leaving."

I do turn to go, but this time Thomas doesn't wait before saying "Stop." His deep voice echoes in the empty space around us, making me shiver.

"What?" I stammer, dazed. "Didn't you just say…" I break off, because the expression on his face suggests that he doesn't want to hear any more questions. I force myself to put aside my pettiness and search his face. I try to figure out if he's still messing with me, but I can't. This guy is unreadable. "Do you want me to stay?"

Thomas looks down and shrugs one shoulder indifferently.

"Say so, or I'm leaving. Seriously."

At that point he looks at me, completely somber, with an intensity that burns me like fire.

"Stay," he says with a sigh.

Eight

WE ARE SITTING NEXT TO one another on the lawn, and neither of us utters a word. A deep silence descends upon us, and the only thing I can hear is the distant chirping of crickets and the hum of other insects far in the background. The dimmed lights of an after-hours campus illuminate this rather awkward moment. Awkward for me, at least.

Thomas seems perfectly at ease as he fiddles with the tab of his soda can. I look around, pull up a few tufts of grass, examine a chunk of my hair for split ends. I should trim these...

"I really make you nervous, huh?" he observes with a hint of smug satisfaction in his voice.

"Of course not," I lie. "So...why aren't you practicing with the rest of the team?" I ask, pulling the sleeves of my jacket over my hands.

"Who knows?" he replies tersely.

Oh, well, that clears everything up.

My gaze snags on his exposed biceps, and I get lost, admiring the tattoos that cover his skin. I get stuck on a sideways hourglass, wrapped in barbed wire. Inside, three small black butterflies are ready to take flight. I wish I could ask him what it means, but I know he'd never tell me.

"You know, I've always wanted to get a tattoo. The idea of permanently imprinting something on my skin fascinates me, but I'm too much of a wimp to really do it. Just the thought of getting stabbed so many times with those little needles gives me the creeps."

Thomas gives me a furtive, indecipherable look.

"You wanna go back in? You're probably getting cold," I fret.

"No."

"Care to tell me why you're in such a bad mood?" I venture, knowing that the answer will be a resounding...

"No."

Of course.

"Thomas, you may not know this, but if you want to have a conversation, you may have to tell me more than just 'no,'" I explain patiently as I would to a small child.

"Never said I wanted a conversation."

"Okay..." I feel a little silly for hoping that he would confide in me. After all, we barely know each other. "Look, you seem tired, and I get the feeling that you don't really want me here. So I'll leave you alone if that's what you want."

"If I didn't want you here, you wouldn't be here," he snaps impatiently.

"All right, then." I'm not sure what to do if he doesn't feel like talking. I take *Sense and Sensibility* out of my bag, and, taking advantage of the flickering light from a nearby streetlight, I let myself get lost in the story.

Out of the corner of my eye, I see Thomas lie down on the grass. He crosses his arms behind his head and turns his eyes to the sky.

"What are you doing?" I ask, surprised.

"I'm taking advantage of the darkness and enjoying the view. Wanna join me?"

"No," I answer in plain disgust. "The lawn is dirty and wet."

"So you're squeamish as well as prickly," he answers, mocking me.

"It's not that, it's just..."

"Shut up and come here," he interrupts, taking the book from my hands. He closes it and sets it on the ground in a way that makes me wince, and then he takes my arm and pulls me down next to him. This unexpected closeness puts me on edge. My heart starts to beat faster, and my breathing speeds up. As I turn my gaze upward, I am amazed at the spectacle above us: the sky looks like a spill of ink, enclosing an infinity of bright stars. They look like innumerable tiny diamonds.

I spot constellations: Cygnus, the swan and, near it, Delphinus, the dolphin. When I was little, Dad used to take me up onto the roof of our house. All, of course, without Mom's knowledge. It was our secret place, where we could sit and stargaze, and he always said that the brightest one was the wishing star. We would race each other to find it and make a wish.

The starry sky has never been the same since he left us.

Thomas and I stay quiet for a few minutes and settle into the stillness around us. A light breeze rustles the trees and sends the taller grass swaying. Although I am inclined to enjoy the moment, I can't hold back a shudder at the idea that my hair is touching the grass that everyone stamps all over with their dirty feet. I try to suppress my discomfort, even though I want nothing more than to run straight into my shower at home and scrub until I've eliminated every last one of the microorganisms that surely must be feasting on me.

"Are you okay?" asks Thomas.

I jump.

Of course I'm okay. I'm just dealing with a very minor nervous breakdown caused by my germophobia.

"Oh, yes. I'm fine," I hiss, crossing my arms over my chest and trying to keep calm.

"Yeah, I can see that." He chuckles. "What's the problem?"

"Nothing! It's just that insects scare me a little bit and lying on the ground kind of...grosses me out," I confess offhandedly. Thomas sits up, shaking his head. He pulls his omnipresent bandana off his wrist, unrolls it, and looks at me. "Lift your head up," he commands, with a hint of amusement in his voice.

"What? Why?"

"Just do as I say and knock it off with all the questions. It's annoying."

"I can't help it, that's just the way I am," I defend myself as I get into a seated position.

"Nosy?"

"Curious."

Thomas gives me an eloquent look but does not reply. He spreads the bandana out on the ground and invites me to rest my head on it. I can't deny that the gesture warms my heart a little.

"Did somebody inject you with pleasantness?" I tease. "Or have you perhaps discovered that you have an incurable disease and now offer good deeds to anyone who crosses your path?"

"It's just a bandana," he grumbles. "You looked like you were on the verge of a hysterical episode."

"That's not true." Sitting next to him, I elbow him in the ribs and bite my lip. He smiles genuinely for the first time since I've known him. I want to point that out to him, but I have a feeling that, if I did, he would instantly stop.

"Yeah, you did. You made the same disgusted face I make every time I have to see your boyfriend in the showers," he says wickedly, and my smile dies on my lips.

"Am I ever going to find out why you two hate each other so much?"

Thomas ignores me.

"Hey, I asked you a question. Did you hear me?"

He sighs in frustration, ruffling that lock of hair that constantly falls over his forehead. "Hard not to hear you…" He's quiet for a moment, before continuing, "Suffice it to say that your boyfriend is a moron. And you should open your eyes."

"Be more specific," I press, feeling a strange sense of foreboding.

"You're together, right?" he blurts out angrily, his eyes full of hate. "If you have any doubts, fucking ask him."

I'm startled by this unexpected aggression. "Sorry, I…wasn't trying to make you mad," I murmur, disheartened.

Thomas lets himself fall back on the lawn, while I am overwhelmed by a thousand feelings and even more questions. I torture myself trying to think of a plausible reason for the intense hatred he harbors toward Travis—and Travis toward him—but I come up empty. I feel like there's just so much that I'm not being told.

It's Thomas who pulls me out of my spiraling thoughts. He picks up the book I was reading and waves it in the air. "*Sense and Sensibility*, by Jane Austen," he reads from the cover. He looks at me out of the corner of his eye. "Why am I not surprised?" I can tell by the way he speaks that he's trying to let me know that his anger has subsided.

"Do you like reading?" I ask hopefully.

"It's boring."

I press a hand to my chest in mock grief. "You have broken my heart."

"It was bound to happen sooner or later," he teases me. I'll allow it, this time.

"You don't know what you're missing."

"Oh yeah? Why don't you tell me about it?" he asks curiously.

"This one is about the lives of two very different sisters. One is passionate and spontaneous, the other more logical."

"And what happens to these two sisters?"

"They fall in love with two men, also very different, and that love changes them all profoundly."

He doesn't answer, instead setting the book down on the lawn again and sitting up before lighting a cigarette.

"You want one?" he asks, holding the pack out to me.

"No, thank you." He smirks, as if he'd been expecting that answer. "Don't you smoke a little too much for an athlete? I thought there were very strict rules about that."

"There are, but I can't help it."

"And your coach is okay with that?"

He laughs a bitter laugh. "If by 'okay' you mean 'threatens to suspend me every other day,' then yes, I would say he's okay with it. He'll never go through with it, though. He needs me. We both know that."

"Have you ever thought of quitting?" I gather my knees to my chest and rest my chin on them.

"You gotta want to quit to make it stick. And I don't want to."

He takes a long drag and, after blowing out all the smoke, gets lost staring at the glowing cherry with a strange and worrisome devotion.

"Nicotine keeps a lot of my impulses at bay. Things I wouldn't be able to control otherwise."

"What impulses?" I ask innocently, and I immediately regret it, because I can see Thomas getting broody again. He runs his hand through his hair, nervous. "Tell me something," I say quickly, hoping to disperse some of the tension, "how long have you been playing basketball?"

"Why do you care?"

"Well, if we're going to be friends, we should know things about one another," I explain, but really he's the only one I want to investigate. There's more to him than he wants to let on, hiding under the surface.

"So you want to be my friend?" he jokes, giving me a sly look.

"First rule of friendship: wipe that smirk off your face."

He snorts in amusement and, after taking another drag on his cigarette, he replies. "I've been playing pretty much as long as I can remember."

"Have you always been so good at it?"

He looks at me as if the answer is a given. "What do you think?"

"So full of yourself…"

"Self-aware, I'd say." For a moment he pauses, clearly thinking about something, then adds, "In all honesty, I am a complete failure. On every front. Basketball is the one thing I'm good at. As soon as I step on the court, everything falls into place, and all the rest of the shit in my life disappears. There's just me, the dull sound of the net when I make a basket, the hardwood floor under my feet, and the adrenaline coursing through my body, guiding my movements."

I look at him, spellbound. "That must be a beautiful feeling."

"You bet it is."

"Thomas…" I pronounce after mulling it over.

"Yeah?"

"You're not… You are *not* a complete failure. Nobody is," I add, fiddling with my shoelaces, because the way he's glaring at me makes me realize that I am touching on something delicate. Maybe another time.

"Don't talk about me. You don't know me," he admonishes me tersely, turning to look away.

"True, I don't know you. But I know you're human, and human beings make mistakes. All of us. You shouldn't be so hard on yourself. You may even be grateful, one day, because our mistakes are what make us who we are. Without them, we would never really understand the essential nature of life—we would just be empty shells." I place my hand on his shoulder to reassure him, but I feel him stiffen. I realize I have pushed too hard, and I retract my hand as if burnt. But I don't give up. "Our mistakes make us human, not failures," I continue.

"Some mistakes destroy people, Vanessa. Permanently." He's so cold as he utters these words, I can't help but wonder what made him so disillusioned.

"Seriously?"

"Never been more serious in my life," he replies, looking steadily into my eyes.

I look away from him, refusing to hear anything else. I'm cold, so I wrap my arms around my knees.

"You're shivering," he observes after a while, tossing his cigarette a few feet away from us. "You should go home," he orders.

"No, I'm fine." I don't want to leave. I want to stay here with the evening breeze on my face and allow this knot in my stomach to slowly unravel.

I lie down, resting my head on his bandana, and look back up at the sky in an attempt to find some relief.

"Whatever you say," he says, lying back down beside me.

"You can go inside if you want."

"I offered for you. It's fifty degrees out, and you're shivering."

"I'm not cold," I insist.

"Tell the truth," he teases me.

"What truth?" I look at him, confused.

"This is all just an excuse to get me to hug you. Sorry, but it's not going to happen," he snickers.

"It is absolutely not an excuse for any—" I start to say, before I realize he's teasing me again. "You are such a comedian, Thomas," I say in a flat voice, narrowing my eyes at him.

A gust of wind suddenly picks up, rustling the trees around us. Some leaves break off and dance in the wind, eventually coming to rest, mostly in my hair. I sit up and try to pick them out but, in my usual bungling way, only manage to tangle them up more.

"Stop. Let me help," Thomas leans toward me, stretching one hand out to my hair while holding my arm with the other. "I'm helping."

"No need, I've got it," I insist. I extract blades of grass and bits of dry leaves with no small amount of difficulty. He lifts a corner of his mouth, amused, but in the next moment, something in his gaze changes. He stiffens and becomes more alert. I am immediately alarmed.

"What? What is it?"

"If I told you to stay still, would you listen to me?"

"Why?" I hiss, almost breathless.

"Because you have a bug in your hair."

What!?

My eyes snap open wide, and I begin to writhe and scream in panic. "Oh my God, that's disgusting! Get it off! Get it off right now!"

"I would if you would stop thrashing like a lunatic." I do not miss the amused tone with which he speaks to me. Clearly this is a great joke. For him. He leans toward me, and my breath catches in my chest. His breath is warm, very close now to my lips. When I feel his fingers move gently through the strands of my hair, I close my eyes fearfully and cover my face with my hands.

"Open your eyes," he urges me after a little while, with a care in his voice that he has so far never reserved for me. But I shake my head no, lips pressed together tight, scared to death.

"C'mon, be brave." He nudges me. I feel his hand grasping mine and trying to pull it away from my face, but I resist. An involuntary reflex. "I got it, you're okay," he murmurs soothingly against my ear.

I slowly lower my hands, coax myself to open my eyes, and I realize suddenly how close Thomas is to me. The tips of our noses are nearly touching. I shiver, my throat drier than the Sahara.

"Are you okay?" He curves his lips into a mischievous smile while I'm trying to remember how to swallow. I give a disjointed nod and, as I feel his gaze sliding slowly to my mouth, my stomach contracts, and a wave of heat sweeps over me from head to toe. I am helpless here, a breath away from his face, completely at the mercy of whatever move he makes.

Thomas inclines his head, as though fighting an impulse stronger than himself. "Fuck..." he curses through gritted teeth, closing his eyes. When he lifts his head up, the cold expression on his face immediately dampens the fire that was beginning to kindle in my body. There is no time to press my hands against his massive chest, no time to put the necessary safe distance between us before I am startled by a familiar voice behind us. My heart stops.

It's Travis.

Nine

"WHAT THE FUCK ARE YOU two doing out here together?" growls Travis, a few steps away from us. I turn to look at him, and I can see his face is already red with anger.

It can't have been an hour already! I grab my book from the ground and spring to my feet in the blink of an eye, as though he'd found me in someone else's bed rather than on the lawn. My heart is pounding, beating right out of my chest.

Travis is flushed and looks like he's ready to explode. All of his muscles are tensed, and his eyes are menacing as he stares at Thomas and me. "Weren't you going home, Vanessa?" He advances on us furiously. Travis has many faults, but violence has never been among them. Yet, in this moment, I am afraid of him. My God, how did I get myself into this situation? What was I thinking?

I try to say something, force myself to spit out some explanation, but panic seizes my throat. I'm so intimidated by Travis's wrath that I instinctively retreat a few steps and hide behind Thomas, who has gotten up by now and is standing in Travis's path.

"You're scaring her, you idiot. We weren't doing anything. Relax," he answers for me in an irritated tone. Then, he lights up a cigarette with all the calm in the world.

"I just caught you all over my girl, and you're trying to tell me it's nothing? You better get the fuck out of here, or I swear—" Travis threatens, stabbing a finger at him.

"What? What are you going to do?" Thomas moves toward my boyfriend until they stand dangerously close, face-to-face. My legs are shaking, and I clutch my book tightly against my chest. I feel like I might faint. I want to speak, to intervene in this madness, but it feels like I'm watching the scene from far above, unable to do anything.

"Travis, please stop," I shriek with tears in my eyes, finally managing to free myself from that fear paralysis. I try to grab my boyfriend's arm, but in vain: in a fit of pure madness, Travis pounces on Thomas, slamming a fist into his gut. Thomas bends double, groaning. Distraught, I bring my hands to my hair.

What really makes my run blood cold, however, is the absent, empty look on Thomas's face as he gets to his feet and growls through clenched teeth, "You're a dead man." It feels like I'm watching the scene through a hazy filter, and before I can even really register their movements, Travis is thrown to the ground with brutal force. I scream desperately for them to stop, but neither boy hears me. They roll through the grass and onto the asphalt, at each other's throats like rival lions, until Thomas gets the upper hand and pins Travis. He towers over my boyfriend with his fist raised, ready to pummel him.

"Thomas, stop! Please, I'm begging you!" I shout again, my eyes blurred with tears, hands shaking with terror. Just when I begin to fear the worst, Finn and Matt burst out of the gym doors. They descend on the brawlers and finally, with effort, separate the two of them.

"What the fuck is wrong with you guys? Are you crazy?" Matt yells.

Travis gets to his feet, and, despite his bleeding mouth, tries to hurl himself at Thomas again. Matt holds him back, putting his body between the two of them. "Calm down, man! You wanna get arrested?" he shouts, moving his gaze to Thomas, who is being restrained by Finn. "What the fuck happened here?"

"What happened is this asshole harassing my girlfriend!" Travis yells, spitting out a mouthful of blood and wiping his lip with the back of his hand.

"'Harassing'?" Thomas repeats with a sinister grin. Finn is still holding his arm in an attempt to keep him from making any wild moves. "Your girl didn't seem too harassed to me."

The implicit accusation lands like a thud in my chest. I give Thomas a murderous glare as Travis takes the bait, furiously trying to charge Thomas again. Thank goodness Matt is still there to stop him.

I move to Travis and plant myself in front of him. Up close, I can see that his eyes are still filled with rage. I take his face in my hands and try to calm him down.

"Travis, nothing happened!"

He pushes me away, furious, and refuses to meet my eyes.

"We were just talking!" I continue, determined to make him listen. "I was on my way home, I saw him out here, and I stopped to chat, nothing more!" I am a big fat liar. I know it, and I am ashamed of it. But, gradually, Travis's breathing evens out. His face is swollen and already bruised. I put one hand on his chest soothingly and, with the other, reach up to softly caress his cheek. "I'm sorry, I shouldn't have done it, but this is all just a huge misunderstanding. Please believe me."

"If I see you with him again, it's over," he says breathlessly.

He looks at me gravely, his mouth a clenched line, and I realize he is deadly serious.

"Okay," I murmur, scared. Travis and I are not in a good place right now, but that doesn't mean I want to throw away what we have for some random idiot who only ever wants to play games.

Behind us, I hear Thomas wriggle out of Finn's grip. In a moment, he catches up to us. "Relax, Captain," he calls out to Travis before pausing. He clicks his tongue, shooting me a look of pure contempt. "This one couldn't get my dick hard if she tried. Otherwise, I would have fucked her already."

"As for you"—his eyes, full of hate, snap back to Travis—"that's the last time you put your hands on me. Try it again and you'll wake up on a fucking stretcher."

I watch as he turns his back on me and walks away toward the dorms without giving me a second glance. He takes with him all of his arrogance, his disrespect, and his pure meanness. Meanwhile, there I stand, humiliated, tears in my eyes, trying to pretend I haven't just been stabbed in the heart.

But I can't let Travis see me hurting. So I put on a brave face and reassure Matt and Finn before wrapping an arm around Travis's waist and guiding him to the pickup truck. I offer to drive, but he refuses, and I don't have the stomach to argue with him. The car ride home is silent, the tension palpable. Travis doesn't speak to me and doesn't look at me. I get it; I had promised him that I would stay away from Thomas and instead I ran right to him like an idiot. I should have listened to Travis. Instead I just lied to him.

How stupid are you? I chastise myself. I allowed my emotions to override my reason, but it will never, ever happen again. *I have a boyfriend, dammit!*

"See you tomorrow," Travis says when we arrive in front of my house.

"Travis…" I try to take his hand, but he recoils and stares at an indistinct spot beyond the windshield.

"I'll get over it."

"I need to know you're okay."

"Do you think I'm okay?"

I lower my gaze, ashamed. "But why did you overreact like that? If anyone else had seen you, you could have been kicked off the team. Or arrested!"

"What were you doing out there with him?"

"I told you, we were talking."

"'Talking'…" he repeats, a note of frustration in his voice. "What, are you two friends now? Why didn't I know about this?"

"We are not friends. There's nothing to know. I ran into him out there and started talking. You know how I am. I'll chat with anybody."

More lies.

"I found you outside, alone with him, inches from his face. Tell me, what am I supposed to think?"

"It wasn't what it looked like. He was—he was just pulling a bug out of my hair," I explain guiltily, tugging the sleeves of my jacket over my hands. A nervous tic.

Sighing heavily, Travis runs his hands over his face, like he's trying to get his mind back in order. There's a sad look on his face, which is still swollen from Thomas's punches.

"I know you, Vanessa." He shakes his head and rests one hand on the steering wheel. His gaze out the windshield is resigned.

"Excuse me? What does that mean? If you know me, then you should know that I would never do anything to hurt—"

"You don't understand!" he interrupts, slamming his hand on the steering wheel.

"What? What don't I understand?"

"He…" He shakes his head knowingly. "He's after you!"

I stay staring at him without saying anything for a good handful of seconds, merely blinking. "That's nuts. He's not after me. Besides, even if he was, I'm the one you need to have faith in. I forgave you for Friday night, can't you let one innocent conversation go?"

Travis laughs bitterly. "Just know that he doesn't give a damn about you. I'm the one he's trying to get at."

"Why would he want to get to you?"

"That's not the point!" he shouts, making me wince. I want to tell him that, actually, I have every right to know the reason for their bizarre hatred, but his anger is scaring me. Instead, I give up and remain silent.

"I expect you to be more careful from now on. Now go," he orders without even looking at me.

"Okay," I whisper. I get out of the car with a heaviness in my chest; I have never seen Travis so angry. Yet, as I watch him drive off into the night, it is not his feelings that I'm lingering on. It is the hurt that Thomas inflicted upon me with his words, which keep swirling relentlessly inside my head.

Ten

WHEN I CROSS THE THRESHOLD of the house, I can smell roasted chicken and potatoes, my favorite dish. Mom always prepares it with a ton of aromatic herbs from her garden. She grows all kinds. It's one of her passions after mud baths at the spa and good wine.

"I'm home," I announce as I take off my shoes. I hang up my jacket and put my bag on the dark wooden bench in the hall. I feel the urgent need to dash into the shower, but first I have to say hi to my mother. I quickly tidy myself up in the mirror, not wanting her to notice how disheveled I've been by the confusion of the past few hours. She would surely start asking questions that I wouldn't know how to answer.

I stare intently at my own reflection. I am pale. My gray eyes are overlarge, and even I can see the wounded, exhausted look in them. The long black hair makes me look even gloomier. Maybe I should stop dyeing it and go back to my natural blond? I sigh heavily and give my cheeks a little pinch, hoping to give the appearance of color. Then, I paste on a fake smile and make my entrance.

From the living room, I can hear the buzz of the television. I head there and find my mother on the sofa with her legs bent to the side and one elbow resting on the armrest, as she flips through one of her back issues of *Vogue*. Her hair is up in its usual chignon, and she's wearing the vintage-style eyeglasses she uses only at home, because, according to her, they age her. She already has her pajamas on, a beige satin set, one of Victor's latest expensive gifts.

The more I look at her, the more I wonder how she does it. How can she so effortlessly exude elegance from every pore?

"I've been waiting all day for you. What happened?"

"Travis's practice ran long. I'm going upstairs for a minute to wash up," I tell her, leaning on the doorknob.

"Hurry up, dinner will be ready in forty minutes," she answers, never taking her eyes off her magazine.

"How come you're not with Victor tonight?"

"He had some urgent work to do."

I can't help but smile a bitter little smile. We have reached the point where she only thinks about me when Victor isn't available. I go up to my room, quickly shed my filthy clothes, and dash into the shower. As the hot water washes over me, I try to let it wash away the bad mood that's been keeping me company for a while now.

I step out of the shower and gather my hair into my usual turban before slipping into my bathrobe. In my room, I put on a clean and nice-smelling pair of pajamas before returning to my mother on the couch.

"Were you watching something?" I point to the television set with the remote.

"No, go ahead."

While channel surfing, I make an effort to strike up a conversation with the woman next to me, who bears only a slight resemblance to me.

"How was the law office?" I ask, resting my head on the armrest and stretching out my legs.

"Oh, fine. They hired a new intern yesterday; it's her first job."

"Why didn't you tell me they were looking for staff? I would have applied right away. I'm good with tasks that require precision," I grumble regretfully.

"And why would you ever do that?" she asks, a little miffed, as she turns the pages of her magazine.

"To contribute to expenses. I need to get myself out there, and I want to start being more independent," I tell her in what I hope is a convincing way, fiddling with the wet hair near my ear that has escaped from my turban.

"There's no need. I manage all the expenses very well, with Victor's help. You just think about studying." She smiles at me and adds, "Besides, your résumé would have been trashed anyway."

"Why?" I frown.

"They don't hire family members of their employees to avoid nepotism."

"Well, in any case, I do plan to get a job, so…"

She pulls her glasses down to the tip of her nose and interrupts me. "I don't want you getting a job. It would hold you back in your studies, and that cannot happen, not after all the effort I've put in to get you this far." She scowls.

Here it comes. She's butting into my life as usual.

"I am perfectly capable of balancing school and work. Lots of students do it. I don't see what the problem is."

"I don't care what 'lots of students do.' You do as I say," she retorts testily, emphasizing the last two words.

"Mom, I'm almost twenty years old. You do realize that you're treating me like I'm twelve, don't you? I'm going to get a job, end of story," I snap, giving her a look that brooks no dissent. I've had enough of people trying to control my life for one day.

She tightens her lips into a hard line and looks at me, enraged. She is about to explode, I can see it in her eyes. But I am ready—more than ready—to face all her wrath. In fact, I can't wait. I'd like to let off some steam of my own. But then, to my enormous surprise, she heaves a giant sigh and pronounces, "Fine. Whatever."

"R-really?" I stammer incredulously.

"Yes. You're an adult now. If you think you can handle it all, I don't see why you shouldn't try."

I look at her, stunned. I must have wound up in some sort of parallel dimension or something. I can't think of any other reason she would just give in like that.

"Okay, well…thanks," I murmur confusedly.

"You're welcome." She dismisses me and returns her gaze to the magazine.

I stare at her skeptically for a few seconds, still put off by her sudden reasonableness. I turn to the television in the hopes of finding a distraction, but all I do is fall into a pit of negative thoughts. One in particular stands out among the rest: Thomas. The spite and shamelessness with which he uttered those disgusting words, his face full of scorn.

I can't help feeling bitter, hurt, reduced to an object. If he had found me appealing, would he have used me for that? Just to get off? And is he assuming that I would have let him, without batting an eye? But since I didn't get his dick hard, he decided instead to use me to goad Travis by putting on that whole charade about wanting to be my friend. How stupid was I to believe his intentions were good? It explained his sudden change of heart when he asked me to stay there with him. He must have planned everything from the start. He knew that Travis would come out shortly and see us together and, like an idiot, I walked right into his trap.

"Are you all right?" my mother asks without looking away from the magazine, bringing me back to reality.

"Yeah, everything's fine," I hasten to answer in as indifferent a manner as possible.

"Are you sure? You were staring off into space like you were in a trance." She tilts her head toward me, looking into my eyes.

"Yes, Mother. I'm sure. When is dinner ready? I'm hungry," I say trying to change the subject.

Fortunately for me, the oven timer trills just then, and my mother gets to her feet. "Now," she says.

Silence hangs heavy over the table during dinner, interrupted only by the small sounds of cutlery on plates. I can occasionally sense my mother's inquisitive glances and wish with all my heart that I wasn't such an open book.

"I've been wondering," I say after a while, hoping to throw her off the scent, "when did you realize things weren't working with Dad anymore?"

She gives me a sideways look, her cutlery suspended in midair over the plate. "Why do you ask?"

"Well, we never really talked about it. I was a little girl when it happened, but I'd like to know more about it now."

"I think it's better not to dredge up the past," she responds with her usual aplomb. Then she looks at me, suddenly alarmed. "Everything is okay with Travis, right?" Her insinuation catches me off guard. Flustered, I start tapping my fingers nervously on the rim of my glass. She would flip out if I told her the truth.

"Yeah, everything's fine," I lie, having no other choice. She releases a breath, relieved.

"I wanted to talk to you too, actually," she continues, crossing her arms on the table. I brace myself for the worst. "Things have been going really well with Victor, you know. We've been dating for a few months now, and I'd like for you to meet him. Officially, I mean. Maybe at a family dinner?"

Stop. What? No. Absolutely not.

"Don't make that face," she rebukes me. "I haven't felt this way— so happy and full of excitement—in years, and it's all because of him," she harangues. "It would mean a lot to me," she insists, stretching her arms across the table to take my hands in hers.

"Mom, you know I hate these things," I whine.

"Please, Vanessa, can you do this for me? To make your mother happy?"

I sigh resignedly. Damn her and damn me for being incapable of saying "no." "Fine, Mom. Plan a dinner."

"Thanks, sweetheart. How about Friday?" she chirps impatiently.

"No, Friday is the game, and right after, we're going to a party," I unenthusiastically explain to her.

"Where? And since when do you go to parties?" she inquires with an arched brow.

"It will be at Tiffany's friend's house. And I go to parties. Rarely. But I do go," I clarify.

"Is Travis going with you?"

I blink, puzzled. "Of course, Mom."

"That's okay, then. I trust him." She raises her hands in surrender. "Could we do Saturday?" she suggests.

"Saturday is fine," I concede with a smile.

"Marvelous!"

We clear the table together and load the dishwasher. Mom invites me to go into the living room with her to watch some TV, but I'm not in the mood. Today has exhausted me. So much has happened that I haven't even had the time to process it all—I just want to sleep and not think.

In my room, I let myself fall into bed. Closing my eyes, I plumb the abyss of my thoughts, searching for a shred of sense. The sense that I have never lacked, until the moment I chose to approach the one person I should have kept far away from.

After a night of restless dreams, I wake up, still a little fuzzy-headed, before the alarm clock goes off. A true rarity. I go down to the kitchen to eat breakfast and find a note under a magnet on the refrigerator. It's from Mom, apologizing because she had to run off to work. I crumple it up and throw it in the garbage. There really isn't much in the refrigerator, but I manage to find two eggs and an almost empty carton of orange juice. I make a mental note to get groceries as soon as possible.

After making breakfast and cleaning up, I go up to my room to get dressed. I decide on a pair of black, high-waisted jeans that are a little more snug than usual. I pair them with a lightweight purple sweater that I tuck in to the waistband before spritzing my favorite perfume on my wrists and neck. For the first time since the semester began, I pull the straightener through my hair and apply light eye makeup. Today, I feel the need to boost my low self-esteem.

Before I go downstairs, I peek out the window to see whether Travis has arrived. His truck is parked in the driveway, and he's waiting for me, leaning up against the front end. I can tell from the frown on his face that he's still resentful about the night before.

I pull on my black leather over-the-knee boots and check out my backside in the mirror. I notice that the jeans showcase it a little too much, so I grab a long cardigan and wear it over my sweater. Now I'm ready to go. I walk toward Travis slowly and, when I finally reach him, he smiles at me, banishing the specter of resentment from his face.

"Hel—"

He doesn't give me a chance to finish but instead wraps his arms around my waist and kisses me passionately, leaving me stunned. So he's not mad anymore?

"You look beautiful this morning." He gestures for me to do a spin. "What's different about you?"

"Nothing!" I squeak, blushing.

"I missed you last night," he says, pressing his forehead against mine.

"Travis, I'm so sorry about what happened, I really am."

He places two fingers over my mouth. "Shh, let's forget about it. I've been thinking about it all night. I went too far. I took out my anger on you when he is the problem," he explains, guilt all over his face.

"I know, it won't happen again," I reassure him. "You are my boyfriend, you don't like him, and I don't like him either. Avoiding him won't be a problem. Besides, you and I are giving each other a second chance now, and I want to focus on us." I press my lips to his, and we kiss tenderly.

"My parents are out of town until tomorrow. You can sleep over tonight," he says mischievously.

"Sure." I stand on tiptoes to caress his cheek.

In the car, Travis seems cheerful, putting on a playlist with Harry Styles songs and reminding me about the concert. For a while, his unexpected good humor manages to make me forget about last night's fight.

When we arrive on campus, however, I immediately catch sight of Matt and Tiffany chatting intently. I hope Matt has kept his mouth shut about the mess yesterday. The last thing I need right now is a dressing-down from my best friend. Travis stops to laugh with them, and I use the distraction to slip away like a thief in the night. I head for my literary criticism class, but, just when I think I'm safe, Tiffany grabs me.

"Missy, you and I need to talk."

My friend is itching for me to tell her what happened. I'm itching to murder Matt.

Since I am only allowed to do one of those things, I tell her everything in great detail as we walk down the hall.

"So. Let's recap." She taps her index finger on her chin. "He asked you to stay with him, and you guys talked for more than an hour under a very romantic starry sky. He gave you his bandana so that you wouldn't get dirty. When he came this close to your lips, he backed off, and, after my brother caught you, he gave you a classic Collins-style snub?"

Collins-style? Is that a thing?

"Yeah, that's more or less how it went. So?" I cross my arms, waiting for an explanation.

Tiffany stands in front of me and puts her hands on my shoulders, her expression both amused and resigned.

"So, what?" I urge her.

She lets out a long sigh. "You're in deep shit, gorgeous, up to your neck."

"What is that supposed to mean?"

"At first, I thought my brother was just being paranoid, but now I'm beginning to think he's on to something."

"What are you talking about? I don't follow," I say, confused.

"Wake up! You've piqued his interest." She punctuates each word with such conviction that I burst into gales of laughter.

"Did you hear what I just said?" I thought my story had been pretty clear.

"Yeah, I heard," she says resolutely.

"He literally told me to my face that he doesn't like me! And in such a gentlemanly fashion too!"

Tiffany shrugs her shoulders. "He didn't say it to you, he said it to your boyfriend. That's completely different."

"It's not different at all, because I was right there, inches away from him. He might as well have said it to me!"

"Look, I know this hard for you to understand, because you've had only one boyfriend in your whole life, and, to your great misfortune, it's been my brother, but you can't listen to what people like Thomas say. You have to watch what they do. From what you've told me, he is showing you something else—"

I interrupt her because it's clear that she has lost her mind. "He hasn't shown me anything! He was making fun of me, bringing out his Don Juan bullshit only to blow me off the next minute. And this surprises me? Why? He's an asshole, and that's what assholes do," I say, raising my voice a little too much.

When I realize this, I look around embarrassed and pull a bit of my hair forward to cover my face.

"How can you be so naive, Vanessa?"

No, sir. I have been, in the past, but now I see everything clearly. Thomas just enjoyed teasing and humiliating me. He even admitted it: "You're easy prey." Tiffany can't talk to me like I'm a little kid who just found out the tooth fairy isn't real. It's irritating.

"I am not naive, I just tell it like it is. Since I met him, he's been giving me nothing but grief, and unless you're five years old, you don't constantly annoy the person you like."

Tiffany doesn't seem convinced, but I ignore her and continue, "Anyway, it doesn't matter whether he likes me or not, I promised Travis that I would stay away from him. It won't be a problem because I don't like him."

She lets out a laugh. "Well, good luck then, you'll need it. All three of you!" She snickers. She pushes me into the literary criticism classroom with a swat on the butt. I stick out my tongue at her.

After class, I decide to spend a few hours in the library. I quickly find my favorite spot, a secluded corner between the window and two rows of shelves. I place my bag on the round table and let myself sink into the chair.

About forty minutes later, I am in "mad and desperate study" mode with my hair pulled back into a low, tousled bun, a pen wedged between my teeth, and my notebook right under my nose.

When I realize that I need two books to delve deeper into the topic I am studying, I get up and head for the correct shelves. I walk down the aisle of books, trailing my index finger across the spines, but no luck. I lift my gaze to one of the topmost shelves and, of course, one of the books is right there. Two shelves above my head. I look around for a step stool but can't find one, so I have no choice but try to reach it on tippy-toes. I extend one arm and stretch my fingers as far as I can toward the shelf, to no avail. I grit my teeth and rest my heels back on the ground, resigned.

Suddenly I feel a presence looming around my shoulders, like a cloak. An arm wrapped in black leather passes close to the side of my face; I feel the solidity of a broad chest pressing against my back, making me wince.

"Why am I not surprised to find you here?" The low rasp of a voice that is becoming all too familiar blows hot on my neck, and it feels like my heart skips a beat.

For a few stunned seconds, I try to regulate my heartbeat and blink repeatedly to bring myself back to reality. Thomas then tucks the book into my hands and moves to the side to lean back against the shelf. He turns his gaze to me and crosses his arms over his chest. "Hello, stranger."

I can't believe it. The audacity to come here and bother me in my happy place! I glower at him, annoyed, before ignoring him to keep searching for the second book. He falls into step beside me as if nothing has happened, with his hands sunk into his jacket pockets.

"You're pissed off," he notes, unflappable, while I resolutely keep my eyes focused on the aisle of books at my left. I do not utter a word.

"So, that's the trick to shutting you up." He lets the sentence hang for a moment and then concludes, "I've just gotta piss you off. I'll keep that in mind."

I grit my teeth, increasingly irritated. I try to convince myself that if I just ignore him long enough, he will go away. I walk over to a stack of books and start plucking them out one at a time in the hopes of finding the one I need. Out of the corner of my eye, I see Thomas to my right, opening a pack of cigarettes and tucking one behind his ear. I release the air I had been holding in my lungs. For a moment, I thought he was going to try to smoke in here.

"Okay, you don't wanna talk. So I'll talk." He looks around, bored, and rubs his chin with one hand. "How's your boyfriend? He was in pretty bad shape yesterday," he sneers. "Did you tend to his wounds?"

"Listen carefully, Thomas," I say, with a threatening look. Once again, he's managed to make me lose my temper, and he seems pleased about it. "People come here to study in silence. Don't you have anything better to do? Like, I don't know, harassing old people at bus stops? Setting things on fire? Maybe attacking people unprovoked? I know you're really good at that."

"I'd rather bother you. It's more fun," he whispers with his usual shit-eating grin.

"Stop it!" I hiss through clenched teeth to avoid being overheard. "Did you come here just to make fun of me? Save it, I'm not going to let you." I turn with the book clutched to my chest and make to walk away. Thomas, however, grabs me by the wrist and pulls me to him.

"What's the matter with you?"

"What's the matter with me?" I growl, unable to hold back my anger any longer. "Do you even realize how ridiculous you are? All you do is harass me, constantly trash-talking my boyfriend. Last night you went nuts on him and then, not content with that, you took the liberty of...ugh, forget it!" If we were outdoors, I would probably have already been screaming at the top of my lungs.

He speaks with the air of one laying it all out clearly. "I'm not gonna apologize to you for hitting him. I'll remind you that he threw the first punch. Did you expect me to just stand there and take it? I was happy to give it right back to him and, for your information, I was holding back."

"I want to be very clear: Don't think for one second that I will let you use me. I don't know what happened between you two, but I won't be put in the middle of it," I hiss.

Thomas looks confused. "Do you think I'm using you?"

"I don't think so, I know so." For a moment, his expression darkens, but I don't understand why.

"You're full of shit." He sighs, rubbing his forehead with his thumb. "If I want something from a woman, I can get it without any tricks."

"What you said to Travis was disgusting," I mutter.

"I'll give you the chance to prove me wrong, anytime you want," he taunts. My eyes widen with indignation and I look around quickly. Fortunately, we are alone in our aisle.

"You...you're really sleazy. And disrespectful."

"Would it make you feel better if I apologized?" he asks, with a new gravity in his voice. He steps toward me, forcing me to step back.

"It would show that you're sorry, at least," I whisper.

"But I'm not. I'm not sorry about what I did. I was pissed off, but I wasn't trying to hurt your feelings. Nor was I trying to use you. However, I needed your boyfriend to get the message loud and clear." He takes another step toward me. I step back, until I run into the shelf and feel it pressed up against my back. He rests his hands on the shelf to either side of my head, caging me in. My throat tightens, and my breath quickens. I feel small under his imposing bulk. "Believe it or not, I was with you last night because I wanted to be with you."

My heart beats faster at the sound of his words. I lower my eyes, unable to hold his gaze. He tilts my chin up with one finger until I am looking in his eyes again. I swallow uncomfortably.

"It doesn't matter what I believe. I can't trust you, and that won't change," I admit. I feel an inexplicable twinge of sadness when I see his eyes darken. "Besides, the two of us have nothing in common," I add. "You don't get along with my boyfriend, and I can't risk ruining what we have for—"

"All right, then," Thomas interrupts me brusquely in a cold, impersonal voice tinged with resentment. "Whatever you want." With a sudden movement that leaves me off-balance, he straightens up and removes his hand from the side of my face, putting distance between us. I realize only now that all the muscles in my body were tensed.

I am filled with a disappointment that I shouldn't feel.

"Okay," I murmur with equal detachment, certain that this is the best solution for everyone. Confused and dissatisfied, I watch him walk away with long strides.

Eleven

I SPEND THE REST OF the morning in limbo, trying to untangle my knotted feelings. Leila doesn't show up at practice, and Thomas ignores me. The cold war is still on, however, between him and Travis.

After class, I tell my mother that I'll be sleeping over at the Bakers'. Tiffany invites me out to drinks with some of the girls in her class, but I'm not in the mood, so I tell her I'll stay in with Travis. But when he starts kissing and touching me in the middle of a movie, I give him the headache excuse. I'm not in that mood either. I still feel restless and even a little guilty about all those strange feelings I allowed myself to feel near Thomas. Travis can't hide his resentment, and so we watch the movie in total silence until we fall asleep facing away from one another.

I wake at the crack of dawn for a change, and I see Travis staring intently at the ceiling. I know what's troubling him: today is Friday. The first game of the season is this afternoon. So even though I can't think straight before my coffee, I sit on the edge of the bed and try to reassure him.

"Everything will be fine. The team is strong," I say, rubbing my eyes. In actuality, I am not so sure. The University of Oregon Ducks are among the best. Last year we came within a hair's breadth of winning the championship, but, in the end, they took it from us.

Travis snorts and sits on the edge of the mattress, running his hands through his curls. "I just want this day to be over quickly. At least this time, my father won't be in the stands." He jumps out of bed and heads for the bathroom.

I can see why he's stressed. His father is always pressuring him to make a good impression in front of the sponsors. But when Travis is nervous, he makes me nervous too, and I can't stand it.

After a silent high-protein breakfast, we get into the truck.

Campus is more chaotic than ever. On game days, the atmosphere is always hectic. Basketball fans are out in force. Lots of students, myself included, wear black sweatshirts with "Go Beavers!" written in orange lettering. Plus, tonight is the first party of the academic year—the electricity in the air is palpable.

In the parking lot we meet Finn and Matt, who greet Travis with fist bumps.

"Vanessa, how are you?" Matt exclaims, giving me a hug.

"Good, how about you?" I look around. "It's a real circus around here, huh?"

"You're telling me. I couldn't even find a decent place to park the car. I had to leave her off campus, and I swear if I find one scratch on her, I'm gonna lose it."

"Wait until the Ducks get here. Who knows if she'll come out unscathed?" I grin and rub it in. At my side, Travis is still tense.

"Shit, they're animals, if they so much as touch her, I swear..."

"Dude, give it a rest," Finn interrupts him. "You parked so far away that you'll have to have someone drive you to pick it up." He punches him playfully in the side, and I burst out laughing.

"Yeah, relax. We have other things to think about today," Travis joins in.

"So," I say a little uncomfortably, trying to change the subject, "are you ready for the game? You guys rocked it at practice yesterday."

"Bet, beautiful! This year we're going to kick Duck ass!" replies Matt with an eloquent hand gesture. "We've got it all locked down and, now that he's back at one hundred percent, we have a true prodigy on the team," he adds proudly.

"Matt, you're exaggerating like always, he's not a prodigy. He's just…passably good," Travis says angrily, giving his friend a dirty look.

"Shit, I want to be passably good like him too."

At these words, my stomach twists. And a strange intuition makes its way through me. They're not talking about…

"Hey, Collins, c'mere!" shouts Matt.

Damn, I knew it.

I can feel Travis's eyes on me, as if studying my every move. I force myself to not, under any circumstances, turn to look at him. I nibble on my cheek instead.

"Nah. I've got better things to do here," Thomas replies from afar.

"Matt! What the fuck are you doing? I don't want that asshole over here. Having to put up with him at practice is plenty," growls Travis. I take advantage of the fact that he and Matt are arguing and allow instinct to override my reason. With utmost discretion, I allow myself to send one furtive glance toward the six foot three collection of muscles and tattoos that sits on the edge of a rusty railing a few feet away from us. He has an unlit cigarette between his lips, his leather jacket open over a tight gray T-shirt that emphasizes his sculpted physique and a pair of dark-wash jeans, a little baggy and ripped. He still has that rough and wild look that never seems to leave him.

He's with Shana, for a change. She has positioned herself between his spread legs, with her back pressed against his chest. I know it shouldn't, but the sight of them bothers me. When Thomas senses my gaze on him, he gives me a contemptuous sneer, the same one Shana also reserves for me. Instinctively, I cling tighter to my boyfriend.

"Knock it off, Trav." Matt's voice makes me wince. "The other night you got outta hand, but it ends there. You're even now, right? Let bygones be bygones and be a man. Team chemistry depends on it."

"You're 'even'? What does that mean?" I stare at Travis, perplexed, waiting for an answer I'm not entirely sure I want to hear. Matt falls silent, awkwardly.

"Nothing. You know we can't stand each other. Let it go," he answers, scratching the back of his head and visibly annoyed.

"Let it go?" The two of them have secrets and a history that I know nothing about, and I'm supposed to just let it go? Does Leila have anything to do with it? Of course she does! I've known it since the first day I saw her in the gym!

"Does it have to do with his sister?" I ask around a rapidly forming knot in my throat.

"What? Jesus Christ, don't start that again!"

"I asked you a question, Travis!" I shout, determined to take it all the way this time. It's what I should have done from the start.

"Yeah, a stupid question, like always. Right now, I'm not in the mood for your ball-busting. Today is stressful enough as it is; don't bring your fucking insecurities into it too," he spits ferociously, leaving me and his friends frozen. I feel tears welling up, but I struggle to keep them at bay. I don't want to start sobbing like a child. Not here, not in front of everyone; this is humiliating enough as it is. So, incapable of responding the way I should, I instead run away before it's too late.

"Nessy! Come back here!" Travis shouts at my back. "Why did you bring that shit up?" I then hear him demand of Matt.

"And why do you treat her like shit every chance you get?" These are the last words that reach my ears before I cross the threshold of the liberal arts building. I run to the bathroom and lock myself inside. Leaning against the door, I finally burst into tears.

I feel so pathetic. I am a sophomore in college, dammit, and here I am locked in a bathroom, crying over a boy who deserves to be slapped in the face. I'm hopeless. I slide to the floor and pull my knees up to my chest. I sob heavily, until I hear someone banging on the door.

Some girls ask to come in. I wipe my cheeks and inhale deeply to settle my nerves before getting up and unlocking the door. I rinse my mascara-streaked face in the hope that a little cold water will get rid of the redness, but it is all in vain. I shrug my shoulders and, despite the pitiful image I see reflected in the mirror, I force myself to act like the mature person that I should be. I have three classes to take today and a game I want to attend. To hell with Travis and his continued lack of respect for me.

I leave the bathroom and head for my philosophy class. Obviously, because I cannot have a moment's peace, I see that Thomas is already seated at the last table. Well, at least this time he won't bother me. His eyes flicker warily over me. He examines me from top to bottom, frowning. But I ignore him, sit in the front row, and do my best to push down the heated sensation I feel whenever his eyes are on my skin, even from so far away.

When Professor Scott enters the classroom, he resumes his lecture on Kant. I hear him speak, but my thoughts are wandering. Matt's words resonate in my head as my logic wrestles with my hope that it's all some big misunderstanding.

"Miss Clark?" Professor Scott calls.

"Yes?" I reply, wincing.

"Class is over, you may go."

What, over? I look around and there is no one left in the classroom. Yikes. I gather my things and hurry out. As soon as I step outside, a strong arm drags me around a blind corner of the hallway.

"What the hell are you doing?" I lash out at Thomas. "Will you stop constantly popping up out of nowhere? It's starting to get disturbing," I exclaim, annoyed, as I try to extricate myself.

He grabs my shoulders and gives me a look so intense that it takes my breath away. "What's wrong with you?"

"I thought we set the record straight yesterday, didn't we? It doesn't concern you," I snap. "In fact, I don't even know why you're here instead of being with your girlfriend," I add contemptuously. But I regret it as soon as I see the corner of his mouth rise.

"Excuse me?"

"Nothing." I tighten my lips into a hard line. "Let me go, please?"

"She's not my girlfriend."

"Believe me, I don't care."

"Sure, I believe you," he says with a wry smile, closing the distance between our bodies. He brushes a strand of hair away from my face and I feel my heart leap. "Either way, that's not my thing," he says, shrugging his shoulders.

"What are you talking about?"

"Relationships. They're a cage I'm happy to stay out of. They all end up the same anyway."

"Meaning?"

"They're soul-destroying," he replies in a rough voice.

"That's crazy…"

"You think so? So tell me, how long have you been with Travis?"

"What?"

"How long have you been with your boyfriend?" he repeats determinedly.

"Two years."

"You know, for some people two years is a long time." He curls a lock of my hair around his index finger. "For other people, however, it's almost nothing…" He stares into my eyes, then his gaze drops languidly to my lips. It seems like he's thinking about something.

"So what? What are you getting at?"

"Are you happy?"

"Of course," I blurt out, but I quickly realize that I'm lying.

He snorts a laugh. "Come on, you don't believe that any more than I do. Two years in a relationship and he's taken everything from you. Your eyes are empty, Vanessa."

His words hit me square in the chest, creating a rift and unleashing emotions I didn't even know I had. This conversation is beyond belief; he has known me for barely a week, yet he can read me better than anyone else in my life. Better, even, than I read myself.

"You don't know what you're talking about," I keep lying, discomfited.

I try to pull away one more time because, all of a sudden, I feel suffocated, but he clasps my hips with both hands and pushes me against the wall.

"Thomas, let go of me," I say with less conviction than I would like.

He ignores me, runs a hand along my neck and looms over me, brushing my ear with his lips.

"I know exactly what I'm talking about," he whispers hoarsely. He caresses my cheek with his knuckles. I want to tell him that he cannot touch me like this, but I can't. My throat is tight and dry. My head is fuzzy, and my heart is beating wildly. I break out in a cold sweat. He moves on to my neck and I feel his lips curving slowly into a barely there smile. He is well aware of the chills he is giving me as I feel a fluttering like butterflies in my lower abdomen.

"W-what are you doing?" I whisper-gasp.

"I'll prove you wrong." He aligns his face with mine, and the way he looks at me makes my knees go weak. Confident. Dominant. Passionate. He carefully hovers his mouth over mine, and my heart begins to beat even faster. Whether it is fear or desire, I don't know. But just as our lips are about to touch, a ringtone brings me to my senses.

My phone.

With a trembling hand I pull it out of the pocket of my jeans. It's Travis.

I stare at it and, in a split second, all my good sense comes rushing back to me. Oh God... What am I doing? I look at Thomas, lost and guilty. Unlike me, he looks perfectly at ease. When he lowers his gaze to the screen of the phone, however, his expression changes. He becomes cold and distant, just like yesterday. Before I can say anything to him, he takes a step back and runs a hand through his hair, tousling it. "Your eyes are more beautiful when they smile, Vanessa."

He walks away, leaving me dazed and staring at the empty space where he used to be. It takes me a few minutes to recover from what-ever was happening with Thomas. I lean my head against the wall and close my eyes as the phone rings for the third time. And for the third time, I reject the call. My mind is in turmoil, crowded with thoughts and torn by guilt.

How did I find myself within a millimeter of his lips once again?

I rub my face and take a deep breath, trying to shake off the memory of his touch, of his eyes burning into me, of his body pressed close against mine. I cannot allow him to take over my thoughts, to destroy what I have built with Travis over the years. I cannot, cannot, cannot.

Guilt forces me to unlock my phone and type out a message for Travis: Meet me at the entrance of the Lit department. Ten minutes later, he materializes on the stairs of the neoclassical-style building where I spend most of my day. I grab him and drag him out to the trees in the garden, away from prying ears.

"I know you're going to yell at me, but just listen for a minute," he begins, clutching my arms. "This morning, I got caught up in the stress. You know, the first game, my father, the sponsors…"

I want to be angry, but remorse is eating me up inside. "I know," I say simply.

"And then you exacerbate things with all that stuff about the Collinses. You make me out to be a liar, but I'm not the one lying to you, Nessy. I may be an asshole, but I'm not a liar." His words hit me like a slap in the face because I'm the one, in fact, who has a guilty conscience. "Do you really want to know why I hate him so much? It's because I overheard him in the locker room a while ago saying some really sleazy stuff about Tiff. His sister is cut from the same cloth. They get their kicks turning other people's lives upside down."

"Hold on…about Tiff? But that's…ridiculous. And Leila… She seemed like a nice girl to me."

"They are good at charming people, that's why I don't want you to get too close to him. Or to her. Look at us, they've already got us fighting."

Indeed, there's a part of me that has to admit everything seems to have taken a wrong turn since Thomas started approaching me.

"Are you telling me the truth, Travis?" I ask suspiciously.

"Of course I am," he answers, looking deep into my eyes. Despite the sense of unease I still feel, I decide to trust him. He would never lie to me so blatantly. Instead, I am the one feeling dirtier than I ever have before. "All right, I believe you," I sigh. Travis hugs me and, although hesitant, I allow him to kiss me.

At lunchtime, I head to the cafeteria, where Alex and Tiffany are waiting for me, while Travis is with his teammates. The Ducks players must have arrived already, because the room is crowded with students in green sweatshirts. I look around and I catch a glimpse of my friends at a table in the back. I walk toward them, but a player from the opposing team—very tall, with dark hair and eyes—walks past me along with a group of other students. He gives me a wink and a flirty smile.

His beauty has me stupefied for a few moments, so much so that I stumble over a bag left on the floor next to a table. Cheeks burning, I hurry and catch up with my friends. I don't understand what is going on these days, why everyone seems to have taken notice of me all of a sudden. What's different about me?

Sighing, I sit down next to Tiffany. Alex studies me for a moment, and I see him start to fret.

"What happened? You look pretty shaken up," he says, stretching his hand across the table to take mine. I don't even know where to start, but I decide to confide in them. At least partially.

"I got into an argument with Travis this morning..." I begin.

They both give me the same resigned expression. "Again?"

I nod and rest my head on Tiff's shoulder. "We cleared it up right away, but I don't know... I feel a little exhausted. This has been the most intense week we've had in a long time," I murmur, distressed.

"You already know how I feel about Travis: you deserve better," Alex replies.

"The thing is, sometimes... I'm not so sure that I do." I steal a chip from his plate and nibble on it.

He looks at me, aghast. "What are you talking about? Why would you think that?"

"I don't know, Alex. Maybe I deserve it. After all, I'm the one letting him disrespect me time after time, always forgiving him."

"But no one should mistreat a person just because they're good enough to forgive you," he exclaims, gobsmacked.

"Alex has a point," Tiffany interjects. "Travis is my brother. But, if I were in your position, I would have kicked him to the curb a long time ago."

"The thing is... You know he was the first and only for me," I confess in a low tone. "I can't imagine being with someone else," I continue. "Sometimes I think that, without Travis, I'd be alone forever. No one wants to waste their time on someone like me," I admit with a hint of shame.

Tiffany's eyes widen. "Vanessa, you are talking crazy."

I shrug. "Why would anyone want to be with me, if they could get everything I have to offer from any other girl? Girls who are much more beautiful, more capable, and more experienced?"

"You cannot be serious right now."

"I am serious, though. There is nothing special about me. Nothing desirable." I bite my thumbnail.

"Have you seen yourself?" Alex cries in amazement. "As a man, I can assure you that is not the case."

I roll my eyes. "Having some curves doesn't put me ahead of anyone else. In fact, the only thing I get out of it are horny looks from creeps."

"Okay, now you listen to me," Tiffany interrupts me. "Nessy, you are completely beautiful, inside and out! You're the sweetest, most sensitive person that I know, you care about others, you try not to hurt anyone, and you always see the good in people. You don't care about outside appearances, and you are always yourself, even when that means being unconventional. Do you realize how much strength of character it takes to be yourself in a society that wants everyone to be the same?" She pauses and continues, "You've been putting up with my brother for two years! Two years! You deserve a sainthood just for that. And when I tell you that my brother does not deserve you, I am being completely goddamned honest! He is constantly being an asshole to you to try and feel superior, but you just are superior. You don't have to be afraid to find out who you are without him, because I am absolutely certain that you will only shine brighter. And he knows it too, that's why he keeps you tied down to a sham of a relationship that no longer has any reason to exist. You are not the one who needs him, Nessy, he's the one who needs you."

Her words move me so much that I have to hug her. "Are you sure you want to be a criminologist and not a life coach? You would be perfect," I joke to disperse some tension.

Alex comes over and sits next to me, squeezing my shoulders with one strong arm as if to infuse me with courage. I really want to be completely honest and tell them all about Thomas and about the strange new feelings he is stirring up in me. But every part of my life that he touches seems to fall apart, so I decide to keep quiet.

We go on chatting about lighter topics for the rest of lunch, and afterward we start heading toward the gymnasium with the other students. The seats in the first row are already all occupied, but in the second row I find Leila. She points to some vacant chairs behind her and invites me to join her. I take the opportunity to introduce her to Alex and Tiffany.

The gym is so full of people that it seems much smaller than it really is. Many of our students have painted their faces orange and black, while others unfurl signs with slogans and cheers on them. On the opposite side of the gym, fans of the Oregon Ducks create an expanse of green. Alex, with his ever-present Canon, begins shooting. When the players finally enter, they are greeted by heated cheers, whistles, and applause.

Travis is nervous. I can tell by the clench of his jaw. I try to catch his eye to reassure him, but he doesn't seek me out. He never does during games, always too focused on going over strategy in his head.

"Hey, hey. I guess someone here made an impression!" exclaims Tiffany, giving me a conspiratorial nudge.

"Meaning what?"

She points to the boy from the cafeteria, who keeps looking up to smile at me from the sideline as he warms up with a few dribbles. I feel the heat on my cheeks, and I know I've turned bright red. My friends laugh at my embarrassment, and I give them both a shoulder check.

"He's definitely looking at someone else," I murmur, biting my nails. I turn to confirm my hypothesis, but behind me I can see only teachers, a few parents, and...a fair-haired boy sitting alone in the back row. As soon as he notices my attention, he greets me shyly with a slight nod of his head. It nags at me—do I know him? I don't think I've ever seen him before, although he does, in fact, have a familiar vibe.

"Oh, knock it off!" Tiffany's wail draws my attention back to her. "He is clearly looking at you! You are a beautiful girl, Vanessa: deal with it. And I'll tell you what's more, lots of guys on campus look at you just like he's doing right now. You would notice if you didn't spend every waking moment moping over my brother!"

Touché.

I take courage from Tiffany's words and return the boy's greeting, smiling shyly at him. We keep looking at each other for a few seconds, but the moment is interrupted by Travis's menacing glare boring into me from afar. As if that were not enough, someone hurls a ball at the feet of the cafeteria boy with the charcoal-colored eyes: Thomas, who gives him a threatening look.

What the...

The surreal scene does not go unnoticed by my best friends or Leila. All three of them look at me, bewildered and incredulous, waiting for explanations.

"Okay, Nessy, what the hell is going on? Since when has your love life become more exciting than mine?" Tiffany asks with a mischievous smile on her lips.

"I-I don't know what you're talking about."

She snorts in amusement and lays a hand on my shoulder. "I'm gonna pretend to believe you only because I know you're probably having a panic attack right now and have plenty to think about. But know that this conversation isn't over, my friend," she concludes in a mocking tone.

I am saved by the referee, who blows his whistle and starts the game.

After an unfavorable first half, we start putting up buckets one after another until we are two points behind the Ducks. Travis maneuvers well; despite a redheaded, freckled boy who is all over him and tries to put him in a tight spot, he is not intimidated. He dribbles confidently, then passes the ball to Thomas behind the red-haired boy's back. Thomas shoots it in the direction of the basket, but a member of the opposing team pushes him. Thomas falls back as all eyes watch the ball swish into the net. With two seconds on the clock, the score is tied and the foul is in our favor.

Thomas goes to the foul line to set up for the free throw. If he makes it, the victory will be ours. Before he does anything else, he bends his knees, rests the ball on the floor, and bows his head, running a hand through his sweaty hair. He is lost, staring at some indeterminate point in the distance, and he squeezes his eyes shut, as though reaching for the focus necessary to better visualize his target. As he does this, he continually worries the NCAA-approved wristband standing in for the black bandana he always wears tied around his wrist, twisting it over and over again. After just a few seconds, he gets to his feet.

When we think he's finally ready to shoot, everyone stands up, all eyes glued to him. The gym, chaotic until a moment ago, plummets into total silence. The tension is palpable. Thomas darts his gaze from the ball to the basket. And, with each practice dribble, the impact of the ball on the hardwood floor is deafening. Suddenly, I remember two nights ago, when we found ourselves outside together and, of his own free will, he told me how it feels every time he hits the court. About the adrenaline that courses through his veins, pushing him through each movement.

Thomas turns my way. He spots me immediately in the crowd, as though we were connected by an invisible thread. Sweat beads on his forehead. There's a flush across his cheekbones and his breathing is labored. But he smiles at me...a barely there smile, but nevertheless it seems to make time suspend, to expand endlessly around us. His eyes, that intense emerald green, are shining. They seem to me to be speaking: Here it is. Here is that most beautiful moment.

Against all common sense, I decide not to break the strange connection that has arisen between us. I smile at him knowingly and, for a moment, it feels like all the spectators around us have disappeared, that there is only me and him. The moment that Thomas turns his attention back to the hoop, I have absolute certainty that he will score. He centers the ball in front of his body, pushes it up, and...

"Ladies and gentlemen! It's a miracle! The Beavers win the first game of the season!" shouts the commentator at the top of his lungs, as all the players on the team—except Travis—pile on Thomas. The crowd is in a frenzy as the Ducks and their fans leave the scene with their tails between their legs. I turn to my friends to cheer, and only then do I notice the identical astonished expressions on Alex, Tiffany, and Leila's faces.

Oh, no...

I can't explain what just happened either. All I know is that, right now, there is a part of me that would like nothing more than to run down from the stands and celebrate with Thomas.

Twelve

AFTER THE GAME, I GET a ride home from Alex. Travis offered, but I told him he should celebrate with his teammates and that we would meet at his house later so we could go to the party together. I needed to buy as much time as possible to figure out what to do. During the car ride, I immediately try to throw Alex off the scent before he can ask me any questions.

"So, Stella is coming tonight?" I say, going on the attack.

"Yeah, she started driving down from Vancouver an hour ago," he tells me with a twinkle in his eye.

"You've got it bad for her, don't you, friend?" I say with a huge grin.

"Shut up!" Alex's face turns purple, and I burst out laughing.

"That's a good thing, Alex! You look happy, and that is already reason enough for me to love her. I have never seen you all aglow like this."

"I am happy. I can't wait for her to meet you; I'm sure the two of you will get along great."

"I have an idea! You should come to my house for dinner tomorrow. Mom wants to 'officially' introduce me to her new boyfriend."

"Ah, the famous Victor, the only man capable of thawing Esther White's icy heart," he replies cheerfully.

"That's the one. So will you keep me company during this torture?" I implore him with my usual doe-eyed look.

"Of course we will. We can't stay long, though: I've got a romantic evening planned," he says suggestively.

"Oh, you're gonna be busy, huh?" I snicker, before turning serious to thank him. "I'm relieved I don't have to face this dinner alone."

"Travis didn't want to come?"

"I didn't ask him. You know how my mother gets around him. The dinner will be awkward enough as it is; I want to avoid piling on."

"That makes sense," he says, smiling.

"I'd better get inside, I need to get ready for the party." I roll my eyes. I don't have the slightest desire to go.

"Speaking of parties, you don't need me to do the safety spiel, do you?" he asks wryly.

"I'm gonna say no. I've got a good head on my shoulders, don't I?"

"I know, but weird things always happen at parties. Just keep your phone on you and call me if you need anything, okay?"

"This is all very thoughtful of you, but I won't call because there will be no need, and because you will be with Stella and an intrusive friend was not included in your 'Couple's Weekend' package." I chuckle. "In all likelihood, I will be home before ten o'clock," I reassure him.

"Have fun, then." Alex rumples my hair with a move that he would call affectionate, and we say goodbye.

An hour later I'm on the bus headed for the Baker house. I walk down the long concrete driveway, bordered by artfully manicured flower beds. When I arrive at the huge wrought-iron gate, I press the doorbell. Lisa, the maid, recognizes me on the video intercom and opens the gate for me. I pass the patio and find myself at the entrance, where Lisa has opened the door for me and stands waiting for me to hand her my jacket. I give it to her and shyly say thank you.

"Please don't thank me, Miss Clark, I'm just doing my job," she says with a pleading look. Inside this house, the words "thank you" do not exist. All this luxury always makes me feel uncomfortable.

"Where's Tiffany?" I find myself whispering, though I couldn't say why. It must be the deafening silence that fills this huge, bright house.

Everything is white here, from the polished marble under my feet to the stone pillars at the entrance to the vast carpet in the living room, which is surely made from the pelt of some poor polar bear...

"You will find Miss Baker in her room, upstairs." The maid bids me farewell with a bow and then leaves.

A bow? Really? This is the reason I stopped coming to this house—it's all a bit much for me.

I climb the stairs and walk down the hallway that divides Travis's room from Tiffany's. I can tell that Travis is in his room by the music blaring from the stereo, so I sneak into the good twin's room. When I enter, I find her curled up on the chaise longue listening to "Like a Virgin," intent on painting her toenails. She's wearing a pink silk robe and looks beautiful even in her lounging clothes.

"There you are! Lock the door, I don't want anyone busting in." I do as she says, then slip off my purse and shoes and throw myself onto the bed, resting my back on the mountain of piled-up pillows. I'd much rather skip the party and stay here to get a good night's sleep.

"Are your folks still out of town?" I ask.

"You know how they are. Work comes first," she says, imitating her father's voice.

"Where did they go this time?" I clutch a pillow to my chest.

"Dad flew to Dubai for a conference, Mom's on a spiritual retreat or something like that. Apparently she's stressed."

"I'm sorry, Tiff," I say simply. I know their absence hurts. The absence of a parent always hurts.

"I've gotten used to it. When your father is the CEO of a big oil company, you don't have much of a choice." She shrugs. "In all honesty, not having them around has its upsides. There's always a lot of tension whenever they're in the house. Especially with Travis, who never misses an opportunity to raise hell to get dad's attention."

"I still don't understand what you guys are doing in this hole of a town. With all the money you've got, I'd be in Los Angeles, New York, San Francisco! Anywhere but here!"

"Father claims that a tiny, godforsaken town like this is more livable. Corvallis is his magic bubble. Also, the grandparents are here. And OSU is a great school, it has nothing to envy from Harvard." She waves her hand over her toes to dry the polish just as we are interrupted by someone knocking on the door.

"It's Travis," he says in a faint voice.

"No, really?" exclaims Tiffany.

"Is Nessy with you?"

Tiff looks at me, waiting for me to tell her what to do. I give her a hesitant nod, and she lets him in.

"Hey," I say as soon as I see him in front of me. I sit up on the edge of the bed and, when he reaches me, he gives me a chaste kiss on the lips.

"We'll be leaving in twenty minutes, you guys ready?"

"Do we look ready?" interjects Tiffany with a raised eyebrow.

Her brother looks her up and down but doesn't dare answer back.

"I'll wait for you downstairs. Make it quick," he says, before closing the door behind him.

"So," she says eagerly as soon as we're alone again. She puts her newly painted feet on the ground and observes the result with satisfaction. "Let's get straight to the point: What is up with you and Thomas?"

I blink slowly at her, pretending not to understand. "T-there is no me and Thomas."

"Oh yeah, sure. I saw very well what happened today during the game." She spreads vanilla-scented moisturizer on her already perfectly smooth legs.

"Nothing happened," I reply, jiggling my foot.

"Nothing? But have you seen the way he looks at you? To say nothing about how he practically incinerated that hot Duck-hunk who was making goo-goo eyes at you. What are you not telling me, Nessy?" She looks at me menacingly, trying to extract information with just her gaze.

"Shouldn't we start getting ready? That way we won't be late," I change the subject.

"Oh, come on! Spill! Since when do you and I not tell each other stuff?"

Since my conscience made me sick with guilt.

"You know I'm going to find out either way."

I give a resigned huff. "Fine! You wanna know what's going on? Well, after my fight with Travis this morning, I was upset, and Thomas noticed, and I don't know how it happened but there was a weird moment between us, and, I don't know how, but we came this close to kissing," I say all in one breath.

"What?" Tiff leaps to her feet, eyes wide. "And you're only telling me this now? I'm your best friend. You should have informed me immediately!"

"Next time I promise to video chat you during the big moment," I retort sarcastically.

"So you think it will happen again?"

"What? No, of course not! I was... I'm just saying."

Tiffany gives me a coquettish look. "But would you want it to?"

"I said no!" I answer wearily.

"Okay, okay."

I let myself sink into the pillows as Tiffany begins to go through some clothes. "Actually, I think he only did it to feed his own ego." I let myself ruminate, my eyes focused on the ceiling.

"Meaning?" Tiff asks calmly.

"To prove to himself that no girl can resist him."

"And is that true?" she asks hesitantly, putting away a green dress.

"Of course it's true! And he knows it. He's a beautiful boy, I'm not blind. But that doesn't change anything. He just caught me in a moment of weakness. And then"—I scrub a hand over my face, frustrated—"I've got a boyfriend, dammit!" A laugh escapes Tiffany at these words.

"I think someone like Thomas is just what you need right now." She takes two sheath dresses from the closet, one red and one black with lace details. After a few seconds of indecision, she chooses the black one, which highlights her fair complexion.

I look at her with a frown. "You shouldn't be telling me these things, Tiff! You should tell me that I am a bad person for letting myself get taken in by someone like him, that I'm disrespecting my boyfriend. You should tell me to leave him alone because guys like him are nothing but trouble."

"Look, even though I can't stand him, I do wish my brother well and I am truly sorry that things between you two are going badly. But it's pretty clear to me that your story has come to an end. I would be a hypocrite if I only told you what you wanted to hear. Should you let it go because guys like Thomas are nothing but trouble? Yes, of course. That's what you should do. But we both know you're not going to. When someone like that sets his sights on you, there's no way out, baby girl."

I rise up on my elbows, ready to retort. "Do you know what separates us from animals? It's our ability to choose how we behave. We can control our instincts, especially when they're leading us in the wrong direction."

"Yeah, maybe you shouldn't do that." She turns around and asks me to zip up her dress.

"I can't tell if you're crazy or what. Are you really pushing me into the arms of someone like Thomas?"

"No, not into the arms of someone like Thomas, but into new experiences. I'm just saying: your love life has been pretty limited. You've only had one real relationship, a long and demanding one. You got into it when you were very young and fragile and now you're going through a period of change. You need to have fun, to live life, make mistakes, try new things. Instead you spend all your time trying to figure out the most correct and responsible thing to do. You will have your whole life to do that; now is the time to be irresponsible." She slips on a pair of rhinestone-encrusted heels and touches up her makeup.

I frown at her. "So what am I supposed to do? Table dance in the cafeteria and get drunk every night at some crappy party?"

"Surely you shouldn't spend every day fighting with your boyfriend, though, don't you think?" She looks at me in the lighted mirror as she runs a styling wand over her coppery hair. She admires herself, pleased.

I am so confused about all of this that I don't even know what to say to her. Sensing the turmoil of my thoughts, she decides not to pile on. "Come on, let's go," she says instead, smiling sweetly. The next moment, however, she gives me a thoughtful look.

"Something wrong?" I ask.

"I'm thinking about what you should wear."

"Oh, but... I thought I would wear this." I look down at the clothes I'm already wearing—a pair of black leggings and a cashmere sweater— then I look at Tiffany again, begging her to take pity on me.

"I'm not letting you go to the party looking like that!"

"What's wrong with my clothes?"

"They're...sloppy!"

"Hey, what happened to all that talk about not caring about appearances? About being unconventional?" I accuse her sullenly.

She shakes her head. "You can be unconventional and wear cute clothes at the same time."

I refrain from answering back; it's a losing battle.

"I'll take care of you," she announces proudly. "Come here, we'll start with makeup."

Oh God, no.

Tiffany sits me down at the makeup station and begins painting me with a product I've never heard of before: primer. After applying foundation and a bit of blush with expert hands, she focuses on my eyes. She chooses a purple eyeshadow and emphasizes the look with a line of black eyeliner, thin and perfect, and no less than three coats of mascara. To finish, she applies a nude lipstick and turns me toward the illuminated mirror.

I stand speechless. The result is crazy. I lean toward my reflection, incredulous.

"See what I mean when I call you gorgeous?" she retorts.

Made up like this, I can in fact see it. I look...sexy. I think she's also done something to my eyebrows because they are darker and more defined.

"You did great, Tiff, but don't get used to this."

"Now we have to think about the dress. Let's see, let's see…" She pulls an array of garments out of her closet and throws everything on the bed. Lost in thought for a moment, she taps a finger on her chin, then picks up a dress, eyeballing it. She gives me a side-eye and pronounces, "Nah, too anonymous."

"Anonymous is perfect!" I squeak, but she pretends not to hear me. She picks up another one and brings it over to me. I can tell from her pleased expression that she thinks this is the one. It is a very short black dress, sleeveless, and the neckline is surrounded by small studs. Eyes wide, I give her a flat "no."

"Try it on!" she orders.

"Tiffany. Seriously, it's not my thing. I'd feel half-naked in that. Where's the anonymous one? Let's give it a shot." I hunt for it among the clothes.

"Stop being a prude and try this dress on." I huff but obey. When I put it on, I see that I was right. It's tight, shows off every curve on my body, and cuts off at mid-thigh. Tiffany hands me a cropped black leather jacket and a pair of Doc Martens. Unfortunately for me, we are the same size. But I suppose it could have been worse: she could have insisted on a pair of dizzily high heels.

"Nessy! I swear, you are so hot!" Tiffany chirps as I straighten up.

I'm ready to tell her that she's wrong, but my reflection won't allow it: she's right, it sounds absurd but… I feel hot.

"It's all you!" I laugh, embarrassed.

"Everyone's eyes are going to be on you tonight!"

What? No. I don't want to have everyone's eyes on me. No. No. No. And just who would be looking at me? I'm going to the party with Travis. In just a few seconds, panic has taken complete control of my body. "On second thought, you know… Maybe all of this is a bit much. The dress…the makeup. Maybe I should just put my clothes back on, I mean, they were comfortable," I babble.

"Don't talk nonsense! You look perfect like this, and we don't have time to change anyway." She slips on her jacket.

"But Tiff…" I grab her by the arm and give her a pleading look.

She takes my face in her hands, as if to reassure me. "You are a stunner. I mean it, you're beautiful. There is nothing wrong with how you look, so just take a breath, relax, and let's go have fun!"

I close my eyes and take her advice. I breathe deeply, desperately praying that this party will end as soon as possible. But then I remember one small detail.

"So, Tiff," I say, trying to be brave. "About what we were discussing earlier... Do you happen to know if Thomas will be at the party? I'd like to avoid any kind of tension between him and Travis."

"You can rest easy. Thomas is going to Matt's party at the frat house," she reassures me as she gives herself a spritz of perfume. I don't know how to feel about this. Disappointed? Relieved?

"Ah, one last thing before we leave," she tells me, planting herself in front of me.

"What?" I'm almost afraid.

"This," She undoes my ponytail and arranges my hair with her fingers. "That's definitely better. Let's go!"

Travis is waiting for us in the living room and, when he sees me coming down the stairs, his mouth falls open. "Wow, you look great."

Tiffany walks past him and snorts haughtily. "You better treat her the way she deserves to be treated." He ignores her and wraps his arm around my waist. I let him. We get into Travis's pickup truck and speed toward Carol's house, just outside Corvallis proper.

A few minutes later, we park in a driveway full of other cars and walk past the open gate. Inside, we find ourselves in front of a very large pool where some guests are already swimming. The garden is as bright as daylight, the lights reflecting off the crystal-clear water of the pool. All around, people are chatting and laughing, underscored by the echo of music coming from inside the house. "Isn't it a little cold for swimming?" I ask, shifting my attention to the luxurious three-story mansion that rises before me.

"They're so drunk, they could probably melt ice with their breath," Travis replies.

"And is it safe to let drunk guys play in the pool? I mean, couldn't they drown?"

"Maybe. But no one will miss them," Tiffany puts in with a careless air. We head inside, leaving the drunk boys behind.

Thirteen

THE LIVING ROOM IS PACKED with people, and a group of freshmen huddle around a drink station the size of my bedroom. Tiffany was right: once we get inside, I feel watched and I curse her for dressing me like this.

"Would you like a drink?" Travis asks us. I had promised Alex that I would stay away from alcohol, but a little sip would be okay. It's just what I need to take the edge off. "Um, yeah. I'll go with you."

"I'm gonna go find some people from my class. I'll be waiting for you there whenever you want, gorgeous," Tiffany tells me with an enigmatic smile.

As we wait our turn at the bar, I look around, a little disoriented. I know almost none of the people here. We are about to get our drinks when a guy comes over to us. "Hey, captain! You guys killed it today. Let me get you a drink." He's a classmate of Travis's. I think his name is Adam. He takes Travis with him and drags him toward a small group of Econ students, Oregon's future ruling class. My boyfriend throws me an innocent smile over his shoulder, as if to say, "sorry, can't get out of this," and I let him go because, deep down, I don't really mind being on my own for a while.

I catch up with Tiffany as hip-hop music resounds in my ears. I chat for a while with her and her friends, sitting on a leather sofa. When the conversation turns to gossip about people I don't know, I take the opportunity to go to the bathroom upstairs.

As I wait my turn, I press my legs together, trying to hold my bladder. When the door finally opens, a girl with messy blond hair emerges. Her lips are swollen, and her cheeks are flushed. She adjusts the hem of her dress, which clings to her slim, toned thighs, and gives a satisfied smile to me and the girl standing in front of me. The latter turns in my direction with a confused air, I shrug my shoulders and shake my head. Immediately afterward, a disheveled boy with eyes as green as the bottle in his hands comes out. My heart catches in my throat when I realize what just happened in that bathroom.

"Hey, stranger." Thomas takes a sip of his beer, making his biceps strain against the tight fabric of his shirt. With his eyes half-closed and his head slightly tilted back, he looks me from head to toe in a manner so brazen that it makes me blush. But wasn't he supposed to be at the frat party?

"Did you just do stuff in there?" I ask abruptly while the girl in front of me walks away with a disgusted grimace.

I don't know what is bothering me more: the strange twinge of jealousy I feel or the small thrill I have at the realization that I've never done anything like this. Maybe Tiff has a point. Maybe, from time to time, I really should lose control and be more daring.

"I fucked her over the sink, if that's what you mean." Seeing my disgust, Thomas tilts his face to one side and looks at me with a small, obscene grin on his lips. "You wanna take a ride on the carousel yourself? The blond used up lot of my energy, but I still have a few tricks up my sleeve."

"Thanks, but I wouldn't be caught dead with you."

"If you change your mind, you know where to find me." He winks at me.

"If I change my mind, I'll find my boyfriend," I retort testily.

Flatly refusing to set foot in that bathroom, I decide to go to the one downstairs. Who cares if there is a huge line?

What an idiot! When I think about what I almost let him do this morning, I want to slap myself. I go back into the room and, through a window overlooking the garden, I spot Travis outside with his classmates. I slump onto an out-of-the-way love seat, and a gentle hand touches my shoulder. I look up and see Leila, green eyes rimmed with long lines of eyeliner, her hair pulled back in two French braids, and pink lipstick to finish the look.

"Hey, am I bothering you? I saw you sitting here all by yourself." Despite Travis's warning, my gut tells me that she can be trusted. I move a little to make room for her.

"No, go ahead and sit down. I didn't even know you were here, I'm glad to see you."

"A girl I know from class asked me to come with her, but she's disappeared somewhere."

"Are you having a good time? You look a little upset."

"Other than the fact that I haven't slept in days and I hate my roommate? I'd say I'm doing great," she complains, collapsing into the cushions.

"What's wrong with her?" I ask with a smirk.

"Every day she brings someone new to party in the room, and at night she snores so loud I want to throttle her." She mimes strangulation with her hands. "Last night I was so tired that, at the umpteenth snore, I seriously thought about smothering her with a pillow." We both burst out laughing. "I'm so exhausted, I could fall asleep right here," she concludes, rubbing her face.

"I'm sorry, finding the right roommate is harder than you think. Hang in there, and if it doesn't work out next year, you can always live off-campus," I advise.

"I look forward to that day," she says with a laugh.

We stand in silence for a while watching the crowd around us. They are yelling and dancing, completely consumed by the mixture of alcohol and the throbbing music.

"Do you do this often?" she asks me after a moment.

I look at her. "What?"

"Isolate yourself in a crowd."

"Let's just say this isn't my scene." I hug my arms against my body.

"Yeah, not mine either." Leila stops talking for a few seconds, then continues, "Look, this might sound weird, but would you like to go upstairs with me? I was hoping to talk to you in private," she adds, clearly agitated.

I follow her up the stairs, unsure of what to expect. We enter a room filled with antique furniture that clashes completely with the rest of the house.

"This is the guest room. Nobody ever comes in here, so we won't be disturbed," Leila explains.

"Have you been here before?"

"My brother knows the owner, and last year we came to some parties here."

"Oh, I see." I ignore the implied information about Thomas "knowing" Carol and turn my full attention to Leila. "Now, what did you want to talk to me about?" I ask, sitting on the edge of the bed.

Leila looks nervous. Very nervous. She keeps rubbing her hands together and biting the inside of her cheek. She tosses her gaze around as if looking for the words. "Okay, it's not easy for me to say what I'm about to say, but you deserve to know."

A flash of fear hits me right in the heart, and I begin to tremble. "I'm listening."

Leila runs her hands over her braids, as if to check that they are in place, and takes a long, anguished breath. "The day we met at the gym, I lied to you. I told you that I didn't know Travis, but that was a lie."

"I figured," I answer immediately in a cold voice.

She paces the room until she stops in front of me and looks at me. Ready to reveal everything. "You know that before I enrolled in college and had access to on-campus housing, I lived at Matt's frat house in the room next to my brother's for a year, right? That's where, one evening this summer in mid-July, I met Travis. Matt was throwing another party; my brother was busy somewhere else. I was trying to stay locked in my room, but I kept hearing the noise from downstairs and the other rooms. You can imagine what they were up to. So, I went out to the backyard to sit undisturbed and write for a while, until this boy sat down next to me. I knew who he was because Travis always came to the frat parties and I had noticed him more than a few times. He'd never mentioned a girlfriend, though, and he didn't that night either, so I always thought he was single.

"We got to talking about a lot of things. He seemed really interested in me, in what I had to say. So when he tried to kiss me a few hours later, I didn't pull away. And I didn't put on the brakes when he asked me to take him back to my room, where I made the terrible mistake of sleeping with him. It was my first time, and he knew it. My judgment was clouded by the emotions of the moment, but I didn't realize that until it was too late."

My blood runs cold as I stare into her eyes, unblinking. "And, sure enough, when I woke up the next morning, he was gone." An unhappy laugh escapes her, and my heart crumbles into a thousand pieces. "I ran into Matt instead, and he knew what had happened right away. He was the one who told me Travis had a girlfriend. I was completely shattered. I promised myself I'd never tell my brother about it, because he would go berserk, but I couldn't hide the pain I was in. When I finally spilled my guts, the inevitable happened. Thomas went looking for Travis all over Corvallis and, when he found him, there was nothing anyone could do. They got into a very heated and violent confrontation. Afterward, I made him swear that he'd never do anything that stupid again. It was only then that he really tried to listen to me, seeing how the whole thing had been terribly humiliating for me. All I wanted to do was forget. During the last two weeks of August, I jumped through hoops to avoid him, but I knew that all my efforts were wasted the moment I set foot on campus."

My ears are ringing, and nausea washes over me.

"I didn't want to go to college anymore, because I knew I would see him again in class, at games, in the cafeteria. Everywhere. The shame was more than I could handle. A few days before the start of the semester, I went to the admissions office to withdraw. But then I caught him flirting with these two freshmen, and something clicked in my head. The idea of him just continuing to live his life with no qualms infuriated me. In that moment, I decided that I wasn't going to let him have any control over my life. So I started walking around campus with my head held high, going to the cafeteria and also to my brother's practices. I refused to be afraid of his presence. If anything, he should have feared mine. But then fate played a dirty trick on me, when a girl with black hair and ash-gray eyes sat down beside me and introduced herself as the girlfriend of the bastard who had humiliated me."

It's like a hand is clenched around my heart, preventing me from breathing. My knees are shaking, and my hands… The world has fallen in on me. I cannot speak or think. Cold shivers run through my whole body. But I don't cry. For once in my life, I don't cry. I would like to cry, I desperately need it, to purge myself of all the disgust, pain, and anger I feel right now. But I can't.

"Vanessa…" Leila's voice rings faintly in my ear and pulls me from the trancelike state I've sunk into.

"I'm so sorry," she says in a small voice, resting a hand on my knee. I hadn't even realized she'd come over to me.

I get off the bed slowly, feeling that at any moment, a chasm might open up under my feet and swallow me down. But maybe I'm already in that chasm?

"Are you okay? Sorry, of course you aren't okay." She peers apprehensively at my blank face. "You're starting to worry me. You're really pale. Do you want a glass of water? Or do you want me to call someone?" Terrified, she pulls her phone from her pocket.

"No," I reply, cold and impassive. I rub my temples, trying to process the information I have just heard. "I'm not okay at all." I breathe slowly. "All of this is ridiculous, Leila. Travis would never do something like that. Yes, he's not the best guy in the world, but he would never do that kind of thing, it's too sleazy even for him. And I would have noticed," I stammer, trying to convince myself. But a terrible doubt creeps into my mind: all those evenings spent at home alone… Travis always told me that his nights were taken up by practices, by his father…

"But he did do it," she replies firmly.

"I don't believe you."

"Why would I lie to you?" I can read the disappointment on her face. She is hurt by my lack of trust. But she's lying. She has to be lying. Travis warned me. He told me to be on my guard around her.

"I don't know, Leila! But I-I-I would have known if it was…like that!" I bury my hands in my hair, panicking. "I would have known if he was cheating on me! I would have known it! You're wrong, Leila. You've got it wrong."

She grabs my wrists in an affectionate squeeze. "I know that it hurts. It wasn't easy for me to tell you. It's still an open wound. But I can assure you that it's all true." She stares intently into my eyes. And all I see in her gaze is honesty, which is what finally makes me break down.

I can't breathe. "I have to—I have to go." I brush past her and move to the door.

"Do you want me to go with you?" she asks, distressed.

"No." I turn toward her. "Excuse me. Forgive me, truly. I just need to be alone right now."

"I'm sorry," I hear her murmur as I close the door behind me.

I hurry down the first few steps, not knowing where to go. Fate is mocking me, because I just happen to find Travis, standing at the bottom of the stairs. He spots me and climbs halfway up to me, but as he approaches something seems to ring alarm bells for him. I look into his eyes and, suddenly, I am fully aware that everything Leila has told me is true. All the times he has told me to stay away from her and Thomas, Matt's phrase "you're even now," Leila's glassy stare when she learned that Travis was my boyfriend… I understand it all now. The truth hits me like a gut punch.

"Hey, what's wrong? Are you okay? Vanessa?" He says my name in an anguished whisper. He moves closer and caresses my cheek.

I push his hand away and slap him so hard that I feel a tingle all over my palm. Fortunately, the loud music covers the sound of the slap, and the psychedelic lights block the view of it from the other partygoers, who continue to enjoy themselves and drink as if nothing has happened.

"What the fuck is wrong with you?" he growls furiously, rubbing his cheek.

"You've been with Leila." My tone of voice is so controlled that I almost don't recognize myself. "And God only knows how many other people."

"What? I already told you, no!" He hunches his shoulders, exasperated.

"That wasn't a question," I reply sharply.

Travis starts to answer but freezes up when Leila rushes to my side. He gives me a bewildered look. "Whatever she told you, it's not…"

"Don't," I interrupt him. "Don't you dare say a single word," I hiss, full of hatred, narrowing my eyes.

"Someone had to tell her." Leila gives him a contemptuous look. "But you're so pathetic, you wouldn't have gotten up the courage to do it even if I gave you a hundred years." She walks past him and goes to the living room. I see her talking to a girl, and I head for the door.

"Vanessa, please let me explain," Travis tries.

"You are the most despicable person I have ever met in my entire my life," I spit in disgust. "It's over. It's over for good."

I run down the last few steps with a lump in my throat, push through the crush, and get out of that hellish place.

As soon as I'm outside, I take a deep breath, inhaling the cool, damp night air. I find an isolated garden wall out back and collapse. It is only at this point that I, finally, burst into tears. I cry my eyes out, I cry out all my tears, all the pain I feel. And it hurts. It hurts like hell.

How could I have been so stupid? It's all been right there in front of my face, but I refused to see it.

I go to the back porch and sit down on the first step. I wipe away my tears and realize that my makeup has smeared. Damn, that's all I need. It takes me a few seconds but, when I finally calm down, a group of boys stagger past me in a cacophony of barely comprehensible words.

I recognize Thomas's voice among them. I watch him walk away, but suddenly he turns to me with a confused expression, as if he didn't recognize me at first. He reaches for me.

"Stranger," he says, sitting down next to me with a beer in his hands. "What are you doing here?"

I let out an unhappy laugh as, slowly, the whole thing dawns on me. Thomas's hatred of Travis...now it all makes sense. I shake my head, despondent.

"I'm reflecting on my life," I say simply, lowering my gaze to the wet grass.

"Bullshit," he snorts, lighting a cigarette.

"Bullshit?"

He takes a long drag, blows the smoke out of his mouth, and then turns to look at me. "Yeah. Bullshit. You, out here all alone, 'reflecting on your life.'"

"Yeah... Maybe you're right." With unusual audacity, I grab the beer out of his hand and take a sip. "Are you leaving?"

I gesture with the neck of the bottle to the group of guys he came in with, who left a moment ago and are waiting for him a few feet away.

He nods, then glances at Carol's house behind our backs. "My sister just went back to campus with her classmate, so I've got no reason to stay. Let's go tear it up at Matthew's."

"Don't do anything you'll regret," I taunt, bumping his shoulder.

"But that's the whole reason we're going," he replies with a teasing smile that makes me embarrassed.

I hand him back the bottle, and, without taking his eyes off me, he downs the rest of it in one gulp. He puts his lips in the exact same spot where mine had been. My heart begins to beat at a manic pace. It's absurd how Thomas manages to provoke such an intense reaction in just a few moments. He senses this and gives me a sly smile. Then he stands up, leaving an empty space beside me that suddenly makes me feel lonely.

I offer a weak smile, sure it's time to say goodbye. Against my every prediction, however, Thomas plants himself in front of me and scrutinizes me carefully. "What's up?" I ask, my voice cracking.

"Come with me."

My heart hammers in my chest. "What?"

"Would you rather sit here, on a filthy porch step, surrounded by spoiled brats and feeling sorry for yourself?"

"I don't know..."

"I won't ask you again. So get up off that cute little ass of yours and come with me." He holds out his hand, waiting for me to take it.

"You think I have a nice ass?" I blurt out automatically, and I instantly regret it.

"I would happily fuck it," he says cheekily. I goggle at him and curse myself for asking that inappropriate question in the first place. He laughs and shakes his head, while I feel my cheeks blazing with shame. "So are you coming or not?"

Hesitantly, I lower my gaze to Thomas's tattooed hand stretched out toward me. Faced with the mischievous glint in his eyes, I am overwhelmed by a rush of adrenaline. And in a moment of madness, I choose to listen to Tiffany. I choose to dare. To break the rules. I choose to sweep away rationality and surrender to instinct.

To hell with Travis, to hell with everything.

I clasp his hand and, in a snap, he pulls me to my feet, just inches from his face, causing our bodies to collide. With his thumb, he traces the contour of my lower lip, and I can't seem to draw any air into my lungs. "Excellent choice, stranger," he murmurs lasciviously, before pressing a kiss to the corner of my mouth and sending shivers down my spine. I smile nervously at him, and a moment later, Thomas drags me away.

Fourteen

WE RIDE IN A CAR with two of Thomas's friends. I don't know their names, nor do I pay attention to the road. My head is foggy, as if the life I am living is no longer my own. Like I'm trapped in a nightmare and cannot wake up. The only thing that makes me feel like a living person right now is Thomas sitting on the seat beside me and the burning heat emanating from his hand, which rests on top of my bare thigh. I force myself out of my stupor long enough to text Tiffany, telling her that I left and not to worry. When I see that Travis is spamming me with phone calls and texts, I turn off my phone and put it in my purse.

We get out of the car, and Thomas takes me by the hand as if it is the most natural thing in the world. He probably holds so many girls' hands that he doesn't even notice it anymore.

The frat house is packed. Through the open windows of the second floor, you can see rooms filled with people drinking, making a ruckus and generally wilding out, swapping spit as they grope and grind on one another.

In the garden, kids are doing keg stands and playing beer pong, and I get a strong whiff of weed when I inhale. The electronic music is booming loud enough to make my chest tremble. This, ladies and gentlemen, is a classic Matthew Ford frat party.

"Don't get too comfortable with these people. Most of them are so stoned they wouldn't even recognize their own mothers," Thomas warns me.

I nod distractedly. I make to advance toward the front door, but Thomas draws me against his body and encircles my waist with an arm, all without letting go of my hand. In an instant I find myself pressed to his chest, and my heart beats uncontrollably. I am so close that I can smell the intoxicating mixture of vetiver and cigarette smoke that he exudes. I lift my head to observe him and, with his gaze fixed on me, I linger on his parted lips.

"Most importantly: don't take drinks from anyone. You never know what they put in it," he whispers a few inches from my mouth.

I blink dazedly and try to recover from the state of bliss into which I had so eagerly sunk. "Reassuring," I reply uncertainly.

When Thomas releases my hand, I take the opportunity to step back, to put some space between us and clear my head. "You can't trust anything in there. And you, dressed like that, you're..." He examines me slowly, biting his lip. "Easy prey." His eyes linger a bit more than necessary on my cleavage.

"No, go ahead. This isn't embarrassing at all," I hiss.

"You're breathtaking tonight," he pronounces hoarsely.

I could say the same thing to him. He's never been so sensual. Lascivious gaze. Full lips. His imposing size. Big, strong, masculine hands that part of me wishes I could feel on my body, on places he has never seen...

I am shocked by my own thoughts. Less than an hour ago, I was crying over the end of a love story that, at one time, I had believed would last forever. And now I find myself thinking about Thomas's hands on me. I must be going crazy.

Thomas takes me by the hand, pulling me out of my thoughts, and leads me inside. We are immediately greeted by a small group of his friends that I think I've seen on campus. He greets them with high fives and shoulder bumps.

"Collins, finally you're here! We've been waiting for you!" exclaims a boy with reddish hair.

"Did you start without me, you assholes?"

"The girls refused. You know they won't do it without you."

I stiffen, puzzled, and Thomas notices. He looks at me apprehensively before getting distracted by his friend.

"What are you trying to do, not introducing us to this piece?"

Instinctively, I loosen my grip on his hand and take a step away from him, tense and intimidated. Maybe it was a mistake to come here after all.

"Perez, I know you're a smart guy, so listen carefully," Thomas says, resting a heavy hand on the other boy's shoulder. "This piece is off-limits. And she's gonna stay off-limits, understood?" The boy, after a moment of bewilderment, nods. "Put the word out, I don't wanna have to get mad at anyone," Thomas concludes, dismissing him with a friendly pat. When Perez walks away, Thomas looks at me and reassures me with a barely there smile. I'm about to thank him, but I don't have time, because some boys—I recognize Finn's face among them—jump him from behind and drag him away with them. In an instant, I find myself alone on the threshold of this madhouse.

Perfect. Great move, Vanessa.

Hesitant, I look around and study my surroundings. Maybe I'll be able to find some hidden corner to hole up in here too. This is not my first time at the frat. During the last academic year I spent an evening or two here, but I was always with Travis then, and I felt safe.

Now, however, I am a fish out of water. As I walk along, dodging plastic cups spilled here and there, I run into Matt. He looks oddly sober.

"Nessy, is that you?" He looks me up and down, and I don't miss the appreciation that shines in his smile.

"Hi, Matt," I greet him tonelessly. "It's me, in the flesh."

"But what are you doing here? Weren't you at Carol's? With Travis?"

"Yeah, we were there," I reply wearily, massaging a temple.

Matt peers at me suspiciously. "Are you all right?"

An unhappy laugh escapes me. "Look, let's cut to the chase here. You knew?" I ask straight-out, crossing my arms.

He doesn't seem to understand. "What are you talking about?"

"About Travis, about his affairs. And about Leila."

Matt stiffens. He parts his lips and lowers his head. Guilty.

"Why? Why didn't you tell me? You knew how he treated me and you didn't say anything..." The words die in my mouth in the face of his regretful expression.

"When I found out, we fought. A lot. I made him promise he'd stop it. And he swore to me that he would. He was remorseful, he seemed determined to repair the relationship between you two. He begged me not to say anything. And I didn't want to get in the middle. I thought I was doing the right thing," he explains to me bitterly.

"I had a right to know. And then...Leila," I say disgustedly. "How can you be friends with a person who is capable of something like that?" My eyes water painfully.

"We have been close since we were kids. What he did was wrong, but he's still my friend."

I shake my head, nauseated. This story is horrifying.

"What would you have done if it had been Alex instead of Travis?" he asks in the face of my silence.

"Don't do that, Matt, don't try to put Alex on that level," I admonish him.

"Would you have turned your back on him?"

Yes! I think... I certainly wouldn't have hidden everything from his girlfriend. Possibly.

"I expected a little more integrity from you. That's all." I bite the inside of my cheek to stop myself from crying.

"I was stuck in a shitty situation. Whichever side I took, I was going to end up hurting someone. I hoped it would end there."

"Oh, it's ended," I spit bitterly.

He runs a hand through his hair. "I'm sorry, believe me."

"It would have ended anyway," I suddenly confess, realizing it is the truth. Still hurts, though.

He lays a hand on my arm and smiles sincerely. "I am your friend too. I'm here if you need me."

"Thanks," I murmur, trying to swallow the lump in my throat.

He stuffs his hands into his pockets and glances around. "You here with someone?" he asks calmly.

"Um, yes." I look around too. "But he's gone now, and I'm regretting not being at home under the covers."

"No regrets. You're here now, so let's have some fun." He gestures for me to follow him into the garden. Apparently, according to Matt, there's no better cure for a broken heart than beer pong. I quickly realize however, that challenging a basketball player to this game is not the smartest choice in the world. So before I end the evening behind some bushes throwing up gallons of beer, I decide to wave a white flag. I leave Matt to play with the others and go back into the house, which is now enveloped by a cloud of smoke. A group of shirtless girls and boys catches my attention.

They are sitting on the floor around a small wooden table. I approach, intrigued. They are playing strip poker. Among the half-naked bodies, Thomas's powerful physique stands out, covered in tattoos. There is one in particular, one I've never seen before, that strikes me—so much so that I get lost examining it. It depicts a child kneeling, surrounded by two huge wings that cover his entire back, while clutching a black anatomical heart in his hands. It's tragic but fascinating at the same time.

Next to Thomas, in tight jeans and a lacy bra, is Shana, with her red hair loose down her back and a joint between her fingers. So this is what you had to do so urgently, eh, Thomas?

When Shana notices my presence, her face twists into a contemptuous grimace. Wasting no time, she pounces on Thomas's lips. He reciprocates as if compelled by inertia but pulls away annoyed after a few seconds.

"Oh, now this is a surprise. Forgot how to get home, little gutter rat?" the redhead chirps bitterly, favoring me with a disdainful look.

I shoot Thomas a quick glance, hoping he will intervene. After all, he was the one who brought me here. But he ignores me completely and confines himself to sipping from a glass containing some unknown clear liquid. I shake my head in resignation; I should have known.

"Yeah, you figured it out: you're not welcome here. Why don't you go hang out with that bunch of losers from student choir? I'm sure you'll have a lot to talk about." She dismisses me with a wave of her hand. Fuming, I am ready to do an about-face.

"Don't listen to her," exclaims a boy with dark eyes, sitting next to Shana. "Why don't you join us, little girl?" he asks with a mischievous grin.

And risk finding myself in nothing but my underwear? No, thank you.

I am about to refuse, but Thomas, with a cigarette between his lips and a deck of cards fanned out his hands, gives the other boy a fiery glare. "Forget I said anything," the boy adds hastily.

"Figures, she wouldn't even undress in front of her boyfriend," Shana snickers with a sneer. "Actually, why don't you go find him? I wouldn't let him out of your sight if I were you, you never know what he might do, or who," she chuckles wickedly.

"Travis isn't my boyfriend anymore." At these words, Thomas stops shuffling the cards for a brief moment and, although he doesn't look at me, I can tell he's listening.

Shana clicks her tongue theatrically. "He dumped you for that freshman? Or for the junior? No, wait! Maybe he just opened his eyes and realized that literally any other girl would be better than you, right?" she says disdainfully, drawing the attention of everyone present. When she hears them laughing, Shana looks at me with a triumphant air.

I feel tears welling up and shame flooding me. I wish I was strong enough to put her in her place the way she deserves, but right now I'm too hurt to do it.

"You really should learn to shut your fucking mouth. And not just when a man does it for you." It is Thomas who speaks up for me, with a severe expression that darkens his face, silencing everyone.

And I shouldn't, but part of me delights in seeing her humiliated. Just as she humiliated me. So I pluck up my courage and reply, head held high, "Quite the opposite, actually. Travis Baker getting dumped by the most boring girl at Oregon State? Ridiculous, isn't it?"

Bolstered by my own words, I am overwhelmed by an uncontrollable need to show this little princess that I do not intend to be crushed by her or her underhanded tricks. I will not go hide in a corner. Not anymore.

"Is that invitation still open?" I cheekily ask the boy with the dark eyes. He doesn't answer me but looks at Thomas as if waiting for his approval. "Yes?" I prompt, resisting the idea of someone else making my choices for me. "I'm ready!"

A mocking smile spreads over the redhead's face, and I am almost certain that I can see a hint of fear behind her mask and...insecurity?

Thomas turns sharply in my direction. "This kind of thing isn't for you."

"Let me decide that," I reply, annoyed. I sit down and get on with it.

I have no idea how, but I soon find myself in just my bra and panties, surrounded by excited boys. Not to be outdone, I raise my plastic cup in the air with each defeat, joining in the boisterous shouts before letting the liquor slide down my throat. The boys toast me and drink along with me. The attention everyone suddenly seems to be giving me has made Shana jealous. Despite all her efforts to cling to Thomas, she eventually leaves, forced to admit defeat.

The eyes of the most handsome and domineering tattooed man I have ever seen are aimed only at me, glaring at me, ferocious and enraged. Or perhaps worried. I am certain I saw him slay a boy with his gaze after the guy tried to reach for me.

After an hour and four drinks, my vision is blurry, my hearing is muddled, and my body feels like it is on fire. People move in slow motion; I need some air.

As soon as I stand up, the room starts spinning and doesn't stop until two large arms hold me up. It takes me a few seconds to realize that it is Thomas, who picks me up as though I were a child.

"What are you dooooooing? Put me doooown," I protest, wriggling.

"Cut it out, you're completely wasted," he snaps. The worried tone in his voice makes me smile. Or at least I think so, it's not like I have a lot of control over my facial expressions at the moment.

"Am I laughing?" I slur with a numbed mouth.

"What?" he asks confused.

"I wanted to know if I was laughing, I wanted to… I wanted to laugh again."

Four green eyes glare at me and two Thomases are climbing the stairs.

"Yes," he mutters. "You're laughing or something like it."

"I'm seeing two versions of you and I really hope that at least one of you turns out to be less irritating, otherwise, I'll be forced to kick both of you…" I laugh for no real reason, and with my index finger, I draw a line that starts at his lip and ends on the lotus flower tattooed on his neck. His mouth is soft, and slight stubble covers his square jaw. The skin of his chest is smooth, his abs sculpted all the way to the edge of his jeans. Damn him, he is beautiful. He mutters something, but I don't catch his words. Exhausted, I rest my head on his chest and close my eyes. "Where are you taking me?"

"Upstairs, to my room."

Stop! What? He is taking me to his room, drunk and half-naked. What the hell does he think he's doing? I kick my legs as hard as I can, until he staggers.

"Stop it, Ness, or your ass is gonna end up on the floor," he scolds me, but I am completely focused on the new nickname he's given me, "Ness." I have to say, I like it. Much better than that annoying "stranger" he keeps insisting upon calling me. Although, to be honest I like that one too. But only because he's the one saying it. And that is something I will never tell him.

"Put me down," I order, summoning the small amount of clarity I have left. "Right now!" I kick again, but his grasp is inescapable. "You want to take advantage of me! I won't let you. Even if I am drunk!"

"Calm your tits. I'm taking you to my room to keep you safe from everything else." Oh. I relax in his arms. He is worried about me, then. He wants to keep me safe. It's so…sweet. I'm almost about to thank him when he adds, "Stupid." I pound my fist against his chest, hard as marble.

"Don't call me 'stupid'!" I say, pouting like a bratty little girl.

"What was that supposed to be? With a punch like that, you wouldn't even KO a baby chick, but we can work on it," he jokes.

Finally arriving on the landing, Thomas opens a door and we enter a dark—very dark—room. I can't entirely trust my eyesight right now, but I think that the walls are black. Everything is shrouded in darkness, with only a faint light pouring in from the window overlooking the courtyard. I can see a desk facing the wall on my left, next to the entrance, and a large dark wooden wardrobe on my right.

"Where are we?"

Thomas walks me over to the huge bed. It's very soft; he helps me lie down on it and covers me with a blanket.

"We're in my room. You can relax." Oh my God! Relax, my ass. This bed will have seen more pussy than a retired gynecologist!

"I want to get off!" I shout.

"You want to do what?" he asks, confused and amused at the same time.

"Down. Right now." I roll off the mattress and end up face down on the carpet. "Ouch!"

Thomas bursts out laughing. Normal Vanessa would find this embarrassing, but I'm too drunk for that. I try to pull myself up, but I feel something churn inside me.

"Thomas…" I call out to him, but he is too busy laughing.

"Thomas!" I say louder.

"What's wrong with you now?" he asks breathlessly.

I put a hand on my belly. "I'm going to…"

He blinks. "Oh fuck, no." He drags me to the bathroom. Yes, he has an en suite bathroom.

I barely manage to squat down in front of the toilet before I start throwing up, with Thomas right next to me, enjoying a front-row seat to the show.

Tomorrow, when I wake up, I will dig myself the deepest grave mankind has ever known. Thomas leans over me and pulls back my hair, while I hold onto the ceramic edges of the toilet with both hands.

"Promise me you won't tell anyone," I plead with him after I've finished, spitting saliva into the toilet and wiping away tears of exertion. When I look at my hand, it is stained black. I wonder exactly how hard Tiffany went with the mascara. My God, what a repulsive spectacle I must be to Thomas right now. Shakily, I get up and go to the sink. I wash my hands and rinse my face.

"It'll be the first thing I do tomorrow after I wake up." He grins.

I widen my eyes at him. "I will kill you. I swear." I lurch menacingly at him, intending to grab him by the collar of his shirt, but I can't, because my stomach is ready for round two.

After what feels like an eternity, I am still in the bathroom, but I feel a little bit better. Except that I smell like death. Thomas is still here with me, and he doesn't look disgusted. He hasn't left me alone for a moment, and I don't know whether to feel grateful or embarrassed about that.

I move away from the toilet. I sit on the floor with my back against the glass door of the shower and hug my knees to my chest. "I'm sorry," I murmur, looking at the ceiling.

"For what?"

For Travis, for what he did to your sister. For the pain and humiliation he inflicted on you both. For not realizing it sooner. For doubting you. For ruining your night. For making you a witness to all of this. I'm sorry for so many things…

I rub my hands over my face and look into his eyes. "For everything. I'm a disaster, Thomas."

He sits down next to me. He tucks a lock of hair behind my ear and caresses my face. A warm, gentle touch. "We all are," he says softly. With tears about to flow, I put my hand over his, still on my cheek, and squeeze it tightly. I want him to know that I am grateful to him for tonight. Really grateful. We stay like this for a handful of minutes.

"I stink," I say disgustedly, interrupting the strange silence that hovers between us.

"A lot." He smiles, and I do the same.

"So, could I...could I take a shower?"

He nods, standing up.

"I'll get you something of mine to wear for tonight."

"To-tonight?" I ask skeptically.

"Yeah, given the shape you're in, you should stay here," he says peremptorily. The alcohol has mostly worn off, but I still feel weak and dizzy, my clothes—or rather, Tiffany's clothes—are gone who knows where, and I have no way to get home. The only sensible choice is to stay. Thomas is right. Sigh.

"Okay, but I'm not sleeping with you."

"Wasn't my intention."

"Oh." I shouldn't, but I feel a little disappointed. Apparently, all the guys around me like to sleep with other girls but not with me.

He looks at me with a mocking smile and adds, "Unless you want to."

"No. I don't want to." Because I don't want to, do I?

"Then we're agreed." He heads for the bathroom exit.

"Where will you sleep?" I ask, following him. He points to a sofa under the window, not far from the bed.

"I can sleep there if you want, it's not a problem. You've already done too much for me." I put my hair in a messy ponytail with the hair band I always wear on my wrist.

"The sofa's not bad. And you need to rest." He takes a pillow from the bed and props it up against the armrest. I would like to give him a hug and thank him, but I'm afraid he wouldn't appreciate it. I opt instead to dash into the shower. After getting myself sorted out and brushing my teeth with toothpaste smeared on my index finger, I move back into the empty room. Thomas is gone. I guess he went back downstairs to the party. He left a T-shirt for me on the bed, black and very large. It goes down to my knees, but it's soft and smells like him, has his unmistakable aroma of vetiver and tobacco. Without thinking about it, I bury my nose in the fabric and breathe deeply. Yes, it definitely smells like him. I get under the covers and stare at the black ceiling. What kind of person would paint the walls of their bedroom like this? A serial killer, perhaps?

I'm immersed in these thoughts when I hear the sound of the door-knob turning. I sit up, clutching the covers to my chest. When I realize that I am alone, wearing nothing more than a T-shirt, in a boy's room accessible to anyone, panic eats me alive. My heartbeat speeds up, and I swallow with difficulty as I look around for an object that I could use to defend myself, if need be. But there's nothing.

The door opens softly, producing a slight creak that makes my skin crawl. As soon as I glimpse the face of the person who is entering, I release a deep breath.

"Oh, my God. It's you." I rest my hand on my chest.

Thomas enters with a small bottle of water in his hand and closes the door behind him before locking it again. "Who else was it supposed to be?"

"At a party full of drunks? Anyone," I point out to him.

"No one else has a key to my room," he reassures me. "How are you?"

"I'm still pretty fuzzy, but at least the room isn't spinning anymore."

"Here, I brought you some water." He hands me the small bottle and I rest it against my sheet-covered legs.

"Aren't you going downstairs to have fun?"

"Nah. Everyone's fucked up, it's not fun anymore."

I raise a skeptical eyebrow. "And you're not?"

"I would have been. But you beat me to it," he snarks. "And I need to be careful for training at the moment."

"Okay." I lie down again and remain silent for a while, while Thomas sits on the sofa, his legs spread and his shoulders against the backrest. He lights up a cigarette without ever taking his eyes off me. "What's up?" I ask, turning on my side to face him, one hand tucked under the pillow.

"What happened?"

Pain clenches in my chest.

"He cheated on me," I confess after a moment of hesitation, expecting to feel a stab to the heart. "But you already knew that, didn't you?"

He doesn't answer. He inhales cigarette smoke with half-closed eyes and blows it upward. Even now, he doesn't take his eyes off mine. "Does he know you're here?"

I shake my head no and watch the smug smile appear on his face.

"Thomas," I whisper. "Would you like to... I mean, can you come here, with me? I know, it's dumb. But it's been a horrible day and I just really need..." Human warmth? Reassurance? Affection? It would be too pathetic if I said any of that out loud. The perplexed expression he gives me prompts me to stop talking. Maybe I'm asking too much. "Never mind, forget I said anything. It doesn't matter."

I go back to staring at the ceiling and calling myself stupid. Surprisingly, however, Thomas lets out a deep breath and gets up. He puts out his cigarette in the ashtray on the nightstand and ditches his jeans, wearing just a pair of black boxer shorts. Faced with the vision of his naked, sculpted body, my ability to speak, think, or breathe is obliterated. My cheeks burn, and I cannot remember my own name. I blink and swallow hard as I try desperately to look anywhere but the most crucial part of his body, currently covered by fabric that is far too tight. So tight that it leaves little room for the imagination.

"What's wrong, Ness?" Thomas's warm, persuasive voice causes me to look up at him. He looks at me mischievously, aware and proud of my embarrassment. Cocky, as ever. "You wanted me under the covers, right? Wish granted." With an insolent smile, he puts one knee on the mattress and slowly approaches me in a catlike fashion, though being very careful not to touch me. It's as though the idea of teasing me amuses him, but he doesn't want to disrespect me in any way or take advantage of my moment of weakness. He puts his hands behind the back of his head and leans back against the headboard. He turns toward me and stares at me with a look so sympathetic and indulgent that it manages to dispel the tension. I was certain that being in bed with someone who wasn't Travis would make me nervous in some way.

Instead, for some strange reason, my body is perfectly relaxed next to him. Moved by an instinctive need, I let go completely.

"Can I...can I just hold you for a little while?" I feel desperate for crumbs of affection. I'm sure it's the alcohol lingering in my body that has made me so open, so free of any boundaries.

He seems bewildered by my request. Then, prompted perhaps by a sense of compassion, he decides to open his arms to me. "Don't get used to it," he grumbles. I curl up and press my face against his warm chest, inhaling his scent. I love it.

Thomas holds me in a grasp that is strong and reassuring as well as protective. And something inside me seems to break loose. Suddenly, I burst into tears. I can't stop. the tears flood out of me, uncontrolled.

"I'm sorry, I...I can't stop," I sob, with my face hidden in my hands.

Thomas doesn't say anything, he just holds me tighter, making me feel as though I am enclosed in a fortress where I can give free rein to all my pain.

"You were right, you know? He took everything from me," I murmur, my lips wet with tears. "And now I can't stop feeling..."

"What?"

"Wrong."

"You're not the one who's wrong," he says brusquely. I tilt my face to look him in the eye.

"But that's how I feel. Wrong. All this time, Travis has been cheating on me. Do you know what that means? That he preferred anyone else to me. I must have disgusted him. Whatever I had to offer him wasn't enough. I wasn't enough. It's always been like that. I've never been enough for anyone."

Thomas pulls away slightly to get a better look at me. "You talk a lot of bullshit. But I'll give you a pass. You're half drunk and clearly depressed."

"No, it's the truth. I don't like myself, and why should I? My own boyfriend didn't even like me," I say, bursting into nervous laughter and then shaking my head in humiliation.

Thomas grabs my chin, forcing me to look at him. "He cheated on you because he's an asshole who couldn't keep it in his pants. That is not your fault. It's his. Get it through your head."

"You don't understand…" I leave the sentence hanging when I realize that he, too, must have inflicted the same humiliation on who knows how many girls.

"Do you think you aren't attractive? If you do, you're fucking wrong."

I feel a shiver down my spine.

Does he really think that?

Dazed and overwhelmed by a thousand emotions, my gaze lingers on his lips. I feel a tingle in my belly at the idea of covering them with mine, of feeling our tongues entwine and our flavors blending together. I wonder how he kisses, Thomas. How he takes control of a woman's body. How he looks at the moment of climax…

An unhealthy idea makes its way into my head.

I want to find out.

My fingers move automatically along his jawline, following his chin before slowly meeting his chapped and parted lips. Hypnotized, I trace the outline of his mouth. My breasts press against his massive, exposed chest. The tips of our noses touch, and for a few interminable moments we do not tear our gazes away from one other, our breaths labored with tension.

"What are you doing?"

"I don't know," I answer, entranced by my own movements.

Longing for more, to feel the effect his skin would have against mine, I push my pelvis slowly toward him; my thighs press against his more muscular ones and the slight bulge covered by the thin layer of his boxers presses against my most intimate parts. My body temperature skyrockets. I bite my lip and close my eyes as I feel him becoming increasingly bulky and defined between my legs.

"This is how you get in trouble." His eyes blaze with desire. "Big trouble."

"That's my specialty." I hold my breath as, with another movement of his pelvis, his erection rubs against a very specific spot between my thighs. In an automatic reflex, Thomas clutches my hair in his fist and tries to suppress a moan of gratification. He lets loose with an actual moan when I begin rubbing myself against him more passionately. I feel like I'm beginning to lose control as well.

"Ness…"

"Give me…" I bring my lips close to his before finally touching them. A series of shivers flood my spine. His lips are soft and full, and I savor their faint aftertaste of smoke.

"You're drunk," he murmurs hoarsely into my mouth. I'm not listening. With my heart beating wildly, I continue this slow torture, elusive and delicate, as if I were playing out a little game of seduction between our bodies. He doesn't retreat but doesn't seem willing to reciprocate either. Instead, he thoroughly studies my every movement with his eyes open wide, his breath short, and his muscles tensed.

To coax him into yielding, I tease him with the tip of my tongue. I lick the edge of his mouth. We both hold back a shiver. I do it again, and again. Only then does Thomas tighten his grip on my hair and move his hips against me. Instinctively, I press my legs together to soothe my arousal.

"You shouldn't be doing this," he growls. But I don't give him a chance to add anything else. At this exact moment, this is the only thing I want to do.

I move to his mouth and kiss him with all the strange passion and perversion that Thomas brews within me. He doesn't reciprocate immediately the way I had hoped. He is using all of his self-control to hold himself back, but I feel the desire he has for me. I sense it everywhere. So I don't give up and decide to be daring… With trembling fingers, I creep down to the elastic of his boxer shorts. I open my palm over his bulge and begin to move up and down, with motions that are relentless, intense, and perhaps a little clumsy. Nevertheless, I feel him quivering, pulsing more and more under my touch. With a brutal growl, Thomas bites my lip, leaving me breathless.

His tongue invades my mouth hungrily, and my body explodes.

I cling to him, kissing him wildly. My mind is foggy with desire and my body burning with passion and urgency. His tongue piercing gives me a new and terribly exciting feeling. When I find the strength to break away from him, I am bewildered. I'm breathing hard. His face is flushed. I thought kissing him would appease this desire, but it has only amplified it.

I move closer for more, and as soon as our lips touch again, I go up like gasoline tossed onto a campfire. I straddle him because contact with just his mouth is no longer enough for me. I feel his erection pressing against me through the thin layer of my panties and, with a lack of inhibition that is completely foreign to me, I grind myself against him, desperate to relieve the devastating heat I feel between my thighs. With one hand Thomas clasps the hair on the nape of my neck, with the other he squeezes my side nearly hard enough to bruise. The pace of my movements increases with the intensity of his grip. We find ourselves moaning together in a whirlwind of arousal. I don't know what I am doing, but I do know that I have never felt better than this.

Our tongues entwine greedily until we run out of breath. We pull away gasping, and I press my forehead to his. Two dilated pupils stare at me longingly; a vein on his neck throbs so hard I fear it might burst at any moment, just like my heart. His erection throbs between my thighs, and I feel the fabric of my panties getting wetter and wetter. I smile at him, pleased with the effect I seem to be having on him and by the feelings that he provokes in me. I move to kiss him again, but Thomas stops me.

He puts his hands on my shoulders and shakes his head. "You're drunk."

"Yes and no." True, the alcohol is probably making me more uninhibited, but I am clearheaded enough to know what I am doing. And I want to do it.

"That doesn't work for me," he replies seriously, as our breathing regulates.

"I don't understand, you don't... You don't want me?" I ask, straightening up away from his face, trying to hide my humiliated expression.

He frowns. "So, according to you, that hard dick you're sitting on means I don't want you?"

"Then don't stop." I pull his hands off my shoulders and draw close to his face, brushing his lips with my own. "Make me forget, Thomas," I beg him in a whisper, moving my pelvis against him. "I need it."

"You'll regret it."

"Don't treat me like I'm a virgin. I'm not." I lean forward and kiss his neck softly, tracing imaginary lines with the tip of my tongue. "It's just sex." I reach his mouth, lick his lip, and bite him hard as he had done to me. I feel him trembling beneath me. I am playing dirty, but I need this. I need to feel desired by someone, even if only for one night.

"All right, I've let you have your playtime, that's enough." He grunts as though annoyed, but I can see in his eyes how much he wants me. As much as I want him. Thomas, however, grabs me by the waist and moves me off him. I fall flat on my back on the mattress, unsatisfied.

I sigh impatiently and prop myself up on my elbows. "You know what? If you don't want to do it, then I'll go find someone who will. That party downstairs is full of assholes desperate to take a turn," I spit acidly, with a language and boldness that surprise even me. I get out of bed, committing to my charade and hoping that it will have the desired effect. I reach the door, but just as I begin to open it, a large, tattooed palm shuts it vehemently. I hide a pleased smile. Thomas grabs me by the shoulders and turns me around.

"Where the fuck do you think you're going?"

"Downstairs."

He takes a few steps forward until my back collides with the door. I find myself trapped, with no escape route.

But why would I want to run anywhere?

"Get your ass back on that mattress," he orders peremptorily, his cheeks slightly reddened.

I am about to refuse and tell him that he can't tell me what to do, but he raises a corner of his mouth impudently and adds, "If you want to get fucked by some asshole, then that asshole is gonna be me..." He grabs my face with one hand and forces me to look him in the eye. "As long as it really is just sex," he says, making it clear.

"Just sex," I reassure him.

He tastes my lip and then sinks his tongue into my mouth. His vetiver scent overwhelms me. I breathe him in deeply. Without interrupting our kiss, he picks me up off the ground, catching me by surprise. Instinctively, I wrap my legs around his waist. He pulls me back onto the bed, where he drops me beneath him. He grabs me by my thighs, spreading them apart and positioning himself between them as I cling to his elbows. He presses his hips against mine, and I am overwhelmed by a wave of heat so powerful that I have to arch my back and inhale deeply into his mouth. He pulls back a bit, his index finger brushing my lips, my neck, and the cleft between my breasts covered by the fabric of his T-shirt. With his other hand, he squeezes my left breast and gently massages the already stiff nipple. I watch, mesmerized, as he bends down and buries his face between my thighs.

He licks me through my soaked panties and then nibbles, teasing me slowly, in such an obscene way that it makes me even wetter.

"Oh, God," I gasp, fisting the sheets in my hands. He pulls my panties down with his teeth, and a devilish grin spreads across his lips.

"Much better without them," he says, kissing my knee, then my inner thigh, moving steadily up and up. He uses his tongue to lap at my most sensitive spot and, for a moment, I cannot breathe. I try to move, but he holds me still, so I sink my hands into his hair and push his head deeper between my legs, urging him to give me more, begging him to calm that heat in my core that makes me gasp. With considerable skill, Thomas rotates his tongue all over my slit, from the top to the bottom. The friction of his piercing against my flesh makes my head spin.

"More...please..."

He presses one finger into me, and all my muscles contract around it. He slides it in and out divinely. He knows exactly when to speed up and when to slow down and applies the perfect amount of pressure the whole time. When he slowly slides a second finger in, I feel a jolt in my lower belly. I am losing my mind with this unbearable pleasure that reverberates through every inch of my body. When he begins to move his fingers faster, I thrust my hips against him, moaning under his smug gaze. He interrupts that pleasure to rip off my shirt and tosses it away to who knows where. Suddenly I feel a pang of shame. I realize that I am now completely naked, in Thomas Collins's bed. And even though I am currently more uninhibited than I've ever been, my insecurities are always alive inside me. My discomfort increases when I notice the hungry way Thomas looks at me: first at my open mouth, then my breasts and belly, all the way down until he reaches the crux of my thighs.

"What are you...what are you thinking?" I bite my lip, immediately embarrassed at myself for asking such a stupid question.

"If I'm being honest? About ten different ways to fuck every part of your body."

Oh God.

He smiles and kisses me on the lips. It is a chaste kiss, nothing like the ones he's already given me. With one hand he hitches up my thigh and wraps it around his waist. I squeeze my knee against his side and I feel his arousal—still covered by his boxers—rubbing against my center. He grabs my butt and tilts my pelvis up to intensify that pleasure. He looks me in the eyes as he does so, his lips slightly parted, a hank of dark hair falling over his forehead and his breath tickling my face. He leans over my breasts and, as he continues to rock my lower body against him, he takes a nipple between his lips and sucks it slowly, meticulously, making me arch into him.

"Please, I need you, Thomas..." I gasp, no longer able to bear the intense pulsations between my thighs. I need him to satisfy the throbbing desire or I will go crazy, I am sure of it. He brings his attention back to me, caressing my leg, resting the full weight of his body on his other arm so as not to crush me.

"Last chance to back out, Ness."

Instead, I take his face in my hands and kiss him, biting his lip so hard that I hear him suppress a moan.

"Fuck me," I breathe into his mouth. "Just fuck me." At these words Thomas dives between my thighs, and I want nothing more than to feel him inside me. With one hand pressed to the mattress, he reaches up to the nightstand and pulls out a silver packet. My eyes widen and I feel dumb for not even having thought of that. Even though I'm on the pill, you can never take too many precautions, especially with a guy like him. Thomas clouds my thinking, which isn't a good thing.

He tears the packet open with his teeth, and that gesture triggers a sudden craving in me. I take the package from his hands. He arches an eyebrow, frowning. "I want to do it," I confess, in a small voice. I don't know what is happening to me. None of this is me.

Thomas, after an initial moment of astonishment, gives me a cheeky smile that exudes unadulterated virility and wickedness. He pulls off his boxers, sits back on his heels, and positions me on him. The sight of his erection towering between us makes me tremble and gulp at the same time. Our faces are aligned, and Thomas squeezes my butt with one hand. With the other he grips himself and starts rubbing the head slowly along my cleft, lubricating it with my fluids and making me shiver with pleasure. Feeling it skin to skin sets me aflame. I see the same fire burning in his dilated pupils. "It's all yours."

I swallow and, with a courage I cannot explain, I wrap my trembling hands around his burning-hot member. Thomas represses a low moan when I caress the moist tip with the pad of my thumb. I slide the condom on him, noting how the muscles in his abdomen twitch under my gentle and somewhat unsure touch. I bite my lip and lift my eyes to his. Heat. That's all I see there.

"Are you still sure?"

I nod.

Immediately, Thomas slams me against the mattress and, with an abrupt stroke that moves me a few inches, he penetrates me. He wrenches from me a cry of commingled pain and pleasure. It is unexpected, strong and invasive. Yet, having him inside me is the most incredible sensation I have ever felt. I loop my arms around his neck and tighten my lips, while he pauses and gives me a moment to get used to his size. When the initial burning fades, I lift my hips and urge him to continue. He grabs my thighs and spreads them even wider. He pulls out slowly and penetrates me again with even more force, making me scream. I dig my nails into his shoulders and scratch hard. Suffused with a savage satisfaction, he continues to move relentlessly in and out of me. Harder. Faster. Making me moan with every stroke. "Goddamn, I could fuck you all night long."

"Do it," I encourage him, unable to help myself.

I run my hands over his pecs, down to his tightened abs, covered with tattoos and small beads of sweat. I worship him, as if I had a god underneath my hands, while he slams me into the mattress with inconceivable force. I crawl my fingers over his hips until I find a raised scar. I feel him stiffen, and the warning look he gives me from under his long lashes tells me I should stop touching him there. Instead, like an idiot, I run my fingers over the tissue gently, solely with the intention of reassuring him. But as soon as I graze the edge, Thomas pulls out of me abruptly, startling me. He grabs me by the hips and, with one move, flips me over. A small cry of astonishment escapes me. I find myself with my cheek pressed against the pillow and my pelvis raised to the height of his groin. With one hand he grabs my hip, and he presses the other against the back of my neck to hold me still. I feel dizzy and hot. What does he want to do?

He squeezes my ass cheeks ferociously and I open my eyes wide when he delivers a resounding slap to my right cheek. It pulls a powerful scream from me and, to my enormous surprise, excites me even more. I feel him bending over me, his chest pressed against my back. He looms over my body, brings his mouth close to my ear and, in a rough, sensual voice, he murmurs, "Tonight I am yours, and you are mine." He gathers my hair into a ponytail and wraps it tightly around his fist. With a jerk, he forces me to tilt my head back, taking my breath away as he rubs himself against my opening. "But there are some lines you are not allowed to cross." He seats himself inside me with one overwhelming thrust that makes me arch my back. My toes curl. "Never," he orders, giving me another hard slap to the other buttock and sending my whole body into a frenzy. To say nothing of my head. My eyes roll up involuntarily, overwhelmed by the mixture of extraordinary sensations. I follow his movements and, pleased, he tightens his grip on my hips. He bites my shoulder, my neck, every bit of skin he can reach.

"Ah...more... I want more," I scream, in thrall to this insane and uncontrolled passion, subjected to his rapid, powerful thrusts. Never would I have thought that sex with Thomas could be so intense. So rough. Animalistic. Above all, I never would have thought that I'd like it so much. It was never like this with Travis. Our sex had always been reserved and contained, even boring at times. It was all because of me, because I got ashamed at the mere thought of taking a risk. Maybe if I had let myself go a little more... Suddenly, Thomas presses his cheek close to mine, continuing his implacable movements. The sound of his soft, gasping breaths reverberates between my thighs.

"What's wrong with you?" he asks frowning, as if he can tell that my mind is wandering.

"Nothing, everything's okay," I reply breathlessly. Thomas tightens his grip on my hair and gives my neck a languid lick.

"If you let me fuck you"—he grunts against my skin—"I want you to be with me." He gives me a yearning thrust and it takes me less than a second to completely forget about Travis and focus on this perfect Adonis who makes me feel things I have never, ever felt before.

"I-I'm with you," I gasp dazedly, completely at his mercy. I feel him smile against my neck. I surrender to his strong, firm strokes again and again and again, accommodating his movements as my knees begin to buckle, and my body contracts with each spasm of arousal. Thomas reaches between my legs with one hand and stimulates my clitoris, intensifying the stabs of pleasure. My God. I could die...

"Are you coming?" he pants into my ear. I barely manage to nod. He flips me over, crushing me underneath him. With my eyes closed, I wrap my legs around his waist and press my heels against his buttocks. Our scents mingle as our bodies merge. This position makes everything more intimate.

"Look at me," he orders, with one hand around my neck in a dominant grip. I do as he says. I look into his eyes and I get lost there.

He leans down and kisses me. His tongue intertwines with mine. His every touch is studied, expert and designed to give me pleasure. Thomas tenses his muscles and pushes into me even more forcefully. I scream and lift my hips to meet his thrusts. I grip his waist with my trembling knees. I cling to his broad, powerful shoulders until I explode for the first time with his name on my lips. Shortly thereafter he stiffens as well, his biceps flexing as he comes, shaking through his orgasm. "Fuck," he exclaims breathlessly, collapsing against me with his face in the crook of my neck. It feels like the earth is shaking, or maybe that's just me. Or Thomas. I don't know. What matters is that I have just had the most intense, most beautiful orgasm of my life. It was incredible. But I don't have the strength to tell him so, because we both sink immediately into a deep sleep.

Fifteen

IT'S THE SUNLIGHT FILTERING THROUGH the window that wakes me the next morning. My head feels like it's about to explode, my eyes are burning, and my stomach is still tied in knots. This is what a hangover feels like, apparently.

I look around and run a hand through my hair, overwhelmed with anxiety.

Damn it, this can't be happening! The little voice in my head suggests that there is only one thing to do: run away. What could I have been thinking? All of this happened because I wanted it to happen. But damn, did I ever take it too far. One-night stands are not for me. And a one-night stand with Thomas Collins is especially not for me. It's much better for my dignity if I leave before he wakes up, otherwise he'll have to kick me out himself. And that would be too humiliating to bear.

Cautiously, I slide the muscular arm off my belly and stand up. In doing so, I feel some very annoying twinges in my lower abdomen. They must be the result of Thomas taking me with such wild abandon last night. I touch my belly and I can almost hear the echo of my ecstatic gasps.

I tiptoe around the room looking for something to wear, but I find only Thomas's boxers and his black T-shirt on the floor. I'm not sure where in the house to look for my clothes. On the other hand, I do find my bag with my phone inside. Thank goodness. At least I can call Tiffany and ask her to bring me a clean change of clothes.

I try to turn it on but it shows no signs of life. The battery is dead. I can't believe this. And I also have to get out of here in a hurry if I want to get to campus in time for my reading group! According to the alarm clock on the nightstand, it's already after eight o'clock. I stick my phone back inside my bag and, unintentionally, I knock a penholder off the desk. The clamor wakes Thomas.

"What...what are you doing?" he mumbles in a voice thick with sleep.

"Where are my clothes?" In one sudden movement, I pick up his black shirt and slip it on, hiding my naked body.

"You going somewhere?" He sits up and rubs his eyes. My gaze drops to his tensed abdominals, the triangle of his pelvic area barely covered by the sheet, above which I glimpse a slim trail of hair. I swallow and bite my lip, trying to ignore the strange sensations that this vision triggers in me.

"To campus," I reply, trying to play it cool. "I have my first book club meeting in forty-five minutes, and I'm stuck here, with no clothes and no memories!" What did he think? That I was going to stay here with him and let him take me for another ride? Take me for a ride? What the hell am I talking about?

"Your clothes are in the wash. After the strip poker, they were in bad shape."

Strip...strip poker? The little voice in my head suggests I not ask any follow-up questions, because I will regret it.

"So how do I get out of here? I can't go to campus dressed like this." I look down at his shirt.

"Why not? It's a lot better than those faux-innocent clothes you usually wear," he taunts me.

"I am not faux-innocent!" I retort acidly.

"Oh, but you are. I got proof of that last night, when you got brutally fucked by yours truly and absolutely loved it." He gives me a satisfied grin and another image rises out of my memory: Thomas taking me from behind, with my hair clenched in his fist, spanking my ass as I begged him to continue. "I suspected that behind that angel facade of yours there was a hidden kinky side. And the idea that you brought it out just for me"—he pauses, full of mischief—"it gets me so fucking hot." He lets his hand trail between his legs without the slightest hint of shame. Meanwhile, my cheeks are on fire.

"Y-you're delusional. I don't have a kinky side. I was just drunk and depressed." I pull down the hem of his shirt, trying to cover as much of my legs as possible.

"You didn't seem very depressed when you came while screaming my name." He chuckles. "I still have scratches from your nails on my back."

I take a deep breath, pinching the bridge of my nose. I try to shake off the devouring sense of shame. Enough. It's time to put an end to this drama.

"What happened last night must never happen again. More importantly, it needs to stay inside these four walls, forever," I threaten. It was a mistake. It was all just a terrible mistake. I mean, it's Thomas Collins we are talking about here. I have no desire to be one of his conquests. The alcohol must have removed all my inhibitions because nothing I did last night with him is me.

"We fucked, Vanessa. Don't make a big deal out of it. You'll have forgotten it by tomorrow." He heaves an exhausted sigh before taking a pack of Marlboros out of the nightstand drawer. He sets an ashtray on one thigh and brings a cigarette to his lips before lighting it.

"Well, I'm glad we agree," I say, clearing my throat and forcing myself to change the subject. "Anyway…I didn't know you belonged to this fraternity." I look around skeptically.

"I'm a man of many surprises." He smiles wryly.

"I don't understand. I thought you were living in the dorms."

"Not much to understand. I'm part of Sigma Beta, but I don't have to live here. I prefer to stay at the dorms during the week because it's quieter."

"But isn't a frat brother supposed to live with the others? I mean, aren't there meetings, services to be rendered, tests to pass, and all that crap?" I sit at the foot of the bed.

"The only obligation I have toward this fraternity is to attend the parties," he explains, exhaling a plume of smoke.

"How come?"

Thomas sighs, annoyed by my chatter. "Because, somehow, my presence at a party guarantees the participation of certain students who matter."

"I still don't understand. Why do you spend the weekend here?"

"Because, I can have fun here however I want," he says cheekily.

"So this is basically...your personal harem?" I ask, disgusted.

"Something like that. My roommate is a real pain-in-the-ass nerd. He doesn't like having women in the dorm because they agitate him or some other bullshit. Last time, he just stood in front of the door to my room until Sarah and Denise left." He shakes the ash from his cigarette and adds, "Right at the best part too."

"You were having sex with two women while your roommate was standing right outside your door?"

He nods, as though that were the most normal thing in the world.

"You're disgusting, you know that?"

He gives me an accusatory look. "And you're a hypocrite."

"Excuse me?" I ask, raising an eyebrow.

"You say I'm disgusting for fucking two girls with my roommate outside the door. But last night, you let me fuck you with an entire frat party downstairs."

I am frozen for a few seconds, staring at him and unsuccessfully trying to find a reasonable retort. "That's...not the same thing," I say simply. "Oh my God, this is so embarrassing." I rub my temples, trying to chase away the negative thoughts.

"Knock it off with all the recriminations, you're getting annoying," he hisses impatiently.

"Easy for you to say. You must have been in this situation a million times, but for me this is new territory! It's not easy for me to wake up in a stranger's room and discover that I've had sex with him merely hours after ending things with my boyfriend," I exclaim. "Ex-boyfriend," I add, correcting myself.

Thomas frowns at me and puts out his cigarette in the ashtray. When he releases the last plume of smoke into the air, I scrunch my nose at the harsh, pungent smell. "Whatever. If you're just going to keep busting my balls, I'm going to take a shower."

I get up, slip on the underwear I found on the chair, and tie my hair up into a tousled bun. "I'd like to take one myself, if you don't mind."

He frowns, before giving me one of his irritating little smiles. "You angling for an invitation?"

"What?" I look at him confused. It takes me a moment to understand.

"No! I-I meant alone. I need to shower, alone."

Thomas slips out of bed in all his nude, sculpted-marble glory. "Relax, stranger, you're too nervous," he says, trying to hide a smile. As he heads for the bathroom, the muscles in his backside contract with every step and I gasp at the mere thought of having touched, kissed and, yes, scratched every part of that body. His shoulders, his hips and even his buttocks are marked with small pink scrapes.

"W-what do I do for clothes?" I ask, dashing after him. He turns around and I almost crash into his chest. I feel his naked member brush against my belly, but I force myself not to show any embarrassment. Although judging by the cheeky smile he is suppressing, I think he is already aware of it.

"You can find something in the top drawer." He points to a dark wooden dresser upon which rests the latest generation of television. I hear the shower running as I open the first drawer. Suddenly, I am faced with a cavalcade of bras and panties.

"What the hell is this?" I scream, disgusted.

"Clothes left behind by girls I've fucked," he answers from under the shower. I imagine him laughing smugly.

I slam the drawer closed with a disdainful sneer before heading for the bathroom.

"You must have completely lost your mind, if you really think that I am going to wear any of these...garments!" I yell at the fogged-up door of the shower. Thomas stops the water, steps out of the shower, and, for the second time within five minutes, proudly shows me his entire naked body. He seems to derive some kind of sick pleasure from making me uncomfortable.

Asshole.

I should turn away, cover my eyes, or tell him to cover himself, but I don't do any of that. I just stand there staring at him, dumbfounded, with my cheeks blazing like some stupid schoolgirl.

Fortunately, Thomas decides to put me out of my misery and wraps a towel around his waist. Then he runs a hand through his wet hair, pushing it back, and approaches me. I back away until my back hits the wall, stuck between it and him. He takes my face in his hands and caresses my lower lip with his thumb. "I knew you weren't going to wear them," he whispers, just a few inches from my face. He tilts my cheek and presses his mouth to the base of my neck. "I just really wanted to see your pissed-off kitten reaction," he breathes against my skin, before lapping a portion of it with his tongue and finally biting down, making me quiver beneath him.

"T-Thomas…" I gasp, squeezing my eyes shut.

With one hand he begins stroking my thigh, then moves up over my belly, until he reaches my breast. He covers it with his palm and I feel like I'm losing my mind.

"Do you have any idea how sexy you look with my shirt on, your hair pulled up like this and your eyes all clouded with pleasure?" he says in a low voice, wedging me more firmly between him and the wall and squeezing my breasts tightly until my nipples stiffen in his hands. A soft moan escapes me, which I try to stifle by biting my lip. "I could take you right here, against this wall, couldn't I? Give you a good reason never to wear anything else…"

My breathing becomes shorter, almost labored, and a familiar feeling of warmth spreads between my thighs. It seems that, after last night, my body has developed some sort of erotic Pavlovian response to Thomas. And now, every time he gets near me, brushes against me or touches me, every fiber of my being vibrates with pure desire for him. With his other hand, he grabs my butt and squeezes it vigorously, lifting me a few inches and wringing another moan of excitement out of me. He bites my earlobe, and the muscles of my abdomen contract, turning me frozen and docile. Is it possible that he is attracted to me enough to make me his again?

The idea makes me a little proud, but also reminds me that we cannot do anything like that again. Which is why, when his mouth draws perilously close to mine, I find myself compelled to put my palms on his damp chest. "Stop…" I was hoping for a more decisive tone, but the tremor in my voice betrays me. Thomas, in any case, shows that he has much more self-control than I do and steps back, putting the appropriate distance between our bodies.

With ragged breathing and nipples that peak sharply against the fabric of his T-shirt, I tuck a few strands of hair behind my ear.

"You okay, Ness? You seem a little…hot," he teases me with a sly little smile.

I give him a sharp look but then my gaze falls on his neck and I start. Did I leave hickeys on him? And did he leave any on me?

I turn immediately to the mirror and realize that the answer to that question is a resounding yes. Freaked out, I bring a hand to my neck.

"That's not the only one," he says mischievously.

My eyes widen. "W-what do you mean?"

Thomas looks me up and down in a satisfied sort of way before winking and leaving the bathroom. I examine my entire body in a frenzy and, sure enough, I find one under my collarbone on the right side, one near my breast, a third on my abdomen, and yet another on my inner thigh. Oh my God.

I join him in the room. "Was that really necessary?"

"I like to leave my mark," he replies calmly, rubbing his hair with a towel. "Anyway, the underwear in that drawer is actually my sister's. Some of her clothes are in the closet too. She lived here in the frat house for a year, in the room next door, and she still hasn't finished taking all her stuff to her dorm on campus," he says, pointing to the wardrobe behind me. I turn to the closet and start looking for something comfortable among Leila's clothes. For pants, I find some skinny jeans that fit pretty well, but I have a harder time finding a top because of my larger bust size. Leila's shirts are all too tight on me, and I don't feel comfortable wearing them.

I turn to Thomas, hoping he can help me, and find he's facing away from me. He is pulling on some black jeans before turning his attention to his sneakers. My gaze lingers on his bare back, muscular and fully tattooed, before sliding to his side, where I notice a scar about two inches across. All of a sudden, I remember touching that part of him, and how he stiffened up and moved me away from that area.

"What are you looking at?" He frowns, catching me in the act.

I gasp. "N-nothing, I was just wondering... I mean, that scar looks pretty deep... How did it happen?"

His face hardens, and I instantly regret not having been able to keep my curiosity at bay.

"None of your damn business," he says shortly, putting on a white T-shirt.

I'm still dumbfounded. "Oh. Yeah, of course, I didn't mean to—" I hesitate. "Sorry," I mutter finally.

I turn around, with my back to him, and pretend to rummage through the wardrobe. I don't like Angry Thomas; it's somehow even more unnerving than the regular cocky one. Shortly thereafter, I hear footsteps approaching and his scent surrounds me. "Did you find something?" he asks abruptly, darting a quick look at me.

"I found some jeans, but no luck with the shirt. Leila is smaller than me." I avoid looking him in the face because I still feel uncomfortable.

"Then keep mine."

"What?" I look at him, wide-eyed. "I can't go to campus wearing your shirt."

"No one's gonna know it's mine," he says in a calming tone.

I think about it for a moment, but I don't have many other options. This is the perfect epilogue for this insane adventure.

"Okay, but now I'd like to take a shower. Could you give me five minutes?" He frowns, seemingly not understanding what I'm saying.

"I'm not going to get into the shower knowing that you're around and could burst in at any moment," I say, pointing out the obvious.

Thomas rolls his eyes and huffs out a laugh. "What am I gonna see that I haven't already seen?"

There he goes again, reveling in my discomfort. Bastard. Resigned, I don't insist and instead go to take a quick shower.

When I come out, I find him leaning against his desk intently typing something on his phone. I still have ten minutes before my meeting with the reading group. That's not much time, but I can make it if I hurry. I quickly put on my combat boots and Tiffany's leather jacket, which Thomas has recovered from the living room. I grab my bag and one of Leila's scarves to hide the hickey. Thomas, meanwhile, stuffs his jacket pockets with his phone, keys, and pack of Marlboros.

As we walk through the hallways and down the stairs of the house, I gather from the cups left on the floor, the empty bottles and joint ends littered here and there, that last night must have been a huge blowout. Arriving downstairs, I see a group of guys sprawled out sleeping on couches, armchairs, and floors. We pass them and head for the front door.

I close the door behind me and let out a huge sigh of relief. Finally, I can put this whole thing behind me. "Um...well, thank you for the shower and for...you know, yeah, all the rest..." I bite my lip, embarrassed. Telling a person *thank you* after having sex is not ideal, but I know he doesn't expect anything else from me.

"You mean thanks for the mind-blowing orgasm I gave you last night?" He quirks a corner of his mouth cheekily. "Don't mention it. Whenever you want another one, you know where to find me."

I roll my eyes, but I can't hold back a smile. "You're an idiot as always. See you, Thomas." I walk down the steps of the porch and onto the sidewalk, heading for the campus library. He continues to walk beside me. He lights a cigarette, slips the Ray-Bans off his head, and puts them on.

I give him a sideways look. "Um...what are you doing?"

"Walking," he says resolutely, apparently heedless of the stares he's getting from some of the female students as we pass them. I, on the other hand, cannot ignore the nasty glares or the suggestive looks from the boys. Fortunately, campus is sparsely populated on Saturdays. To avoid giving the wrong impression, I move a little away from Thomas. I don't want to be seen as some naive little girl who fell into his clutches.

"Are you… Are you headed for some extracurricular too?"

"To the dorm." He puffs out a cloud of smoke around his head.

"Is it really necessary for you to walk beside me?"

"We're going in the same direction, Ness."

"People are looking at us, Thomas," I point out to him in annoyance.

He takes a quick look around before turning his attention back to me. "So?"

"They might get the wrong idea about the two of us, they might think…"

"That we fucked?" he finishes my sentence. "Do you think we're the only ones doing it?" He chuckles, dismissing my discomfort.

"I don't care what other people do, I care what they think of me."

"And what do you think they think of you?" he asks.

"They look at me like I'm your new little slut."

Thomas stops suddenly, as if I had just slapped him in the face. His smile fades, leaving a different expression. Almost disappointed.

"If you were really my slut, they wouldn't notice you at all. So stop it with this bullshit."

Go tell that to my conscience, which is making me feel so dirty. I'm even afraid of what my friends will say when they find out that I wasted no time in throwing myself into someone else's bed right after I broke up with my ex.

"There are some things that a person like you could never understand," I say simply, before I leave.

Sixteen

THE MEETING WITH MY READING group at the library ener-
gizes me. We choose the novel we'll read this month and sketch out a
meeting schedule; I am happy to have a small space where I can talk
about books. I also manage to borrow a charger for my phone. When
it finally turns on, I see calls from Travis, texts from Alex, and, with
perfect timing, I get a new notification from Tiffany: In the garden,
ten minutes. We need to talk.

Damn, I was hoping for a clean escape, but apparently I'm due a
full-blown lecture for walking out of the party, sending her one vague
message, and then disappearing all night. In retrospect, I realize that it
was pretty irresponsible of me.

When I get to the garden, I look for her among the picnic tables,
and a copper-colored head of hair immediately catches my attention.
I head for her but as soon as I see that Alex is right next to her, I turn
pale. What is he doing here? Isn't he supposed to be with Stella?

Oh God, I don't have the guts to tell Alex that Travis wasn't just
the asshole he had always thought but was actually much worse. I
definitely don't have the guts to tell him that I got nearly blackout
drunk and ended up sleeping with Thomas. The very same guy he had
warned me about and I had reassured him, telling him he should trust
my judgment. Instinctively I take a step back, trying to slip away, but
Tiffany's voice pulls me back.

Damn!

I squeeze my eyes shut and turn around slowly. My friend waves her arm to get my attention. I smile at her through gritted teeth and, resigned, I walk over to them.

"Heeeey, hi," I murmur, tense as a violin string.

"Hi, my ass," Tiffany immediately interrupts me. "What the hell happened last night?! Do you have any idea how I felt when I read your message and found out that not only were you no longer at the party, but you weren't even reachable! I didn't know who you were with, where you were, why you ran away!"

"And do you have any idea how scared I was when Tiffany called me in a total panic asking me if I had heard from you and, guess what, I hadn't?" Alex adds in a stern voice.

I bend my head and cover my face with my hands, then take a big breath and say, "Guys, I'm really sorry for worrying you, it was wrong of me. But everything happened so fast that I didn't even think about it. I was safe, though. I wrote you just to let you know that you shouldn't worry. I was at Matt's," I confess, leaving out the small detail of Thomas's presence.

"At Matt's? What were you doing there?"

"Well, I…" I look from Alex to Tiffany, ready to tell them everything, when just a few feet away I see a furious Travis approaching.

My stomach churns, and that familiar nauseous feeling returns to keep me company. Why is he here?

He catches up with just a few long strides, and I begin to tremble. "Where have you been? I spent the whole night trying to call you!" he thunders, making us all gasp. "I asked everyone about you, but no one knew where you'd gone!" He pauses, waiting for an answer that he will not get from me. "I was about to call the police, or, even worse, your mother. You can thank Tiffany for holding me back!"

"Travis, calm down," his sister interjects in my defense. But it's time for me to speak up. They need to know the truth.

"Do you really have the nerve to come here and lecture me?" I burst out, gathering my courage.

"I was worried!" He gives me a look that burns with anger. Worried… What a hypocrite. He must not have been so worried when he was slithering into another girl's bed.

"I can take care of myself. And, for your information, I was at your frat house," I reply in a scornful tone.

"You're kidding," is all he says, as if refusing to believe me. He lets out a deep sigh and starts pacing. Tiffany makes to approach me, when Travis spits out all his vitriol, "You ran off to go to some stoner party? That's insane. No, it's stupid. That's what you are, an idiot!"

The swollen vein in his neck throbs, his eyes blazing with anger.

"Hey! Watch your mouth!" Alex insists, approaching him cautiously.

"Yeah, Trav, calm down," his sister urges him.

Travis scrubs a hand over his face and takes another deep breath. "Why did you go there?"

"Oh, were you hoping I would stay at Carol's with you after what I found out? Or maybe you thought I'd go home and cry like a heart-broken little girl?"

"Okay, be straight with us now. Travis, what did you do?" interjects Tiffany.

"Yeah, I'd like to know too," Alex backs her up.

"Stay out of it!" Travis snaps, glaring at me. Oh, no. He's not getting off that easy. Not anymore.

"What happened is that, last night, I found out that Travis has been cheating on me all along! He even lied and tricked an innocent girl, Leila! That's what happened."

"Travis, tell me she's joking," his sister begs him, stunned. I hear Alex curse through gritted teeth.

"No…" He struggles to speak, rubbing his pale face with both hands.

"Do you still have the nerve to speak to me? To show up here, face me, and make a scene like this?" I wipe a tear away from my cheekbone and make to leave. Travis steps in front of me, blocking my way.

"Move aside!" I try to push past him, but he stops me.

"Nessy…" He tries to put his hands on my shoulders, but Alex doesn't let him. He stands up and shields me with his arm.

"You'd better leave," Alex commands, without any niceties.

"Now," Tiffany agrees in a glacial tone.

"Mind your own fucking business. This doesn't concern you!" Travis growls, out of control.

"What happened to you?" Tiffany turns a disappointed gaze on her brother. "It's getting worse every day. I don't even recognize you anymore." But Travis is so caught up in his rage that he's not listening to her.

"It's not like that, Nessy. You know I never wanted to hurt you." He takes a step toward me, and I freeze.

"You never loved me, Travis. It was just convenient for you to have someone easy to control. Someone stupid enough to let herself be fooled, someone who would believe whatever lies you told. Well, my eyes are open now."

"I made a mistake, but we can overcome it together." He moves as if to touch me, but I push his hand back. I see my friends tense up, ready to intervene. And that's when I snap to attention. My stomach clenches as though trapped in a vise, and an intoxicating scent envelops me. I don't need Travis's furious expression to tell me who the person behind me is; I know it from the adrenaline that courses through my veins. From the unmistakable scent that has lingered around me all night long, infused in the shirt I'm still wearing. I can feel it on my skin.

It is Thomas who stops beside me, crossing his arms over his chest. The tension he exudes passes through my body like an electric current.

"Is there a problem here?" His icy voice resonates in the space between us, and a shiver of fear runs down my spine.

His presence will only make things worse. And he knows it. Maybe that's exactly why he's here; to needle Travis, and fully relish his defeat. I tilt my head and glare at him, as if to say, "What the hell did you come here for?" But he doesn't reciprocate. His whole attention is on Travis. He stares straight into his eyes.

"Everything's fine. You can go," I say hastily, doing my best not to stutter. I really don't need to witness a second fight between these two.

"What the fuck do you want?" Travis snaps after a moment of hesitation.

"She doesn't want you to touch her, asshole." Thomas inches toward him, and I instinctively block him, grabbing him by the arm.

Travis shifts his sharp gaze to me. "Are you going to let him defend you now?"

"I'm not letting anyone defend me!"

"Then explain why I'm looking at him right now!"

"I don't know!"

"You sure? Because I'm beginning to understand," he says mockingly.

Panic takes over my body.

Travis looks at Thomas and then immediately back at me, staring at me pensively for what feels like the longest second of my life. Something in his face changes, as if he has just solved a riddle. "You've really hit rock bottom, haven't you?"

"Excuse me?"

"You let this asshole fuck you!" he shouts in front of everyone with a disgusted grimace on his face, and I am paralyzed.

"Travis, you're out of your mind!" Tiffany lashes out at her brother, yanking him back roughly.

"What is he talking about, Vanessa?" asks Alex, baffled.

"N-no..." My voice shakes, and I pray that Thomas doesn't embarrass me in front of everyone.

"Do you think I'm stupid? You're wearing his shirt! I spent the night worrying about you, and you were hooking up with him? I can't believe it." Travis runs a hand over his face, red with anger. "Did you want to be one of his whores or were you just looking for someone experienced so you could work on your subpar skills?" he rants hatefully. My heart skips a beat. My tears well up, blurring my vision.

"You are such a son of a bitch." Thomas is about to lunge at him, but Alex gets between them in time to avert catastrophe.

"Everyone, calm down," he orders sharply. "Vanessa, you're leaving with us now." He takes my hand gently, as if I were some delicate crystal ornament ready to crumble at his touch. And he keeps talking, giving Travis a threatening look. "From now on, you will stay away from her. And you are done mocking her." Travis is motionless. I know him well enough to realize that he is repentant. But I won't let him manipulate me again.

"You are such a disappointment," Tiffany whispers, with tears in her eyes. It is so rare to see her cry.

"Okay, guys, show's over!" shouts Alex irritably, addressing the students who have crowded into the garden. Then he leads me away, while Tiffany wraps an arm around my shoulder.

"I'm sorry, I didn't think it would go that far." She holds me tightly and I lean on her shoulder as I try to push back the tears and soothe the pain and shame that I feel.

But we don't make it to the exit before Thomas comes after us. Alex and Tiffany turn their heads in surprise, and I can't help but wonder why he keeps following me. Why can't he just leave me alone?

Alex stands between me and him and puts his hand on Thomas's chest. In response, Thomas looks down at the other boy's fingers. "Move it," he orders with a clenched jaw.

"Vanessa doesn't need any more messed-up people in her life," my friend says, but Thomas is not even listening. His green eyes are fixed on me and they scrutinize me intently. "She'll be fine," Alex adds, sensing his thoughts. "We're with her, her friends. Her family. She doesn't need anything else," he concludes.

"You done?" Thomas silences him with a raised eyebrow. "Now move over."

"No, dude, I know your game, and I'm not letting you do it." Alex is immovable.

"Fine, I'll bite: what's my 'game'?" Thomas crosses his arms over his chest, looking down at him.

"You took advantage of her at her weakest moment. Low, even for someone like you."

"Alex, it wasn't like that…" I put my hand on my friend's shoulder to calm him down. If there is anyone to blame for last night, it's me.

"Don't defend him, Vanessa!" Alex exclaims, turning to me. "We all know what kind of guy he is."

"I didn't make her do anything she didn't want to do," Thomas replies through gritted teeth, anger glimmering in his eyes.

"Guys, can you give us a couple of minutes alone, please?" I ask, looking from Tiffany to Alex.

"No," Alex snaps, never taking his eyes off Thomas.

"Alex, it didn't go the way you're thinking, believe me. Thomas didn't do anything wrong. Really."

"Come on, let's give them a minute," Tiffany urges him. I owe her a huge thank you. Alex takes a deep breath as they walk away. I walk in the direction of an isolated tree while Thomas, beside me, seems to have calmed down.

"What do you want?"

He shoots me a worried look. "I want to make sure that the shit that idiot said didn't stick in your paranoid little brain and convince you that he's right."

I hesitate for a few seconds, but then I have to admit it. "Of course he's right."

He shakes his head in resignation. "What we did last night does not make you somehow in the wrong."

"Are you sure?" I dump my bag at the foot of the tree. "Can you really say that all the girls you slept with weren't subsequently labeled 'easy' solely because they had been with you?" His prolonged silence is telling. "Yeah. That's what I thought."

"It doesn't matter what other people say. All that matters is what you think!"

I almost envy him; he is so sure of himself and he doesn't fear the judgment of others. I, on the other hand, have to struggle with my own harsh self-assessment every day before I even try to face the outside world.

"The thing is, Thomas, 'what I think' is not that different! And I know that it's hard for someone like you to understand. You change girls as often as you change your underwear, but for me it's not that simple!"

"Then make it simple and ignore the judgments of people who don't matter."

"Ugh, never mind, I give up! Instead, why don't you explain to me what you came here to do? Didn't we just establish that we were going to keep our distance from one another? Instead, you keep tormenting me." I can feel myself losing my patience.

Thomas's face wrinkles in surprise. "I torment you?"

"If you hadn't caught up with us, Travis wouldn't have suspected anything! So thank you, thank you so much! I hope my public humiliation has served your purpose!" I throw the accusation at him, my thoughts and feelings a confused whirl.

"My purpose?"

"It's obvious, Thomas, stop pretending. You've been dying to tell Travis about us from the moment I agreed to go with you to the frat house, admit it!" Saying it out loud severs the last tether on my temper and, moved by an anger that I cannot control, I shove him.

"That's not what I did," Thomas replies, unflappable.

"Only because you chose to be cunning, to play it underhandedly. Just us being seen together would have been enough to make people suspicious. You know, maybe everyone is right, maybe you are just a selfish asshole who doesn't give a shit about anyone else!" I explode, angry as I have never been before.

My words land hard. Suddenly, though, something in his gaze changes, and it sends a chill through me. His eyes become hostile and he takes deep, short breaths, like a bull before a red cape. He approaches me slowly, looming over me with his height, and then touches my chin with his thumb. I swallow and stiffen before this seemingly gentle touch, in such sharp contrast to the menacing look on his face.

"You think you're so much better than me, don't you?" His voice is low and intimidating. "You're right, I'm not afraid of what I am. I enjoy life, I fuck whomever I want, and I don't give a damn about the judgment of fake moralists. You, on the other hand... You put up this front as a good girl, hiding your true self even from yourself because you are incapable of accepting what you really are. Well, I'll let you in on a secret." He comes close to my ear, and my heart rate increases. "That doesn't make you honest or respectable, Vanessa." He looks me in the eye again, annihilating me with a glance. "It just makes you a fucking hypocrite," he says bitterly.

Thomas's words cut me to the core, but, drawing on an inner strength I didn't know I had, I force myself to keep my guard up.

"Who do you think you are to talk to me like that?"

"Who do you think you are to judge me?"

My God, my head is going to explode.

"You know what? I'm not surprised that this is so difficult for you to get your head around. I mean, your whole life revolves around two things: fuck and run. No one expects anything else from you; it's who you are and you've never made any secret of it, it's true. But that's nowhere near who I am. That's why I don't I want to be around you and that's why I was running away this morning. Because I deeply regret having made such a mistake. Don't confuse hypocrisy with awareness!" I burst out. I leave him there, just as furious as I am. And as I walk back to Alex and Tiffany, with anger blurring my vision, it only takes me a few moments of clarity to realize what I have just done: I vented all the frustration and pain I felt about Travis onto Thomas. I said terrible things to him, which I didn't really mean, just to hurt him. I was mean, and I'm ashamed of that. Seized by a profound feeling of guilt, I turn around, ready to go back and apologize, but there is no longer any trace of him.

Seventeen

I SPEND THE MORNING IN a catatonic state. After dropping Alex off with Stella, Tiffany gives me a ride home. She hugs me tightly and swears that Travis won't be a problem anymore. I know that she has the means to keep him in line whenever she wants. Before saying goodbye, I promise that I'll retrieve her clothes from the fraternity. I hope they are still intact, at least.

Returning home, I discover to my relief that Mom spent the night at Victor's place and therefore knows nothing about my "disappearance." After a pistachio ice cream binge for lunch and a monumental sleep, I wash and dress up for tonight's dinner: an olive-green turtleneck and white jeans cinched at the waist by a gold belt. On my feet are my beloved unicorn slippers. My mother won't appreciate it but, what the hell, we're not the royal family.

I gather my hair into a high ponytail and use a curling iron on the ends. I give myself a light layer of foundation, a little peachy blush and a smack of nude lipstick. I'm ready to welcome our guests, although I would much rather stay curled up in bed.

I had to lie to my mother and tell her that Travis couldn't join us because he had practice. And she certainly didn't jump for joy when she found out I invited Alex and Stella in his place. It doesn't matter. I need the support if I want to make it through this.

At six o'clock sharp, a black Mercedes pulls into our driveway. I pull back one side of the curtains and peek out my window to watch the arrival of this man who has captured my mother's heart. He gets out of the car and walks toward the house with a confident and determined stride. He is very tall, wearing a dark gray suit and elegant shoes.

Before ringing the doorbell, he adjusts the knot of his tie.

"Nessy, come down! He's here!" my mother chirps. I roll my eyes heavenward.

I join them in the living room and do my best to seem sociable. "Hello, Victor. Welcome," I say, extending my hand to him. This is the first time I've spoken to him for more than two minutes; we've only ever met in passing when he brought Mom home after nights out.

"Hi, Vanessa. Thank you for inviting me to dinner," he replies in his Canadian accent. "I'm happy to be here tonight. Your mother speaks highly of you."

Surprising. My mother doesn't usually speak well of anyone but herself.

"Oh, um, I'm sure she exaggerated," I say, embarrassed.

The doorbell rings, saving me from this awkward impasse. I run to open it and find Alex and Stella. Alex is wearing a pair of jeans and a white wool turtleneck under a tweed blazer. Stella, by contrast, is wearing a leather jacket, with an elegant powder pink blouse underneath, skinny jeans and over-the-knee boots. I hug them both simultaneously. I am so relieved they came.

"Thank God you guys are here," I whisper to them both as I squeeze them tight. "Stella, I am so happy to meet you in person," I say, offering her my hand. When she reciprocates, her grip is warm.

"I was looking forward to it too. Alex told me all about the wonderful friendship you two have," she says in a sweet and joyful voice.

We join my mother and Victor in the living room, and I take my friends' jackets.

"Thanks for the invitation, Mrs. White," Alex says.

"Thank you for coming," my mother answers in a sugary, slightly forced tone. "Come on, don't just stand in the doorway, get in here."

"Mom, Victor. This is Stella, Alex's girlfriend. They met this summer in Santa Barbara."

"Santa Barbara? Do you live there?" my mother asks as she shakes Stella's hand.

"No, I live in Vancouver. We were both in Santa Barbara with our families, and we met purely by chance." Stella exchanges a look with Alex, and her cheeks, still tanned, turn scarlet. Alex wraps his arm around her waist and pulls her close in a reassuring gesture.

"Oh, first love is so magical," my mother squeals. "Too bad it's always doomed."

What?! I shoot a look at her.

Victor intervenes, alleviating our embarrassment with a friendly wave of his hand and introduces himself to both of them.

"Sometimes fate surprises us," he concludes with a smile. Having finished the introductions, Mom ushers us into the dining room, where we find the table already set with serving dishes.

"Wow, Mom, when was the last time you did a setup like this?"

"I was inspired..." She smiles broadly at Victor. Nauseating. "Honey, Victor and I will sit here," she says pointing to the seat at the head of the table and the one next to it. "You can be next to me, Alex and Stella on the other side."

We sit down, and my mother busies herself filling plates with slices of roast turkey and baked potatoes before uncovering the serving trays, which contain vegetable side dishes. Finally, she brings out a basket filled with sliced bread.

Dinner proceeds peacefully, Alex tells us about the trip to China that his parents are taking, Stella about her life in Vancouver. Older than Alex by two years, she is in her last year of college and has decided to take a gap year after graduation to travel.

After a moment of silence, Alex turns to my mother. "Dinner is delicious, Mrs. White. My compliments to the chef."

He's right. My mother has outdone herself this time. She put a lot of effort into impressing Victor. Mom gives him a pleased smile.

"Thank you, Alexander. But I didn't do anything special," she answers, cutting a piece of turkey with disarming grace.

"So, Vanessa," Victor interjects, patting the corners of his mouth with his napkin, "your mother says you are an excellent student. Is she right?"

"Excellent? The best, you mean." Alex grins. I blush and lower my eyes at my friend's compliment.

"I just do my best," I retort with a smile.

"You're very humble as well," Victor adds.

I frown at him. "Is that bad?"

"No, not at all. But if you are lucky enough to be good at something, you shouldn't be afraid to say it out loud," he answers with conviction.

"It's not fear. I just think bragging is, how should I put it...conceited," I say emphasizing the last word and add, "And I personally don't like conceited people."

"But if it's true, there's nothing you can do about it," he insists.

"Sure, but there's no need to shout it from the rooftops," I answer, arguing my point.

He shakes his head, impressed. "Esther, you were absolutely right. Your daughter is a tough nut to crack," he quips, stroking her knuckles as they exchange knowing smiles. "Are you enjoying college?" he continues, keeping his hand over my mother's. She gives me a joyful look.

"Yes, I like it very much. It's a nice environment," I say shortly.

"What are you majoring in?"

What's with all these questions? Someone should tell him that it's considered impolite to interrogate a person in her own home.

"Oh, I'm still thinking about that." My answer leaves him flabbergasted.

"You still don't know? Esther, how can she not know?"

Is that a crime now?

"Of course she knows! Vanessa will major in law. We've known that ever since she was born. Her innate sense of justice will make her the best lawyer in the state!" she exclaims, laughing.

I, on the other hand, want to cry. "Actually, Mom, I don't know. I'm still thinking about it. After all, sophomore year just started. I have plenty of time to decide what to do with my future."

"Don't be ridiculous, Vanessa." My mother shakes her head with a fixed smile.

"I'm not, Mom. I intend to make the most of this year." I ask Alex to hand me the tray with the vegetables, and I put a spoonful on the plate.

"Coming into your second year of college and still not knowing which track you'll take is unusual, but it's not the end of the world, Esther," Victor interjects, trying to defuse the steadily building tension. "Tell me, do you belong to any sororities or clubs? I belonged to Phi Gamma Delta. It was one of the most important fraternities at our university. We were quite a group of guys, each one crazier than the last, but boy we were smart! We made that fraternity the most prominent on campus!" He adjusts the lapels of his jacket proudly.

"Phi Gamma Delta? Some of my father's friends were brothers," Stella interjects.

"Really?" Alex and I ask at the same time.

"You don't say!" Victor presses.

"Does the name Chad Mitchell mean anything to you?"

"Of course! I can't believe it. That guy was a genius. Once, he managed to hack into the central server of the university and changed the entire school's schedule. There was so much chaos that they had to cancel classes for the day!"

We all laugh at this anecdote.

"Chad is a legend! He works with my father. In the office he is equally loved and feared," says Stella, taking a sip of wine.

"That's Chad, all right!"

"To answer your question, no. I don't belong to any sorority, too many constraints. But I have joined the university book club and am thinking about applying to work on the paper," I interject to resume the conversation.

My mother gasps, dropping her fork to the floor.

"Sorry, I'm so clumsy." She gets up abruptly and goes to the kitchen to get clean cutlery.

"Would you like to be a journalist?" Victor asks curiously.

"I don't know, that's what I'm trying to figure out. I dream of writing, but I'm waiting for the right story. I think working on the school newspaper, even though it's very different than an actual newspaper, is still a good way to practice," I explain.

"Absolutely, but it is a difficult field to make it in, you know?" I nod, and he continues, "I know very few writers or journalists who have managed to turn their passion into a sufficiently high-paying job that allows for a good standard of living."

I shrug one shoulder and frown slightly. "I am very aware of that."

On her return, my mother listens without uttering a word until, taking advantage of a moment of silence, she exclaims, "You know dear, I'm sorry you didn't get to meet Travis, my daughter's fiancé. He comes from a very respectable family; Vanessa is so lucky."

Now it's my turn to drop cutlery onto the plate this time. Alex gives me a disheartened look and I consider ruining the whole dinner, telling my mother that her precious Travis turned out to be a first-class asshole. I wonder how she would react if she knew that the boy she always treated like he was the second coming was nothing but a cheater. She'd probably pass out. Yet part of me is convinced that she would never turn on Travis, not even if she was faced with the ugly truth. Instead, she would probably disown me for daring to leave the richest daddy's boy in all of Oregon.

I open my mouth to spit out the whole truth, but Alex, who seems to have read my mind, taps me on the foot under the table, shaking his head. I reflect for a few seconds and, in the end, I keep my mouth shut. Maybe he's right, this is not the time.

"Yeah, yeah, too bad. He was busy," I babble.

"We'll have a chance to make it up. Maybe next week?" my mother chirps with a smile on her lips.

"I doubt it."

"Why not?" she asks, confused. Across the table, Alex and Stella freeze.

"Because..." I clear my throat. "Because he's really busy right now."

A moment of silence follows in which my mother turns in her chair to observe me. "Everything is okay between you two, isn't it?"

I plaster my fakest smile on my face, inhale slowly, and nod. "Yeah, Mom, everything's great."

"Oh, thank goodness, I feared the worst for a moment." She laughs in relief, bringing one hand to her chest. With the other she squeezes Victor's fingers. "You know, his father, Edward Baker, is the CEO of an oil company."

Oh my God. Again? I slump back against my chair inelegantly. I could use a whole bottle of wine right now. Too bad my stomach revolts at the very thought. "He owns a lot of property here in Oregon as well as in a variety of countries. He's a very important man, so he's always away on business. His son is already working hard to follow in his footsteps," my mother concludes, while I stifle the urge to burst into hearty laughter.

"He sounds like a great guy, this Travis," Victor says, turning to my mother.

Give me a break.

"Mom, please. Can we stop talking about Travis?"

"You're right, dear. It is not nice to talk about someone when they aren't present," my mother says.

The conversation turns to Alex's mother's work. Because my mother, it seems, is only interested in talking about money and careers. When we finish dinner, Mom gets up and starts clearing the table. Victor offers to give her a hand, but she insists that he is a guest and should join Alex and Stella in the living room. Left in the kitchen, I am about to load the dishwasher when my mother sneaks up behind me.

"Honey!"

"Mom! You scared me," I gasp.

"Shh! So, tell me: What do you think?" she murmurs enthusiastically.

"Why are you whispering?" I whisper back.

"I don't want them to hear us. Come on, tell me: Do you like him?" I toss a glance at Victor in the other room. Only the hallway separates us.

"Victor?" She nods impatiently. "He seems like a good person."

She hugs me. "I knew you'd like him! Now go be with your friends, I'll finish cleaning up."

I join them, and Victor takes my place in the kitchen to help my mother. I chat a bit more with Alex and Stella before telling them to go enjoy the rest of their evening together. They have scheduled a trip to Siuslaw National Forest tomorrow, so I don't want to take up any more of their time.

"Do you want to come with us tomorrow?" Stella asks.

"No, thanks. I think I need to be on my own for a while."

"Are you sure?" She looks apologetic.

I nod. "We'll do it again some other time." I smile at her.

"Are you okay?" Alex asks me. I really appreciate that he has given Stella a heads-up about the situation with Travis.

"Yes, don't worry. I'll be fine." He pats me, tousling my hair in his usual way. I hug Stella, who reciprocates warmly. She is just as I had imagined her: sensible, sweet, and easygoing. Perfect for Alex.

"Good night, guys, and thanks for coming."

Alex smiles at me, and then he intertwines his hand with Stella's, and they leave.

I spend Sunday at home. The weather outside is gloomy, so I hole up in my room and read. After lunch, Tiffany keeps me entertained with a sprawling phone call. The afternoon, however, I spend studying. I start drafting some papers that I have to turn in within the next week and, before I realize it, it's already dark outside.

After dinner, my mother asks me if I want to go for a walk downtown with her and Victor. I cheerfully decline. I have absolutely no desire to play third wheel with my mother and her new boyfriend, who has just had dinner with us for the second time.

Here I am, then, alone in this deserted house, which suddenly feels too quiet. I decide to go to my room and get ready for bed; I really need it. A bit early, I know, considering that it is only half past eight—the last time I went to sleep at this time I was approximately seven years old—but I think it might do me some good to catch up on a few hours of sleep. I lie on the bed and stare at the ceiling above me, waiting to fall asleep. But my thoughts won't give me any respite.

In less than a week, my life has changed completely. At this very moment, I was supposed to be at the concert in Portland with Travis, singing along until I was blue in the face. Instead, I'm lying in bed tossing and turning, looking for a comfortable sleeping position. I can't seem to banish the memory of Thomas, which has been haunting me ever since yesterday morning. When I'm near him, I feel confused and vulnerable but, at the same time, I feel better than I ever have before. When I told him that the night I spent with him was a terrible mistake, I really meant it. Not for the reasons I think he assumed, though. Because now there is a part of me that feels connected to him. And no sane person would want to get entangled in Thomas Collins's life.

Yet no matter how hard I try, my mind refuses to bury the memory of his lips on mine, of his warm and rough hands that seemed to crave my body, of his soft and good-smelling hair, and of the way that, every time he said my name, my heart would pound.

I kick off the comforter and go downstairs to the kitchen. If I can't sleep, then I'll have a nice *Shameless* marathon—that should keep my mind occupied. I pop some popcorn in the microwave, pull a can of Coke out of the fridge, and throw myself into the recliner, covering my legs with a fleece blanket.

After a few episodes, that tattooed reprobate continues to occupy my thoughts. I check my phone every two minutes in the hope of getting a message from him, which I know I won't because he doesn't even have my number. And why would he text me? After the things I said to him, and the way I treated him, I wouldn't want to see me either. Oh, to hell with it. Enough. I want to see him. For a moment, I am surprised by my own admission, but it is the truth.

Before the heat of the moment passes, without overthinking what I am about to do, I rush out of the house. Fortunately, Mom has left the Toyota here. I start the car and fifteen minutes later I find myself in front of his dormitory on campus. I ask some guys in the lobby for Thomas's room number, and I don't miss the amused expression they give me. As if to say, *Here's another girl looking for a good time.*

I have to make a tremendous effort not to get upset by that thought.

I arrive in front of door D37 on the fourth floor and stare at it for a few moments, trying to muster up the courage to knock. My stomach is in knots, and anxiety is eating away at me. What if he refuses to see me? The last time we saw each other, I yelled at him and ordered him to leave me alone. He'll think I'm more confused than he is. Not to mention that I've just realized I am still wearing my pajamas. I left the house so fast that I didn't even change. Fortunately, I have a coat that covers me to my knees.

I take a deep breath and knock softly. I wait a while, but no one answers. I knock louder. I hear footsteps approaching from behind the door and my heart beats faster.

When the door opens, I am confronted by a short, awkward guy with a bag of chips under his arm. He's definitely not Thomas.

"H-hello," I say, confused.

"He's not here," he replies irritably, crunching a potato chip.

"W-what, sorry?"

"You're looking for Thomas, aren't you? They're all looking for Thomas! But he's not here. He's never here on weekends."

Right! It's Sunday and he had told me that he stays at the frat house during the weekend. The thought disturbs me. Is he with some girl? I immediately imagine him tangled up with Shana or some other more beautiful and more experienced girl. Stupid! This is definitely a sign. Thomas Collins cannot be a part of my life, not now and not ever. I have to leave.

"Ah, um, sorry for the inconvenience, then." I turn to leave but the boy stops me.

"Don't you want me to tell him you came by?"

"H-huh?"

He pushes a lock of brown hair off his forehead and repeats, "If you tell me your name, I'll text him and tell him that you are looking for him." He licks his fingertips with an expression of pure delight.

Should I tell him he has crumbs in his hair?

"No. No message, thank you. In fact, do me a favor and don't tell him I stopped by. It's nothing important. Sorry I disturbed you while you were…doing whatever you were doing."

"I was just finishing *Full Metal Panic*."

"Okay…" I say, pretending to know what he's talking about. "Sorry again." I back away and leave. This guy really is weird…

Before I get into the car, I text my mother and ask her to bring me two scoops of pistachio ice cream with chocolate syrup and whipped cream.

I would go and buy it myself, but I didn't bring my wallet with me when I had the brilliant idea of jumping out of this plane without a parachute.

My mother confirms with an emoji.

Great, I'll need all the calories I can get to swallow the humiliation I have just subjected myself to.

In just two days, I found out that I was cheated on, broke up with Travis, had sex with Thomas, and now I am washing my hands of him as well. Well, not that there was anything real between us, just…ugh! Two scoops of ice cream will not be enough! I send another message to my mother and tell her to get a pint.

Arriving home, I take off my jacket and shake off the chills. I tie up my hair haphazardly and scroll through my music app. Now more than ever, I need pining and pain. I scroll through the various songs included in my "Recovery" playlist and hurl myself onto the couch with the lights off. I listen to Sum 41's "With Me," followed closely by "Echo" by Jason Walker and a long series of heartbreaking songs while I ponder the mess my life has become.

A few minutes later, the doorbell rings. Finally, my three scoops of pistachio bliss and regret has arrived. I go to the door with my head still bent over the phone, intent on choosing another song. I'm ready to go back to the couch, but something snaps me to attention. Or rather, someone. I look up from my phone and stare incredulously at the person in front of me.

Sweet. Merciful. God.

He's here.

Eighteen

THOMAS COLLINS STANDS IN MY doorway wearing a gray sweatshirt that clings to his powerful shoulders. He worries his tongue piercing between his teeth and has a lit cigarette in his right hand as he looks me up and down with those eyes that make me so uncomfortable, so intimidated. Because when Thomas looks at you like that, you can't help but feel a little naked and a lot vulnerable. The fact that he actually does know what I look like naked doesn't make it any better.

With an evil grin, he drags his gaze from my pink PJs with the teddy bears all the way down to the fuzzy unicorn slippers I'm wearing. He pauses for a moment on my hair, which looks like a bird's nest. I blink repeatedly, still incredulous, as I try to get my bearings.

"Are you going to stand there and stare at me much longer? I mean, I know I have a certain allure, but I'm starting to feel violated here." His smug insolence brings me back to my senses. I had hoped I'd be getting the nice version of Thomas now that I know such a person exists, but apparently, I've got his asshole twin instead.

"Thomas, wh-what are you doing at my house?" I try to hide my astonishment but fail miserably.

"You were looking for me?" he asks calmly, taking a drag from the cigarette.

"What?" Earth to Vanessa. Wake up!

"On campus," he specifies impatiently. He must still be mad at me for yesterday morning's meltdown. "Larry, my roommate, said a girl with dark hair and gray eyes came to see me." He gives me a wink. Wait a minute, did he seriously just wink at me? So he's not angry with me, then? "He said you were blushing pretty hard, reminded him of a giant Red Vine."

What is this guy's deal?

"So, what did you want?" he asks.

Oh my God, why couldn't Mr. Red Vines have kept his mouth shut like I asked him to?

"Nothing, I was just in the neighborhood."

"You were in the neighborhood," he repeats, making air quotes. "Of my dorm. Alone. On a Sunday night?"

Well, when you say it out loud, it sounds more ridiculous.

In one of her films, Greta Garbo once said that any lie will find believers as long as you tell it with enough force. So come on, Greta, let's see if you were right. "Yep," I said.

Thomas gives a resigned sigh and shakes his head, as if he didn't believe a word I said. "Let's hear it, then: Why, during your questionable visit to 'the neighborhood,' did you end up at my door?"

"I came to return Leila's clothes to you," I replied, congratulating myself on managing a plausible, spur-of-the-moment lie.

"You could have gone straight to her. She lives in the building next door."

"I didn't know that."

"Bullshit. You also could have given them to me tomorrow. Why'd it have to be tonight?"

"Enough with the questions!"

"Don't get worked up. I'm just trying to understand. Yesterday you make a scene, saying I'm tormenting you, and now you're showing up at my room in the middle of the night." He pauses and continues in a more soothing tone: "What is going on inside that little head of yours, Ness?"

He tilts his head slightly, waiting for my response, and reveals what is obviously a lipstick stain on his neck. My breath catches. Seriously?

He has the nerve to show up at my house wearing clear evidence of his most recent sexcapade? Suddenly, I am filled with rage.

"I don't know!" I snap, and it's the truth. If I'd known that, while I was beating myself up over my outburst, he was out getting laid, I would never have gone looking for him. No way.

He takes one last drag on his cigarette and, looking me steadily in the eyes, tosses the butt to the ground, where he crushes it with his toe. "While you come up with a more believable excuse than that, why don't you let me in? It's cold out here," he adds, blowing a final plume of smoke into the air.

"No way. Good night." I make to close the door, but he blocks it with one foot.

"I wasn't really asking," he says, pushing the door open with one arm and stepping over the threshold. He advances on me until we are far too close, just inches from each other. He dips his head slightly to whisper in my ear, "For the record, you look hot..." I can feel his eyes sliding along my body, lingering on my breasts, and I remember too late that I'm not wearing a bra. Instinctively, I cross my arms over my chest. Thomas caresses my cheek. His knuckles are cold and the contrast between his skin and mine makes me shiver. "even in pajamas," he concludes in a whisper.

Breathe, Vanessa. Breathe. Everything is under control.

I gesture for him to leave, before the tingling in my belly overwhelms my rational mind. But he pretends not to notice. "Thomas!" I squeal, as he brushes past me without a care in the world.

"Get out. Right now! You can't just go walking into people's houses uninvited!" I dash after him as he makes his way further inside.

"Hmm...I don't recall inviting you to my dorm, and yet you showed up there." He stands with his back to me, hands in his pockets, peering around the room.

"No, of course not. You were clearly...busy." I clench my fists and immediately regret saying it. I sound jealous, and wouldn't that be stupid? He turns around, giving me a confused head tilt. "You have lipstick on your neck," I say, trying to sound unbothered.

No reaction. Not even a twinge of surprise or shame at being caught out like that.

"Oh, this?" He wipes the smudge from his neck with one hand. "A dalliance."

A dalliance. That's all women are to him, I guess. Just something to do. Something to pass the time.

"All right, now what's wrong?"

"Nothing's wrong. It's good to see exactly how much you value the women you sleep with. There's something to like about you, Thomas: you're always consistent," I spit venomously before turning my back on him to shut the front door.

"I value them exactly as much as they want to be valued."

"I don't care what you do, Thomas." I needlessly arrange some business cards stowed in the drawer of the hall cabinet; anything to avoid those eyes. "You are free to do whatever—or whomever—you want. It's none of my business."

"Whatever you say. Anyway, I'm still waiting."

I look at him, confused. "Waiting for what?"

"I'm waiting to hear whatever new excuse you're going to come up with to explain your visit to my dorm in the middle of the night."

"Fine. I came to your dorm because I wanted to apologize to you. Are you happy now?"

Thomas looks surprised.

"I was being unfair yesterday. I lashed out at you instead of dealing with the real source of my anger, and it wasn't okay. That's all." I shrug indifferently.

"Apology accepted."

"Excellent," I say, feigning an enthusiasm I don't feel. "Now that we've resolved all our issues, you can leave."

"Nah. Don't feel like it."

"What do you mean you don't feel like it?"

"I mean, I. Don't. Feel. Like it."

"Look, I'm sorry Larry wrecked your night. But you and I have buried the hatchet. We're done here. You can go back to whatever it is you were doing." I try not to look directly at the place on his neck where the lipstick was.

Ignoring me entirely, Thomas gives the house a bored once-over. "So," he says, "this is where you live." He turns to face me. My God, I am never going to get him out of here. "Not bad. Looks like someone with taste furnished it. Although there is something…a little *off* about it."

"Order," I supply.

"What?" He gives me a puzzled look.

"Order," I repeat. "Tidiness, neatness, whatever you want to call it. A place for everything and everything in its place. My mother is like that. She obsesses over details. There's never a book out of place, a crumb on the table, or a speck of dust on the furniture. People sometimes find the house kind of…sterile because of it."

Curious, he runs a finger over one of the shelves and then looks at his fingertip. He finds exactly what I knew he'd find: nothing. His skin is perfectly clean. "That's nuts. You do know that, right?"

"Sure, if you're not used to it, it can seem weird, but it's actually harmless. It's just this quirk she's had for years and, when my parents separated, it intensified. Her therapist says it's how she gains a sense of control over her life or some crap like that."

"Well, I am glad to hear she's seeing a professional."

I roll my eyes at his predictable sarcasm and decide to try playing hostess in hopes that he'll leave afterward. "Would you like something to drink?"

"Water." Right, Coach is always watching. He follows me into the kitchen, and I pour him a glass. He sits on the counter and downs it all in one go, while I think about how bizarre it is to see him in my house.

"You want more?"

He shakes his head, and I put the bottle back in the refrigerator. "So, your folks are separated?" he asks.

For a moment I freeze; I don't like to talk about the divorce, the whole situation in general. So I just nod and close the refrigerator door, leaning against it with my arms behind my back. Thomas grabs an apple from the fruit basket on the counter and starts tossing it in the air, catching it easily with one hand. "You get along with them?"

"With whom?"

"Your folks," he says, watching the apple rise and fall.

"Not really. With my mother, it's...complicated. I think we're too much alike in some ways and too different in others."

"Yeah, I've witnessed your shared obsession with order. But what about your dad?"

I stiffen. "Well, to get along with him, I'd have to occasionally see him, so..."

He raises an eyebrow and looks at me, confused. "What do you mean?"

"He doesn't live here. He moved out a few years ago," I answer regretfully.

"Where?"

"Honestly? I don't know. One day he just up and left us, made a brand-new family and decided to disappear, forgetting all about the old one." I hope Thomas doesn't start looking at me with pity in his eyes. I hate being pitied.

"What a bastard."

"My father cheated on my mother, Travis cheated on me. You want me to believe this moves you deeply?" I chuckle. "Don't make me laugh, we all know how you feel about 'relationships.'" I mime the quotation marks.

"Don't compare me to them," he says sternly. "I don't promise anything to anybody. The girls I fuck know exactly who they are dealing with, they know what I want from them, and they know that, whatever it is, it won't last." His coldness is disconcerting. Yet part of me admires his honesty. He doesn't pretend to be someone he's not just to please other people.

On the other hand, it is alarming to know that sex really is all that matters to him.

"How about you?" I try to change the subject because we have talked about me far too much. "What's your relationship like with your parents?"

Suddenly he frowns. The surly expression on his face is the same as the one he wore when I tried to ask him about the scar. "None of your business," he snaps, hopping off the counter and heading into the living room.

"None of my business?" I retort irritably, after catching up with him.

"There's no need for you to know," he says resolutely.

"You asked me, though."

"You could have chosen not to answer if you didn't feel like it." I don't know what's more annoying, his biting voice or his punchable face.

"So you are allowed to ask and get an answer, but I'm not? That's not how it goes."

"Stop pushing." He glares at me, and for a moment I catch a glimpse in his eyes of some emotion he is trying to suppress. Anger? Sorrow? Resentment, perhaps? "You're not missing anything anyway."

"Fine." I tighten my lips into a thin line and cross my arms over my chest. "So, now that we've said everything we have to say to each other and you've seen my house and learned all about my family's flaws, it's time for you to go," I say curtly.

"Are you kicking me out because I won't answer your question?" he asks with a sarcastic smile.

"I am kicking you out because my mother will be back soon and, believe me, you don't want to be here when that happens. Especially in your condition."

He frowns and peers down at his clothes. "What's wrong with me?"

"I can smell the weed from here," I say disgustedly.

"I haven't smoked anything, I'm clean." I believe him, but he is imbued with that frat house smell.

"You may be clean, but your clothes aren't. My mother would go crazy if she found me at home with a boy who isn't Travis, especially one who is covered in tattoos and smells like weed and Jack Daniel's. She would immediately call a rehab facility and have you committed, though not before having you bludgeoned by the orderlies," I calmly explain to him.

He looks at me dumbfounded. "Your mother doesn't need a therapist; she needs a psychiatrist. I'm starting to get seriously concerned for your well-being. Is it safe for you to live here?"

I laugh out loud. "With my mother, nothing is certain, but I'm not taking any risks for now." After a moment of silence, I continue, "Thomas…"

"Yeah?"

"How did you know where I live?"

He walks over to me with a mocking smile and touches my chin. "Friends of friends…" Then he walks past me and heads for the hallway, where he stops to look at the antique paintings hanging on the wall.

"Which friends of friends?"

"Does it matter?"

"I'd like to know. Do you know who shows up on someone's doorstep without that person having given them their address?"

"Who?"

"A stalker," I retort dryly, making him laugh under his breath.

"Maybe I am a stalker, have you ever thought of that?" He turns to me with a mock-intimidating look.

I watch him with narrowed eyes, playing along with his game. "You are quite a weirdo, aren't you? You have wild mood swings, you show up at my house in the middle of the night, you attend my classes, everywhere I turn I find you." I advance on him. "You wait for me in blind corners of hallways to make sure that I'm okay, you defended me in the garden even though no one asked you to. Tell me, Collins," I continue, standing right in front of him. "Should I be worried?"

He steps forward, closing the distance between us. "Oh, you should definitely be worried. But generally, I don't like to harass anyone who doesn't want to be harassed. I like consent." I hear an edge of provocation in his voice. "You should know that." I blush and avert my gaze. Why does he make me always feel so exposed?

"I see you get it," he says smugly, then continues, "So, you really aren't going to give me a tour? You're being a terrible hostess." He smiles.

"Didn't you hear what I just said? You have to leave, I can't risk my mother finding you here."

"Yeah, I heard you," he answers, climbing the stairs.

"Excuse me, where are you going?" I call after him.

"For a tour," he answers calmly.

"There's nothing interesting upstairs, just bedrooms," I shout, as he climbs the last few steps.

"The best part, then." He smirks mischievously at me before disappearing upstairs.

Damn, he's not planning on going into my bedroom, is he?

There are a lot of pictures of me as a child up there, back when I looked like a raccoon. I rush up the stairs to stop him, but I'm too late. He is already inside. I clench my fists and wrinkle my nose in frustration.

"Who...gave you...permission to come in here?" I pant.

"I took it," he replies with his usual arrogant air. "I always take what I want," he adds.

I put one hand to my hip and use the other to point to the door. "Out. Now."

Cocky as always, and with no intention of listening to me, he takes an amused look around before examining the framed photos on the shelf next to the bookcase. In the first one I am just a few months old, in the one next to it I am blowing out the candles on my third birthday cake. Then there is a picture of me at nine, completely drenched, with the German shepherd we had back when Dad was still living with us, Roy. We were at a friend's barbecue that day. Dad and a friend of his had the bright idea of giving Roy a bath and they soaked me along with him. It was Mom who had captured that particular moment.

Thomas points to the picture, puzzled. "I don't fucking believe it. Are you blond?" He looks at me in genuine astonishment.

I shrug. "You caught me."

He looks at me, then at the picture, then back at me. "I never would have guessed."

I managed to surprise Thomas Collins. Score one for me. In another photo, Alex and I wear our robes on graduation day, both of us sticking our tongues out at his mother, who was taking the picture. In the next one I am standing between Travis and Tiffany, also on graduation day. The last one is just me; Travis took it for me about a year ago. I am sitting in a rocking chair on the porch, kissed by the spring sun, with my legs crossed and a peony in my hair, immersed in a copy of *Pride and Prejudice*. Thomas picks this one up and looks at it thoughtfully, preparing who knows what idiotic comment.

"You look very beautiful here, Ness."

"Thank you," I reply, surprised and embarrassed.

A few seconds later, he grabs the picture of me at three years old and says, "And here, you look like a ghost." Ah, here is the idiotic comment. It felt weird without one.

I snatch it out of his hand, annoyed. "Well, I was sleepy and I had just finished eating I don't know how many pistachio brownies. I mean, I was going through an emotional time and no one understood that!" I defend myself wryly.

We look at each other for a few seconds, then he admits, "Your room isn't what I imagined. Everything is a bit too pink for you, no?"

"It's my childhood bedroom. At seven years old, girls love pink," I explain, wondering why he was imagining my bedroom.

He nods vaguely, approaches my bed and asks me with a grin, "And who are these guys?" He points to three stuffed animals settled against the pillows.

Oh, no.

"What do you take me for? I'm almost twenty years old, Thomas, I don't name my stuffed animals." I chuckle nervously.

"Come on, give me the names." He sits on the edge of the bed, certain that he's guessed right.

"Momo, Nina, and Sparky," I confess after a moment's hesitation.

"Momo. Nina. And Sparky?" he repeats, clearly trying to hold back an explosion of laughter.

"Hey! You can't just barge into my room without permission and start ridiculing my things! You'll hurt my feelings."

He tries to make his face serious, with little success. "So, let's see if I've got this right." He rests Sparky, my stuffed bunny, on his lap. "You still sleep with stuffed animals, which means you're a big baby. You like TV shows." He points to the shelf above the TV, where a variety of box sets are stored. "Which tells me that your real life bores you. You're an incurable romantic," he continues, gesturing to my bookshelf full of romance novels. "And you probably suffer from the same disorder as your mother." He looks at me smugly. "How'd I do?"

I frown. "The same disorder as my mother? Why do you think that?"

"I don't know, maybe it's the books arranged in order of height or the shoes in order of color... Or maybe it's the military precision with which you organize your desk during class. Seriously, your family has a real problem," he insists.

I'm beginning to feel annoyed. "Give it a rest. I like things to be in their place, in the right way. I'm a tidy person, nothing more," I say, trying to minimize the issue.

"What if I were to, purely by accident, make a mess of everything right now? Here, maybe?" He gets up and walks toward my bookcase.

"That depends: do you have a death wish?"

"Actually, I've got another kind of wish..." He gives me a cheeky smile. I blush but force myself to glare indignantly. Which only amuses him more. "Or I can just sit in this chair and contemplate the ceiling." He makes himself comfortable, crossing his arms over his chest and spreading his knees. He drops his gaze to my legs, a mischievous gleam in his eyes. Instinctively, I cross them, feeling a wave of heat invade my body.

Dammit, why does he always have to be so attractive?

"You're not contemplating shit. Now, you can get up and go back to the dormitory, or you can go back to the party, but you can't stay here," I retort when I manage to recover from the visual aphrodisiac he presents.

"The frat party wasn't much fun. Just when it was about to get fun, my roommate called me. Does that ring a bell?"

"Oh, no!" I press a hand to my chest, pretending to be pained. "I'm so sorry I ruined your night. But in all honesty, Thomas, no one asked you to come to my house. You could have just stayed there and… scratched your itch," I retort acidly.

"Yes, I could have. In fact, I should have," he underscores the point. "I'd be having a much better time."

I am shocked by his lack of tact. "You're an asshole, Thomas." He's an insensitive, arrogant, mercurial jerk who enjoys testing my patience.

"I've been holding myself back quite a bit with you. You should be thanking me, not getting pissy." The satisfied expression he gives me is enough to make me lose my patience. Without a second thought, I throw one of the stuffed animals in my hands and I hit him square in the face.

"Shit, you got me right in the eye. What's in this thing?" He brings a hand to his face.

Oh no. Caught up in the heat of the moment, I threw Nina at him, the mother kangaroo in which I keep my earrings and bracelets. He rubs his forehead as I leap to his aid. I reach out and take his face gently in my hands.

"Sorry, I didn't mean to—" But I don't get a chance to finish my sentence, because Thomas gets up, grabs me by the waist, and throws me onto the bed.

"You really are too naive, little one." He straddles me, pinning my wrists above my head with one hand and tickling my side with the other.

"Oh God, stop!" I laugh so hard that the words come out strangled.

"Were you trying to kill me with a stuffed animal, Ness?" He teases me mercilessly.

"Thomas, I'm begging you, stop!" I writhe, trying to free myself from him. I can't. He's too strong; his fingers tickle my neck, my sides, my belly. I can't resist any longer. "Okay, okay you win! Enough!" I say with tears in my eyes. Only then does he loosen his grip.

"I always win, remember that."

"You're twice my size, and you lured me in under false pretenses. That's what is called an easy win," I answer, pretending to be offended.

"You gotta play the cards you're dealt." He *boops* me on the nose with one finger, then we hold still and look at one other as the smiles fade from our lips. A few minutes ago, I was so angry at him, and now I have tears in my eyes from laughing. "You should do that more often."

"What, hit you with stuffed animals?"

"No. Laugh," he whispers, dangerously close to my mouth. "It puts you in a different light." It's breathtaking and, when he touches my lip with his free hand, I shudder. Instinctively, I part my lips.

"Everything okay?" he asks with an insolent little smile.

"Everything okay?" I've lost the ability to produce saliva and my heart has gone crazy. I feel pinned by the intensity of his gaze, overwhelmed by the sheer scale of his body as it is pressed against mine. Stunned by his unmistakable vetiver scent.

Nevertheless, I manage to nod. He grins, pleased with himself. He gets even closer and my heartbeat speeds up dramatically. He confidently positions himself between my parted legs. Every cell in my body quivers.

"What-what are you doing?" I gasp.

"What do you think?" he whispers hoarsely.

"Thomas…" I swallow and think I should stop him… I should push him away…or at least try.

"Vanessa…" He brushes his lips against mine. Once, twice, three times… His touch is intoxicating, so much so that I close my eyes and clench my knees around his hips in an instinctive motion. Then he traces a line of slow, delicate kisses along my jaw, increasing in intensity as he reaches my throat.

I have a machine gun for a heart.

"You should…you should go…"

He moves his lips to my ear and nibbles on my earlobe before lapping at it with his tongue, setting off a shiver in my lower abdomen. "No, I shouldn't."

"Please…" It's more a desperate plea than a request. Part of me really does want him to go away. But there is another part that just wants to throw myself on his mercy and let him do whatever he wants.

"You're talking too much," he cuts me off, pressing his hips against me with an untamable fervor. A wave of chills runs through my entire body, a sensation I have experienced with him before, but it is even stronger now. His tongue captures mine with determined ferocity. I had hoped to put up more resistance, but I return the kiss instinctively, needy and hot.

He releases my wrists, and I take his face in my hands, deepening the kiss. He seems to become even more excited, circling one arm around me and squeezing so tightly that I gasp for air. I cling to his powerful shoulders, his muscular neck, as his hand descends to my thighs. He parts them impatiently. "I'm going to fuck you here, Ness," he says against my lips, rubbing his erection between my legs and tearing a soft moan from me. He suffocates the sound, pouncing on my mouth ardently. "On your childhood bed," he concludes lewdly, perversely. I blush, feeling the burning need to have him inside me again. Suddenly, however, the little voice in my head reminds me that this is all wrong. He can never give me what I need, and I can never give him what he wants. I have to stop or I will regret it; I cannot allow this boy to mess up my life any more than he already has.

I put my hands on his chest, stopping him. His heart is pounding, just like mine. "Thomas, wait…"

He pulls away from my mouth, eyes hazy with desire. We are both out of breath, our faces flushed, our lips red and swollen from kisses. We stare at each other for a long moment and while he seems to immediately sense what I am thinking, I have completely forgotten.

"You think too much…" His hoarse tone sends me over the edge. He runs a possessive hand over my neck and then lavishes it with his mouth, scratching it with his teeth, biting and licking. "Live in the moment," he continues, sliding his hand under my pajama shirt, up to my breasts. I feel his lips curving against the hollow of my neck. "I knew you weren't wearing a bra as soon as you opened the door." He squeezes my breast and presses his erection against my most sensitive spot. "Stop thinking, Ness. Just stop," he orders and, without giving me a chance to answer, goes back to devouring my mouth. My uncertainty is swept away like grains of sand scattered by the wind. Instinct gets the better of reason. I let myself be overwhelmed by those impulses that only he seems to awaken in me. I sink my teeth into his upper lip, eliciting a guttural groan from him. This time I won't be able to blame it on alcohol when, after having sex with him, I see him in the arms of another. It will be my fault, just mine. I press my pelvis harder against him. I put one hand in his hair and, with the other, I begin to unbutton his jeans. His hand pushes below the elastic of my pajama pants, insinuating itself over the damp fabric of my panties, but then something stops us, forcing my heart into my throat.

Three words. Three simple words that make me regain all my lost clarity.

"Nessy, I'm back!"

Nineteen

"OH MY GOD! MY MOTHER is back!"

I throw Thomas off the bed and jump up, trying to straighten my disheveled clothes and hair.

"I noticed," he sulks, getting up from the floor with an extremely visible erection in his pants.

"Excuse me?" I ask in a soft voice.

"I got your ice cream. I'll wait for you downstairs," my mother calls from below.

I open the door and, after clearing my throat, I shout, "Um, thanks, Mom. But, well... I'm not hungry anymore." I squeeze my eyes shut tightly and pray that she believes me.

"But you asked for it less than an hour ago," she answers, confused.

"I know, I'm just too tired now. I almost fell asleep." Meanwhile, I hear thumps behind my back. Thomas wraps his arms around my hips and starts peppering kisses on my neck. Is he insane? I try to push him away, but he tightens his grip and his mouth on my skin makes me waver.

"Are you sure?" my mother continues. "I got exactly what you asked for: a pint of pistachio ice cream with chocolate syrup and whipped cream. I also got you some of those little rainbow cones you like so much." I feel Thomas's chest twitch against my back in an attempt to suppress laughter.

My cheeks ablaze, I turn my head slightly toward him and murmur, embarrassed, "I was a little hungry."

"Oh, I could tell." He laughs and nibbles on my earlobe, grinding his pelvis against my bottom and giving me goosebumps.

"Thanks," I turn my attention back to my mother. "But I really don't feel like it right now. I'll eat it tomorrow," I say firmly, with my head peeking through the narrow space between the door and the jamb.

"Whatever, I'll put it in the freezer. I'm going to take a hot bath. If you need anything you know where to find me."

"Okay," I tell my mother quickly, before the Thomas Effect makes me completely lose my mind. I shut the door and try to think of a way to get Thomas out of here without my mother seeing him. I turn to him and put my hands on his chest to push him away. "I don't know what depraved ideas are going through your head, but you should forget them. You absolutely must get out of here without her seeing you."

He ignores my words, moves my hands and presses me against the door, pinning me with the weight of his body. "Am I wrong or did you just call me depraved?" he murmurs under his breath, lifting my chin with one finger. His green eyes stare at me greedily, full of danger. Those eyes should scare me, and yet I am drawn to them. Almost hypnotized.

"I-I..." I swallow hard, feeling my throat suddenly become dry.

"Shh..." He presses two fingers to my lips before pushing them slowly inside my mouth, inviting me to open up. And I, helpless victim of some strange spell, do so. Completely dominated by him. By his confidence. By his beauty. "Let me show you just how depraved I can be." He latches on to my neck with his lips, sucking the sensitive skin, leaving his mark, just the way he likes it... My knees are shaking and heat blossoms between my thighs. Thomas stops torturing me just long enough to let down my hair. It falls disheveled over my shoulders, releasing the scent of my berry shampoo.

He breathes it in greedily, half-closing his eyes and smiling appreciatively. Then he gathers my hair into a fist and pulls backward until I tilt my head. He goes back to tracing a small, scorching trail down my neck with his tongue, ending on my shirt-covered breast. He bites it hard, giving me a small preview of what he's about to do to me. I gasp with pleasure and pain.

"My...my mother is downstairs," I pant without much conviction. I can't tell whether the thought makes me more anxious or aroused. Thomas, unfazed, drops to his knees. He caresses my stomach and my ribs under my shirt, all the way up to my breasts, where my nipples are already stiff and swollen. He envelops them in his large hands, squeezing and licking a stripe between them. He obliterates my last ounce of sanity.

"Then you'll have to be very good at keeping quiet," he murmurs, a devilish smile on his face. He stands up, towering over me, then pulls my shirt over my head and tosses it to the floor. I suddenly find myself naked and vulnerable before his lustful gaze. The cold of the door against my bare back makes me shiver. My heart beats wildly, and my cheeks burn with embarrassment. Insecurity takes over and I try to cover myself, but he stops me, grabbing my wrists with one hand and pinning them above my head. He takes a long moment to examine my soft, languid body. "Don't hide," he says in a deep voice. "I want to look at you." I lower my eyes and hold my breath, unable to believe that someone like him, used to far more sensual bodies, could find anything appealing in mine. My insecurities are swept aside, however, when Thomas falls upon my breasts. He tortures one nipple with his fingers and takes the other between his lips. When the cold ball of his piercing lingers on my skin, I erupt into goosebumps. He slips one of his legs between mine and presses his thigh against my sex. I close my eyes and clench my lips, suppressing a moan. I feel dazed, aroused, ravenous. So much so that I begin to shamelessly match his movements. I ride his thigh, rubbing myself against his muscular leg. He pushes harder against me, allowing me to feel him even more. All of my muscles tense at once and my legs give way beneath me. When he releases my wrists, I am forced to cling to his powerful shoulders to keep from collapsing to the floor. "That's how you like it, isn't it?" he asks, his voice raspy with desire. He abandons my breasts and attacks my mouth, invading it with rough kisses, crushing me between the door and his embrace.

My thoughts short-circuit, my breathing is out of control, and arousal rises within me, becoming almost unbearable.

"Thomas..." I gasp into his mouth, embarrassed and overwhelmed. But he gives me no respite. His kisses, if possible, become even more ruthless and savage. He then lets his free hand slide down, under the elastic of my pants, until he reaches the now completely sodden fabric of my panties. He smiles at me with burning eyes. He pushes my panties aside to stroke my warm flesh with slow movements. He goes from the bottom to the top, an agonizing, tormenting touch. "Oh, God," I moan in despair. He continues to move his hand deftly, rubbing my clit with his index finger before pressing down hard on it with his thumb. This expert, unexpected touch tips me over into delirium. Thomas continues his slow torture, determined not to sate the incandescent need that is driving me mad. "Please..." I beg again, panting between desperate moans.

"Please what?" he asks greedily. Before I can answer, he presses a finger inside me. He pulls it out quickly, giving me a single surge of pleasure that sweeps me from head to toe and makes me cry out. "Shh, did you forget we aren't alone?" he whispers into my ear, warm and sensual. He slips a finger in again, but only for a moment.

My God, I'm going crazy. Frustrated, I close my eyes and rest my forehead against his chest. "You're going to kill me..."

Thomas lifts my face, forcing me to look him in the eye. He grabs my wrist and guides my hand to his groin. I shudder and become somehow even more aroused when I feel his erection pressing against his jeans. "Feel how hard you make me." He thrusts his hips forward and invites me to get familiar with his thick bulge. I give it a firm squeeze and only then do I hear him emit a soft, guttural gasp—the first I've heard since he decided to absolutely ignite me with desire. My legs are trembling, and my brain is so clouded with pleasure that when Thomas pulls my pants down along with my panties, I furiously kick them the rest of the way off. Thomas kneels before me and touches my calf, making his way up my entire leg.

He strokes the sensitive skin of my inner thigh, intensifying my need until he reaches my mons. I tremble at the sight of his fiery eyes staring up at me.

"I want to kiss you here, taste all of you." He looks at me, waiting for my consent. I nod shyly. He moves closer and closer to me and then, slowly, he presses his lips against me. He laves me with his tongue, lingering on my clitoris. It is more agony than pleasure, just a taste of what's to come. Suddenly, he fills me first with one finger and then two, tearing the air from my lungs.

"Oh, yes," I gasp, finally satisfied.

"I can feel how tight you are," Thomas murmurs. He slides in a little deeper. His eyes darken as he feels my core contracting greedily. "You were like that the other night too. So tight and wet…"

I stiffen, struck by an immediate insecurity. He understands and strokes my cheek. "Relax, I'm just trying to get to know you. Getting to know every part of you." He pushes his finger deeper, giving me an intense stab of pleasure. Something about the reassuring sound of his words makes me trust him.

"I don't know, it's just…" Vision clouded with desire, I stop, consumed again by the thrust of his fingers. I grab both his wrists to steady myself. "I've never had a lot of self-confidence," I confess, my face aflame with the discomfort of revealing something so intimate to him. "And after what Travis said yesterday…"

He draws closer to me, kisses me delicately before biting my lip. Softly at first, then harder. "I'm gonna have to work hard to help you get your confidence back then." With these words, he ends the conversation and begins to move his hand masterfully against me, driving every single fear of being disliked, of not measuring up, straight out of my head. I close my eyes and let myself be carried away by the pleasure he gives me, by the desire he has for me, the need he has to make me his own. I cling to his shoulders, I sink my nails into the fabric of his sweatshirt and bite my lip to keep from screaming. Thomas slides his fingers in and out of me, never quite reaching the exact place I want. He stops halfway and pulls back. I gasp for breath. I dig my hands into his hair, trying to communicate something that I'm not able to express in words.

"Do you want more?" he whispers, licking my increasingly slick folds.

I confirm with a breathless nod as he continues to move inexorably inside me, torturing me.

"Say it," he demands.

I look at him with wide eyes. I am not used to being so explicit about these things.

"Say it, or I'll stop." He gives my clit a lingering, protracted lick. My body is crying out for mercy. "And, believe me, I really don't want to stop." I suck in a breath but cannot speak.

"Why-why do you want to hear that?"

"Because I want you to shed all your inhibitions when you're with me."

I look at him, biting my lips. His breaths come in short pants like mine, his mouth glistening. His eyes are full of arousal, and a few locks of black hair fall over his sweat-slicked forehead. He's beautiful. Then he presses a kiss to my stomach, his eyes locked on mine, and one corner of his mouth curves into a smile. I dissolve.

"Do it, please," I burst out, finally.

As soon as I feel his hot tongue on my sex, I gasp. I close my eyes and throw my head back. I thrust my hips into his mouth and I feel so starved and desperate that I almost don't recognize myself. He plunges his fingers in and out of me, coaxing a wave of sensation that makes my legs tremble.

He presses his thumb to my clitoris and sucks it hard, while his fingers keep going in and out, faster and faster, ever deeper and more intense. I grab his hair and yank on it, lost in ecstasy. Thomas does not stop me. In fact he seems to grow more excited, lapping at me. I tremble and pant against the door, struggling to hold back a scream. When I finally feel that I am on the precipice of orgasm, Thomas slows down just enough to panic me.

"Not yet." He starts moving his fingers inside me again, finding a rhythm that makes my senses blur. I don't know if it's the thought of having my mother right downstairs, or the fact that I've been brought to the edge for a second time before being denied, but the mixture is so potent that I could pass out from bliss.

"Thomas, I'm begging you. I'm almost there, I'm about to…" Thomas lifts my right thigh and lays it on his shoulder, still holding me over his mouth. He looks down at me and continues to move his fingers in targeted circles, each time touching a magical spot that sends me into ecstasy. Suddenly, a wave of pleasure hits me and every muscle in my body contracts. An overwhelming heat sweeps me from head to toe as I am shaken by small, violent aftershocks. I try to pull myself away from Thomas because the idea of letting myself go like that, on him, is incredibly embarrassing, but he holds still. He wants to make me come just like this. He increases the movements of his tongue until I explode on his mouth with the most intense orgasm I've ever experienced. I feel like I am shattering into a thousand pieces. I cry out, but Thomas presses his palm to my mouth. Muddled with sensation, I sink my teeth into his hand, muffling my moans. Thomas fingers me relentlessly through my climax, until my breathing regulates and my legs stop shaking. Only then does he loosen his hold on me. He lifts himself slowly off the floor and draws a trail of kisses over my belly, to my right breast, then on to the left one. On my neck. Then my jaw and finally, delicately, on my mouth. He brushes the tip of my nose with his own and smiles at me. I look at him, stunned. I want to say something to him, but my whole body is paralyzed, and my head continues to swirl with the last tremors of orgasm. My legs are going to give way at any moment.

"You look wrecked." He picks me up with his powerful, tattooed arms and puts me gently on the bed. I curl up, dazed. Thomas surprises me once again by pulling back the covers and tucking me in. I stare at him in sheer confusion and it's only now that I realize he's still fully clothed.

He heads for the door and for a crazy moment, I think he's going to try to leave. "You can't go out there, my mother might see you," I say. But he only turns off the light and joins me in the bed. As he pulls off his sweatshirt and his sneakers, I begin to feel a little uncomfortable at the idea of being naked—and sober—next to him. Wrapping myself in a quilt, I get out of bed and search the floor for my pajamas. "I need to get dressed. Could you...could you turn around?" I ask shyly.

Lying on the bed, with his arms crossed behind his head, Thomas gives an amused snort. "You do realize you just came in my mouth, right?" he points out arrogantly. I choke, my eyes widening in embarrassment.

"Thomas!" I scold him.

"I'm not gonna turn around, so you do what you have to do."

"Thanks so much for your understanding!" I sulk. I turn my back to him and wrap myself in the sheet so he can't see me. I can practically hear him grinning behind me, but I ignore it. Maybe I seem funny to him, or childish, but I don't care.

"You don't need my understanding; you need to realize that there's nothing wrong with you."

I shake my head. "You couldn't understand even if you wanted to." Shielded once more by my pajamas, I sit cross-legged on the edge of the bed, in front of the TV. "So, while we wait for my mother to go to sleep, we have two options: watch a movie or chill." Or hash out exactly what just happened between us and what it means. But of course I don't waste my time asking him about that. He would just dismiss it and the very thought of that hurts me. He stares into my eyes, his own eyes so fathomless it makes butterflies erupt in my stomach.

"Neither of those. I want to talk."

"What?" I ask in amazement.

He pats the mattress to invite me closer. "C'mere. Tell me a little about yourself." He smiles sweetly at me. Guarded, I lie down alongside him. The darkness of the room somehow makes the atmosphere more intimate.

"There's not much to know." I shrug.

"Did you finish reading that book about the two sisters?"

I nod, surprised that he remembered it.

"Did you like it?" he asks with a crooked smile.

"Very much. But I'm biased, I love everything she wrote. I'd probably fall in love with her shopping list too," I say dreamily.

"Why do you like her so much?" he asks, seeming genuinely interested.

"Because she used her novels to rebel against the restrictions of English society, and she always did it with the utmost irony and intelligence." I play with a lock of hair, propping myself up on one elbow.

"Hmm, and let me guess: *Pride and Prejudice* is your favorite, right?" He casts an amused glance at the book open and overturned on the nightstand next to me. I had started yet another reread of *Pride and Prejudice* just this afternoon. I had to inaugurate the edition that Alex's mom got for me.

"All of her novels are masterpieces, and the way she draws you into the story is disarming, but yes." I look up at him. "*Pride and Prejudice* holds a special place in my heart."

"What are her books about?"

"Love." His face twists derisively, but I ignore him and continue, "Love and all its many facets. Tormented, painful, sometimes impossible. Unconventional, but authentic. Take Elizabeth Bennet for example: she rejects a marriage proposal that would have guaranteed a comfortable future, both for herself and for her family, even going against her mother's wishes all because she wasn't in love." Thomas is paying close attention to me now, although he does have the hint of a smile around his mouth.

"Well, you know how I feel about that."

Here, Vanessa, just in case you forgot who he was...

"Tell me, what else do you like?"

"I don't know." I lie on my back and look up at the ceiling. Biting my lip, I think about what to tell him. "Well, I like books, TV series, journalism fascinates me, I love pistachios...but you may have figured that out." I look at him, amused and embarrassed at the same time. "I like the rain. The sound. The smell. The feelings it gives me. It is melancholy and romantic. I feel I have a connection with it."

"Are you like that too? Romantic and melancholy?"

I think about it and then, as naturally as anything, I answer, "Yes."

He stretches out his arm and gestures for me to come closer. He slips his arm under my neck as if to act as a pillow, and a shiver runs through my whole body.

Why is he acting this way, so…so…affectionate?

"Do you like the sea? You seem like the kind of person who would hang out on a seaside cliff, searching for meaning. Maybe with some bummer song in the background," he teases me. I pinch his side in answer.

"I like the sea but…"

"But?"

"Okay, confession incoming." I prop myself up with my elbow and rest my cheek on my palm. "First, though, you have to swear you won't laugh at me." I give him a menacing look.

"I never make promises I can't keep."

Go figure.

"The truth is, I…I don't know how to swim."

I hear him stifle a laugh and close my eyes in shame.

"How is that possible?"

"I don't know. I love the sea, but the idea of swimming in deep water gives me a panic attack."

"You are such a wimp. I learned when I was three years old," he boasts. It's so funny, almost endearing.

"Wow, do you want a round of applause, Captain Nemo?" He laughs and the low sound of it warms my heart. I want to take a picture of him in this moment and keep it under my pillow so I can fall asleep every night with a smiling Thomas underneath me.

"It wasn't as fun as you might imagine. My uncle took the 'rip the Band-Aid off' approach. Without telling me anything, he took me to the water and threw me in. No floaties," he adds.

I look at him bewildered. "Seriously?"

He nods. "Bit of a crude method, but effective."

I want to ask him more about his childhood, but I know it's difficult to break through the walls he's put up. So I offer up something else about myself. "I do, however, know how to ice-skate. When I was little, my father used to take me to the ice rink every Sunday, and we would spend hours there. Until one day I had the bright idea of improvising a loop jump. Instead, I fell and got this." I show him a small scar on the back of my left calf. "The cut wasn't very deep, but there was enough blood to scare my father. I don't know if he was more worried about the wound or about having to tell my mother. After that day, he never took me to the rink again." I laugh along with him, and the domesticity of this scene feels so surreal to me. Something about the situation makes me want to tell him about a tradition that Alex and I have been carrying on since high school. "And then there's the thing I do with Alex, my best friend: we collect tickets."

"Tickets?" he repeats skeptically.

"Yeah. Train tickets, theater tickets, movie tickets. At the end of the year we have this tradition of looking at them all together."

"That's bullshit, you know," he snaps, hurting my feelings.

"Excuse me?" I murmur, dismayed. His phone is audibly vibrating in his pocket, but he ignores it.

"You heard me. That whole collection thing is ridiculous. Your little friend probably just wants to get in your pants, but he hasn't had the balls to try."

I sit up and give him a dirty look.

"How dare you insinuate such a thing? Alex and I have known each other for thirteen years. We're like brother and sister. We love each other with all our hearts, without ulterior motives. It's called friendship," I emphasize. "And, believe it or not, not every human interaction is about sex! But I don't think you can understand, 'Mr. I Don't Do Relationships.' And for the record: our collection is not ridiculous. You're the ridiculous one, Thomas," I snap back, offended.

"Are you mad now?" He heaves an annoyed sigh and shakes his head.

"I opened up to you and you immediately assumed the worst. On top of that, you take it as a given that a guy could only want one thing from me." I cross my arms and look away. He has ruined a perfect moment.

"You're acting like a child." His phone starts vibrating again but again he lets it go.

"And you're a superficial asshole."

"I'm superficial? Need I remind you that I'm in here because your crazy mother is out there and you don't want to run the risk of her seeing me because who knows what would happen if she found you with 'a boy who isn't Travis' who is 'covered in tattoos.'"

I take a deep breath, trying to calm down. "For your sake, I will pretend that you didn't just insult me, my best friend, and my mother all within the space of two minutes," I say sourly. "And for heaven's sake, pick up your damn phone!"

He huffs but answers the phone. "What do you want? I left. No, I'm not on campus. None of your damn business. Yeah, I'll see you tomorrow. Your place." He hangs up.

"Who was that?" Dammit, I cannot help myself.

"Shana," he replies tonelessly, showing no emotion. I can feel him watching me, waiting for a reaction.

My heart leaps into my throat and I start to feel hot. "So, you're seeing her tomorrow?" I ask with feigned nonchalance.

"I don't think that's anything new."

A pang in my heart catches me unprepared, but I try to hide how his frankness hurts me. Suddenly I feel like such a fool. Tomorrow, he'll go back to Shana, and I will be eaten up with regret for letting him do all this to me. I don't even have the right to get mad at him because he has been clear from the beginning. It was stupid, falling for it again, hook, line, and sinker.

"Well, no wonder you two get along so well. After all, you have so much in common. You're both assholes and the same kind of petty." In response, I get only silence. I get out of bed and head for the window opposite. I need a moment to clear my head. Was Alex right? Am I messing with Thomas to escape the pain that Travis caused me? Part of me is tempted to believe it. Yet, the other part of me knows full well that whenever Thomas is nearby, I can't think of anyone but him. His haunted emerald eyes pull me in like a magnet. Did I let this happen because I'm weak? Naive? Or am I just a masochist? I wipe two traitorous tears from my cheeks. "Why did you come here,

Thomas?" I ask faintly, with my eyes turned to the dark night sky outside the window.

"I felt like it."

"You felt like it," I repeat with disappointment in my voice. "You wanted a...a dalliance?"

He remains silent for a few seconds. Seconds in which my heart breaks.

"If I wanted a dalliance, I would have stayed where I was."

I close the window and turn around, thankful for the darkness of the room that keeps him from seeing my tear-streaked face.

"I don't understand why you didn't," I mumble. I reach the bed, feeling his eyes on me. "You'll stay here until my mother has gone to sleep. In the meantime, get out of the bed. I would like to sleep." I grab the quilt and cover myself up to my chin before turning my back to him.

"Ness..."

"Good night," I answer shortly.

I hear him sigh. A few seconds later he wraps an arm around my waist and pulls me against him. I feel his warm, muscular chest against my back.

"Thomas, let me go." I try to fight him off, but he holds me even tighter, burying his nose in my hair. I hate the effect he has on me. He annihilates me. He manages to make me feel things I shouldn't. He makes me feel light and desired one moment, wretched and disconsolate the next. And now—now I want him to hug me, to hold me against him all night long, because I need it. Especially after the intimacy we shared, a connection that I've never had with anyone before. Not even with Travis. But I am not allowed to do any of these things, because he is not my boyfriend and, worst of all, he'll never be a boyfriend at all. This is the punishment I deserve for allowing Thomas Collins into my life.

He exhales exhaustedly, as if he has read my mind. With his face still in my hair, he murmurs, "What do I do with you..."

"What do you mean?" I murmur, my voice trembling.

"Nothing, Ness. Sleep now." He presses his lips to the nape of my neck, placing a delicate kiss there, which makes me shiver and makes me angry at the same time. I want to kick him out. I should kick him out. Instead, I end up basking in his warmth, surrendering myself to a deep sleep.

Twenty

I WAKE UP TUCKED BETWEEN sheets infused with Thomas's scent, but Thomas himself is gone. A wave of disappointment sweeps over me, especially when I notice the note left on the pillow next to mine. *Got out before the bloodhound woke up. See you around.*

I bite my lip nervously; did he really just blow me off with a note? I cannot believe it. I crumple up the paper, get out of bed, and toss it angrily in the trash can. Go to hell, Thomas.

After a nice hot shower, the smoky smell of bacon from the kitchen draws me downstairs, where I find my mother navigating the stove.

"Good morning, dear. Did you sleep well?" she asks, loading a plate with two slices of bacon and some scrambled eggs. "I've prepared you a breakfast rich in fats and carbohydrates to start the week off right." She hands me the plate and invites me to sit down at the table to eat.

"Thank you," I reply, softened by the gesture.

She smiles at me. She pours a cup of coffee and hands that to me as well. "Here, how long until your first class?"

"An hour, but with the bus ride, I have to leave in fifteen minutes," I answer her, sipping the coffee.

"Victor is picking me up today, so I can leave you the car if you want."

"Oh, thanks." She takes the keys out of her purse and leaves them on the kitchen counter, next to the fruit basket. Right where Thomas had sat yesterday. Great, now this house is full of things and places that will always make me think of him. And it's absurd to feel so torn up over someone I've barely known for such a short time.

"Good, now I have to run." She turns to leave but stops in the doorway. "Ah, one last thing: the next time Travis sleeps over, tell him there's no need for him to sneak out in the middle of the night. It's not like he's never stayed with us before." She disappears upstairs with a sardonic smirk, leaving me speechless.

Before starting class, I stop by the cafeteria in the student union to meet Alex for our usual 8:30 coffee. The atmosphere, however, is almost gloomy. Which is unusual. Stella's departure must have robbed Alex of his usual good humor.

"Have you heard from Travis again?" he asks after interminable minutes of silence in which we both do nothing but stare blankly at an indefinite spot on the table. We really look like a pair of depressives.

"I blocked his number. Just the thought of hearing from him makes my stomach turn. I hope for his sake I don't cross paths with him; I can't be held accountable for my actions."

"If he's smart, he'll know to stay away from you."

"In any case, Tiffany assured me her brother wasn't going to be my problem anymore." Speaking of problems, mine has just entered the cafeteria in the company of Shana. The way he loops his arm around her waist immediately triggers my anger. I can't help but think about those hands which, less than six hours ago, were on my body, holding me, wanting me... It's enough to make me cry.

I feel the urgent need to flee. I stand up, trying to hide how upset I am, and ask Alex to walk with me to my next class. I know I won't be able to get away from Thomas forever, though, because I am headed right for philosophy. My friend intuits the source of my upset, but he doesn't say anything; he merely accompanies me down the hallway.

I take my usual seat in the front row and wait for the professor. Ten minutes later, the classroom is beginning to fill up, and Thomas sidles up next to me. The nerve of this guy.

"Hello again, stranger. Same place, same time." He smiles. As soon as he notices that I have no intention of responding to him, his enthusiasm wanes. Out of the corner of my eye, I can see him scrutinizing me carefully. "What's the matter with you?"

"Leave me alone, Thomas," I say in a clipped voice with my gaze fixed on my already-open notes. But his proximity gets on my nerves. "Hey, is that seat free?" I ask a blond guy in the third row. A pair of blue eyes give me a perplexed look, but then the boy smiles at me. I realize suddenly that he's the same guy who said hello to me in the stands before the basketball game. How had I never noticed him in this class before?

"Yes, of course. Come here."

I gather all my things and change seats.

"What the fuck is wrong with you?" Thomas grips my wrist tightly, but I manage to wriggle out of it.

"Nothing," I lie. "Everything is just fine."

I sit down next to the blond boy and position everything I need on the desk in my usual maniacal order.

"Nice to meet you, I'm Logan."

"No one asked you, dumbass," Thomas says testily, turning in our direction.

I lean forward and glare at him. Logan starts, caught off guard. "Ignore him," I tell my new neighbor, who listens and turns back to me. "And I'm Vanessa." I smile at him.

"Yes, I know who you are, but this is the first time you've ever spoken to me. We had a class together last year, but you never even said hello."

I am embarrassed by the implicit accusation.

"Damn, sorry. Please forgive me. Believe it or not, I don't talk to a lot of people. But that's not a you-problem, it's a me-problem." I shake his hand. "Nice to meet you, I'm Vanessa. The most awkward and introverted person on the face of the earth. Sorry again," I babble begging for forgiveness with my eyes.

"Of course, don't worry about it, it's not like you're the only one."

He smiles shyly. "But, if the guilt is eating you alive, you can always make it up to me with lunch, maybe in the cafeteria? How about that?"

I'm about to agree but Thomas interrupts us. "Shit, your pickup game is mind-blowing. What are you gonna do now? Slip her a note that says 'do you like me? Check yes or no?'"

I am flabbergasted.

"Please, pardon me. In fact, pardon him," I say, turning to Logan. When I realize that Thomas is still looking at me, I snap, "What the hell do you want?"

"Why did you move?" he asks angrily.

"I'm sorry, I didn't realize that you two are...uh...together," Logan says awkwardly.

"We're not together," we answer in unison. At least we agree on something.

"Clark, Fallon, and Collins? If it is not too much of an imposition, I would like to start class," Professor Scott chides us, having just made his entrance.

I clam up, purple with shame. This is the first time I have ever been reprimanded by a professor. Logan smiles reassuringly at me. Thomas seems unfazed. He gets up and joins us. "You, find another seat. I have an issue to resolve," he orders, standing behind Logan.

I place a hand on Logan's arm and insist, "No. Stay here."

Thomas looks at my hand clasped around the blond boy's forearm. He shifts his angry gaze back to Logan, who is now visibly uncomfortable. "I'm not going to tell you again," he threatens him, furious. I see Logan turn pale.

"Vanessa, listen, maybe it's better if I—" he murmurs, but I don't let him finish his sentence.

"He. Stays. Here." I turn to Thomas challengingly. We glare at one another for a handful of seconds, each of us waiting for the other to give in. Between us sits Logan wishing, I'm sure, that he was anywhere else right now.

"Miss Clark, outside," Professor Scott declares.

"Excuse me?" I ask incredulously.

"Get out of my classroom right now."

I can't believe it. I've just gotten kicked out of class because of this idiot!

"Thanks so much!" I whisper sourly as I get up.

I leave the classroom and am about to walk down the hallway when I hear the professor's muffled voice, "Collins, where are you going?"

I don't believe it.

I walk as fast as I can, hoping to lose him.

"Ness!" I hear him shout as I head out of the building, but I don't turn around and continue walking briskly. "Will you fucking stop?"

He catches up to me and grabs me by the arm, forcing me to look at him.

"Do you realize this is the second time this week you've ruined a class for me?" I shout, smacking him on the shoulder with the notebook I was holding tightly in my hand.

"Fuck the class. You wanna tell me what's going on with you?"

"I could ask you the same question! You were so rude to Logan for no reason!"

"You left me no alternative," he says with an unruffled air that enrages me.

"Just because I didn't want to be near you?"

"No, because you keep acting like an immature child! Instead of running away, tell me what the problem is."

I'm immature? That's rich, coming from him.

"There is no problem." I snort, ignoring the insult, and trying to wriggle out of his grip. But Thomas won't let me escape.

"You sat next to Logan so you wouldn't have to talk to me. So I'll ask you one more time: What is the problem?"

"You seriously don't know?" He doesn't answer. "For as long as I have known you, you have done nothing but mess with my head. First you play nice with me, then you say you don't like me. You defend me to Travis and then you call me pathetic. You show up at my house, we have sex, you make arrangements to meet another girl, and then you disappear in the middle of the night without a word, leaving a lousy little note that says *see you around*. You'll see me around? Really, Thomas? And, to end this farce on a high note, I see you wrapped around some other girl like I don't exist," I yell. I realize too late that we have attracted the attention of some nearby students. Perfect.

"And that's your problem?" He seems surprised and annoyed at the same at the same time.

"My problem is that I don't understand you!" I lash out, a twinge of pain in my temples warning me to calm down. After taking a deep breath, I look at him. "What game are you playing, Thomas?"

He runs a hand through his hair, as if struggling to get his thoughts in order. "No game."

"Then what do you want from me? You keep hanging around me but you won't ever stay for good."

"I don't know," he confesses in a half-whisper.

"You don't know? Really?" I shake my head bitterly and make to leave, but he stops me.

"No, Ness, I don't know." He takes a deep breath. "When I'm with you... I do things I shouldn't do."

"What things? Running away in the middle of the night? Or using me as a sexual release valve, like I'm one of your bimbos?"

My voice cracks but I force myself not to cry.

"What was I supposed to do? You were terrified that your mother would find me there. I only did what you asked me to. And I didn't use you as a release valve. Need I remind you that you were the one who got off?"

"You made me feel used, Thomas. I shared a piece of myself with you and, just a few hours after you slipped out of my bed, you had no problem at all showing up here with Shana! How am I supposed to feel?"

Thomas bites his lip and looks around nervously. It seems like he's about to say something, but then his expression changes, hardens. It is an expression I have never seen on his face before, and it doesn't bode well.

"Showing up at your house was a mistake. Forget about it. Pretend that never happened."

What...

"Forget?" I repeat in a broken voice, trying to choke down the lump I feel in my throat.

"Yeah, this thing between you and me." He moves a hand between me and himself. "You're acting like a jealous fucking girlfriend, but you're not. I'm not with you, I fucked you a couple of times, and we had fun. But that's all it was!"

I remain stunned by his words as I feel tears welling up. I back away, incredulous, deeply humiliated, ashamed, and hurt once again.

After a moment of bewilderment at my brimming eyes, Thomas seems to sadden. He takes a step toward me, reaching to take my hands, but I shy away from him.

"You told me yesterday that you don't want to be compared to Travis, but the truth is, you're not that different from him." I blink rapidly, trying to chase away the tears. "From now on, stay away from me." I turn to leave and, as I walk away, I'm no longer able to hold back the tears. I feel like the dumbest person in the world. How could I misunderstand his intentions so grievously? Had I really believed that an insecure, bookish, awkward girl like me would be able to capture his attention? Yes. For a tiny fraction of a second, last night, lying on my bed with him beside me... I had believed it. But I was wrong. I shouldn't have done any of the things I did with him. I knew what he was like from the beginning. I knew I was just a dalliance for him. That whole thing about wanting to know me, it was pure fiction. It was all part of his game...

I run past the campus buildings with tears blurring my vision. I get into the Toyota and, when I finally manage to stop weeping, I start the car. I park in the driveway, enter the house, close the door behind me, and slump against it. The silence in the empty room is broken only by my sobs, which I no longer try to hold back. I put my hands in my hair and cry, disappointed in my own naivete. As soon as I manage to calm down, I go take a shower and then throw myself on the couch, not even making an effort to assemble a lunch. When my mother comes home around five o'clock, I beg off with an excuse about studying and lock myself in my room.

But I don't have the wherewithal to actually study, preferring to continue reading *Pride and Prejudice*. I reach out to the bedside table but...it's not there. That is where I left it, though. Mom must have put it away in the bookcase when she was dusting. I don't have time to go over to the shelf before the sound of the doorbell makes me jump.

What fresh hell is this?

I run down the stairs so I can answer the door before my mother does. I find Logan standing on the front stoop, with an awkward smile on his face.

"Um...hey, Vanessa," he greets me.

"Hi, Logan," I say, equally embarrassed and surprised at this unexpected visit.

"I thought I should bring you the notes from today's lecture, if that would be useful," he says sweetly, handing me a USB stick.

"Oh, thank you very much. I meant to ask someone for notes. I also meant to apologize to you for the scene. You were in the wrong place at the wrong time—you didn't do anything wrong," I explain uncomfortably.

"Don't worry, it's Thomas Collins. What can you expect? Even though, at one point, I did think both of you were about to blow up."

I put on a fake smile, but I just want to sink into the floor. "Well, in any case, I do apologize on his behalf. And thanks again, for the notes," I repeat, hoping to dismiss him.

"No problem. You know..." He rubs a finger over his eyebrow, self-conscious. "I was thinking, if you wanted, we could get coffee one of these days?"

"Vanessa, is everything okay over there?" My mother's voice breaks in from the kitchen, saving me from further awkwardness. "Dinner's ready!"

"Um, I have to go now, Logan. See you in class, thanks again!" I say in a hurry. I don't have time to close the door before my mother appears behind me, looming.

"Who was that, honey?"

"A classmate. I had to give him some notes," I lie.

"Mmhmm, I see. And does Travis know that your classmates are showing up at your house and inviting you for coffee?" she asks me as we head back into the kitchen.

"You shouldn't eavesdrop." I sit down at the table and nibble on a piece of bread. Mom brings over two plates of macaroni and cheese and sits down across from me. "And with Travis..." I leave the sentence hanging, wondering if I should talk to her about it now. Knowing her, she will flip out when she hears about our breakup. I trust, though, that when I tell her why, she'll finally understand what kind of guy he was.

"Did something happen? Did you have a fight?"

I take a deep breath and silently pray that my mother will be reasonable for once. "You're not going to like what I'm about to tell you," I warn her in a trembling voice. I take a pause before letting it all out in one big breath. "It's over." I gasp for breath, as though there's been a brick lying on my chest all this time, and I've finally pushed it off.

"What, dear?" she asks, perplexed.

"Between Travis and me," I add, looking her in the eye. "It's over." A stony silence settles over us. "What did you say?"

"You heard me," I reply, trying not to be intimidated.

She stares at me in disbelief. Then she shakes her head, twisting one corner of her mouth. "Don't joke."

"I'm not, I'm serious."

"You can't," she says, setting her fork down on her plate.

"That bastard cheated on me, Mom," I explain. She just keeps looking at me, lost, panic in her eyes. "He lied and cheated on me," I repeat. "He seduced a girl just to use her for one night."

My mother blinks, as though awakening from a deep sleep. "What are you talking about? Travis is a good boy. He comes from a very respectable family; he would never do something like that!" she says, putting her hands on her hips with an accusatory look.

"Yeah, that's what I thought. It was a shock to me too."

"What you're saying is impossible, he must have been under the influence of alcohol, maybe those troublemaker friends of his peer-pressured him."

I wrinkle my forehead. "What movie are you making up in your head? He was completely lucid. And, even if he had been drinking, how can you justify something like that?" I shout, slamming my fist on the table.

My mother won't stop babbling. "Honey, listen." She runs her hands over her face, as if trying to organize her train of thought. That train has been off the rails for a while now. "I know that you are in shock and hurting a lot right now, but think about this for a minute... You can't throw away two beautiful years over one momentary mistake."

I look at her, dumbfounded. "He disrespected me constantly, cheated on me regularly, and tricked an innocent girl into sleeping with him only to disappear the next morning!"

"Vanessa, did you consider for even a second that he might have been going through a difficult time? You know he's under so much pressure, you've never been able to fully understand it. He must have felt so lost. You can't condemn him for that."

I am struck speechless. So this is my fault now?

"You...you...you're crazy, Mom! Of course I can condemn him. In fact, that's exactly what I did. I left him. It's over! I have no intention of ever going through what you went through with Dad!" I get up, turn on the faucet, fill a glass with water, and drain it all in one go.

"Vanessa, if you allow pride and anger to win out over the bond that you two share, you will end up regretting it bitterly. Do you really think you'll get another chance like this again?"

My eyes widen in disgust. "You know what, Mom?" I slam the glass down furiously on the kitchen counter and turn to look at her. "I knew this news would upset you. I knew that you would go into a rage and that you would do your damnedest to change my mind. But— and who knows why?—a part of me actually believed that, confronted by the enormous lack of respect that boy showed your daughter, you would have understood and supported me for once! But I was stupid to think that, because the only thing that matters to you is money!"

"Vanessa!" she scolds me.

"No, Mom, don't 'Vanessa' me! You have made up this idea of him that has nothing to do with reality, but we all know why you did it. He has something the others don't, doesn't he? Ten figures in the bank! And that is more than enough for you. Who cares if your daughter is demeaned, humiliated and betrayed! What really matters is that she marries a billionaire who will lock her up in his luxurious golden mansion where she can live the most miserable existence in human history! But, hey, she'll be able to do it surrounded by caviar and champagne!" I take a breath. "You can put your mind at ease. Travis and I broke up days ago, and I have no intention of going back, not now or ever!"

"D-days ago?" she starts. "Then who was in your room last night?"

I swallow with difficulty as I stare at her with wide eyes.

"Leave me alone, it's all over anyway!" I spit. I leave the kitchen without giving her a chance to say anything else. I run to my room and shut myself in. I turn the lock and throw myself onto the bed. With my head sunk into the pillow, I burst into my second inconsolable crying jag of the day.

PART TWO

One Month Later

Twenty-One

"OKAY, READY?" TIFFANY ASKS IMPATIENTLY.

"No!" I scream, my eyes closed in terror.

"On the count of three!"

"No. No. No," I beg her, trying to block her hands.

"One, two..."

"Wait, wait! Give me a minute. Just a minute," I whine.

My friend snorts, rolling her eyes. "You say the same thing every time. We've been here twenty minutes, Nessy, my hand is cramping up." Then, without warning, she shouts "three" and rips the wax off my crotch.

"Ah! I hate you!" I scream, squeezing my legs together and covering my face with my hands.

"There you go, smooth as a baby's butt." Tiff grins, proud of the job she's done after twenty minutes of tears (hers) and protests (mine).

"Is she still in one piece?" I ask.

"Ready to go for a ride!" she says enthusiastically, closing the jar of wax.

I get up slowly from my bed and pat her arm.

"Don't you know? I closed up shop and threw the key into the sea."

She bursts out laughing. "Oh, come on, we all know you're hiding a spare in your bra." She winks at me as I get dressed. "You want me to believe that after no fewer than three dates with Mr. Boring you still intend to keep her locked up in your panties?"

"First of all, don't call him that. Also, excuse me for preferring to build a certain kind of relationship before giving him my virtue," I inform her haughtily.

"Your virtue was gone years ago. And I don't seem to recall you going to all that trouble with Thomas."

I could kill her for bringing him up. It's been a month since we last spoke. Or rather, yelled. "Yes and look how well that turned out. I don't want to rush it this time."

"I get that, but you're going at a snail's pace. You and Logan have been out three times and you haven't even kissed him yet. Why not just admit you're bored stiff?"

"Because I'm not."

"Come on, Nessy, we all know. He's perfectly nice, of course. But not what you're looking for," she says.

"And what exactly am I looking for, Miss Mind Reader?" I ask, crossing my arms over my chest.

"I don't know, but I think a pair of green eyes and a lot of tattoos might crystallize the idea in your head." She giggles as I glare at her, curling my lip.

"You're wrong. I'm over that." I turn my back to her and stand in front of the mirror to fix my hair.

"Of course. And I'm Mother Teresa of Calcutta. Just look at the way you blush every time you accidentally pass by him," she teases. "Or the way that, every time he sees you with Logan, he suddenly becomes more unbearable than usual. I don't know why you two try so hard to stay away from each other, when even the scenery can tell that you want to do the exact opposite."

"I don't care how it looks. He behaved badly with me and didn't even pretend to be remorseful. All he did was rub my face in all his conquests. Logan, on the other hand, is exactly the kind of guy I need right now: he's good, sweet, polite, thoughtful, romantic..."

"Boring," she mumbles, covering the word with a mock-cough.

I ignore it.

"Do you realize that he has shown up for every one of our dates with a rose? I have never in my life received roses, and it's wonderful. It makes me feel important!" I tell her, my eyes dreamy. Tiffany turns her back to me and pretends to retch.

"I can see you, you know," I say dryly.

I throw a pillow at her, which comes right back at me.

Tiff opens the bag of gummy bears I brought from the kitchen, sits down on the bed, and pops one into her mouth with an expression of delight. "So where's the big boy taking you tomorrow night?"

"We're going out for Indian food and then to the movies."

Tiffany's eyes widen. "But didn't you tell him that you don't like Indian food?"

"It's not that I don't like it; I just find it a bit too spicy for my taste." She nails me with a "who are you trying to fool?" expression. "Okay! I don't like it, but I don't see the problem. I can just order plain rice."

"Ah, so it'll be a nice dinner of nothing for you. That's sure to be unforgettable," she mocks me. "Why didn't you tell him the truth?"

"Because he was so happy to take me to this Indian restaurant with 'inimitable cuisine,' which, according to him, I can't miss. You should have seen him, even you wouldn't have been able to say no to him."

"Doubt it. Anyway, what are you going to wear?" she asks, blasé, while eating another gummy bear and sitting on the bed.

"I don't know, something simple. Logan likes me as I am; I don't need to twist myself up to get his attention—"

Tiff rolls her eyes and I glare at her. I join her on the bed, lying down next to her and stealing a candy.

"Tell me, what did he ever do to make you dislike him so much?" I ask, chopping a bear in half with my teeth.

"Nothing, it's just...he's too perfect, you know?"

I give her a confused look and shake my head.

"Believe it or not, Prince Charmings don't exist, honey. Very often, they're just hiding behind clever masks and they turn out to be the worst of them all. And you can be so naive at times, that..."

"That you worry about me," I finish the sentence for her, gently.

"Maybe." She looks at me sideways and laughs affectionately.

"You don't have to, Tiff. It's true, I was naive with Travis and Thomas, but only because I was blinded by emotions."

"I wasn't talking about Thomas. He was an asshole to you, but he never tried to pretend he wasn't an asshole. He showed what he was from the start. Can you say the same about Logan?"

She's not completely wrong. Thomas never promised me anything; I was the one who believed it could be more than it was. And when it comes to Logan...I think for a moment and then nod. "My instinct is to trust him, but I promise you I'll give him the third degree tomorrow night, if that will help you feel better...Mom," I tease her, nudging her with my elbow.

Not only have I cut ties with Thomas for the last month, but Travis also seems to have finally disappeared from my life. I haven't heard from him since Tiffany threatened to tell their father everything if he didn't stay away from me. Of course, I have also avoided any Beavers games like the plague, since the team is filled with guys I'd rather not see, but apparently I've come out of it otherwise unscathed. Well, except for the tiny detail that my mother and I only speak to each other in monosyllables ever since I confessed everything to her. Everything except the identity of the boy who was in my room that accursed Sunday night. If I had told her that while she was taking a bath, I was achieving ecstasy in the arms of a "ne'er-do-well" (as she would surely call him) she would have kicked me out.

"So, are you ready? Alex will be here any minute," Tiffany announces, shaking me from my thoughts. I'm very ready. In fact, I can't wait. After a month of looking for work, Matt was finally able to get me a job interview at his uncle's bar.

"Waxed, primped, and perfumed. Let's go!" I reply, full of enthusiasm.

Twenty minutes later, we find ourselves in front of a bar north of the city. A buzz of rock music emanates from the building. Strange, bars are usually pretty empty at this time of day. Parked outside are two Harley-Davidsons, one red and one black. I've never been to this place before.

I leave my friends to wait for me in a nearby park and, as soon as I enter the bar, I am hit with the smell of hops, lumber, and fried food. To my right is a long, solid wooden counter with a set of taps and leather stools, upon which a few patrons are seated. The walls are also wood-paneled, with small, darkened windows.

"Hey! Do you need a seat?" asks a girl with a head full of blue and black braids.

"Hi, I'm Vanessa Clark. I'm here to talk to the boss; I have an appointment with him in five minutes."

"He's in his office." She points upstairs. "I'll go grab him now. Is there anything I can get you in the meantime?" she asks as she finishes arranging some clean mugs.

"A soda, thanks." I smile at her. She pours the soda into a glass and hands it to me along with a bowl of chips. Then she heads upstairs.

After a few minutes, I hear footsteps behind me and a deep, British-accented voice exclaims, "Vanessa, at last we meet! Matt tells me many good things about you. Pleased to meet you, I'm Derek Ford." He extends his hand, and I take it. He's probably in his forties, well groomed, with a thin beard covering his chin and jaw. He has the same dark eyes as his nephew only with more crow's-feet around them. "Come, sit," he says, and we settle at a dark wood table. "Tell me, what brings you to these parts?" he asks, folding his hands on the table.

"I'm a sophomore in college, and I'm looking for a job that will allow me to have a bit of independence," I say with a certain nervousness as he watches me attentively.

"That's a mature move, it does you credit. Most kids your age only think about having fun and ruining their livers. What is your availability? I'm guessing college takes up a lot of your time."

"A part-time position would be ideal."

"You should know, during the week it's busy here but manageable. On weekends, it's pure chaos. I can offer you part time in the evenings with the possibility of more hours on the weekends if there are extra events. What do you say?"

"Yes, I can do that," I reply enthusiastically.

"Very good. Have you ever poured draft beer?"

"Erm, no," I admit, embarrassed. I regret not having attended more parties. "But I'm a quick learner!" I hasten to add.

"You know that a lot of OSU students come in here, right?"

"Oh, yes?"

"Is that a problem? I mean, serving your classmates could be unpleasant."

"No, no problem." Apart from Alex, Tiffany, and Logan, and two blowhards whose names begin with T and end with S, no one at school knows I exist. Serving a few students won't tarnish my nerdy loser rep.

"All right, then. I'd say we can set up a trial week and see how it goes."

"That would be great, thank you so much, Mr. Ford."

"First thing: if you start working here, I want you to call me by my name," he says, smiling.

"Gotcha, Derek." I smile in turn.

"Second thing, much more important: remember to always bring that smile with you. It'll be your calling card with every customer you serve. If you use it the right way here, you can ensure yourself some good tips by the end of the day." He winks at me.

"I'll keep that in mind," I reply, trying to sound as convincing as possible, torn between enthusiasm and performance anxiety.

"Excellent!" Derek slaps his hand on the table. "I don't think there's anything else. The locker rooms are downstairs. After last call, we clean up and close out the cash register, but Maggie will explain all those boring things in more detail." He gestures to the blue-haired girl who had just greeted me. "Your uniform will be given to you on your first day, come a little before opening hours if you can. Are you okay to start tomorrow?"

I nod fervently, all the while with a dumb grin plastered on my face. For the first time in months, I feel confident and proud of myself.

After two weeks of work, the Marsy has become almost like a second home. Sure, my under-eye rings are at their peak, and I have to study on the bus to keep up with my classes, but having a little independence is an achievement.

As I wipe down the bar, the front door jingles. I look up and spot a man in the doorway. It's James, a regular who comes in to watch the football game on our screens. His presence reminds me that, despite the skimpy yellow cheerleader uniform that I am forced to wear to get tips, I do actually enjoy this job because of all the new people I am getting to know, who chat and share stories with me. I watch him head for the bar and sit in his usual seat. He's wearing the same sort of elegant, designer clothes that he typically wears. The Bluetooth earpiece he always wears and the black leather briefcase he carries make him look a bit self-important—and definitely out of place at the Marsy—but I only had to exchange a few words with him to see that he is not nearly so haughty as he appears.

"Hey, James!" I greet him with a smile. "Shall I get you the usual?" A creature of habit, he always gets the same thing: barbecue wings and a nice cold pint.

He confirms with a nod, returning my smile. He's handsome for a guy in his fifties, with light hair and blue eyes, and just a few frown lines on his face.

"You sure know how to keep your customers satisfied." He chuckles, lays his briefcase on the counter, pulls out his laptop, and starts typing away on the keyboard, without even looking. If I understand correctly, he works in the publishing industry, and someday I would like to ask him for advice. When he flexes his arm, the sleeve of his jacket rides up a bit and, for the first time, I catch a glimpse of a tattoo on his wrist.

My mind immediately goes to Thomas, and I feel my heart clench. I would be lying if I said that I was immune to his charms or that I don't long to be near him whenever I think of him. After the way he treated me, though, and especially after the Travis ordeal, I vowed to make better choices when it comes to men. And this is the mantra I repeat to myself every morning before getting out of bed. Then all I have to deal with is my heart beating wildly, my legs shaking, and my stomach turning upside down every time I see or hear about him.

Twenty-Two

MONDAY MORNING FINDS ME IN the student union cafeteria reading the latest novel chosen by the reading group while I wait for class to begin.

"You're gonna break it." Thomas's deep voice makes me gasp. It's the first time in exactly forty-five days that I've heard it so close to me.

"What?" I turn to look at him, confused and nervous. I realize only now that he is already sitting beside me in his usual swaggering pose, with one ankle balanced on his knee, his arm resting behind my shoulders.

With a jerk of his chin he indicates the pencil I hold between my teeth, which I use to underline the sentences that strike me most in the book. "You keep torturing it like that, it's gonna break," he reiterates.

I place the pencil on the book and look back at him, impassive. "Is there a reason you're talking to me?"

"Is that how it's always gonna be between us from now on?"

I frown. "Like what?"

"You ignoring me, me doing the same to you…"

"It's worked so far."

Thomas cracks a faint smile. "You never get tired of denying the truth to yourself, do you?"

The nerve, showing up here after weeks of silence and presuming to know how I feel! I snort, shaking my head, and put the book back in my bag. "You're ridiculous, Thomas. You've been here less than five minutes and have already made me lose my patience."

"A record," he retorts proudly.

"Are you kidding me? What exactly do you want from me, Thomas?" I demand with a sharp look. "You come around here after all this time, talking to me like nothing happened, after having thrown every one of your new conquests in my face, and you expect me to laugh and joke with you?"

He shrugs a shoulder. "Seems to me you also didn't miss any opportunities to show me how into that idiot you were, no?"

"That's not the same, not at all!"

"Yes, it is, and you know it." He stares at me grimly.

Okay, it is possible that I got a little closer to Logan than I really wanted to when Thomas was around, but I never kissed Logan in front of him. He did that, though, with his lady friends.

"Forget it. And Logan has nothing to do with it anyway," I answer, certain.

"He definitely has something to do with it."

"No, it's not about him! It's about you. My God, how can you not get this?" I put my face in my hands before looking at him wearily. "You hurt me! I let you into my house, I told you about me, about my life, about my father. And you... You belittled everything," I admit, re-opening a wound that hasn't yet healed. Thomas frowns seriously at me, but I see his face through a veil of humiliation. My eyes are filled with tears, and I'm forced to bite the inside of my cheek to keep them from falling.

"I know," he says, bowing his head, his voice full of regret. "I have a bad habit of saying things I don't mean when I'm pissed off," he defends himself in a small voice. And I let out an unhappy laugh because I feel like I'm having déjà vu.

"Yeah, I've heard this story before, for a good two years..." I shake my head. "I have no desire to relive the past."

Thomas releases a sigh, surrendering, and the features of his face soften. "I know I hurt you and, whether you believe it or not, I'm not proud of it." Something about the tortured way in which he speaks tells me that this is his way of apologizing to me. Although it's not the best excuse in the world, I can sense an underlying sincerity that makes me let my guard down. "Can we..." He runs a hand through his hair. "Can we stop all this and start over again?" he asks, his voice uncertain.

What?

"Start over again? What does that mean?"

"I don't know. We could be like...friends?" he ventures, leaving me stunned.

"Friends?" I repeat skeptically.

"Don't make that face," he scolds me. "It's a fair compromise."

A fair compromise? To have him back in my life, without actually being able to have him? More like a fair punishment if anything.

"I don't think that will work."

Thomas frowns. "How do you know?"

"Have you ever been friends with a girl without benefits?"

He looks at me for a few seconds, caught off guard. He thinks about it before giving a troubled shake of his head. "No."

"I figured. I'm not going to pretend to be your friend just to make it a bit more convenient for you to try to sleep with me."

"That's not what I want to do." He sounds almost offended. "It's true, I've never been friends with a girl without benefiting, but there's a first time for everything, right?" He pauses and smiles sweetly at me, before inching closer. I hold my breath. "Do you want to be my first, Ness?"

A laugh escapes me. "Do you realize how absurd that sentence sounds coming out of your mouth?" I smile and he does the same in return. The light that illuminates his face melts my heart.

Damn you, Thomas.

"It definitely sounded better in my head," he adds.

"I don't know," I say, getting serious. "Friendship is important. You can't just wing it. It takes commitment, consistency, respect. For someone who doesn't want relationships, forging a bond of friendship could be a real problem," I explain, firmly convinced of what I am saying.

"Then teach me how to be a good friend."

My eyes roam over him. "Do you really want to do that? You actually intend to be my friend?"

He nods decisively. "Friends, Vanessa, just friends." But the glint in his eyes is in stark contrast to the words he is saying. Yet I decide to believe him anyway. Tiffany was right: I can't let go of him.

A moment later, a friend of Thomas's pulls him aside. They stop to talk for a few minutes, and I take the opportunity to pick my reading back up from where I had stopped. I need something to relieve the tension, but not even one of my beloved books seems to be able to do it. Thomas returns to sit at my side and, out of the corner of my eye, I can see him staring at me for a long moment. I force myself to keep my eyes on the page, so as not to let him see how his proximity puts me off-kilter, but my constant worrying of my lip and wild jiggling of my foot betray me. And Thomas decides to make matters worse by placing his hand on my thigh. The unexpected contact startles me. "Don't be nervous, stranger. We haven't talked in a while, but it's still me and it's still you," he reassures me.

I look up at him and nod, as tense as a violin string.

"Want a coffee?" he suggests with his usual cheeky smile, saving me from short-circuiting entirely.

"Yes, great idea."

I watch him get out of his chair and pull a pack of Marlboros from the pocket of his ripped, black jeans, and stick one cigarette behind his ear.

As soon as he notices me looking at him, he gives me a wink. It's a harmless gesture, but one that makes me blush nonetheless. I look down and pass him quickly to keep him from noticing the flush on my face.

"What classes do you have today?" I ask as we head to the cafeteria.

"Law. Two Hours. With Thompson, who's going to enjoy reading me the riot act."

"And why exactly will she do that?"

"Are you sure you want to know?"

I nod, preparing for the worst.

"I had a good time with her granddaughter this summer. Apparently Thompson found out about it recently and didn't like the way I ended things," he explains simply.

"Can you blame her?" I mutter, avoiding his gaze.

"She's convinced that her granddaughter is a little Goody Two-shoes; she has no idea what the girl is really like. So yeah, she's wrong," he replies, all conviction.

"She's still her granddaughter," I point out to him. "And, either way, you should show more respect toward women," I admonish him. He rolls his eyes, so I add, "Don't worry, I don't expect you to stop talking like a caveman just because we're friends now."

I can feel a few passing female students staring at us. Ugh, not again. I wonder how Thomas manages to stay sane.

"Don't give it too much weight," he snaps me out of my musings, as if he's read my mind.

"It's annoying. I mean, apparently me just being seen with you is enough to antagonize half the school." For a month, I had spared myself Shana's dirty looks, but it took just one walk down the hallway to reignite the fuse. "I just wish they could understand that I am not a competitor in the bare-knuckle brawl for Thomas Collins's heart."

"The only brawl they can hope for is the one in my bed."

"Well, even then, I pose no threat."

Thomas gives me a sidelong grin, before opening the cafeteria door and letting me through. "And you, do you have classes today?" he asks, ending our previous conversation.

"English literature, why?"

He shrugs as though his question were completely unmotivated, yet the thoughtful look that creases his brow makes me think the opposite is true.

"I'm going to get some coffee," he says.

"Okay, can you get me a sugar-free long shot?" I ask. I sit down at the table and check my phone for notifications.

I'm scrolling through social media on my phone when Thomas returns with coffees and a muffin.

He hands me the steaming mug and sits down across from me. Then he slides the saucer with the muffin across the table and I realize it's pistachio. "It was the last one. I know you like pistachio," he states casually, rubbing the nape of his neck where his hair is cut short. It's clear that he's trying to downplay this uncharacteristic courtesy. My mouth drops open in surprise, but I decide to pretend that the gesture has no effect on me whatsoever and just thank him instead.

"So, I heard you started working at the Marsy. How are you liking it?"

I tell him how many mugs I had to fill before I learned how to properly pull a tap beer. I complain about how hard it was at first to carry several plates at once and how much I detest dressing up like a cheerleader.

As we chat, a curly-haired girl with amber skin walks past our table. She casts a sly glance at Thomas, who either doesn't notice, or pretends not to notice. "Hi, Thomas," she calls.

"Hi…" he answers uncertainly, his eyes half-closed as if trying to dredge her name up from his memory.

"Nancy," she says, irritated. "Two weeks ago you tattooed my sister's name on my wrist, and then took me to the backroom to get to know each other."

I am not surprised to hear that something happened between the two of them, although it does sting a little. But what really amazes me is something else: I had no idea Thomas did tattoos.

"I have lots of sex. With lots of different girls." He takes a sip of his coffee, wipes his mouth with the back of his hand and continues. "I can't remember every one of you. What do you want?"

And here we have Thomas Collins, the primordial bastard version. The girl looks mortified and, although I don't know her, I can't help but empathize with her. I get it, it's hard not to fall into Thomas's trap. This is exactly why I will never cross the line with him again. I can't imagine being treated like that by someone with whom I had shared the most intimate part of myself.

"So?" Thomas prompts her irritably, without the slightest bit of tact.

From the furious expression on Nancy's face, I could swear that she's thinking seriously about pouring a cup of hot coffee all over him. Honestly, he would deserve it. But, in the end, she just chooses to walk away, shooting him a look filled with hatred. Thomas turns to me with an imperturbable shrug. "Where were we?"

"Did you have to treat her like that?" I frown, crossing my arms over my chest.

"It was the only way to get rid of her. We had a good time, but that's where it ended."

I raise my eyebrows. "Wait, so you did remember her?"

"I remember them all. Some more than others." He winks at me. I try not to blush.

"If you remembered her, then why did you humiliate her like that?"

"Because otherwise she wouldn't have left so easily, and I wasn't in the mood to deal with a pain in the ass. Is that a good enough answer for you?"

I bite my lip, ready to deny it. But even though it's wrong, a part of me is pleased to know that he would rather interact with me than spend time talking to someone else. Although I still don't like the way he went about it, I choose to bite into my muffin and, instead of answering, I change the subject.

"How's Leila? I haven't seen her in a while." It's not that I blame her for what happened with Travis. In fact, I'm grateful to her for being honest. But I haven't seen her since that night, partly by accident, partly because I try to avoid her so as not to relive my humiliation when I look into her eyes.

"Ever since she started working for the paper, she's been off my radar. She's started to climb the ladder and now she's convinced she's the next Mika Brzezinski."

I laugh under my breath. More for the fact that he knows who Mika Brzezinski is than for the comparison itself. "I'm glad she was able to join the staff. I'll be eagerly awaiting her first article." I clasp my hands around my coffee cup to warm them.

"You'll be the only one, believe me," he says, annoyed.

I smack him on the arm. "You're her brother, you should be her number one fan!"

But I don't hear his reply because I catch sight of Logan at the counter. He is giving us a confused look. I wave hello but as soon as Thomas turns to look and notices that Logan is coming toward us, the smile fades from his lips.

"Is he coming over here?" he asks, annoyed.

"I'm gonna say yes."

Thomas glares at me. "I don't want him here."

What?

"We're dating, Thomas, I can't stop him from coming to see me." My reply seems to irritate him.

"Are you actually serious about Logan?" he exclaims, disgusted. "You don't know shit about him."

"I know enough. I know that he's kind and polite. And, most importantly, he knows what he wants." I underscore the sentiment by lifting my chin, proud of this small, but effective, dig. "And if we're being honest, I don't know anything about you either. The one time I tried to find out, you shut me down."

He clenches his jaw: he has taken the blow.

"Listen." I take a deep breath and try to calm down. "I don't want to argue with you now. If you're worried about me, you have no reason to be, okay? We've gone out a couple of times, I assure you he's a good guy."

"There are weird rumors going around about him. So no, I'm not comfortable knowing that you're with him." He looks me straight in the eye as he says it, and I can't help but wonder why everyone seems to have something against Logan?

"I don't know what you've heard, but he's been nothing but good to me so far. He's nice and well-mannered. People always talk, they say all sorts of things, but that doesn't mean they should be believed."

As soon as Logan reaches our table, Thomas gets up abruptly. "I've got class, I'd better go," he blurts out, obviously on edge.

"Thomas..." I mutter dejectedly. I would like to grab his hand to stop him from leaving, but I restrain myself. After all, he's the one who wanted to be friends. And he can't throw a fit every time Logan gets near me.

Thomas rounds the table and comes up behind me. He leans over me, grabbing my chin with one hand and urging me to tilt my face toward him. I gasp at the unexpected gesture and, when his rough jaw draws close to my cheek, I shudder. It is the first real contact I've had with him in more than a month. Without giving me time to understand his intentions, he plants a kiss just a little too close to the corner of my mouth.

"See you around, stranger," he whispers in my ear, never taking his eyes off Logan. Then he leaves.

I sit there, stunned, trying to decide what just happened even though I'm pretty sure I already know.

He wanted to mark his territory.

This realization triggers a wave of anger in me. He has no right to lay claim to me! What the hell?

"Hey," Logan greets me in a small voice, embarrassed by the scene he was forced to witness. "Are you two talking again?" he asks me, his blue eyes boring into mine as he sits down next to me.

I sigh and try to shake off the familiar tension I feel whenever Thomas is around. "It seems so, but to be honest, I don't know how long it's going to last."

"I don't know why you're still wasting your time," he says with ostentatious nonchalance, but I can tell by the way he clenches his jaw that he's trying to suppress some irritation. And who could blame him? Thomas was doing his best to provoke him. He takes my hand, intertwining our fingers and kissing the back. If there is one thing I like about Logan, it's that he lets me set the pace; even though we've been on four dates already, he's never tried to kiss me. He wants me to take that step. Even physically, he's Thomas's opposite. No piercings, no ink on his skin, no intimidating appearance that makes you uncomfortable. He's a good guy, the kind that makes your life easier.

"This thing between you two…" He looks at me, growing serious. "I don't have anything to worry about, do I?"

"No, of course not." I take a sip of coffee, shifting in my seat. I wasn't expecting that kind of question.

"Are you sure? Because I got a vibe that… I don't know, I don't like it. And I certainly haven't forgotten the way he treated me that day in class. Not to mention the way he looked at me just now: he looked like he wanted to take me apart. He doesn't seem like someone who's playing with a full deck."

"He…he's not so bad." I feel compelled to defend him; even though he did hurt me emotionally, he was never a danger to me. "In any case, you have nothing to worry about, really. We've settled our differences, but it's nothing more than that." I smile to reassure him.

"I always wondered why you guys fought. I mean, I was with you at the time, but I admit to not having understood much about it." He looks at me expectantly, waiting for an answer.

"Oh, the usual stuff, you know… His temper meets my stubbornness and, boom, the bomb goes off. Nothing major, in any case." I seem to have convinced him.

"By the way, I have bad news. Unfortunately, I have to cancel our bowling date for tomorrow." He rubs his forehead.

I give him a sad look. "How come?"

"I have to go back to Medford. My grandmother's birthday is at the end of October, and the whole family gets together to celebrate. It's a tradition. But it had slipped my mind when I suggested going out to the bowling alley."

"I understand. How long will you be gone?"

"A week, I leave in the morning."

"Oh, then you could come see me at the bar this evening," I suggest, smiling.

"You know I don't like that place. Besides, you'd be working. I can't get the time with you that I'd like."

"I know, but during the week there's not as much hustle and bustle. And we aren't going to see each other for days…" I say, doing my best impression of a pleading doe.

"Okay, okay. It's impossible to say no to those big eyes. Now I've got to go, I need to pack my bags."

"Hey, I can give you a hand if you want. I love packing."

"Don't worry, I have everything under control," he tells me, standing up and burying his hands in his pants pockets.

"Oh, okay. See you this evening, then?"

"Yes, I'll see you later." He kisses me on the cheek gently and we say goodbye.

After my last class of the day, I walk off campus headed for the bus stop, when suddenly a hand grabs me, pulling me backward. I almost lose my balance but two muscular arms prop me up.

"You are so uncoordinated." A tattooed man with emerald eyes smiles at me.

"Thomas, what are you doing here?" I give him a dazed look.

"I'm out for a walk." He brings a cigarette to his lips and lights it before looking at me. "And you're coming with me."

What? This morning he stormed out of the café and now he wants me to leave with him? I'm afraid I'll never be able to keep up with his mood swings.

"Actually, I'm going home."

"Don't be a buzzkill." He blows out a cloud of smoke. "Let's get a change of scenery. I promise to get you home by curfew," he teases me with an angelic expression that doesn't suit him at all.

"But what about your classes? Practice?"

"No practice today, and Professor Thompson was my last class of the day."

"Good for you. But I'm working tonight, so sorry but I'll pass."

"What time do you start?" he asks point-blank.

"Six-thirty."

"You'll be there by six-thirty."

"Thomas, I'm serious. I don't feel right about it…"

"Because?"

"Because I know what you're trying to do, and I have no intention of—"

"Ness," he interrupts. "I'm not trying to get into your pants. I just want to spend some time with you." He circles an arm around my waist and moves closer. My heart leaps into my throat, and I nearly stop breathing. He peers intensely into my eyes and, with the hand that holds the cigarette, he brushes aside a strand of my hair that has fallen over my left collarbone. "I've missed you, stranger."

And this is how weeks of self-control, determination, and Herculean efforts to repress my emotions crumble. The warm, seductive way he says these words makes me falter for a few moments. Until the little voice in my head reminds me that he must have really been missing me every time he stuck his tongue in someone else's mouth. That thought alone is enough to bring me back to planet Earth.

"I didn't miss you at all."

"Liar." He quirks a corner of his mouth smugly.

Arrogant as ever. Without giving me a chance to consider his proposal, he hands me a helmet.

"What is this?" I ask with a grimace.

"Probably a helmet, don't you think?" he replies teasingly.

"Yes, I get that. But what am I supposed to do with it?"

"Wear it. Let's leave with her." He points to an aggressive-looking black motorcycle parked a few feet away from us.

I burst into hysterical laughter and hand the helmet back to him. "No way. It'll rain gold from the sky before I get on that thing."

"Don't tell me you're scared," he teases with a mocking smirk.

"It's not fear, it's a survival instinct. Besides, I don't like motorcycles."

He frowns and takes a drag on his cigarette. "All right, let's hear it: What's your problem with motorcycles?"

"They're dangerous," I explain earnestly.

"That's the beauty of it." He cocks his head and gives me a mischievous grin.

"I am not getting on that thing."

"Don't talk about my baby girl like that," he retorts, pretending to take offense.

"Baby girl? What is it with men and vehicles?" I laugh.

"It's the same as you and your stuffed animals."

Thomas stubs out his cigarette with his shoe and slips on his Ray-Bans. "Move your ass or I'll carry you myself."

"I won't tell you again. I'm not getting on that bike, I swear to—"

I don't finish the sentence because he grabs me and throws me over his shoulder. "Took too long, Ness." I can't see it, but I bet he's got his slyest smile plastered all over his pretty face.

"Thomas! Put me down right now! You are making a scene!" I rain small punches down on his back, which don't faze him at all. He sits me down on the bike's seat and restrains my arms and legs, holding them firmly against his body.

"You've got two options here," he chuckles. "You can choose to come with me or you can come with me anyway."

"I'm sorry, what happened to free will?" I shrill, irritated. I tuck a few strands of hair behind my ears and cross my arms.

"It's on vacation." He folds the corners of his mouth up and I crumble in the face of that smile. Damn me! Thomas, pleased with his win, slips my helmet on and adjusts the chin strap.

"I'm capable of putting on a helmet, Thomas," I inform him sourly.

"I see you're still a shrew," he retorts. I hit him softly on the chest.

"And you're still a swaggering douchebag," I say, but a small laugh escapes me. He tries to restrain himself, but soon bursts out laughing along with me. The interior padding of the helmet presses my cheeks, and I feel quite awkward. I expect Thomas to start teasing me at any moment, but it doesn't happen. Instead, he takes off his leather jacket and hands it to me.

"Put it on, you'll get cold." When I wear it, I feel enveloped by a comforting warmth and the scent of vetiver and tobacco. A scent that, I have to admit, I've missed.

"So, where are we going?" I ask, zipping up the jacket while he slips on his helmet and chews a piece of gum.

"I don't know. Baby Girl will be our guide." I roll my eyes skyward while Thomas gets on the bike. I settle myself behind him, holding his shoulders and resting my feet on the small pegs on either side of the bike. At that point, Thomas starts the engine, letting it roar a couple of times before the bike suddenly jolts forward. Letting out a little cry, I plaster myself against his back and hug his sides. I hold my breath for a few seconds and listen to him chuckle.

Then he rests both feet on the ground and places a hand on my knee. "All right there, stranger?"

"Don't be an idiot," I admonish him, gently punching his back as I try to control my anxiety and look for something else to hold on to, but I can't find anything. "Thomas...where do I put my hands?"

He turns his head slightly toward me, then takes my hands and moves them around his waist. "Right here. Hold on tight," he orders.

I don't have time to tell him that he should go slow, because with a sharp flick of his wrist, we are speeding across the asphalt at full speed. I close my eyes fearfully and squeeze him as tightly as I can, praying that I arrive in one piece.

Twenty-Three

WE TRAVEL A FEW MILES north, on a small road made up mostly of stomach-twisting curves. Eventually we find ourselves on a long, deserted road, bathed in the light of the midday sun. Thomas turns off the engine, and I leap for the safety of the sidewalk. I tear off my helmet and set it on the ground.

"You are out of your mind! Were you trying to kill me?"

He looks at me, amused. Extending the kickstand and parking the bike, he gets off before removing his helmet and fixing his hair. Only now do I notice the Kawasaki lettering on the lower part of the vehicle and Ninja on the upper part.

"I didn't go that fast," he claims, chuckling under his breath.

"If that wasn't that fast for you, I dare not imagine what fast would be," I answer, fixing my tangled hair.

He moves closer to me, shaking his head and moving a strand of hair behind my ear. "You've got no reason to worry when you're with me," he whispers. As if hypnotized, my gaze falls involuntarily on his full lips. Strange and dangerous thoughts sprout within me. I wonder if it's all from the adrenaline I can feel in my body or if there is very simply a wild and seductive charm about Thomas that will never cease to put me on my back foot. "Come on, let's go this way." He takes me by the hand and I, stunned at the skin-to-skin contact, follow him.

We walk down a path through the trees and bushes, which Thomas pushes aside to clear my way. The sky above our heads, incredibly clear for a late October day, is crisscrossed by birds. The ground beneath our feet is covered with red and orange leaves. We hear them rustling with every step.

"Where are we?" I ask curiously, looking around as we enter the dense forest.

"Outside the city, beyond the edge of Chip Ross Park, isolated from the outside world," he tells me distractedly, leading me who knows where.

"Wait a minute." I pull my hand from his grasp and stop. "What are we doing in a remote forest outside of town?" I ask suspiciously.

He scrutinizes me seriously for a few seconds before saying, "Haven't you figured it out yet?" I shake my head. He takes a few slow steps toward me, watching me predatorily. "I brought you here because I intend to fuck you in every corner of this forest until you regret ever following me."

I look at him in horror, my heart hammering in my chest. "Wh... What?"

Seeing my disturbed expression he bursts into shoulder-shaking laughter. "I'm just fucking with you."

"That's funny to you?"

"Your face certainly is." He shakes his head, then resumes walking with his back to me.

"Well, one never knows what's going on in your head," I reply testily.

"What's the matter, Ness, don't you trust me?" he asks mildly, looking around for something.

"Of course not. I'd be crazy to trust someone like you!" I blurt out immediately. Thomas turns sharply with an anguished expression on his face. He stares at me and with one stride closes the distance between us. He seems disheartened by my words.

He gently touches my cheek, and I have to resist the urge to grab his hand and squeeze it. "I'm not the best person you'll ever meet, but you shouldn't be afraid when I'm around. I wouldn't harm a hair on your head," he tells me seriously, his eyes fixed on mine.

"Okay," I breathe apologetically. We move further into the woods, passing centuries-old shrubs and trees. "Do you come out here often?" I ask after a few minutes of silent walking.

He nods thoughtfully.

"Why?" We advance a few yards until the vegetation thins out a bit and we come to a small wooden bridge. I rush to lean over the edge, watching the river flow by below. It is beautiful, with the play of light and the reflection of the trees on clear water.

"It frees my mind," he says, joining me at the railing.

"Frees your mind?" I ask, turning around to look at him. This is new to me.

"Yeah, I stop thinking." He rests his forearms on the rail and watches the river.

"You stop thinking?" I ask, even more skeptically.

"Stop repeating what I say," he snaps impatiently.

"Sorry! It's just that, usually, people isolate themselves precisely because they want to think. You, on the other hand, do it to not think… You're a walking contradiction, Thomas." I shake my head, stifling a laugh.

"Do you think it's weird?" he asks, turning to me. "That our brain does nothing but process thoughts. We think all the time, all day long. Isn't it a pain in the ass sometimes?" I slowly shake my head.

"For me it is. Sometimes, all I want to do is stop thinking. There are people who cut themselves to do it, some people fuck, some people get drunk, some people do drugs…" He stares blankly, looking at some empty point in space. "When I get that feeling, I come here."

In a way, I think I understand it. This place is for him what books have always been for me: a refuge from reality.

"Why do you feel the need to stop thinking?"

He gives a troubled sigh. "Because when I do, I feel free."

"Free from what?" I'm asking too many questions, I know I am. But I can never figure out what's going on in his head, and I want so badly to know. His hard eyes linger on mine, and I am unable to resist them. And, for a split second, I even think that he is about to let me into his inaccessible world.

But then for some reason he looks away and just says, "From lots of things."

Disappointment washes over me. *Bravo, Thomas. Keep it up. Keep closing in on yourself. We'll make great strides this way.*

"And what does that have to do with me?"

"What do you mean?" He bends his head slightly toward me, confused.

"I mean, this is your little piece of paradise, right? You should guard it. Or is it just another way to impress girls?" I ask, in more sour a tone than I would have liked.

"I don't need to impress you if that's what you mean. I already know you like me, I'm not stupid," he says with his usual bravado.

"Thomas…" I laugh nervously and bend down to tie my sneakers as a distraction. "I don't like you. Not anymore, at least."

"Don't waste your time trying to bullshit me. I can see it in the way you look at me, the way your body reacts every time I touch you." My hands tremble at this observation. "We both know what's going on here."

I get back to my feet and clear my throat. "And what exactly is going on here?"

"I like you and you like me. But that's all it is: attraction."

"If that's all it is, why are you so set on wanting to be my friend? You're attracted to a lot of girls, Thomas. But you're not friends with any of them," I point out indignantly.

He takes a step toward me, coming so close that I feel his fresh breath on my face, it smells like the mint gum he's always chewing. "Because I am selfish, and I'd rather have you in my life as a friend than not have you at all," he admits without hesitation.

I shake my head. "That doesn't make sense."

"It does, though."

"Then explain it to me; I'm all ears." I cross my arms, waiting to understand.

He snorts and then decides to come clean. "I'm used to getting what I want, whenever I want it. But I suppose there are limits, even for a piece of shit like me."

"A limit you no longer intend to push with me?"

"Exactly."

"Why?"

"Because... You're different from the other girls I'm used to being with." He lowers his gaze, then raises it again and gives me a slight smile. "You're funny, simple, and naive. A pure soul. I like that about you, and I want you to keep being that way. My getting close to you would ruin you." He pauses, then adds, "And to answer your question, I've never brought anyone here."

"You brought me..."

"Yeah, and don't get any ideas about that. We're here because I didn't know where else to go." He lights a cigarette and then sits down with his legs dangling out over the river. I shake my head and finally give up on the idea of understanding him. I sit beside him, and we're silent together for a while. The river below us flows rapidly, and it is pleasant to listen to the splashing of water, the flow of the current, and the occasional honks of the waterfowl. Soon, though, the atmosphere grows heavy. I notice that Thomas is hunching his shoulders, his jaw clenched and his head bowed, as though brooding over something.

I want to ask him what he's thinking, but I know he won't tell me. I would like to hug him, to hold him tightly to me, but that would be inappropriate. I feel useless, I wish I could do more for him. Be more. It is for this reason that I decide to break the silence, even knowing I'm probably making the wrong move.

"Thomas..." I whisper after a while.

"Mhm?"

"Let me get to know you. For who you are, not who you pretend to be."

The way he looks at me, like a cornered animal, cowering but ready to attack, throws me off.

"I am exactly who I seem to be."

I shake my head in denial. "You don't fool me, Collins. I'm sure you are much more than that. I've thought so since the first time I sat next to you, that night outside the gymnasium, and I got confirmation when you came to my house."

"You should stop reading all those fucking romance novels. You're getting a completely skewed idea of men and feelings."

"Never. I'm sure that somewhere out there in the world, there are still men brave enough to fall madly in love with a woman and give themselves to her unreservedly. Fight for her, respect her, protect her from all the evils of the world. Make her laugh out loud. Make her theirs, for every minute of their lives. Just like in those 'fucking romance novels' that I love reading so much," I conclude proudly.

Thomas lowers his head, grinning. "You are completely doomed."

"So will you let me get to know you?" He stares at the river below us, ignoring my question. "I don't really know anything about you," I continue. "But you know a lot about me. I don't think that's fair."

"It's better for you this way," he cuts me off.

"That should be my decision, don't you think?" I draw small circles on the wood of the bridge. "If you really do want to be my friend the way you say, you should confide in me. At least a little bit," I insist earnestly, after more silence. "Otherwise, this relationship will just be a big joke."

He scrutinizes me silently, forehead wrinkling in a frown, as if he is mulling over my words. Then he takes a deep breath and, against all odds, gives up. "What do you want to know?"

I straighten up in disbelief. "Really?"

"I'll give you ten minutes, you little busybody. But don't get used to it."

"Okay! Well, let's see. First of all, I didn't know you do tattoos."

"I don't do them, not professionally, at least. Sometimes I'll do one if I'm at my friend's studio, but that's about it."

"Did you take a class?"

"No, it was my uncle who taught me. He has a studio in Portland,

and I used to stop by his place after school. Or before. Or during," he says with a wink.

"Did he do your tattoos? When did you start getting them?" I ask impatiently.

"I got my first one when I was fourteen." He shows me an anchor between his thumb and wrist. "He did almost all my tattoos, but the designs are mine."

His? Holy shit, he's a real artist.

"So, in addition to being a basketball god, you also know how to draw? You never cease to amaze, Collins. I told you that there was more to you!" I exclaim with conviction.

"Is the interrogation over?"

I pretend to think about it, tapping my index finger on my chin. "No. Not yet."

"Don't your batteries ever run out?" It seems that this curiosity of mine amuses him, because he looks at me with a tender expression, while still remaining his usual grumpy self.

I stick my tongue out at him and continue. "Favorite food?"

"What bullshit…" He shakes his head in resignation.

"I'm waiting…"

"Stew, maybe?"

"Really? I wouldn't have thought so. I, on the other hand, love oven-baked lasagna. Mom makes it from this finger-licking, real Italian recipe."

"Am I supposed to care?" He gives me a confused look, and I roll my eyes. I ignore his lack of interest in this conversation, and I barrel on.

"The ocean or the mountains?"

"You're really making me regret giving you the opportunity to ask questions."

I smile and try to move the conversation onto more personal topics in the hopes that he will let me. "Why did you come to Corvallis?"

Thomas rubs the back of his neck, staring straight ahead and growing suddenly tense. "I don't know. I got the scholarship, so we went."

"And do you go home often?" I ask in a softer tone of voice, trying to sound understanding rather than intrusive.

"Never. I haven't considered it my home for a long time."

"So, you came here to start over?"

He turns to look at me with his jaw set, making me dry swallow. "You can't escape the past," he answers grimly after a moment. "But I had been restless for a while already. My sister wanted me to stay with her. And I did, until I couldn't anymore. Then I left. Leila decided to come with me at the last minute."

"She turned her whole life upside down just to stay with *you*? She must love you a lot." I give him a tender look.

"I don't know how, but apparently she does," he murmurs penitently.

"Why shouldn't she?" I put a hand on his shoulder and feel all his muscles tense up. But this time, I don't withdraw. "You're her brother, and you're a good person." I pause for effect. "Sometimes."

"I know I'm not a good person, but I've been this way for so long that I don't know how to be anything else."

"Hey, look I was just joking... Of course you're a good person." But he remains silent, absorbed in who knows what kind of dark thoughts. "Do your parents know you're here?" I continue. When I see him shake his head and stare at a distant point on the horizon, my heart aches.

"They must be worried sick with their children missing, scattered who knows where."

"They are not, I assure you," he says resentfully.

"What happened?" I dare to ask.

In response, Thomas takes a big breath and gets to his feet.

"Your ten minutes are up." He wipes his hands on his jeans. "Come on, I want to show you something." He extends a hand to me and I take it gladly, squeezing slightly. Even though he refused to answer all my questions, I'm happy that he gave me the chance to discover something more about him.

"Where are you taking me now? An enchanted valley?" I hear him chuckle. He leads me up a slope until we come to a stop in front of a giant oak tree.

"There he is. That's him," he announces, raising one corner of his mouth.

"Who is he?" I ask, looking around bewildered.

"The tree." He slaps his palm against the bark as if it were the shoulder of a friend.

"I'm not following you."

"My piece of paradise." I let my gaze wander to the top of the tree. "It's him."

"An oak tree?" I ask, puzzled, and he nods. "You worry me."

"Get up," he orders.

"Excuse me, what?"

"Climb up." He points to the tree and I look at him incredulously.

"Are you seriously asking me to climb a tree? What'll you have me do next, find a banana?" I retort skeptically.

"I'll think about it. Though I could just give you my banana; I'm sure you'd appreciate it." He gives me a suggestive grin and my eyes open wide in indignation, my face in flames.

"Thomas!" I shout, hitting him on the shoulder and making him laugh with gusto. "You're still a crude perv."

He shakes his head and tells me, "You can't see it from down here—it's hidden by foliage—but there's a little tree house up there. You'll like it."

"And how am I supposed to get up there?" I cross my arms over my chest and wait for an explanation. Thomas takes me around the tree. "You see this?" It's a rope ladder, just barely hanging from the tree. "You put your little feet on the rungs and climb up."

I burst out laughing. Hysterically.

"Thomas, that must be more than fifteen feet up! The last time I climbed anything that high, I was taking the escalator at the mall."

"You'll get to the top in no time, you'll see," he answers, unconcerned.

"Are you blind, perhaps? Can you not see how huge that thing is?

I can't handle that!" He looks at me with a wicked grin, and I redden as I realize what I've just said.

"Stranger, you're really serving them up to me on a silver platter today."

"I didn't mean... I was obviously referring to the tree." I shake my head vigorously. "And I have no intention of climbing this tree, unless our little jaunt today also includes a detour to the hospital."

"I'm right down here. If you fall, I'll catch you."

If you fall, I'll catch you? That's it?

"Is that supposed to reassure me, King Kong? What if you don't catch me?"

"I lift heavier in the gym."

I see he never misses an opportunity to brag about his performance.

"Perfect. I'll die splattered on the ground like a cockroach, just because some hotheaded egomaniac wanted me to experience the thrill of climbing a freaking tree!"

He approaches with determination and looks at me intensely.

"I said I'll catch you. I promise," he reassures me. I examine the oak tree from the roots to the highest branches with a certain reluctance, and I force myself to think of a good reason to give in to him. I can't think of a single one. Yet, for some stupid, crazy reason, I do.

"You better hope to God that there really is an enchanted valley up there or I'm going to make you pay," I threaten, poking a finger into his chest.

"And how exactly do you intend to make me pay?" he asks, looking down at my finger and laughing.

"I don't know yet, but it will be terrible." I narrow my eyes to two slits.

"Mmh," he murmurs mischievously. "I can't wait."

I take a deep breath and try to concentrate. Then I think about the fact that I'm about to climb a tree. I cannot believe it!

With trembling legs I begin to slowly climb up, grasping the rope ladder in both hands as it sways with my every slightest movement. In some places, I even feel some resin sticking to my hands. Gross. I climb higher and higher, with the sun filtering through the foliage. After a minute, I stop to see where I am but I regret the impulse instantly.

Too high.

Too. High.

Another deep breath. I can do this.

"You're doing great, Ness." Despite the affectionate tone of his encouragement, all I want to do is throw a shoe at his head. Stupid, jerk-faced idiot. When I've almost reached the top, I catch a glimpse of a small wooden house, hidden among the leaves. I'm stunned—it's so beautiful!

"I think I've found it, Thomas!" I cry out, elated like a little girl.

"Oh yeah? It's not Wonderland, it's a tree. How many houses did you think you'd find up there?"

I lean down slightly to glare at him. "Don't you dare crap on my enthusiasm! Not after you forced me up a tree full of ants," I shout. "And stop looking at my ass like you want to…"

"Fuck it?" He interrupts me, making me flush with embarrassment. I glare down at him, while he smirks.

Five more steps and I finally reach the house, wedged between sturdy branches. With a little momentum, I manage to climb in without breaking any limbs. Inside, I find a blanket, a couple of empty beer cans, some snacks, and a notepad with some sketches in it. I settle in, and, while I wait for Thomas to join me, I give in to my curiosity and examine the notebook. I find several drawings there, each one more incredible than the last. Out of all of them, I am most enchanted by a winged snake, a phoenix rising from flames, and some sketchy tribal designs.

A few seconds later, Thomas arrives.

"You're fast."

"Or simply more agile and less wimpy than you," he answers with typical arrogance, snatching the notebook out of my hands and giving me an admonishing look for being unable to resist the urge to snoop.

"They're beautiful," I say sincerely, wiping bark residue from my hands.

He doesn't answer me. Instead, we sit silently in the doorway. I pull my legs up to my chest while Thomas stretches his out, letting them dangle in the air. "Is this stuff yours?" I ask gesturing at the junk lying all around. He nods. "Aren't you afraid someone will come and take it?"

"Hasn't happened yet. This little house is well hidden by the leaves, and the few people who pass this way after a hike don't pay it a lot of attention," he explains, swatting away some midges with his hand.

"It's like standing on top of the world's tallest mountain and having full control," I say captivated by the beauty of nature that surrounds us.

"Do you like it?" He smiles at me with a sweetness so unusual that it makes my stomach curl.

"A lot," I answer dreamily.

"I figured."

We spend the rest of the time lying side by side and, to my enormous surprise, I manage to extract a little more personal information from him. He tells me about the small group of friends that he used to shoot hoops with every afternoon as a child. How much he hated the Sunday lunches that his whole family attended. A simple life, seemingly quiet. Yet, as I listen to him telling me about it, I can't shake the feeling that he is giving me a distorted version of reality, omitting some parts while changing others. Fundamental parts, which I get the impression contain the source of all his cynicism and torment. And I think that is the real reason he left everything and moved to Corvallis. In any case, I don't want to push it. I've finally managed to get him to talk, and I don't want to risk ruining the moment.

He continues, telling me about the deep bond he had with his grandparents, who practically raised him and Leila and had passed away five years ago. In school, it was a classic case of a boy who had all the capability but didn't apply himself, he tells me. In fact, his steel-trap mind actually allowed him to goof off as much wanted, because he only ever needed to read someone's notes to get everything. He had a girlfriend. Yes, indeed, Thomas Collins had a girlfriend. At the age of sixteen. The first and only one: Elizabeth. It lasted more than a year before they broke up, but they still saw each other from time to time, until he moved to Corvallis and broke contact for good. I pretend to be indifferent to these revelations, but I am actually burning with jealousy knowing that there was a girl who got to enjoy a privilege that he no longer grants to anyone. Finally, I discover that he hates licorice and that his life's passions—besides basketball and drawing— are his irreplaceable motorcycle and his car, which he learned drive at age fifteen courtesy of his uncle. As he talks, he fiddles with a lock of my hair, a sunbeam warms our faces, the leaves move slowly above us, and the peace that hovers in the air makes it feel as though time has stopped.

"Ness?" He shakes my shoulder gently.

"Hmm…"

I hear him chuckle tenderly next to my ear. "We've gotta go."

"What?" I slur.

"It's six o'clock. You fell asleep."

What? Six o'clock?

I sit up immediately, rubbing my eyes.

"I fell asleep? But how? When?"

"You took a three-hour nap."

What the hell…

"I am mortified. You take me to this beautiful place and what do I do? I fall asleep."

"Don't worry. I didn't wake you up because of the way you were sleeping. You seemed pretty tired. Are you sure you can stay on top of your work and school?"

The way I was sleeping? I didn't drool, did I? Or worse, snore?! Oh God, please tell me I didn't snore. "Everything's under control, I just haven't gotten as much sleep lately," I explain as I check my phone. There's a text from Alex asking how I am and two from Tiffany; one to show me the new pair of stiletto heels she bought and another to ask what happened to me. There's nothing from Logan. It's strange, ever since we started dating, he's been texting me nearly every day. I reply to Alex and Tiff and stuff the phone in the pocket of my jeans.

"Why aren't you sleeping enough? I thought you were a sleepyhead."

He stands up, grabs the pack of cigarettes and holds out his hand to me to pull me up.

"It's a timing issue. My shift at the Marsy ends late, and I have to ride home on the bus, which takes a longer route at that time of night. Same thing goes for the morning when I have to go to school. Everything would be simpler if I lived on campus."

"There are still vacancies, why don't you apply?"

"My scholarship money doesn't cover funding for the dorms, but I'm hoping to be able to pay for housing with my salary from the Marsy. I just have to wait a few more months." When I start to crawl out of the tree house and look down, panic seizes me.

"Oh God, was it this high when we came up?" My legs tremble in the face of that long drop. Thomas nods, looking at me as if I had just asked the stupidest imaginable question while I swallow with difficulty.

"I...I can't go down," I stammer fearfully.

"Bullshit. You managed to get up here, you'll be able to get down."

"Going up is easier."

"Knock it off. In thirty minutes, you've got to be at work and I have shit to do," he tells me absentmindedly, his eyes fixed on his phone, texting intently with someone.

"Thomas!" I squeal, like a child who can't find the solution to a problem. He rolls his eyes and joins me, standing up with his back to me. What is he doing?

"Jump up," he demands impatiently.

"What?"

"Get on my back, I'll take you down."

"You really are out of your mind!" I blurt out.

"You got a better idea, Miss Chickenshit?"

"I don't know! But I'm not going to get on your back and increase the risk of breaking every bone in my body!"

"If you don't get on, I'll leave you here."

"You wouldn't."

"Try me," he challenges.

"You would really leave me here?"

He doesn't even reply. Impatient, he heads for the trunk, ready to go down.

Is he for real?!

"Thomas! Come back here! All right, all right, I'll get on your back!" I see his lips twist into a teasing smile. Within two seconds, he loads me on his back. I wrap my arms around his neck, my legs around his hips, squeezing tight. We get into position, and I close my eyes as we descend. This ladder is going to break, I am certain of it, and we will both crash to the ground.

As soon as Thomas's feet touch the ground, I release a huge sigh of relief and jump off him.

"Sorry," I murmur, adjusting my jeans.

"For what?"

"I get a little unbearable when I panic." I shrug, embarrassed to have appeared so cowardly.

"Don't worry, you're also unbearable when you're relaxed," he taunts me. I give him the finger in return, and he pretends to be shocked. We retrace our steps back to the bike. Ten minutes later, I find myself in front of the Marsy.

I get off, remove my helmet, and pause for a few seconds before returning it, just staring at him. "Do you always have two helmets on you? Isn't that cumbersome?"

Thomas lifts the black visor to get a better look at me but remains seated on the bike with the engine running. "Do you honestly think I walk around carrying two helmets all day every day like some kind of dumbass?"

Okay, maybe my question wasn't the smartest, but still...

"You had two helmets this morning before you even knew whether I would agree to come with you."

"You were leaving, and I wanted to be with you. So, before I caught up with you, I quickly asked Finn for his helmet. How do you come up with this shit?" He chuckles. My heart does a somersault at this little confession.

The alarm clock on my phone rings and reminds me that there's only five minutes until the start of my shift. "Now I have to go." I jerk my thumb toward Marsy's entrance behind me. "Thanks for today. It was...nice." I really think so.

"Have a good shift, stranger," he says with a smile. "And don't let them ogle you too much." He winks, lowers his visor, and leaves.

Twenty-Four

CONTRARY TO MY PREDICTIONS, THE bar is packed today because of the football game. All the tables are already occupied by fans who, between their conversations and laughter, create a general din. The only upside is that evenings like these are always big for tips.

"And this makes seventy, beautiful!" During a lull, I slam a wad of bills down on the wooden counter, each one of them earned with a strategic smile and a well-timed wink. Getting tips at the Marsy turned out to be easier than I expected, especially after I realized that the customers we serve are nothing more than brain-dead morons, who only need to see a flash of leg before they're ready to give away their life's savings. And then, with every dollar I earn, a little bit of that insecurity I've been carrying for as long as I can remember slips away from me.

"You're unbelievable, Nessy, with those cat eyes and that sexy mouth, you always hustle 'em," Maggie says, giving me a high five.

"Child's play." I try to make a haughty face and roll my eyes, but I burst out laughing instead. To be honest, the first few days I was like a plank of wood. Then Tiffany gave me some tips and, by God, they worked great. I fold the bills up and tuck them inside my bra.

"It's the pigtails," interjects our colleague Cassie in her usual vapid tones. "They give us that hint of innocence that contrasts with the sexy cheerleader uniform. And they literally lose their minds." Cassie is the quintessential sexy girl, her slender yet curvaceous physique nets her double the tips the rest of us make. She is perfect for this job because, unlike Maggie and me, she gets off on the attention.

Halfway through the evening I'm clearing a table for some new customers when I hear a familiar voice calling out to me.

"Hey, Vanessa." I turn around with my hands full of crumpled place mats and see Logan walking toward me at a brisk pace. He's wearing khakis, a blue sweater, and a pair of two-tone loafers. His facial features are tense, though, and his rapid stride makes me think he's worried.

"Hey! I'll be right with you." I place the wrappers in the dish tray, give the table a wipe down with a damp rag and seat the customers. Then I head for the bar, followed by Logan.

"What's going on, are you okay?"

"I was just about to ask you that question," he retorts worriedly.

"What do you mean?"

"I've been looking for you all afternoon. What happened to you?"

I let out a sarcastic laugh. Is he kidding me?

"What do you mean 'I've been looking for you all afternoon'? I didn't get a single call from you in the afternoon. In fact, I haven't received any calls or texts from you all day. But you were busy packing, I understand." I smile at him and grab everything I need to set up the tables in my section.

"No, wait a minute. I was busy packing until lunchtime, that's true. But as soon as I finished, I called you. Three times. I even left you a voicemail, but you never responded."

What is he talking about?

"Maybe you were calling the wrong girl," I say sardonically, but he doesn't seem to be in the mood for jokes.

"No, I'm pretty sure I called you." He takes his phone from his pocket and shows me the calls and the message.

Yet, I didn't receive anything. Maybe I didn't have bars at the top of a tree?

I shrug apologetically. "I was probably in a spot with poor cell reception. I don't know what else to think." I leave him waiting at the bar while I go fetch an order.

"Why, where were you?" he asks me when I return to him.

I'm silent for a moment, considering what to say. If I tell him that I spent the whole day with Thomas, he might misunderstand, and that's not what I want. But lying to him would be worse. "I took a nature hike. The rest of afternoon I spent sleeping." It's true, in a way.

"You had me worried. I was about to go over to your house to make sure everything was okay." He smiles and touches my cheek.

"Bad move. You would have found my mother and left bitterly repentant." We both laugh.

"Look, I can't stay long, I have to get back to campus in less than an hour. My roommate is waiting for me, I promised him some *Call of Duty* before I leave. Can you take a little break?" he asks with a twinkle in his eye. I take a quick glance around the room and make sure the tables in my section are all served. Then I nod to Maggie, who is on the opposite side, and ask her if she can cover for me. She gives me the thumbs-up and looks at Logan approvingly. I smile and we walk outside. We decide to go to the parking lot behind the Marsy for more privacy. We stop at a more secluded corner, and I lean back against the wall of the building. Logan stands in front of me, entwining his hands with mine.

"Hi," he whispers softly.

"Hi," I repeat just as softly.

"I like these pigtails." He takes one and plays with it a bit. "And this uniform. I'm not a jealous guy, but I have to admit that it really bothers me that everyone can see you dressed like this." He examines me from head to toe.

"I hate these stupid braids, they make me feel ridiculous."

"You say that because you don't see yourself with my eyes. You're so beautiful."

"Stop it, come on, you're making me blush." I lower my eyes, embarrassed.

"I asked you to come out here because I wanted to give you something."

He pulls a small square box out of his pants pocket and places it in my hands. "These are for you, I wanted to give them to you this afternoon."

I come away from the wall, thrilled, and open the box. Inside I find heart-shaped caramel chocolates. I look up at him, amazed. "Did you buy me chocolates?" I ask. It may seem trivial to him, but I've never received any from anyone in my life.

He shrugs. "I'll be gone for a few days. If you're missing me, you can eat one and think of me. Because I will be thinking of you all the time." He strokes my cheekbone with his thumb.

"You know these won't last more than an hour in my possession, don't you?" I joke.

"Are you telling me that I need to find a more effective way to make you think about me?" Without giving me a chance to reply, he closes his eyes and slowly brings his face closer to mine.

Oh, no, this is the moment. He's going to kiss me.

His lips land on mine. They are soft, warm. He caresses one cheek and slides his other hand down my ribs, pressing his body against mine. He kisses me slowly, sweetly and it is wonderful. But I don't feel anything. No tingling in my belly. No trembling in my knees. My mind is clear, not scattered across some unknown galaxy. Kissing Logan is pleasant, but not overwhelming.

"I really like you, Vanessa. I've wanted to do this since the very first day I saw you," he whispers against my lips.

"I like you too." And that's the truth. Even if we didn't ignite with passion right away, that doesn't mean it won't flare to life in the future. In fact, it doesn't even have to be there, necessarily. With Travis, the passion had faded so quickly. With Thomas, there was way too much of it, as far as I'm concerned. And things ended badly in both cases. I wrap my arms around his neck, he slides one hand along my bare thigh, lifting it a little. We continue kissing until a group of boys passes us, hooting and hollering and telling us to get a room. I pull away from Logan and bring a timid hand to my lips. He laughs softly.

"Maybe we'd better go back inside." He takes me by the hand and we make our way toward the entrance.

"Vanessa?"

I turn sharply.

"Matt?" I exclaim in amazement.

Okay, now this is awkward.

My boss's nephew just caught me making out behind the bar. But things somehow get worse when I notice the guy next to him. Thomas is staring at us with fury in his eyes.

"H…hey," I stammer, trying to tamp down the anxious feeling growing inside me. I smile at him, but he doesn't smile back. He leans his elbow on Matt's shoulder and, turning to Logan with contempt, sneers: "Your uncle ought to limit the number of rich dicks he lets in. They steal the waitresses and won't even buy a fucking beer." He passes us, shoulder-checking Logan roughly.

For a few seconds, I'm dazed. Why does he feel the need to be such an asshole whenever I'm with Logan?

"Excuse me?" Logan demands furiously, but Thomas ignores him.

"Don't pay too much attention to him," Matt suggests, "he's having a bad night."

I should have guessed that this afternoon's version of Thomas would become just a fleeting memory. Matt waves at us and goes inside, while Thomas stops to finish his cigarette. He leans his back against the wall and crosses one leg over the other, looking right at me. Logan notices and takes me by the hand. I instinctively pull back but then, stung by guilt, I interlace my fingers with his.

"Nice legs, Ness. You should show 'em off more often." Thomas winks at me, blowing out a lungful of smoke when I pass by him.

"I see you're back to being a troglodyte," I say acidly.

He shrugs and watches the cigarette smoke rise.

I start to go inside but Logan reaches out a hand to stop me.

"I'm curious, Thomas: How does it feel, wanting something that you can't have?"

Oh my God. Why, Logan, why?

With one move, Thomas is on him. He stops short, just an inch from his face. "What did you say to me?" he growls through gritted teeth.

"Thomas, stop it," I interject, trying to push them apart, but neither of them seems inclined to listen to me.

"You heard me," replies Logan calmly, looking him right in the eye.

"Tell me." Thomas slaps a hand to his chest and says in an almost imperceptible whisper, "What can't I have?"

"Seems obvious to me," Logan says defiantly, throwing a glance in my direction. "It's why you hate me. It must be frustrating, huh?" My mouth drops open in astonishment, and I frown at him. What the hell is wrong with him? Thomas takes a deep breath, looking like he's about to explode. And at the exact moment when I think he's going to attack, he pauses, a sinister grin painted on his face. He looks at me for an interminable moment, and I silently beg him to remain calm.

Then he looks at Logan, clicks his tongue against the roof of his mouth, and proclaims, "I could fuck her right now if I wanted to. Right here in front of you, just to show you how fucking wrong you are. You can fool her with that choirboy face, but not me. The truth is, you're a fucking psychopath pretending to be a gentleman. You can fuck every waitress in the state of Oregon, but none of them will ever belong to you either," he spits at Logan with such hatred that it leaves me horrified.

"The facts suggest otherwise," retorts Logan with an icy calm that only stokes Thomas's anger. Logan puts a hand on my waist and pulls me close to him.

What the...

I don't have time to pull away before Thomas is grabbing him by the collar of his sweater and slamming him against the wall with unimaginable violence. He punches Logan square in the face, splitting his lip.

I gasp and clasp my hands over my mouth in fright. Before I can think twice, I put myself between the two of them. I close my eyes and cover my face with my hands, ready to absorb the next punch headed for Logan. But it doesn't come. I uncover my face slowly, and I see Thomas's arm raised a few inches from my face, his angry eyes boring into me. "Move," he orders peremptorily. At that point, seized by an uncontrollable rush of adrenaline, I grab his leather jacket and push him back with all the strength I have. I don't know how, but I actually manage to get him away from Logan. I am about to lash out at him with all the fury in my body, but then I freeze. His gaze is glassy, cold. Full of suffering. There is a gleam in his eye that is completely foreign to me. Matt's right. Something is wrong tonight.

I press my hands to his chest in an attempt to calm him, but he pulls back wildly. "Thomas! What's the matter with you?" I stare at him, alarmed.

"This asshole provokes me, and somehow I'm the problem?" he rants, gesturing at Logan behind us.

"You started it!"

Thomas's breathing is labored as he begins to pace back and forth in an attempt to control the anger that seems to be devouring him from the inside out.

"You're getting fucked behind a bar and expect me to be cool with it?"

"That's not what I was doing!"

"Then what the fuck were you doing?"

I scrub my hand over my face and shake my head. "Thomas, I don't know what is going on with you tonight, but you can't just take your anger out on other people! Just because you and I are friends now, that doesn't mean that what I do in my personal life is any of your business!" I burst out.

He looks like I've stuck a knife in his chest, and I almost feel guilty in the face of such suffering. Then, without another word, he walks away around the side of the bar, and I hear him go inside: the sound of a violently slammed door echoes across the parking lot.

Confused and disturbed, I turn to Logan. I am angry with him as well, but when I see his bleeding lip, I reach for him.

"Oh my God, I...I'm so sorry. Are you okay?" I lift his chin with my trembling fingers and he grimaces in pain.

"No. I'm not okay. He's out of his mind, that guy." He uses his thumb to wipe a dribble of blood from the corner of his mouth.

"Yeah, well, he...he's not in a good headspace right now. And you were provoking him. Why did you do that?" I ask, distressed.

"Are you excusing him and blaming me? Let me remind you that I'm the one who got punched in the face!" he shouts, massaging his jaw with a surly look.

"Yes, I know. Sorry…" I lower my eyes, mortified. "I'm not excusing him, but this whole situation could have been avoided. Why did you have to goad him?"

"Because in case you didn't notice, he was doing the same to me." I fall silent. "Tell me the truth: What is going on between you two?"

Panic seizes my throat. My eyes grow wide. "Nothing."

"But there was…wasn't there?"

"No." I stare at the asphalt underneath my feet.

"Vanessa…" he says, urging me to say more.

"It's not a big deal, Logan."

He tilts his head and lets out a frustrated sigh, sensing that this will be my only answer. He's silent for a moment before asking, "Do you like him?"

"We're friends."

Logan purses his lips. "You have to be honest with me. It's clear that he likes you, but I can accept that. I have to know, though, if you like him back. Because in that case, I'm just wasting my time."

"It doesn't matter whether I like him or not. What matters is that I could never be with someone like him. I already had a guy like that, one who didn't respect me enough, and I learned my lesson. I want to feel good, Logan, and you make me feel good. You worry about me, you treat me with kindness. You hold doors open for me, and you even got me chocolates." I smile. "Small things, but no one has ever done them for me before," I admit in a whisper.

He moves a pigtail behind my shoulder and touches my cheek. "Okay, if you say Thomas is not a threat, then I believe you." He kisses my lips gently, and I reciprocate.

"I want to be your boyfriend, Vanessa. I won't force you to decide right now, but I am asking you to give me an answer when I come back to Corvallis, if you can."

An answer…about us?

Suddenly, it feels like there's a heavy weight on my chest and I struggle to breathe. I'm happy with Logan, but I don't think I can feel for him what he feels for me. Fortunately, Maggie pops out of the back door and calls me back in, allowing me to put the subject on hold for a little while at least.

"Are you coming in too?" I ask.

"No, I have to get going." He gives me a sincere smile. "Plus, Thomas is in there. Best not to poke the bear." What the hell is wrong with me? Why am I not madly in love with this guy who looks at me like I'm a goddess?

"Okay then...see you when you get back?" I ask, a bit melancholy.

"You can bet on it. And I'll call you. Frequently," he smiles.

"And I will answer. Frequently. And don't worry about Thomas." We exchange a knowing look and kiss each other for the last time.

When I enter, I see that Thomas, Matt, and their group of friends have taken a table in my section. I curse under my breath and head over to take their order. "Please explain why all your customers are incredibly hot dudes while mine are all well north of forty and wearing dentures?" asks a particularly whiny Cassie when I return to the bar.

"We can switch, if you want," I suggest as I start pouring two pints of beer for their table.

"What?" Her eyes light up.

"You'd be doing me a favor, actually. There's a guy over there I really want to avoid." Cassie looks at me like I've lost my mind. I slide the pints toward her, along with an order of chicken wings that just arrived from the kitchen. "Go ahead, these are for them."

She adjusts her cleavage and, not needing to be asked twice, hurries over to their table.

An hour later, I am still working all my tables, except for number eleven. Thomas does nothing but stare at me and, every time I walk past him, I have to resist the urge to meet his eyes. I head to a table that is finally about to leave and exchange small talk with a guy not much older than me, implementing some of my tried-and-true tip-getting tactics. Before he leaves, the boy puts an arm around me and pulls me close to him, smiling up at me. He pulls some bills out of his wallet and wedges them between the band of my skirt and my skin. I gently move his hand from my hip before smiling at him and walking away.

I am about to pass table eleven, when a tattoo-covered hand grabs my wrist, sending a shiver along my spine.

"Stop."

Frowning, I slowly lower my gaze to him. "I suggest you take your hand off me, otherwise you'll have to deal with our bouncer, Sean. And, believe me, he doesn't care if you're here with the boss's nephew. He will throw you out one by one," I say, with deliberate emphasis.

Thomas raises an eyebrow, not remotely intimidated. "Come outside. I need to talk to you."

"I can't. I'm working."

"Yeah, I can see that. Are you enjoying yourself?" he asks with a nasty grin, looking pointedly at the bills sticking out of the top of my skirt.

I roll my eyes. "They're just tips. Stop acting like an overprotective big brother," I snap in annoyance.

He purses his lips and tugs my wrist, forcing me to bend closer to him until my ear is near his mouth. In doing so, I cannot help but breathe in his masculine, sensual scent: vetiver, bodywash, and…Jack Daniel's? Has he been drinking? How did I not notice? His lips are touching my skin; my stomach twists, and I employ every bit of will-power I have to keep myself from getting swept away by the tingling sensation underneath my skin.

"Big brother? Seriously?" He rasps.

"That's what you're acting like. Leave me alone, Thomas, you've done enough damage for one evening." I straighten up and try to free myself, but he only tightens his grip.

"You're still pissed off about earlier, aren't you?"

"No, of course not. What would make you think so?" I answer with a sarcastic grimace. I can feel the discomfort radiating off of Matt and the other boys at the table.

Thomas loosens his grip on my wrist and runs a hand through his hair. "I talked a lot of shit, I know. But I was pissed."

"And, as always, that seems to be reason enough for you to completely lose control," I reply, pretending to be impassive. My response seems to irritate him because he releases my wrist entirely and lets me go.

"Do not tell me that the guy you're avoiding is that giant hottie with all the muscles and tattoos?!" Cassie demands in a shrill voice when I join her behind the bar. I remind myself that murder is illegal in all fifty states.

"Bingo."

"You've got to explain that one to me."

"There's nothing to explain," I mutter.

"I just saw you two talking. One minute, I thought you were going to rip each other's clothes off, the next minute, I thought you were going to start throwing hands. What are you two? Sworn enemies? Friends? Lovers who can only love each other under the covers and must hate each other in the light of day?" She titters.

I roll my eyes with a huff. "Friends, Cassie. Just friends." With poor results, I might add.

"That is excellent news, because I've been daydreaming about biting his lips ever since he walked in here. I don't think I've ever seen such a perfect body. I want to taste it. How about giving me his number, eh?"

"I don't have it."

Her eyes bulge in disbelief. "How is that possible?"

I shrug. "We never exchanged numbers. But, if you want it so much, just ask him. He's only a few feet away." Cassie raises her eyebrows and laughs as though I've said something ridiculous.

"Babe..." She pats my back with a red-nailed hand and gives me a big smile, as if I were a child to whom an elementary concept is being explained. "I can't just ask him for his number. It's the second most important rule of the dating code."

I look at her, dumbfounded. "What are you talking about?"

"Never ask a guy for his number: if you do, he'll know you're into him and he'll think he's hooked you and then—poof!—he'll suddenly lose all interest in you."

I frown. "And the first rule would be...?" I ask, though I'm not at all sure I want to hear the answer.

"Don't look at him. Ever."

"But if you never look at him, how do you let him know you're interested?" I ask, increasingly confused.

"Yes! That's the trick. He shouldn't know."

How idiotic. I don't have time to discover any more made-up rules because Maggie interrupts to tell us that her shift is over. That means in an hour Cassie will also be gone, thank God. And, finally, in just two more hours I can get out of this place. I'm exhausted.

Twenty-Five

HALF AN HOUR BEFORE THE end of my shift, I find myself in a nearly empty bar with only Thomas still sitting at his table. Matt and the others have already left and, to tell you the truth, I'm surprised that Thomas didn't take the opportunity to go back to campus with some new bedpost-notch.

Irritated, I join him at the table. "Thomas, I'm about to close up. Go home." I gather up the last empty glasses on the table and leave his, still full of amber liquid.

"Don't feel like it." He turns a cigarette over in his hands.

"Maybe you don't know this, but a bar is really the last place you should seek refuge when you're feeling sad." I look at him and see nothingness in his gaze.

"This is not a real bar," he snorts unhappily.

"Same concept."

"What makes you think I'm sad?" he asks in a teasing tone.

Your goddamned eyes.

"Are you?"

He shrugs in response, avoiding my gaze.

"Why did you come here?"

He sighs and straightens his spine. "For this." He raises his glass. "And these." he looks at my legs, brushing my right thigh with his knuckles. I wince, ready to move away immediately.

I raise my eyebrows. "Are you drunk?"

"I don't get drunk, Ness," he insists with a mocking smile.

"Yeah, sure. How many have you had since you got here?"

"Five or six. No, maybe eight or nine. I lost count... I've been here a while."

"You're definitely drunk. Let me take you home on the bus, it'll be for the best."

"There's no way I'm leaving my car here. I'd find it stripped to the wheels tomorrow, maybe not even those." He gestures slowly.

"Are you planning on spending the night in here? I'm warning you, Derek won't be pleased."

He pulls his keys out of his jacket pocket and dangles them in the air. "Drive me."

"Thomas, if I drive you, I'll miss the midnight bus. The next one doesn't come until one o'clock. I can't, I'm sorry. I'll call you a cab." I pull out my phone and start dialing, but he blocks my hand.

"I said I won't leave the car here. Forget it. I'll get back to campus on my own." He gets up, wobbling a little, and downs the last bit of Jack Daniel's before heading for the exit.

"Where are you going? You're in no condition to drive!" I shout.

He turns toward me just enough for me to see him smirk. "Suppose I'll have to do it anyway." He opens the door but then, as if suddenly remembering something, he marches back inside and walks up to me. "F-forgot to pay," he mumbles. He pulls a couple of bills from the pocket of his jeans and lays them on the table. He folds one, places it between his middle and forefingers and then slips it into my cleavage. "Just the way you like it." He grins, so pleased with himself that, if he weren't drunk, I'd gladly slap him in his smug face. But as he can barely stand upright, I take a deep breath and keep my composure.

"You're completely out of it... Sit down. I'll take you home," I order sternly.

He doesn't object. He does what I tell him and sits down, crossing his arms and resting his head on top of them.

I go back to the bar, thoroughly irritated. I wipe it down one more time with a damp cloth, take out the garbage and recycling, and put the last of the dirty glasses in the dishwasher. I grab a small bottle of water from the refrigerator and bring it to him.

"Here, pretend it's Jack Daniel's. My shift ends in twenty minutes. Then we're leaving."

He lifts his head and two shiny, reddened eyes look at me. He slurs something, but I don't catch half the words.

After counting the cash three times, I put the money in an envelope and scribble the date on the outside before putting it in the safe. I collect my tips and Logan's box of chocolates, and I head to the changing room downstairs. I try to grab my spare clothes from my backpack but I notice that they are damp. I don't believe it. I left a water bottle in my bag without checking to make sure it was fully closed. Good thing I didn't bring any books. I resign myself to the idea that I will have to go home in this damn cheerleading uniform and slip on my jacket. I untie the stupid pigtails and join Thomas at the table.

"Wait here for me, I'm going to throw these away," I tell him, nodding at the garbage bags I have in my hands.

"I'll take care of it." He starts to get up, but I push him back down.

"No way, you can't even stand up."

I don't give him time to answer back before I'm already outside the bar.

The air is cold and biting, though I suppose that being basically half-naked doesn't help at all. Looking around the Marsy's parking lot, I see a black SUV. I guess that's Thomas's, as it's the only car left. It looks like it just rolled out of the shop, so shiny and perfect. One thing is certain: if I scratch it up, he would deserve it. I resist the urge, however. I've had enough trouble today already.

I duck back inside the bar and signal for him to follow me. "Come on, let's go." I want to sound stern, but there's a softness in my voice that betrays me.

"You leave work dressed like that?" He looks at my uniform with disapproval.

"I don't have a choice. My change of clothes is in here, and it's soaked," I say, showing him my backpack. With one hand I help him up, but he falters. I put his muscular arm around my shoulder to support him. "You're so stupid, Thomas." I shake my head. It's not just anger that moves me to scold him. The truth is, I don't like seeing him reduced to such a state.

"Once at a party, I met a pretty okay girl who had more alcohol than blood in her body. When I told her she was stupid, she tried to knock me out with a punch," he whispers in my ear, bringing back the memory of the night I got wasted at Matt's frat house.

A hit, a very palpable hit.

"Well, I'd say you were both stupid, then." I look at him, stifling a laugh.

Thomas rests his cheek against my head and mutters something unintelligible in a thick voice. I load him into the car and I lean over him to buckle his seat belt. "Always so cautious…" he teases me with a slightly crooked smile on his face. Even dead drunk, he remains irresistible.

"You can never be too careful," I tell him firmly. I turn my head in his direction and find myself just inches from his face.

"I agree. Why don't you stay in this position and make sure everything is…rock solid," he murmurs, reducing his voice to a sensual hiss.

What?

It takes me a few moments to grasp his meaning, but when I get there, I immediately pull myself out of the passenger seat, banging my head against the roof in my haste.

"Ouch!" I rub my head, wrinkling my nose. He explodes with laughter. "You're such a pervert!" I say, punching him lightly in the shoulder. I walk around the car and get in the driver's seat. There's a huge gap between my feet and the pedals, so I slide the seat as far forward as I can, raise the seat higher and then I adjust the side mirrors.

"You're messing up my whole situation," he protests, frowning.

Listen to him—I'm messing up his "situation."

"Maybe you'll think about that next time before you get wasted at my workplace," I admonish him.

He doesn't answer but only closes his eyes and rests his head against the slightly open window. I place Logan's chocolates in the center console and notice Thomas looking at them askance.

"Who gave you those?"

"Logan."

A kind of angry huff escapes from his throat. He grabs the box with his usual casual entitlement. For a moment, I'm afraid he's going to fling it out the window. Instead he flips it over. " Caramel…" he mumbles. "He doesn't know shit even when it comes to chocolates." He opens the box and, without asking permission, unwraps a piece and brings it to his mouth.

"Hey!"

"What?"

"He got those for me."

"I'll have to send my apology in writing," he taunts, plucking another one.

"Didn't you just say they sucked?"

"I need the sugar."

Sure, right. He devours each chocolate with a sinister satisfaction that gives me the shivers. It's as though the box of caramels has somehow wronged him.

I decide not to push it. Thomas is drunk, and I don't really want to argue.

The trip is smooth, the streets are empty and silent, and this car drives like a dream.

"Ness, you need to know something," he mutters after a while. "Something that'll piss you off. A lot." He takes a pause and I see him looking at me sideways.

"What?" I demand with my eyes fixed on the road. Now I'm on high alert.

"This afternoon, while you were sleeping… That dickhead wouldn't stop calling you."

It only takes me a few seconds to understand what he's saying and, before he even finishes explaining himself, I'm braking hard. The wheels slip on the asphalt, and the car skids slightly.

"What the fuck, are you crazy?!" He straightens up, pale, and looks wildly in all directions. "Somebody could have run into us! Get out, you're a hazard. I'm driving!" He fumbles with his seat belt and moves to get out of the car, but I activate the child safety locks and stop him.

"Don't you dare get out of that fucking seat, Thomas!" I yell, surprising him with my language. I pull over, unbuckle my seat belt, and lean toward him, my eyes smoldering with rage. "Did you or did you not put your hands on my phone?"

"I was trying to tell you."

I look at him in shock for a handful of seconds, silent, just blinking. "You...you...you're joking! Tell me you are joking! You took it upon yourself to reject calls from the guy I'm dating while I was asleep? What is wrong with you?"

"I don't know why I did it, okay?" he says, annoyed.

Annoyed. He's annoyed. Suddenly I am overcome by a blind fury. I leap over the seat and perch on his legs. I lash out at him, hitting him repeatedly in the chest.

"What the fuck are you doing, stop it!" he shouts at me, in shock.

"No, I won't stop it! You're sick! Presumptuous! Possessive! Who the hell do you think you are, huh? You reject calls for me on my phone, you threaten Logan, you punch him." I hit him again, for emphasis.

Thomas tries to grab my wrists but fails. His reflexes have been deadened by alcohol. "Calm down! You're overreacting!"

I know, I'm going crazy because of you!

"Tell me why you did it!" I scream, ready to hit him again but he finally manages to grab my wrists, pinning them both behind my back.

"Because I can't stand to see you with him. I can't stand seeing you with anyone," he confesses forcefully, his mouth inches from my own.

I freeze instantly, breathless. Thomas releases my wrists. I could try to parse that sentence, but I won't. Instead, I rub my face and tuck my hair behind my ears. I take a breath to calm down, and only then do I realize that, caught up in my outrage, I have straddled Thomas. His hands are resting on my thighs. I look up and realize that he is staring at me with eyes full of desire. I feel that strange tingling in my belly that only he seems to cause. I know what is about to happen. But no. I won't allow it.

"Don't do it."

"Don't do what?" He challenges me with his usual smartass look, sinking his fingers into the exposed flesh of my legs.

"Don't kiss me. Don't touch me. You're drunk and clearly worked up about something. Don't use me as a release valve. Do it with the other ones, but not with me." It's almost a plea, because there is a part of me that desperately yearns to be kissed by him, but the rest of me knows that would be a grave mistake.

After lingering for a few seconds, Thomas lets his head fall back against the headrest and sighs in frustration. He removes his hands from my legs as if it costs him a great deal of effort, and I get back in the driver's seat, adjusting my skirt. I sit motionless for a moment, staring out at the dark, empty road ahead of me, trying to put my thoughts in order.

"Why did you tell me?" I ask finally, gripping the steering wheel tightly in both hands.

"What?"

"About the phone. You could have not done it, pretended not to know anything…"

"That was my plan," he admits. I turn to look at him and watch his Adam's apple bob. "You said you don't trust me. And I don't blame you, I pull a lot of shit, I'm unreliable and unmanageable. But I want your trust. Being honest with you is the only way I can think to get it."

He secretly deletes calls and messages from my phone and then he wants me to trust him… My God, it's so hard to keep up with him. I can't pretend that I didn't appreciate his honesty, though.

"Will you do it again?"

"Probably."

"You are hopeless." I shake my head resignedly. "I'll take you to campus." Thomas slumps back against the window. We drive in silence but, from time to time, I can feel his burning gaze on me. "Every guy in that bar was drooling over your legs. You've filled their spank banks for years to come," he says suddenly, brazenly, giving my legs a sneaky look.

"Come on… It's just a work uniform." I shrug it off, embarrassed.

"It took all the self-control I have not to grab you and slam you down on a table every time you passed by. Give every creep in that place something to really look at."

His vulgarity takes my breath away. His insolence makes me blush. My body, though, quivers at his words, at the possibility of them becoming a reality. Is it possible that some part of me is secretly attracted to this barbaric and shameless side of him, so at odds with my own preoccupation with decency?

I clear my throat, trying not to let any emotion show. "That's because you're a primitive troll." Arriving on campus, I put it in park and turn off the engine. "We're here." I get out, walk around the car, and try to help him get upright.

"I may be a primitive troll. But you…" he whispers, his lips pressed almost to my ear, so close that I shudder. "You are too beautiful."

I bite my lip, trying to keep the storm inside me at bay. The little voice in my head comes to my rescue, it reminds me that he is drunk and that I must not under any circumstances make the same mistake again.

"I'll take you back to your room," I tell him in a low, trembling voice.

"That was your plan all along, wasn't it?" he snickers, grinning arrogantly. I ignore him and lead him past the common area, which is completely deserted. We take the elevator up to the fourth floor and walk down the hallway until we reach his door.

"The key is in the back pocket of my jeans. You have to get it, I can't reach."

I snort. "That was your plan all along, wasn't it?" I tease.

Not that the idea of touching his butt bothers me all that much, actually. He smiles faintly. I open the door and I realize that his dorm suite is huge. The living room is furnished with a coffee table, a sofa under the window and a small kitchenette. My room was a hole in comparison.

"Where do you sleep?"

He nods to a door on our left.

The opposite room belongs to Larry, who is asleep and snoring loudly. I was expecting a pretty macho space, but instead I find myself in a sterile, white-walled room with a basic bed, a desk, and a shelf with a picture of Thomas and Leila hugging each other. She is smiling, he is not. The frame is pink and glittery, and I can tell right away that this photo is only here at Leila's behest. I smile to myself.

I hear Thomas fumbling around behind me so I turn to help him out of his jacket. His movements are slow and awkward. Light-years away from the way I usually see him. He throws himself onto the bed still fully dressed and stares blankly at the ceiling.

"Are you okay?" He shakes his head but doesn't answer. "I'm guessing you don't want to talk about it." I meant for it to be a question, but it comes out like a statement. He ignores me and closes his eyes. A clear signal: it's time for me to leave. "Suit yourself. It's late, I'm leaving."

"Wait." He lifts his head and throws me his car keys, which I surprisingly manage to catch. "Here, bring it back to me tomorrow."

"I'm not taking your car." I chuckle.

"I'm not letting you take the bus at this time of night, dressed like that. Take the car, end of discussion. Or stay here. Your choice."

"I choose the car."

"Careful with the paint job."

I roll my eyes. Before I leave, I bring him a glass of water and fish out a bottle of painkillers from the cabinet in the bathroom. I set it all on his nightstand along with a packet of tissues. I retrieve a bowl from the kitchen and put it on the floor next to his bed. Finally, I slip his phone out of his jacket pocket and rest it beside him. As I am doing all of this, I feel his eyes on me and do my best to not blush.

"What are you doing?" he asks cautiously.

"Uh...um...I've put some things in easy reach for you. You know, if you need to throw up, you've got it all right here." I worry the ends of my hair. I must seem like a complete idiot to him. I'd better disappear before he starts making fun of me.

He sits up with his knees slightly apart and reaches out a hand toward me. He pulls me closer, into the space between his legs. "You're sweet…" He wraps his arms around my waist and presses his forehead to my partially exposed midriff. The skimpy uniform shirt ends just below my ribs. Suddenly I feel the need to give him a hug, to comfort him. I slide my hands into his hair and stroke his scalp. I can feel his mouth curving into a smile against my skin. Before I realize what he's doing, his lips are on my belly. I startle, and the heat is rising again, under my skin and between my thighs. Unable to react, I narrow my eyes and watch him trace a trail of slow, wet kisses down my belly. His hands slip eagerly under my skirt, until he reaches my butt; he squeezes it firmly and pulls me down, forcing me to sit on his lap. He rests his forehead on mine, sinking his fingers into the flesh of my buttocks. An electric shock runs down my spine. I grip his hair tighter and he grinds me against his pelvis. The friction makes me moan. My body is drunk on the touch of this tattooed, arrogant, tormented boy. He is like a drug for me, impossible to resist.

"You are not a release valve," he hisses through clenched teeth. Then he kisses the hollow of my throat and the contrast between his warm tongue and the cold metal of his piercing scrambles my brain. Our breaths quicken, excitement grows inside me and merges with his, but when his tongue moves dangerously close to my lips, the smell of alcohol calls me back from the edge I was about to pitch over.

"Thomas, stop…" I put my hands on his chest and push him away. His eyes, pupils dilated, fill with bitterness and frustration.

"Fuck," he murmurs in a soft voice, as if aware that he was in the wrong. I get up and adjust my skirt.

"I-it's okay. You're not yourself right now."

With a frustrated sigh, he buries his face in my belly again and clenches his fists against my back. He has the body of a broken man, but the soul of a lost child. Seeing him like this destroys me. "What's wrong, Thomas?"

"I'm grieving, Ness. And it's my fault."

My blood runs cold. I take his face in my hands and force it up to look him in the eye. "What are you talking about?"

"Nothing. Go home," he orders. He lies down on the bed and collapses immediately into a deep sleep.

I remain paralyzed before him. What the hell does that mean?

Twenty-Six

I STAY UP ALL NIGHT thinking and rethinking his words. Thinking about his sad eyes and his arms that held me so desperately. I don't know which is more galling, the mystery of his ominous words or the knowledge that I want to feel those arms around me all the time. I wanted to lie down beside him, to stroke back the tousled hair that fell over his forehead and get lost cataloging every tiny detail of his perfect face. But I couldn't—I shouldn't. Before leaving the room for good, I took a few minutes to scrutinize that powerful body, laid out helpless on the mattress, completely defenseless. I touched his forehead, let my hand slide over his cheek, on to his chin and, without realizing it, my thumb came to rest on his lips. I don't know what was going on in my head, perhaps it was the knowledge that he would never know? That it would remain my little secret.

I moved closer and gave him a gentle, closemouthed kiss, enjoying the softness of those lips. It was only then that I realized how much I had missed them. As soon as I pulled away, I felt an instant sense of loss. And a frightening truth revealed itself: Thomas has somehow, in some way still unknown to me, managed to creep inside me, and no matter how hard I try to believe otherwise, I don't want to drive him out.

By the time my alarm clock goes off, I have been awake for several hours already. I turn it off and stare at the ceiling and just keep touching my lips, which still taste of him. I take a deep breath and go start a shower.

The water has been running for a while already, but it's still ice cold. I'm shaking like a newly hatched chick.

"Mom!" I shout, hoping she's still at home.

No response. I get out of the shower, teeth chattering. I wrap myself in a towel before scurrying downstairs.

In the kitchen, I find a note on the refrigerator: *The water heater's broken. I've already called the repairman and he's coming this afternoon. Be home by five o'clock.*

"Damn it!" I curse, crumpling the note in my fist. I throw it in the garbage and go back upstairs to get dressed.

I open my closet and stand in front of it contemplatively. I am about to grab my usual clothes, which Tiffany would call dull, but suddenly I change my mind. I look at myself in the mirror and, for some strange reason, I want to feel more attractive today. I decide to wear a fitted coffee-colored skirt that ends just above my knees and perfectly cradles my backside. I forgo my usual shapeless sweater for a blouse that I leave a little open at the neck, and on my feet, I have my ever-present Converse.

I get into Thomas's car and, since I am early, I decide to meet him at his dorm to return the keys. As I'm walking toward the building, two hands land on my shoulders and squeeze.

"Hey, Nessy. How're things?" Matt falls into step beside me, and we walk together.

"Hi, Matt. They suck, how about you?"

"Great, as always." He smiles smugly. "What happened to you?"

"The water heater is out at home. I couldn't take a hot shower. Mom is at work, and I'm here with no car and no hot water," I explain, getting angrier as I do.

"Ah, good ol' Murphy's Law," he replies calmly, pulling a little packet of mints out of his jacket pocket.

I think for a second. "Whose law?"

"You know: 'anything that can go wrong, will go wrong.'"

He throws a mint into the air and catches it in his mouth.

"Oh, yeah. Murphy's Law."

"Thomas really didn't want to leave the bar last night. I couldn't do anything about it. Did he cause any problems?" he asks, concerned.

"Don't worry about it, he didn't bother me," I reassure him.

"I shouldn't have taken him there when he was in that condition."

I put a hand on his chest to stop him.

"Wait, was he already drunk when you guys got there?"

"He'd already had some shots of Jack, yeah."

"Does he do that a lot?" I frown at him.

"What, drink?"

I nod, clutching my books more tightly to my chest.

"We're guys, Nessy. You know how it is."

"Yes, Matt, you are guys, but you also have brains in your heads, I hope. Having a few beers to celebrate is one thing, but getting wasted every time you get the chance doesn't seem wise," I admonish him in a tone that brooks no argument. He looks away from me with a hint of shame on his face, and I immediately feel bad for putting him on blast like that. "Sorry, I'm not mad at you, I just don't like seeing him like that," I explain quietly.

Matt rubs the back of his neck. "Listen, how about I make it up to you with a shower at my place?"

I raise an eyebrow, confused. "What?"

"I have class until the afternoon and practice after that. I'll give you my keys and, after you finish class, you can go take a nice hot shower without anyone hassling you. You won't even need your car, it's a five-minute walk off campus," he turns, pointing toward the fraternities.

"But you don't have anything to make up to me." I give him a smile.

"I feel a little responsible for last night." He shrugs.

"Don't worry. Thomas is an adult, he should be able to handle himself. As for your offer, um, I don't know..."

"Come on, Nessy, I insist. You can't go a whole day without

bathing." He teases me by pulling a disgusted face. He's not entirely wrong, though. My shift at the Marsy starts at six thirty, and the repairman comes at five. I have no idea how long it will take him to fix the water heater, but there's a good chance I won't make it in time.

"Okay, but aren't all your frat brothers there? I don't want any nasty surprises."

"Not a problem, I'll let them know. You should still lock the door, though." He walks backward away from me and throws me a ring of keys as he does it. "Purple's the front door key. Green's my room. Make yourself at home."

I stick them in my bag and check the time. That little chat with Matt took me longer than I'd thought. I have class in about five minutes, and I really can't miss it. I'm going to have to give Thomas his car keys in class. Or maybe now, since he's just a few feet away, chilling in the entrance of the building. His back is turned, and he's wearing sweatpants and a black sweatshirt with the hood pulled up over his head. Even from behind, I can see that he is agitated as he argues with Leila. They both look very nervous. I am too far away to hear what they're saying, but when I see Thomas haul off and punch the wall to the right of him, I rush over to them.

"Hey." I gently touch his arm, in an attempt to calm him down. He shies away from me like a mad dog. I stay by his side and look at him, his expression furious, so I turn my attention to Leila, whose eyes are glittering and red.

"I've already told you, I'm not coming," he rages at his sister, ignoring my presence.

"This could be the last time. He would like to—" she presses.

"Have you already forgotten what he did to us?" He reaches out toward her in a furious gesture, but Leila doesn't seem at all intimidated.

"Please, if you just—"

"I said *no*!" Thomas is about to unleash another punch at the wall, but this time I grab his arm with both hands and stop him. Only at this point does he seem to notice my presence.

"Thomas, calm down. We are on campus," I remind him. He twists out of my grasp and leaves without giving me a backward glance. I watch him walk away as I try to put the pieces of this puzzle together, but I can't figure it out. I turn toward Leila, who looks as astonished as I am.

"Vanessa...I'm so sorry," she whispers, running her hands over her face in an exasperated gesture.

"Don't worry about it. Are you okay? What happened?" I ask, a little uncomfortable.

"It's impossible to reason with him!" She slams her palm against the wall in front of her. The Collins siblings have a serious problem with anger management.

"What were you trying to reason with him?"

She sighs, massaging one temple. "Our father is not doing well. Our uncle got in touch with us. He's trying to reunite the family, a family that fell apart long time ago." She leans her back against the wall and looks up at the ceiling.

"Is that why he's so angry?"

She nods. "He doesn't want to go. He doesn't want to hear anything about it..." She shakes her head, dejected.

"Why?"

She looks hesitantly at me, as though debating how much to tell me. "It's complicated." I hate that word. I hate it with all my heart. Typically people use it when they've done something wrong and don't know how to come clean.

"Leila, I'm just worried about him. Yesterday we were together all afternoon and he was fine. Then in the evening he came to the bar where I work, got drunk, and started babbling nonsense... He said... He said he was grieving," I whisper, looking around to make sure no one is listening. Leila seems to freeze.

"He told you that?"

I nod, my heart in my throat.

"Listen, this isn't a good time for Thomas. Not really for anyone in our family, but for him in particular. He'll get over it, but maybe it's better if you stay away from him for a little while."

"Why are you telling me this?" I ask defensively. I don't like at all the idea of having to back away from him again. Especially if he is going through an emotional time.

"Because I know that you guys are friends, or whatever you are trying to be. And I know that my brother, when he's at his worst, destroys every good thing around him." I'm about to protest but her miserable look stops me.

"I don't know about…"

"I'm saying this for your own good," she cuts me off.

I lower my eyes mutely. "Okay…" I murmur in surrender.

Leila looks hastily at her wristwatch. "I have to go now, but I'd like to see you again. Under better circumstances, if possible." She smiles sweetly at me.

"Of course, I'd like that."

Thomas doesn't show up for art history class. I spend most of my time staring at his empty chair and reflecting on the fact that this the first class I've had without him. Even when we weren't talking to each other and he was sitting in the back, I still knew that he was just a few feet away from me and that knowledge was enough for me. I hope he's not getting into trouble. He was pretty angry earlier, and Leila's words were not at all reassuring.

When I leave the classroom, the only thought in my head is that I have to find him. I have to give him back his car keys but more importantly, I want to make sure that he is okay.

"Hey, where are you going in such a hurry?" Tiff asks, as she and Alex try to halt me at the exit.

"I need to see someone, sorry," I answer hastily, not even stopping.

Arriving in front of his dorm room, I suddenly feel nervous. I take a deep breath and try to shake off the feeling. I knock but no one answers. I knock again. I press my ear to the door and hear noises inside, then his voice cursing.

I bang more energetically on the door. "Thomas, it's me, Vanessa," I call. After a few seconds, the door opens. I can tell by his drawn features that he's in no mood for visitors. If I were smart,

I'd probably get out of here quickly. He stands at the door, silent, his jaw clenched.

"Will you let me in?" I know it's a gamble. Although clearly reluctant, he moves out of my way and closes the door behind me. The room is silent. The leaden sky outside the windows gives it a gloomy air. There are a few empty beer bottles scattered on the carpet, and I'm pretty sure that smell I'm getting is weed. I look around, staring at Larry's door.

"Are you alone?"

He nods and walks further into the room, leaving me behind. "I'm gonna tell you this before you get going: don't stress me out with a bunch of bullshit questions," he blurts out, not even looking me in the face.

"I wasn't going to," I lie, swallowing a mouthful of saliva.

"So what were you going to do?" he asks with arrogant disregard.

I take his keys out of my bag and throw them at him. He catches them on the fly, puts them on the table, and sits down on the couch. "Anything else?" He slumps against the sofa back, shakes out a messy lock of hair and lights a cigarette. On closer inspection, it's not just a cigarette.

"What is that? A joint?" I ask, irritated. I set my bag down on a chair.

"That's what they call it." He lifts it toward me. "Want a hit?"

I raise my eyebrows. "It's ten thirty in the morning. Doesn't that seem a bit early?"

I walk into the kitchen and lean against the counter, my arms crossed over my chest.

Thomas, holding the joint between his thumb and forefinger, takes a drag and then watches the cloud of smoke dissolve. "Never too early for weed."

We look into each other's eyes for a few interminable moments, during which I struggle to suppress the urge to ask him what is wrong. Finally, the intensity of his gaze forces me to avert my own.

Uncomfortable, I let my eyes wander over the rest of the room and I linger on the door to his room. Just a few hours ago I was sitting on his lap, he was touching me longingly…kissing my warm skin… Suddenly

I feel short of breath. I turn around and fill a glass with water. I drink it all in one gulp.

He was drunk, Vanessa. Nothing he said or did was dictated by his rational mind, but instead by sheer desperation. I, on the contrary, was fully conscious of what I was doing, every fiber of my body was. And every fiber of my body wanted it like crazy.

"Isn't that skirt a little short?" he asks impassively.

I almost choke.

I swallow hard. "Seems perfect to me," I manage, trying to sound self-confident.

"On your ass, it sure is." I keep my back to him so he won't see my burning face. "Did you do it for him?"

"What?" I ask when I decide to finally look at him.

Thomas glances at my neckline, before focusing on the skirt. "You don't usually dress like that."

The little voice in my head keeps pointing out that I did want to get noticed by someone, yes. But that someone is not Logan. I'd be lying if I said I've thought about him for more than two minutes since he left. Which perhaps makes me a bad—very bad—person.

I shake my head. "How could I? He's not even in Corvallis."

Thomas remains silent and continues to smoke, watching me. "Where is he?"

"He went back home for a few days." Despite his serious expression, I catch a fleeting flicker of satisfaction cross his face. I hasten to change the subject. "Why didn't you come to class?"

He takes one last drag and stubs out the joint in an ashtray on the small coffee table in front of him. "Wasn't in the mood."

"Yes, I can see that." He gets up and joins me. Correction: reaches into the refrigerator next to me.

"Did you miss me?" he asks with a cocky air that makes me roll my eyes.

He grabs a beer, brings it to his lips and downs it in a few drinks, never taking his eyes off mine. His eyes are the same as last night: reddened, sad, and empty.

"No, I was just worried."

"About me?" He lifts one corner of his mouth in a mocking fashion. "Don't be, I'm fine."

"Fine?" I echo in amazement. He nods and gets another beer. Oh yes, this is definitely typical "fine" behavior. "Is this what you intend to do all day? Lock yourself up in here drinking and smoking?"

Thomas sets the bottle down on the table, annoyed, and advances on me. "That's the idea." He pronounces each word with an unbearable arrogance. I cross my arms over my chest and lift my chin.

"Well, let me just say: your idea sucks."

"No one asked you." Another step toward me. Only inches separate us. The room, previously spacious, seems to have suddenly shrunk. I am forced to tilt my head back slightly to get a better look at him.

"But if you have a better idea…" He strokes my neck with his index finger, moving down to my cleavage. "I'm listening." He stares greedily at my mouth. "Maybe you want to pick up where we left off last night, Ness…" The deep rasp of his voice lights up all my senses. "Or maybe, you'd rather go from where you left off…"

I look up at him, blinking like a scared doe. "Wh-what?"

He approaches my face and twists a lock of my hair around his finger. "Did you like it?" he whispers, warm and raspy.

I'm breathing heavily. "I-I don't…I don't know what you're talking about."

"Yes, you do…" He brushes my earlobe with his lips and then takes it gently between his teeth, making me gasp. I feel my cheeks flush and my body shiver at his touch while a warm feeling flares between my thighs.

"Thomas…" I croak in a vain attempt to stop him. But he pushes me back until my backside collides with the kitchen cabinet. He rests his hands on either side of me, caging me in. "You owe me a kiss, you little sneak," he grunts, pressing his body against mine. I look up at him, overcome by his renegade charm and his intoxicating scent. His mouth is touching mine. And he's so close I can smell the mingled scents of weed and beer. My stomach tightens, and I feel almost dizzy.

"No." I push him away with a determination that surprises me and stuns him. Thomas frowns in annoyance. I put my palms on his chest, and for a moment it seems like I can feel his heart beating faster. "Don't try to seduce me just to run away from your problems. Talk to me. Whatever is hurting you, don't let it make you into…this."

His eyes narrow into two slits and I realize that I've said the wrong thing. The atmosphere changes dramatically, suddenly icing over. Thomas heaves a sigh and takes a step back. "Fuck, Vanessa. You just can't help yourself, can you? Always have to look for the deeper reason for everything, Jesus Christ!"

"No, I'm just trying to figure out what's going on with you!"

"Nothing." He runs his hands through his hair in an anxious gesture.

"Nothing? You call this 'nothing'?" I point indignantly to the empty beer bottles and the full ashtray.

"What's wrong with it? Relax, you sound like my fucking mother!" He snaps back, his face hard.

"Just because I think it's a bad idea to numb your pain with alcohol and drugs? You're suffering, but you're dealing with it in the wrong way."

He lets out an unhappy laugh. "My pain. What, now that your little boyfriend is gone, you need to fill the void by playing Sigmund Freud with yours truly?" he says contemptuously. I know he's just trying to embarrass me, but I won't fall into his trap.

"I'm not playing anything, Thomas." He brings the bottle to his mouth again and gives me a challenging look. Overwhelmed by a surge of anger, I snatch the bottle from his hand and throw it into the sink, spilling the contents.

He frowns and points a finger at me, threatening. "Don't you ever do that again."

"Or what?" I challenge him.

He stares at me furiously for a few seconds, until his mouth curves into an evil grin.

"I pity you. Look at you, coming here convinced you were going to what? Lift poor Thomas's spirits? Patch up my wounds? When are you going to get it into your little head that just because we hooked up, that doesn't mean you matter to me?" His mouth spews poison, but his eyes are filled with sadness.

"You are suffering. You don't really mean what you're saying." I want with all my heart to believe that's true. Otherwise, yesterday would have been just another lie. Still, I can't ignore the little voice in my head that insists on reminding me of the saddest truth: he doesn't form attachments to anyone. My eyes begin to burn, and I bite down on the inside of my cheek to stop the tears from falling.

"Do yourself a favor. Get out." He waves a hand at the door. I know very well that I should have left long ago. In fact, I shouldn't have come here at all. But in spite of everything, this is the only place I want to be. With him. Even if it means fighting. Even if it means suffering. Even if it means weathering his wrath, the worst of him.

"I'm not leaving," I murmur.

"Should I throw you out?" he growls, leaning into me.

"You wouldn't do that."

He reaches me in one step and, for a moment, I fear he might actually attack me. I stiffen with fear and back up, crashing into the cabinet. When he is just inches away from me, his expression turns into one of pure bewilderment. He takes my face in his hands, a desperate, needy grasp, just gentle enough to let me know that he won't hurt me. He presses his forehead to mine, closing his eyes. "Why are you being so difficult, huh? Why?"

"I want to help you," I whisper, so close to his lips.

"Why do you want to do something stupid like that?" He grips my cheeks with more force.

"Because," I murmur with shining eyes. "Because I'm your friend. And friends support each other." I offer him this half-truth, convinced that I am reassuring him, but he pulls away from me instead, his eyes bloodshot. And I quickly realize that, for the second time in this conversation, my words have only made the situation worse.

"Get out," he orders.

"What?" I widen my eyes in confusion. Our conversation is

interrupted then by a couple of knocks on the door. A shrill voice calls Thomas's name and makes my skin crawl. There's only one person who can hit that unmistakable high note: Shana. I turn toward the door and then look back at Thomas, who stands motionless in front of me, never batting an eyelash.

"Thomas, open up. I want to be with you." Shana stops knocking. "I know you're in there. I heard voices." She knocks again. "Come on, don't make me wait. Please?"

"Well? Aren't you going to let her in?" I ask indignantly.

Thomas shakes his head. "No, I don't need another pain in my ass." He pronounces each word clearly and cruelly, looking me straight in the eyes. "But apparently none of you understand that. You in particular."

And it's as if he had punched me in the stomach. "*Me in particular.*" Even I have my limits.

I push him hard, grab my bag from the chair, and beeline for the door.

Thomas lets me go and lights a cigarette. "And while you're out there, tell her the same thing," he continues maliciously before dismissing me with a wave of his hand.

I look at him, deeply saddened. "Fuck you."

He leans his back against the table, crosses his legs, and stares at me. His eyes are alight with anger. "Maybe I'll fuck Shana instead. That's what she's here for, after all," he says with a sinister smirk.

For a moment, I can't breathe. Tears spill over my eyelids, but I turn away before he notices. I close the door forcefully behind me, putting all my pain into the movement.

Once outside, I come face-to-face with Oregon State's biggest bitch, who is looking at me with an expression that is both surprised and mocking.

"Uh-oh, look who's sneaking out of Thomas's room." She strokes the long smooth hair that falls over her shoulder. "I've always said that the ones who pretend to be angels are the worst of all. You're just a little whore." I feel an anger boiling up inside me, so intense that I could rip that annoyingly perfect hair right out of her head. I advance on her and stare brazenly into her eyes.

"Yeah, maybe you're right." She blinks in astonishment. "But at least I didn't have to beg him to open the door for me," I point out contemptuously. She remains motionless as she stares at me, taken aback. She tries and fails to hide the humiliation that shines in her eyes.

I give her a murderous look and walk away.

With shaking legs and a churning stomach, I get into the elevator, and I don't look back. I should have listened to Leila. Whatever is troubling him, it is rotting him from the inside out. And there's nothing I can do to save him.

Twenty-Seven

AFTER TWO HOURS OF SOCIOLOGY, my skull feels ready to explode, but at least being forced to focus on immigration trends and human rights means I don't have time to be distracted.

"I've been trying to figure it out since this morning..." Tiffany whispers beside me, tapping her chin with her index finger. I detach my pen from my notebook and turn my attention to her.

"What are you trying to figure out?"

"What's different about you today. I think I just got it, though."

Instinctively I lower my head and look at myself. "I'm the same as always, Tiff."

"Never, never, in the four years that I've known you, have I seen you wear a skirt that goes above your knees. And this shirt? I've never seen you wearing anything remotely low-cut. Your hair looks particularly gross today, but your clothes, darling, look like you want to impress someone. Now, the question arises: Who?" She tilts her face to the side thoughtfully. "Certainly not my asshole brother. For a moment, I thought it might be Logan, but you're the one who told me that you don't need to twist yourself to get his attention. So at this point, I'm wondering: it can't be for a particular bad boy with green eyes and bulging muscles, can it? No, of course not, my best friend would never, ever dress up to attract the attention of that arrogant prick." She blinks in a faux-innocent manner. "Am I right?"

I look at her in amazement. I don't know how to respond to this insinuation, but she knows she's hit the mark. I know too, and it plunges me into a pit of shame. Since when do I wear tight clothes just to impress a guy? A guy who, need I remind myself, treats me like crap on any given day.

"What were you smoking before school today?" I pretend indifference, nibbling on the cap of my pen.

"What aren't you telling me?" she responds with a question in her eyes.

I shrug. "You know everything there is to know." I barely manage a smile, but I can tell from the way she looks at me that I am a terrible liar.

"You sure? The wrinkles on your face say otherwise."

"What? What wrinkles? I don't have wrinkles!"

"You do have them. This one here, for example." She points to a spot above my eyebrows. "It gets more pronounced when you're surprised. And this one shows up when you are worried," she continues, touching my forehead. "And this," she points to the corner of my mouth, "wrinkles when you're nervous. And right now, my dear, you are really nervous."

I give up. Exasperated, I drop my head into my open notebook.

At the end of class, as the other students file out, I sigh and spill everything. "Yesterday I spent the whole afternoon with Thomas in a forest. We had a good time, talked about lots of things, until that evening when he showed up at the bar and saw me kissing Logan. He flew into a rage and got super drunk. Actually, he was already drunk when he arrived at the bar. Apparently he's having a hard time, so he's back to being his usual insufferable arrogant self."

Tiffany stares at me for a few seconds with an incredulous look on her face. "Sorry, since when are you two talking again?"

"Since yesterday morning. He proposed a truce and apologized, in his own way. We decided to be friends." She bugs out her eyes and bursts into thunderous laughter. I give her a blank look.

"What are you laughing about?"

"S-sorry, but"—she sheds a tear—"do you realize"—another

tear—"what you just said to me? You and Collins are friends?" She bursts out laughing again. "Okay, let's hear it, what kind of friends are you? The kind who have sex with each other or the kind who paint each other's nails?"

How about the kind who insult each other every other day?

"Neither of those. And, believe it or not, friendships between men and women do exist. Look at me and Alex, we have been friends for more than ten years and we don't have sex or do manicures."

"You two spend your time reading novels and watching TV shows. And that's totally different; you guys are like siblings." She stows her laptop, a couple of books, and a small bottle of water in her bag. "But never mind that. We'll come back to this topic another time. Right now, I want to focus on the part where Thomas caught you making out with Mr. Boring. What happened?" she asks, vibrating with curiosity.

"In my opinion?" I say flatly. "They challenged each other to a pissing contest, and Thomas punched him in the face." Tiff's mouth drops open in surprise. "And there's more. Logan told me that, when he gets back, he wants an official answer about the two of us, and then a few hours later, I found myself sitting on Thomas's lap and letting him squeeze my butt." I put my hands over my eyes, ashamed. Ever since Thomas came into my life, I have been doing things I am not proud of. I don't recognize myself anymore.

"Oh. My. God." She stares at me in shock. "Did you get the name of the spell that boy has clearly cast on you?"

"I don't know, Tiff. I was very tired and he was very drunk and, I don't know... It just happened."

"Did it just happen?" she asks, quirking one eyebrow. "Honey, continuing to deny how you feel about him won't make your feelings any less real."

Another direct hit. I could try to deny it but what good would that do? She's right, as always.

"I know." I pause to collect myself before continuing. "I know I feel something for him, I just really wish I didn't. Whenever I'm with him, I feel I'm riding this pendulum. One minute, I'm in heaven, the next, it's hell. And he is always the one who decides which way it swings. I don't like it. I don't want to feel so enthralled by someone who uses other people's weaknesses as a weapon when he's feeling defensive."

"I know, honey." Tiff hugs me and lovingly strokes my hair. "But you know what he's like. You've always known. You want hearts and roses, but he's only got darkness and thorns. No one can change that reality." It might have hurt less if she had just stabbed me.

"How could I have been so stupid? How could I have bonded with a person who categorically rejects any kind of human bond?" I murmur with my cheek pressed against her shoulder.

"Because we can't control what we feel. Our emotions run right over us. They overwhelm us. Sometimes they bleed us dry. They render us helpless and all we can do is go along for the ride, hoping not to get destroyed along the way."

We pull away from our embrace and I look at her sadly. "Feelings are a bitch."

"True. But sometimes it's the bitch that makes life worth living." She tucks a strand of hair behind my ear. "What are you going to do about Logan?"

"I have no idea. The closer I get to Thomas, the more I realize that he'll never be able to give me what I want. Logan, on the other hand, is attentive, sweet, and caring. And I'm pretty sure I'm not going to find a girl waiting around in front of his door. Logan can give me everything I need, and I don't even have to ask him to, you know?"

"But he can never give you what you really want."

"I can't get what I want anyway. Not in the way I would want it," I say passively, shrugging.

"But... You can't be with Logan if your heart beats for someone else."

"The feelings will go away, sooner or later. But Thomas will always be the same."

The heartbroken expression that suddenly darkens her face makes me realize that, unfortunately, she agrees with me. "You know what we should do now?" She sits up straight. "Let's drown all our sorrows in a giant plate of tacos, the really greasy kind. What do you say?"

Her attempt to lift my mood does my heart good. I smile at her. "I say that sounds perfect. I'll text Alex to come too."

She stands up, gives me a kiss on the cheek and pulls me to my feet.

During lunch, Tiffany tells us that Carol is celebrating Halloween with a pool party—intentional this time—and invites us all to go together. I am not entirely convinced that I want to go. The idea of showing up in a bikini in front of this avalanche of people terrifies me. "The last time didn't go so well, remember?" I remind her, taking a sip of water. Inevitably, my mind turns to Thomas and the night I spent with him. Strange, that night should have been devastating because of my breakup with Travis, yet the first thing I think of is that tattooed lout. That guy has monopolized my thoughts. Sometimes, it scares me the way he manages to make me forget about everything, becoming the single point around which I orbit.

"I know, honey, but the situation is completely different this time. First of all, Travis won't be there. I've been very clear about that. Secondly, I'm sure we'll have fun."

"Hmm, and what do I do about work?"

"I can pick you up when your shift is over," she answer easily.

"Tiff is right, between school and work, you barely have time to breathe these days," Alex adds.

"And what about you? Will you come?" Tiffany asks him.

"I'll think about it. School started two months ago, and I haven't been to any parties yet. Not that I think it's so fundamentally important, but it is Halloween. What the hell, I've gotta do something, right?" Alex chuckles.

"See?" Tiff squeals, giving me a fierce look. "Alex is coming. You can't refuse!"

"Ugh, fine," I say resignedly. I wonder why, after all these years I still try to argue with someone like Tiffany. I always end up doing as she says.

When my classes are over, I drop by Matt's to shower. I've been looking forward to this for hours. It feels strange to be here at the frat house again, in the same place where I gave myself to Thomas for the first time. Just thinking about it conjures this heaviness in my chest. Luckily for me there is no one here at this time of day. I climb the stairs to get to Matt's room and find myself forced to walk past Thomas's. For a second, I am almost tempted to go in. The last time I was there, I had no idea that I was about to spend some of the most beautiful hours of my life in that room. Without really thinking about it, I lay a hand on the door and close my eyes, remembering those moments. Remembering him. Him, holding me tightly. Him, sitting on the cold bathroom tiles, taking care of me at my worst. Him, touching me passionately and kissing me gently.

"Damn it..." I whisper, resting my forehead against the wood. The squeak of a door opening downstairs, accompanied by masculine laughter, brings me back to my senses. I jump back and scurry to take refuge in Matt's room, closing the door behind me.

The room is very large, strangely neat and bright. The walls are painted canary yellow, the bed at the back is large, but not like Thomas's. On a white cabinet, there's a television, a laptop, and a gaming console.

I head to the bathroom, and I am pleased to discover that it's identical to the one in Thomas's room, only it doesn't smell like him.

After showering, I slip back into my black cotton underwear. I am about to dress when my phone, which I had left on the bed, starts ringing. I reach for it. It's Logan. A sudden feeling of guilt floods my chest. I hesitate before answering, biting my lip. If he knew what I did with Thomas, he probably wouldn't want to hear from me again.

"Hey sweetie, how are you?" he greets me.

"Hey, I'm good. How are you? Did you get home okay?" I press my knee into the mattress, biting my nails.

"Yeah. I've been here four hours and I'm already regretting it." I hear a buzz of voices in the background.

"Is everything okay?"

"Now that I've heard your voice it is. Is it too corny to tell you that I miss you already?"

My mouth turns up in a small smile. It fades instantly, however, when I hear the door open behind me.

"What the…"

An angry voice startles me. I turn sharply and nearly fall off the bed. Thomas and Finn are looking at me from head to toe with their mouths wide open. I immediately end the call with shaking hands. I'm so frightened that I drop the phone and it falls to the floor. "What the hell are you two doing in here?" I scream, trying to cover my entire body with my arms.

"What the fuck are you doing in here half-naked?" Thomas lashes out at me furiously.

"What does it look like?" I angrily wave a lock of my wet hair at him.

"Are you with him?"

My eyes widen. Him who? Matt?

Like a lunatic, Thomas rushes into the bathroom to find him. Once he's figured out that no one is there, he returns to us with a heaving chest. Finn and I stare at him in bewilderment.

"The water heater at my house was broken this morning. And Matt was nice enough to offer me a hot shower." Why am I bothering to explain myself to him? "Now, why did you two barge in here without knocking?"

"We heard some noises coming from this room. We knew Matt wasn't there and came to check," Finn explains more calmly.

"I certainly wasn't expecting to find you in here in your underwear," says the cantankerous, tattooed man next to him.

"I don't mind," Finn interjects with a pleased expression. He stares shamelessly at my legs. "In fact, if you wanted to turn and get into that position you were in when we came in, you'd be doing me a real solid. Love the Brazilian panties," he continues, as I try to cover myself up as much as possible with my hands.

Thomas turns to him with his jaw tense, grinding his teeth. "Stop looking at her, or I swear I'll throw you out and beat your ass."

Finn continues to stare at me, biting his lip. I'm starting to get really embarrassed. I don't have enough hands to cover all the bare surface area on my body. My clothes are in the bathroom, but to go get them I would have to turn around, and I have no intention of showing my butt to that degenerate Finn. Thomas moves to stand squarely in front of Finn with his arms folded, blocking his view.

"Knock it off," he warns him, grimly. "You're pissing me off."

"Okay, okay," Finn says, raising his hands innocently. "You know what? I think I'll head downstairs and have a nice, ice-cold soda. I'll wait for you, but don't get any ideas; they're expecting us in the gym in twenty minutes." He shifts his gaze to me and smiles. "Nice to see you again, pretty girl." He winks at me as Thomas pushes him out the door and locks it behind him. I take a deep breath, trying to relax. Everything is fine. Except that Thomas turns toward me, enraged.

"You didn't even lock the door, are you out of your mind?"

Damn, I forgot about that!

I pick up the phone from the floor and put it back on the bed. "I must have forgotten; I thought I had," I explain myself calmly. In reality, I am anything but calm. I was stupid.

"You forgot?" He widens his eyes. "You're in a frat house. Anyone could have walked in."

I roll my eyes. I can't stand it when he treats me like a child. "That's what I said. Stop it," I answer angrily. I turn my back on him and go to the bathroom to get my clothes.

"Why didn't you tell me?" he says from outside the bathroom door.

"Tell you what?" I ask as I move back into the room. I head for the bed, avoiding his gaze as if it might petrify me.

"About the shower. You could have done it at my place," he says in a feeble voice. If I were in a slightly better mood, I would have burst out laughing.

"After the lovely treatment you gave me? Don't make me laugh." I slip my skirt on, wiggling it over my hips and then pull on my shirt.

Thomas scrubs his face with his hand. "About this morning..."

I sit down at the foot of the bed to slip on my Converse. He comes over to stand next to me. "I don't want to talk about it," I cut him off before he has a chance to add anything else. I have no desire to hear anything he has to say. Not after all the nasty words he's thrown at me.

"Well, I do." He kicks his foot onto the bed, rests his elbow on his knee, and leans his chin on his palm, staring at me until I return his gaze. When he knows he has my full attention, he sits down on the floor, facing me. For a moment, my bare thighs are just inches from his face, and it seems to distract him. But he quickly averts his eyes back to me.

"I'm sorry."

My lips twist as I give a bitter laugh. "For what? For saying that I don't matter? For making it clear that having me around was a pain in the ass?" I slip on a shoe angrily. "For asking me to courier messages to your fuck buddy, who never misses an opportunity to treat me like shit? Which, by the way, you know very well?" I put on the other shoe. "Or was it for letting me know that you were going to fuck her the minute you kicked me out?" I glare at him.

Thomas runs a hand through his hair bitterly. "For all of that. I was an asshole, and I shouldn't have been." He sighs, looking into my eyes. "I didn't do anything with her. I sent her away as soon as you left."

I gather my still-damp hair and put it in a high ponytail. "I don't care; you're free to do whatever you want." My voice sounds cold and detached, but just the thought of that stupid girl's mouth touching his sends a rush of hot blood to my head. Knowing it didn't happen does soothe me.

"I know I am," he says with his usual swagger.

"Actually, I feel sorry for her. Imagine going to all that effort for nothing. Must be a hard pill to swallow," I say testily, smoothing the bed covers with feigned nonchalance.

Out of the corner of my eye, I see him trying to hold back a laugh. "You feel sorry for her, do you?"

"Very."

"Don't. She'll be luckier next time."

I suddenly fall silent. "I don't like leaving horny girls unsatisfied in front of my door." I open my mouth, ready to yell at him, but then I think better of it. I struggle to push myself off the bed and leave, but he holds me down by the wrists. "Where are you going?" he asks, stopping me with an amused smirk.

"You're disgusting and I can't stand you, Thomas. I cannot stand you at all!"

"What's the matter? You're not jealous, are you?" The smug way he says it irritates me to my core. He knows that I am, yet he torments me mercilessly.

"Jealous? Me? Of a bitch whose only ambition in life is to crawl into your bed?" I shrug. "You know I don't care."

I cross my arms over my chest and look out the window to my right. When Thomas tries to touch my face, I brush his hand away with my forearm. "Don't touch me," I growl, offended.

For some strange reason, my response makes him chuckle.

"The last time a girl crawled into my bed, she was drunk and desperate." Is he referring to me? Has he forgotten all the times I've watched him stick his tongue down another girl's throat in the last few weeks? Does he really expect me to believe that he hasn't been with anyone since our night together? Does he honestly think I'm that stupid?

"I suppose that happens to you frequently," I say, still avoiding his eyes.

"No, not that often. Usually they're clearheaded and pretty excited," he says, pleased with himself. He gets so much joy out of torturing me. He moves closer to my ear, pressing his hands against my thighs. I try to ignore the surge of heat that his touch kindles in me, but I get lost in the low whisper of his voice, shivering as he speaks. "I haven't had a proper fuck in I don't know how long. Every goddamned thought that pops into my brain is focused on just one girl."

I stare at him in dismay. Does he actually have the nerve to come here and tell me that...he's fallen for someone else?

I push him away more firmly. "You just keep hurting me, and you don't even realize you're doing it. It's getting late, I have to go." I try to get up again but he stops me and forces me back down, again.

"What did I say wrong now?" he asks, genuinely confused. I do not answer. I turn my head away from him, trying not to cry like an idiot. He looks down for a few seconds, then shakes his head with a smile.

"Look, you misunderstood…"

"You've been very clear: you've fallen head over heels for someone else. I'm so happy for you, thank you for letting me know."

"First of all, I haven't fallen for anyone. I said that a girl occupies all my thoughts; that's different. Second, let me try get something straight: Who do you think I'm talking about?"

I goggle at him, incredulous.

"I don't know, Thomas! You want us to sit down and gossip over milkshakes like old friends?" I snap.

"You just don't get it." His expression, resigned and vulnerable at the same time, bewilders me. "Forget it. It's not the reason I'm here. I don't like that you saw me in that condition, nor do I like the way I treated you this morning. You didn't do anything to deserve it, except worry about me." He rubs my knee and looks into my eyes with such intensity that all my barriers are dissolved.

"It won't happen again. I've learned my lesson," I say waspishly.

"I like that you care about me, it's just that…" he mutters, looking at the floor. "I'm not used to it."

It breaks my heart to see him so fragile. How is it possible that I was so angry at him until just a few seconds ago and now all I want to do is hug him tightly? Instead, I take a deep breath. I place two fingers under his chin and lift his face so I can look him in the eyes.

"Is this how you do it? First you pull some crap and then you beg for forgiveness, playing the poor, misunderstood boy?" I fold my arms over my chest and frown. "Tell me, how many girls have you bagged this way?"

"None that really count."

"Ah, because I count?"

"Yes, you count," he answers guardedly, as if startled by his own admission.

"That's not what you said before."

"I say a lot of things I don't mean."

I'm not willing to accept being treated badly just because he can't hold his tongue when he's mad, but right now he seems so sincerely sorry that I can't help but forgive him. I snort, puffing my cheeks out slightly. I let myself fall back on the bed, cover my face with my hands, and try to figure out what to do. All logic goes to hell when Thomas Collins is involved.

"Ness?"

"Mhm," I mumble with my face still covered.

"You're not a pain in the ass. Well, not all the time." I jerk my foot forward, hitting him on the chest with the toe of my shoe. He laughs, and the sound of it makes me laugh in return. He stretches out on top of me, holding himself up on his elbows and making room for himself between my legs in his usual arrogant and overbearing way, as if that space was rightfully his. Unlike the other times, however, I don't sense any ulterior motives in this gesture, intimate and overwhelming though it may be. All I feel is an extreme need to be close to him, a need that seems to grow more and more urgent. I welcome his body by bending my knees and pressing them against his hips.

He moves my hands away from my face, and I lose myself in the green of his eyes. "But even when you are a pain in the ass, it's the kind I always want to have around, the kind I don't want to give up." The kind he doesn't want to give up...

I frown and take his face in my hands to make sure he is sober. I look closely at his eyes. They are not red, and the pupils are not dilated. "Are you high?"

"No, why?"

"Because you just said..." The words die in my mouth.

"I know what I said."

My heart seems to burst in my chest. Yet, the small rational part of me won't let me just be happy or simply believe him. How can he say that he needs me, when the moment I try to get close to him, he pushes me away in the cruelest way possible? "Sometimes I just can't understand you," is all I can manage to say.

"Then don't. I have a hard time understanding myself most of the time," he admits.

"Will you ever tell me what's troubling you?" I stroke his eyebrow, moving the tuft of hair that always falls across his forehead and resisting the impulse to lean forward and kiss his half-open mouth. He stiffens a little at my touches, but he doesn't pull away.

"No, Vanessa. That's an off-limits topic for me," he says firmly. "I need you to understand that. Tell me you can accept it."

He's almost begging me with his eyes. Knowing he is in so much pain devastates me. I wish I could just be indifferent to him. I wish I never got those feelings in my stomach when he talks to me, when he looks at me or touches me… Everything would be so much simpler. Even ignoring his suffering.

"Why do you want to keep me if you can't let me enter into your world?"

"Because it hurts less when you are with me."

His words always have the power to send my thoughts into turmoil and make my heart beat like mad. "I can accept it, then," I say, surrendering to him. Thomas releases a sigh, as if a part of him was already preparing to meet more resistance from me and this capitulation has reassured him.

He gets up off me and we both sit down: me on the edge of the bed, Thomas kneeling on the floor. He reaches out for my hips and pulls me toward him. I'm startled at this unexpected gesture as he wraps his arms around my back and hugs me so tightly that, for a moment, I struggle to breathe. I hug him in return, because I have the feeling that he really needs it, and I hope, deep in my heart, that I can alleviate just a little bit of this untouchable pain that is weighing him down. He buries his face in the hollow of my neck and inhales deeply, smelling my skin. I do the same. He smells so good that I wish I could bottle it and keep it with me always.

"You smell like a dude," he murmurs after a while.

I laugh out loud. "That's what happens when you wash yourself with a dude's shower gel."

"I like it better when you smell like me." He brushes my nose with his own and looks at me for a few seconds before speaking again.

"Come to me the next time you need something. It doesn't matter if we aren't talking. Or if you're mad at me for yet another fuckup. Just come to me."

"Okay," I agree softly, wondering how it's possible that this is the same guy who spewed all that bile at me this morning.

The phone lights up next to me. It's a text from my mother, reminding me to be home by five o'clock. "Now I really have to go."

We both get up. Thomas reaches the door before me and turns the knob. Before he leaves, however, an enigmatic expression moves over his face. "So," he tells me, "I'm gonna see you in a bikini tomorrow night." He pauses for effect and continues, "Finally I'll get to see you the way I want to."

I frown. "Excuse me?"

"The party at Carol's."

I am paralyzed. I am overcome with panic. The idea of him seeing me in a bathing suit makes me incredibly nervous and I don't understand why, since he has already seen me naked twice, and in my underwear just now.

"W-will you be there too?" I ask, embarrassed.

"I wasn't planning on it. But then someone told me you'd be going, so I thought...why not?" He gives me a big, challenging grin.

I approach him suspiciously. "Who told you that?"

Thomas clicks his tongue on his palate. "I'm not gonna name names." He winks at me and *boops* my nose. "Don't be nervous. We'll have lots of fun." He grins derisively and leaves.

I stand there, heart racing, wondering why the hell I ever agreed to go to that party in the first place.

Twenty-Eight

BETWEEN CLASSES AND COFFEE BREAKS with Alex and Tiffany, Wednesday passes quickly. After lunch, Thomas kidnaps me again and takes me to the tree house, taking advantage of the unusually nice weather. We spent two hours there in comfortable silence, him sketching out a design for a future tattoo and me reading. Periodically, I get lost watching his hand move confidently over the blank sheet of paper, his gaze focused and intense.

I've thought a lot about what Thomas said yesterday. Even though he wouldn't tell me about the problem that is plaguing him, he did admit that he needed me. He admitted that he wants me in his life because I make him feel better. Hearing him say that made my heart beat wildly. But he is so mercurial that I can never tell if he really means what he says or if he just gets carried away by the moment. I would not be at all surprised if, by the end of the evening, he's shouting in my face about how pathetic I am to have taken him at his word. Not that I want to reopen the topic and ruin the unusual serenity of the moment.

At the end of my shift, Tiffany picks me up from the Marsy, and we go to my house to get ready. The beaming smile and the duffel bag she brings with her don't bode well for me.

"Hi, Mrs. White!" she shouts from the entranceway.

"Don't waste your breath, she's busy with Victor. For a change," I tell her as we climb the stairs.

Once in my room, Tiff empties the contents of the duffel bag on my bed: a mountain of skimpy bikinis.

Oh, dear me.

After carefully sorting through everything she brought, Tiff makes me perform a long series of try-ons to choose the most suitable bathing suit. I have never been more embarrassed.

"Um, no. Not this one either. It shows my breasts too much," I say fifteen minutes later, peering at myself in the mirror. "It barely covers my nipples," I sputter, ignoring Tiffany's exasperated face.

"Nessy. That's the twelfth bikini you've rejected. If you keep this up, you'll be going to this party naked," she warns.

"Don't you have anything with more coverage? A one-piece, for example?" I whine in frustration.

"Yes, sure, of course. Wait here, I'll go ask my grandma if I can borrow one," she answers sarcastically.

I give her a dirty look. "Don't be cute. I'm on the edge of a panic attack and you're not helping me at all! Do you have any idea how many people will be there tonight?"

"And why is that a problem?"

"Oh, come on! Have you seen me? Have you seen these hips? And this ass? Look! Jiggling like a Jell-O mold! You know what? Let's forget it, I give up. Put it all away, I'm not going." I throw a bathing suit at her indignantly and sit on the edge of the bed.

"You're delusional. I don't understand what you're worried about. Your ass... Half the university is jealous of it, and the other half would like to tap it."

"Tiffany!" I blanch, embarrassed.

"Vanessa!" she mimics, laughing at me. "We're going to this party and you are going to wear a bikini, whether you like it or not. Everyone else will be wearing one. No one is going to pay attention to you." She's trying to cheer me up but she can't, because I know for certain that at least one person there will be paying attention to me: Thomas. He's going to see me, and then he'll see all the other girls, and the comparison will be inevitable. Actually, it's really his fault that I'm so worried about this.

"Come on, come over here. I think this one might do the trick."

I listen to her and try on a simple black suit. The top is bandeau-style with a ring in the middle that shows my cleavage. There's the same kind of ring on either side of the bottoms. And yet, out of all the suits I've tried, this is the one that covers me the most.

Tiffany grabs me by the shoulders and drags me over to the mirror. "Wipe that frown off your face and look at the girl in front of you. She's magnificent." She shakes me gently until a small, forced smile appears on my face.

"I really don't know what I was thinking when I agreed to go to this," I mutter.

"Stop your whining. It's time to move on to makeup!" she shushes me.

I wear a cream-colored sweater over the swimsuit along with the same skirt that I had on yesterday and, of course, my trusty Converse sneakers. After what seems like endless preparations, we finally go to pick up Alex.

When we arrive, we are immediately overwhelmed by the roar of dance music. The garden and pool are illuminated by jack-o'-lanterns resting on the grass, the candles inside them creating a soft atmosphere. A cardboard skeleton dangles from the door; some already tipsy person has amused themselves drawing a mustache on him. In the entrance, someone calls out exuberantly: "Tiffany! Finally you're here!" Carol and her friends join us, all in a clamor. Alex and I look at each other for a few seconds. We are both thinking the same thing: How in the hell did we end up here?

"We're here," Tiffany specifies, pointing at me and Alex.

Carol turns her attention to Alex. "Oh, right, we take Performing Arts together. And you, you're the one who was with Baker, right?"

I nod stiffly. I don't like being remembered just for that or still being associated with him, but I am going to have to live with it.

"Anyway, you're all welcome, you can get changed in the pool house." She points to a paved pathway on our right and invites us to enjoy the evening. The last time I was here, I was so enchanted by the grandeur of the house that I hadn't even noticed the pool house.

Tiffany and Alex walk around in just their suits. I, on the other hand, couldn't do it. Against Tiffany's will, I forced Alex to lend me his T-shirt, which goes all the way down to my butt, because mine doesn't cover enough.

An hour later, Tiffany and I find ourselves sitting at a table, surrounded by a bunch of her friends who are chatting about some new influencer I've never heard of. Alex is in the garden with some of his friends from class, and I am—surprise, surprise—bored out of my mind. There's still no sign of Thomas. I decide to go and stock up on food. I grab a paper plate and start selecting from the dishes set out. An imposing figure appears to my right, holding out a slice of lemon cake.

"I looked for something pistachio flavored but couldn't find anything." I recognize Travis's voice even before I even lift my eyes. I almost drop my plate. I cannot believe that he is here, but more importantly, that he actually has the nerve to speak to me.

"I would like to be left alone." I walk past him, leaving him and the slice of cake hanging.

"I already left you alone, thinking I was doing the right thing. But all I did was push you further away."

I turn to look at him with a raised eyebrow. "Push me further away? I didn't drift away from you, I cut you out of my life. It's a very different thing," I point out.

"Do you still hate me that much?"

"Hating you would mean that I still had feelings for you. I don't feel anything for you anymore," I declare, as I fill my plate with a pretzel mix.

"I deserve your contempt. I deserve all of it."

"Not just mine." I slip a napkin under the plate I'm holding and continue. "Did you ever apologize to Leila for what you did to her?"

"I am guessing I'm not on the list of people she wants to see right now," he says with a flippancy that makes me sick to my stomach.

"So you haven't done it, then? I know you well enough to know that the real reason you haven't done it isn't anything to do with being disliked. It's that you simply don't care."

"How can you expect me to just go see her after everything that happened?"

"The same way you just took her to bed while you were with me." The volume of my voice has risen dramatically.

Embarrassed, Travis tries to put a hand on my shoulder, but I push him away contemptuously. "I will apologize to Leila. I fully intend to do that. But I wanted to make things right with you first."

I gape at him. "You're still not getting it: there is nothing to make right anymore! You know what, Travis? I came to this stupid party to have fun, but if I'd known I'd find you here, I would have spared myself!" I drop my plate of appetizers on the table and leave without giving him time to respond. Behind me, he throws the cake into a small trash can and storms out of the pool house, furious.

Tiffany runs to intercept me. "Oh, shit. I swear, he promised me he wouldn't come," she exclaims apologetically. "He should be gone now; I'll text him again to really hammer in the point."

"Don't worry, Tiff. I can manage," I spit the words resignedly, as from a distance I watch Travis refilling his glass and draining it in one gulp.

"If I had known he was going to show up, I wouldn't have done what I did." She runs her hands over her face, stroking her perfectly defined eyebrows.

I frown. "Why? What did you do?"

We sit down at a table, and she crosses her legs, hugging herself as her long, wavy hair falls over her shoulders. "When you left after lunch, I went to the coffee shop and suddenly Thomas barges in after me, asking about you."

I clear my throat. "About me?"

"Yes, he wanted to know where you were. After the way he treated you, I wanted to make him squirm for a while and not tell him anything. He was getting super annoying, though, so I just let slip one small irrelevant detail: that he could find you at this party." Well, there's one mystery solved.

"Well, don't worry about it. I already knew Thomas would be here.

I saw him yesterday afternoon, and he told me. But I'm beginning to think that he won't come after all. Maybe it's better that way," I lie. The truth is, I perk up every time I hear new voices coming from the hall.

"Oh, don't despair," Tiff says with a wave of her hand. "He always comes late to parties."

I don't have time to investigate further, because Alex calls out and invites us to join him at the pool, where he is playing water polo with some classmates. We sit on the edge, dangling our legs in the water, cheering every time they score a point. When the game is over, Alex approaches me.

"Did you see that shot?" he enthuses, resting his crossed arms on my lap.

"You were great," I encourage him proudly. Alex sits beside me and we observe the chaos around us in silence for a while.

"So..." he says vaguely, "I heard there was a little commotion yesterday, on the fourth floor of the men's dorm." I immediately stop swinging my legs in the water.

"Really?" I ask, hoping Alex won't notice the way my breathing just sped up.

He nods his head and keeps looking away from me.

"Apparently two girls were arguing in front of Collins's room."

I bite the inside of my cheek, nervous. "Oh, uh...seriously?"

"Yeah... So, I got curious and asked around a bit about who the girls in question were...and the description that emerged was pretty odd."

"Odd h-how?" I stammer.

"Because one of the girls sounded a lot like you."

"Me?"

"Yes, Nessy, you."

"Why?"

"You tell me."

I huff. "I have nothing to tell, Alex." I shrug. "It wasn't me."

"Are you lying to your best friend?" he asks, draping a wet arm around my shoulders.

"Alex!" I groan, but that only seems to amuse him more and he pulls me tighter to him. "Okay, okay! It was me!" I admit, and only then does he free me.

Alex gives me a tender look. "You really wanna hurt yourself this time, don't you?"

I shrug. "Apparently, I can't help myself."

"Tell me about it."

"Where do I start?"

"Wherever you want."

"Okay, but you're not going to like it. It's not like me…" I rub my palms on my thighs.

"How long has this been going on?" he prompts.

Sigh. "Since the night at Matt's frat house."

He gives me a disgruntled look.

"I know you think he was the one who came on to me, that he was using me, but it wasn't like that, Alex. I had just learned the truth about Travis. He suggested I leave the party with him, but I was the one who said yes, I was the one who got drunk, and I was the one who insisted that he should…help me forget. As unlikely as it may seem to you, Thomas actually tried to reason with me, but I wouldn't listen to him. I actually kind of…jumped him," I admit in a shame-filled whisper.

From the way he looks at me, I can tell he's trying not to judge me. He twists the hem of his Bermuda shorts as he seems to mull over my words. "So, since that night…" he repeats, almost to himself. "Are you together?"

I let out a thin, unhappy laugh: Thomas and I together…not even in my dreams. I am sure that, even there, Thomas would show up with all his insolence and would manage to make me feel like an idiot for daring to dream of him.

"No. We're friends. The thing is, it's so hard to keep up with him… One day he says one thing, the next day he does something else entirely. Not only can I never understand him, I hate him ninety percent of the time; he tries my patience constantly. Yet, for some inexplicable reason, a part of me is tied to him. I know, Alex, I know I'm getting myself into big trouble. But I can't help but feel that there is something more inside him. I know I can be good for him. And, in his best moments, he makes me feel so good." I lower my eyes bitterly, waiting for his verdict.

He rests his head on my shoulder and says, "You know, I'd like to think that this is just one of your bad jokes. Like that time when we were kids and you called me in the middle of the night and pretended you were a creeper watching me from the driveway, but you forgot to mask your phone number. Or when you tried to get me to eat Roy's food by telling me it was tuna fish, but you left the can of dog food open on the kitchen counter." We both laugh. "But I can see from your eyes, that's not the case. I'm not going to tell you to stay away from him, because I already did that once, and it didn't do anything. I don't know much about him, except what everyone knows and what you definitely know. But I do know a lot about you, and if he has somehow managed to make a good person like you love him, then maybe he's not all bad. I'm just afraid you're going to relive everything you went through this past year with Travis. But I trust you, Nessy. If you see some good in him, I believe in you."

I look at him, stunned. I thought for sure he was going to be angry and that he would make me feel like a complete fool for losing my head over the most obnoxious tattooed asshole in all of Corvallis.

"So you're not mad at me? I feel guilty for not telling you anything; I was afraid of how you'd react," I admit in a faint whisper.

He lifts his head. "You have terrible taste in guys, but you're my friend. I'm always on your side."

I hug him tightly and he hugs me back.

"Guys, how about we liven up this evening a bit with that game they're playing in there," Tiffany interrupts us, pointing to a small group inside the mansion.

"I don't think that's our thing," I start to say, before Tiffany grabs Alex and me by the hands and pulls us up without giving us a chance to argue. "We're here to have fun, not to be bored to death." She drags us into the house, where some boys and girls are already sitting in a circle on the floor around a low table. In the middle of the table rests an empty bottle.

"Let's play truth or dare," says one of the girls already sitting cross-legged on the floor.

Not gonna happen.

"Truth or dare? Come on, that's for—"

"For kids," a warm, sensual voice interrupts from behind me. Two hands wrap around my hips and a mouth rests against my ear, making me shiver. "Hi, stranger." Thomas kisses me on the cheek, then passes me by, leaving only the trail of his overwhelming scent behind him. He wears a gray sweatshirt, which highlights his powerful biceps, and a pair of dark jeans. His hair falls disheveled over his forehead. My God, he is breathtakingly beautiful. He picks a bottle of beer off the counter, opens it with the steel ring he wears on his middle finger, and takes a sip.

"Collins, are you gonna watch or are you gonna join these 'kids'?" Tiffany asks.

Thomas stares at me for a few seconds, then gestures at me with the neck of the bottle. "If she plays, I'll play." He winks at me, and I can't help but smile in return. *Vanessa, dignity is not optional*, my conscience reminds me.

Then, Tiffany turns to me. "Nessy? What are you going to do?" Suddenly, everyone looks at me as if I'm the wet blanket here.

"Sure, I'll play," I say resignedly.

We all sit around the table. Alex takes a seat to my right, while Thomas sits across from me. "I'll start," exclaims a girl with long brown hair to my left. "Nash. Truth or dare?"

"Truth," answers a boy wearing a pair of hipster-y glasses.

"Let's start with a softball. How was your first time?"

What kind of question is that!?

Nash seems to ponder it for a moment. "Definitely too brief." We all burst out laughing. The game proceeds merrily, between Thomas admitting that the strangest place he did it was inside an old-timey phone booth, me confessing that I have never masturbated (which earned me a cheeky look from Thomas's side of the circle), some spicy revelations, and big laughs. Thomas and I both chose "Truth" at every turn, and I must confess I'm surprised that he doesn't take advantage of the dares to have a little fun.

Everything seems to be going smoothly, until Alex is dared to kiss the person in the circle that he has known the longest—namely, me. We both try to weasel out of it, Alex out of respect for his girlfriend Stella, me, both because of their relationship and our friendship, but most of the others around the circle tell us not to be buzzkills and that it's all just a silly game. So, with embarrassment gnawing at us, we kneel facing one another. We are both bright red and constantly giggling, despite how uncomfortable we both are. After a few moments of hesitation, Alex takes the reins and wraps one hand around the back of my head, pulling me to him and kissing me. We pull away from one another, laughing a little and wiping our mouths with the backs of our hands. However, my amusement fades the moment I see Thomas's glacial expression.

He can't seriously be mad about this totally innocent kiss, from a boy who might as well be my brother, can he?

Next is the brown-haired girl's turn. I can't even remember her name. Her gaze lingers on Thomas and alarm bells sound in my head, warning me to prepare for the worst. For the first time, Thomas chooses "Dare." And as he does so, he stares straight into my eyes with a challenging look. My heart begins to pound in my chest at an unprecedented speed.

The brunette casts a mischievous glance at her friend, a girl with dyed pink hair sitting next to me and pronounces: "I dare you to give Malesya a hickey." I stop breathing. Malesya goes to meet him amid the hoots and shouts of those present. Thomas, still looking at me, makes her sit on his lap, resting both of his hands on her butt. I begin to feel a kind of nausea. Alex and Tiffany look at me sympathetically. I just want to disappear.

Thomas brushes aside her pink locks and starts enthusiastically kissing her neck. She sighs ecstatically, grinding her pelvis against his lap. Amid giggles from the circle, someone tells them to get a room. Finally, they break away. Malesya returns to sit beside me, and I can't help but stare disgustedly at the bruise he has left on her neck; nor can I banish from my brain the image of her rubbing herself on Thomas as he eagerly indulged her.

My legs are shaking, my eyes are burning, but I refuse to cry. I clear my throat. I shrug my shoulders and tell myself that I am going to avoid Thomas's gaze for the rest of the evening. For all the days to come! He's an asshole down to the DNA level, and that won't ever change.

After several rounds, it's Tiffany's turn. She gives everyone a long look, but to my enormous surprise, Thomas is the one she points out.

"Truth or dare?" asks Tiffany.

"Dare," he answers immediately. As if he's been waiting for exactly this question from her. Instinctively, I lift my eyes to him and see a wicked expression light up his face.

"Good, good," Tiffany exclaims victoriously. Too victoriously. I look at her and frown. I know all too well that rush of megalomania she gets when she thinks she has total control over a situation. I silently beg her not to include me in the "Dare." Thomas also looks at her but appears to be wishing for the exact opposite. Tiffany darts her gaze between us. Then she stops on me, smiling. When she murmurs, "You're gonna thank me," I wince. Oh my God.

"Thomas, I dare you to spend ten minutes locked in a closet with Nessy," she orders.

"What?" Alex and I cry out in unison.

"Come on, let's go," Thomas demands, standing up.

"I'm not going to lock myself anywhere with you. What are we? Kindergartners?" I reply acidly.

"Rules are rules, Vanessa. And they must be respected," he replies with a singsong voice and his most punchable face.

"He's right. So far we have all followed the rules," Nash interjects, before explaining where the closets are.

Damn Tiffany. She'll pay for this. Oh, how she's gonna pay. I breathe deeply and then huff the air out through my nose.

"Let's go to this damn closet."

"After you, miss," a smug-faced Thomas mocks. I pass him with a glare.

I go in first, and he closes the door behind us. For some reason, the light is on. Maybe someone's already been in here before us. This little room is claustrophobic. I turn my back to him because, even though I am furious at him, having him within a few inches of my face would make me lose my mind and I know it. So I'll just stay here, staring at the greenish walls around me, for ten minutes. In front of me there's a dusty set of shelves with some books and a few ceramic dolls on it. Creepy. I notice a cord hanging from the ceiling. I pull it and the dim light goes out. I immediately pull it again. Light. I need light.

"It's better in the dark, don't you think?" Even though I have my back to him, I can imagine his lips curving in his usual goading way.

"No. I don't think so," I answer sharply.

"Let me guess, you're pissed."

What a brilliant deductive mind, Collins. "No."

"That wasn't a question, it was an observation."

You know where you can put your observations? I sigh and turn to face him. "Yes, Thomas. I'm pissed. What's new, am I right?"

"Yeah, what's new?" he replies, annoyed, rearranging the disheveled hair on his forehead with his fingers.

"Is it really so hard for you to stop being a jerk for more than five minutes at a time?" I go on the attack, making no effort at all to rein in my anger.

"When did I piss you off?"

Is he making fun of me? Of course he's making fun of me, because it's clear as day that he knows exactly why I'm pissed off. But evidently, if he's not mocking me, he's not happy.

"I don't know, maybe when you put that girl on your lap and practically screwed her in front of everyone? I hope it was good for you, at least," I conclude with a contemptuous grimace, trying to ignore the pang in my heart.

"And what about you? Did you enjoy kissing your little buddy?"

Is he seriously trying to make me believe that performance was all just to get back at me?

"Don't call him 'my buddy' like that. And, just to be clear, it was just a stupid kiss. He didn't clamp on to my neck like Count Dracula."

"If yours was just a stupid kiss, mine was just a stupid hickey. I don't see what the problem is."

I give up. He just doesn't get it. "Forget it," I mumble, turning my back on him again.

"Turn around."

"Nope. I'm good like this."

I hear him advancing on me, and my heart leaps into my throat.

"I want you to look at me when you talk to me," he demands in a hoarse voice.

"And I want you to stay away from me."

"No, you don't." He rests his hands on my shoulders before gliding them down my arms, all the way to my hips. His rough touch on my smooth skin makes me shiver. My brain tells me to pull away and maintain a safe distance between us, but my body is increasingly drawn to his. "You want me to touch you." He lifts the hem of my shirt, running his fingers over my stomach. "You want me to kiss you," he murmurs against my hair. "And do you know how I know?" I try to answer, but I can't. I just shake my head mutely instead. "Because your mouth can lie, but your body can't." He pulls me to him, making my bottom collide with his pelvis and tearing a moan from me.

"So," he pulls my hair away from my neck and presses his lips to my skin there. "Did you enjoy kissing him?"

"What did it look like to you?" I retort, trying to appear confident. I pray with all my might that I can somewhat hide the incredible destabilizing effect Thomas has on me.

"You seemed pretty into it."

"Like you were with Malesya? You seemed pretty attached...to her ass, mostly."

I hear him chuckle into the crook of my neck. If I weren't so completely subsumed by him, I probably would have slapped him by now.

"But she didn't get me hard the way you do." He pushes his erection against my butt to illustrate his point. "And she didn't make me want to bend her over the coffee table and fuck her breathless." His hand tightens on my left hip, fingers sinking into my flesh as he licks a spot behind my earlobe. I am overwhelmed by a powerful electric shock that seems to be completely concentrated in my lower abdomen. His fingers move down to settle between my legs, which I close and tighten automatically. "Good job, tight around me is the only way I want to feel you," he murmurs obscenely, moving his fingers to apply more pressure to my center. A warm and intoxicating sensation makes me quiver. He slides my bikini bottoms to the side and slips a finger between my lower lips, already slick with fluids. I groan and, surrendering to his magical touch, I close my eyes. He makes small circles on my clitoris, and I go boneless. I drop my head back onto his shoulder, and Thomas puts the palm of his other hand against the wall in front of me, panting against my ear. I slur his name and squeeze his wrist between my thighs. I would like to be able to push him away, but instead I move with him. I'm doing it again, making another mistake I'm going to regret. Why? Why can't I seem to live without this? I feel like a moth that is inexorably attracted to the light, even knowing that, if I get too close, I'm going to get burnt.

"Let go. I know you want it; I can feel on my fingers how much you want it."

His words short-circuit my brain. As soon as he feels the muscles in my legs give way, he dips one finger into me. I arch my back and push my ass against his groin, causing him to let out a low grunt of excitement. Thomas licks my neck and then sucks it. He bites me, rubbing his ever-growing erection back and forth against my ass.

I feel his breathing getting heavier as, with one quick motion, he unzips his jeans and releases his erection. He rubs it against the cleft of my buttocks, with only the thin layer of my bikini between us. I feel the hot, wet tip of him teasing my slit, sliding back and forth. The hoarse sound of his moans and the sensation of warm, moist skin rubbing against me make me even wetter, so much so that I feel an overwhelming wave beginning to build. He picks up the pace with his fingers, teasing me until my legs are shaking from another jolt of pleasure. I almost want to tell him to stop because the stimulation is too intense, but a third wave of sensation causes a spasm of pleasure so intense that the only thing I can do is squirm, sputtering incoherently.

"Spread your legs a little wider. I want to look at you and I want to…feel you." He crushes me between him and the wall, repeating filthy things that are about to push me over the point of no return, when a knock at the door makes me jump.

"Time's up, guys!" someone yells from beyond the door.

I blink, wide-eyed. What? That's not possible.

"Shit," Thomas curses, grinding his teeth in frustration. He pulls his hand out of my swimsuit bottoms, leaving me dazed, yearning, and more unsatisfied than I have ever been before.

I look around blearily and slowly lift up my head. I gasp with parted lips, breathing in the stale air of this closet. Thomas turns me toward him abruptly. Only now do I see how his eyes are hazy, filled with an excruciating desire that he is forced to repress. He grabs my jaw and tells me, "The next time you let me touch you like that, I'm gonna make you scream my name until you lose your voice."

Feeling almost drunk, I watch him painstakingly arrange his still stiff member in his jeans and walk out of the closet. Meanwhile, I try to figure out how I got myself into this situation again.

I let him use me again, like a puppet on a string. Thomas smelled my weakness and took advantage of it without a second thought. I slump onto the floor, disappointed in myself once again.

Twenty-Nine

I HAVE MY FACE IN my hands when Thomas reappears in the doorway, flooding the closet with the light from the room outside.

"Why aren't you coming out?" he asks with a calmness that grates on my nerves.

"Why?" I repeat, still panting, my cheeks on fire. "Explain to me what the hell was going on in your head! Why did you do that? What were you hoping to accomplish, huh?" Thomas stares at me in astonishment before crossing the threshold of the closet again and closing the door behind him.

"I wasn't hoping to accomplish shit. I did it because I wanted to." He pauses and gives me a cocky look. "We wanted to," he emphasizes.

"Are there no boundaries? Or was all that 'I want to be your friend,' 'oh, I'm a selfish bastard, but with you it's different' stuff just a big lie?"

He squares his shoulders and tightens his lips into a hard line, glaring at me. "You didn't seem to hate it."

"Don't treat me like this." I clench my hands into fists at my sides. "Who do you think you're dealing with, Thomas? You kiss another girl in front of me and twenty minutes later you're slipping into my panties! Is that how little you respect me?"

"I didn't kiss anyone. It was just a stupid hickey; you're the one who kissed someone! And you're the one who let me slip into your panties. If we hadn't been interrupted, you would have let me fuck you too. So, instead of getting mad at me for doing what I honestly wanted, get mad at yourself for insisting on keeping this goddamned act going," he shouts, the veins in his neck throbbing.

I frown. "What act are you talking about?"

"Which act? The one where you are as attracted to me as I am to you, but for some stupid reason you won't let yourself go. You let your customers touch you for a few bucks, you let the first dickhead who makes cow eyes at you and tosses a few compliments your way hump you against a wall, you even kiss your best friend. But if I do it, I'm a piece of shit, right?"

Of course! Because none of them have the power to destroy me with a word like you do, you idiot!

"It's not about that," I say instead in a low voice.

"And what is it about?"

"Leave it alone."

"Tell me." He takes a step toward me.

"Need I remind you what happened the last time I let go with you? You made me feel so pathetic that I was ashamed of myself. I won't let that happen again. You and I want different things. I want stability, you want freedom. I want a relationship; you want to avoid ties. You are careful not to take on any kind of responsibility. I get that, and that's fine with me, but you can forget about using me as one of your dalliances."

"The fact that I don't want relationships doesn't mean I don't want you," he replies seriously.

"Oh, no? And what does it mean, then? That you'll use me, but then you can just leave because you have no moral obligation toward me? Does it mean that you can sneak out of my bed and, only a few hours later, play grab-ass with another girl in the university cafeteria without thinking about how that makes me feel?" By the end of my speech, I'm shouting so loudly that for a moment I imagine a whole crowd of people outside the door, intently eavesdropping on this pitiful scene.

He lets out an annoyed sigh. "I've already told you, I haven't had a real fuck in weeks."

"And you really expect me to believe that? I saw you all over I don't how many other girls while we weren't talking. Don't treat me like an idiot, I'll take offense." I cross my arms over my chest and look away from him.

"Yeah, you're right, I fooled around with some of them because, guess what? I'm a man and I have urges. But whether you believe it or not, I haven't been able to go all the way with any of them. And do you know why? Because all the time, my fucking head is full of—"

I cut him off angrily. "Some other girl. My God, you've already said that! And that only proves my point: you're thinking about someone else but you demand that I—" He slaps his hand over my mouth to shut me up.

"Of you! In my head, there's only you. Stupid shrew that you are."

I remain frozen for a handful of seconds, attempting to process his words. He looks at me, waiting for a reaction. Then, with a sudden jerk, I pull his hand off my mouth.

"What did you say?"

He takes a step toward me, and I take a step back. He advances again, stalking me. "Stop running away."

"Stop saying bullshit."

"Does it sound like bullshit to you?"

"Need I remind you that yesterday morning you were the one who told me that you were about to have sex with Shana? And now you tell me that you couldn't do anything with anyone because you were thinking about me? Yes, I think it's a load of bullshit."

"I only said that because you made me."

I bring my hand to my chest. "I *made you*? And how did I do that?"

"You wouldn't stop talking about how you were my friend," he says, leveling a deadly stare at me. "A friend, Ness? Do you act like this with your friends?"

"But I am your friend. Or at least, I'm trying to be."

"Jesus Christ…" Frustrated, he runs a hand through his hair. "Are you my friend?" He approaches me aggressively and, without asking permission, slips his hand between my legs. I gasp, caught off guard. "You let your friends do this to you?"

He applies more pressure to my most sensitive spot; pleasure tears through me. "Do you enjoy feeling your friends' hands on you?" He slides my bottoms to the side, penetrating me with one finger. "Inside you?" he asks hungrily, his breath on my skin.

"Stop it!" I push him away forcefully, hitting his chest. "You're an animal, Thomas!"

"And you're a liar!" he yells, the vein in his neck swollen with rage. Then he steps back abruptly, wiping his fingers on his sweatshirt nervously.

My head is spinning. We are both out of control. I take a deep breath to calm my nerves. He turns away and I let myself collapse on the floor. I tuck my knees up against my chest, rubbing my temples with my head bowed. "What the hell do you want from me?" I ask him finally, exhausted.

"I want to figure it out," Thomas replies after a few moments of silence.

"Figure what out?"

"Why ever since that fucking night, no other girl can hold my attention."

I press my head against the wall and stare down at the floor. "And how do you plan to figure that out?"

He gives me an indulgent look and squats down to look me straight in the eye. "With you."

I stare at him, dumbfounded. I am dreaming. I can't see any other explanation.

"With me? What does that mean? Do you...do you want us to date?" I stammer, afraid, as always, of being rejected.

He nearly laughs right in my face, making me feel like complete dope. I almost fell for it.

"No relationships, you know how I feel about that." The frigid way he says it chills my blood.

"Then what the hell do you want?" I shout at the top of my lungs.

"I want you."

"And in what way do you want me? Tell me that," I say irritated.

"You know how," he answers seriously. Yes, Thomas, I know. You want me in a way where you don't belong to me. In a way that hurts me.

"You want my body, but not me," I murmur bitterly. "And what would I be to you? The naive little girl you fuck when you're bored? Or pissed off? Or horny? No, thank you. If I'm going to feel like a nonentity, I'd rather do it alone," I say with a lump in my throat and my eyes misted with tears.

"You wouldn't be any of that."

"And what, then? What would I be?" My voice is heavy with disappointment.

"Why is it so important for you to classify the relationship? Does it connect you to the person? It's just a word. A fucking word. Trust me, you can have fun with someone without necessarily being with them," he says without hesitation.

"This is ridiculous. Are you seriously asking me to start a non-relationship with you based purely on the physical without any emotional involvement? That is your pitch?"

"I know it's hard for you to understand…" He pushes a strand of hair behind my ear. "You see relationships differently than I do. You dream about true love, that romantic and all-encompassing kind you read about in your novels. But I will never be able to give you anything like that, I can't give you anything close to that kind of love. And you shouldn't want it from someone like me anyway."

"Why, Thomas?" I ask in a broken voice. I don't care whether I sound desperate or pathetic to him. It's not like his opinion of me can get worse.

He bows his head, and for a moment, he just stares at the floor. Then he looks at me. Very grave.

"Because I'm broken inside. And there's no cure, no treatment, for people like me. If I were a better person, I'd keep you far away from me and the way everything goes to shit around me. But the problem is,

I'm greedy. Selfish. I'm so selfish that I want you, even though I know how wrong it is. Even though I know it won't last and that nothing is ever going to change. And I'm sure that, sooner or later, you'll find someone who is prepared to give you everything you've ever dreamed of and gone after and wanted. And when that happens, me and Travis, Logan, and all the other assholes who come along will only be able to watch as you walk away. But, before that happens, I want to be able to enjoy everything about you. Everything."

I am incredulous. My heart seems very loud, even to me. "I-I don't understand. If that's what you want…then, why don't you want to be with me?" I ask, looking into his eyes.

"It's not that I don't want to be with you. It's that I don't want you to be with me. I'm a complete mess. Tying the two of us together would mean involving you in my life. And then you couldn't help but end up ruined just like me. And none of this takes away from the fact that I want you for mine. All mine. Only mine."

"And while you'd have me, what would I have?" I cannot believe that I'm even considering this proposal.

"You'd have sex with me." He cracks a small smile but quickly realizes that I'm not in a joking mood.

"I can have sex with anyone."

"But you want it with me, don't lie. I feel it every time I touch you."

"And what about the other girls?"

"I'll stop seeing them," he says resolutely. It seems like the only positive note in all this madness.

"So, it would be just you and me…with no responsibilities or feelings?" Feelings that I already have, while he has, at best, an attraction accompanied by an inexplicable possessiveness.

"No ties or responsibilities," he confirms.

We stare at each other in silence for a few moments. I bite my lip, not knowing what to say or even what to think.

"I don't know, Thomas…"

"It could be better than you imagine."

Or worse than you think…

I draw in a deep breath and blow the air out of my nose. "I'll think about it."

For a moment, he seems surprised by my answer. "You will? Really?"

"Yes."

"Okay." He clears his throat and pulls himself together. "Now let's go. You can't fucking breathe in here."

He extends his hand to me and I, though hesitant, take it. Before we leave the closet, Thomas stops, turns and looks at me. He puts his arm around my waist and pulls me into him. Only a few inches separate us. He takes my face in his hands and caresses my cheekbones gently. His eyes scrutinize me. I wonder what he is thinking about.

Suddenly, he wraps his giant arms around me, and I take refuge in this seemingly indestructible fortress. He rests his chin on top of my head, while I press my cheek to his chest, deeply inhaling his scent. We don't say anything to one another, but words aren't needed. We remain like that, embracing, for a few moments that I wish could last forever.

Thirty

WHEN WE TRY TO RETURN to the others, we find that the truth-or-dare group has disbanded. In our absence, the party seems to have gotten into full swing; everyone is tipsy. We go out and find Tiffany and Alex by the pool. They both give me *we'll talk about this later* looks. I smile weakly.

Thomas sits on a small patio sofa and lights a cigarette with all the ease in the world, as if we hadn't just spent the last ten minutes lusting after each other, tearing into each other, and then... I don't know. I couldn't even define it. Whatever it is though, it's still turning my mind upside down.

I drop into a vacant chair a few feet away from him. A girl with an inflatable pumpkin under her arm suggests we get in the pool. Everyone else seems enthusiastic, but I'm feeling extremely anxious at the idea of getting undressed in front of all these people.

Thomas stands up and, in a matter of seconds, has taken off his shoes, jeans, and sweatshirt, remaining in just a pair of blue Bermuda shorts, which put his sculpted, tattoo-covered midsection on full display. Wait a minute, are those nipple piercings? Those are new, right? The last time I saw him without a shirt on, he definitely didn't have them. My God, that's somehow even sexier.

"Done drooling, Ness?" asks the absurdly overconfident man in front of me.

"W-what?" I stutter, trying to shake the dopey look off my face.

"You should know by now: I'm a shy and insecure boy. You can't stare at me like that, I'll be intimidated."

"I was just looking at your piercings, stupid. Did they hurt?" I babble, feigning indifference.

"I felt them. But that's the downside of beautiful things: they hurt." He smiles crookedly at me. "Come on, I want to see you darting through the water like a minnow."

"Um, to be honest, I don't really feel like getting wet right now." I lower my gaze to my nails, worrying at my cuticles.

"Didn't seem that way a few minutes ago," he answers mischievously, without an ounce of shame.

I turn purple in a split second. "Thomas!" I scold, throwing the first empty plastic bottle I see at him. It hits him on the shoulder, and he bursts out laughing. He leans over me and rests the palms of his large hands on my thighs. It is fascinating to watch the contrast of my pale flesh with his own completely tattooed skin. "Come on, don't make me beg."

"I won't. Just go, I'll stay here. Besides, this—"

Before I can finish my sentence, I find myself hanging upside down over Thomas's shoulder.

"No, Thomas, let me go!" I slap his back wildly, but all it gets me are his fingers tickling my side. I try not to, but finally I cannot help laughing.

"I can't swim, remember? Besides, I'm still dressed."

"Are you asking me to undress you? I thought there were certain things you preferred to do away from prying eyes. What a dirty little girl you are," he pats my exposed butt cheek as he continues walking.

"And you are still a caveman." I kick my legs in the air, trying to free myself. "I'm not taking off my shirt."

When we get to the poolside, he puts me down. "Why not? It looks like shit on you."

"Lovely," I scoff, crossing my arms over my chest.

"Who gave it to you?"

"Alex."

His jaw tightens, but I pretend not to see it.

"All the more reason to get it off your back."

After thinking about it for a few seconds, I decide to go for it. I take a deep breath and pull up the hem of my shirt. But just as I'm about to take it off, I freeze. I can't do it. It feels like a thousand eyes are on me.

"What's the problem?" Thomas asks.

I lean toward him and confess in a low voice, "I'm extremely ashamed."

Thomas looks at me in astonishment. "What are you ashamed of?"

"Of my body," I answer awkwardly.

He huffs a laugh. "Bullshit. Take these clothes off or I'll do it for you."

I sigh again but gather all my courage and just do it. I am immediately uneasy. I feel exposed. Too exposed. Thomas fixes me with an indecipherable look that makes me want to hide.

I prepare to cover myself again, but he frowns at me. "What are you doing?"

"Getting dressed. This is exactly how I don't want to be seen," I mutter.

"Yeah, you should get dressed," he says, glancing at someone over my shoulder. "Maybe then all these assholes would stop eye-fucking you. But I'm too greedy for that. Because if you get dressed, then I can't look at you. And fuck, do I want to look at you. I want to look at you 'til it hurts."

I look down, even more embarrassed. "How deep is the water?" I ask, trying to change the subject.

"Dunno, I've never been in. But we'll find out soon. Get on my back, we'll dive in together."

That seems like a really stupid idea, but it does have a certain appeal to me. Mainly because I really want to feel his skin against mine again. With a leap, I cling to his back. His hands reach back to grasp me firmly by the thighs, as I lace my arms around his neck.

"You okay?"

"Yes, why?"

"You're shivering."

"Uh, um, yeah, it's just really cold, that's all," I lie. The truth is, the idea of diving into the water scares the shit out of me, but Thomas's presence somehow manages to alleviate a bit of my fear.

"You don't have to if you don't want to. We can go back in and play a round of beer pong. Though, fair warning: I will crush you. Or we can even go home. Your choice." It makes me smile, the way he tries to put me at ease and the way he takes it as read that we will leave this party together, even though we arrived separately.

"The pool is fine, but I warn you: if you leave me underwater to drown, I swear I will return from the afterlife just to slap you!" I threaten, poking his shoulder muscle with one finger.

He cocks his head slightly to look at me. "Are you telling me that I finally have a chance to get rid of you and your big mouth for good?" He clicks his tongue against his palate with an amused air. "That's very tempting..." I swat the back of his head and we both laugh.

I bring my mouth close to his ear and feel him stiffen. "You wouldn't last a single day without my big mouth. You'd miss it too much," I whisper in his ear. He remains silent for a few seconds, seemingly pondering my words.

Then he murmurs, "More than you know."

I smile shyly. Never did I think I would hear him say something like that.

"Ready?"

I nod and hold my nose. Thomas laughs and shakes his head.

He takes a short run-up and then, the next moment, we are underwater. The pressure of the plunge briefly separates us, but he grabs my hand and uses it to pull me to the surface. I gulp air, and when Thomas pulls me into his arms, I wrap my legs around his waist. He carries me like this to the shallow end of the pool, where the water comes to my clavicle.

"I think I just gave you a good reason to hate me." He smiles, moving closer to me.

"Just the one? Let's hear it, what is it?"

"Your eye makeup is melting." He chuckles.

Damn it, Tiff. I wipe my eyes quickly. "Is it all gone?"

"Yeah, now you look like a panda." He laughs. Thomas draws very close to me and whispers, "Your eyes are a work of art, don't hide them with this crap." With his right thumb, he rubs my face from cheek to chin. Immediately, even underwater, a feeling of warmth suffuses my body. My God, I really have to stop melting like a jellyfish in the sun every time he touches me. Or looks at me. Or smiles at me...or compliments my eyes. To break the tension a bit, I splash him, catching him off guard.

He gives me a bright look, with just a hint of fiendishness. "I wouldn't do that again, if I were you."

"Or what?" I challenge him.

He approaches with a wild look, and I retreat. I half smile and, hit by a sudden wave of courage, I splash him again. "Bad choice," he announces with a devilish grin.

I turn away, ready to take cover, but in the blink of an eye, he pounces. He wraps his arms around me, and I hurry to plug my nose; I already know exactly what he's got planned. And indeed, Thomas lifts me up before dropping me back into the water. I resurface a few moments later and, with my eyes still closed, I feel his hands pushing me right back under. When I get back to the surface, I can't stop laughing. He draws me close to him, trapping my back against his chest.

"Do you give up, little shrew?" he asks, amused.

"Never!" I windmill my arms, throwing water behind me. I drench him relentlessly, then turn to face him and grab him by the shoulders. I try with all my might to push him under the water, but there is no budging him. We both cackle at my miserable attempt.

Incredibly, we spend the next half hour laughing and joking around, talking about everything and nothing. We start with the disgusting cafeteria food, which the school chefs are inexplicably proud to present. They're so scary that not even Thomas has the courage to point out how bad the food really is. He tells me about the time he found his roommate soaking in the tub, sprinkled with mineral salts and encircled by candles, romantic music playing in the background. I point out to him how strange Professor Scott's voice is, even improvising an imitation that's not too far off the mark, and he bursts out laughing. I'm having such a good time that I don't even notice the people around us, drinking, laughing, shouting, and diving. From time to time, I catch curious glances from Alex and Tiffany, and I think I see them talking to each other, pointing at Thomas and me. But he's the only thing I can focus on.

When, later, some guys suggest a swimming competition, I curse them in my head for breaking the spell we'd taken refuge inside. I demur, but Thomas accepts. He swims along with the others, while I go over to the edge of the pool and watch his every move. How he shakes away the hair that falls onto his forehead when he emerges from the water, the veins on his arms that stand out thickly when he tenses his muscles, the movement of his shoulder blades with each stroke. The broad shoulders, the muscles in his back entirely covered by that tattoo so forbidding as to be fascinating and tragic at the same time. And, almost imperceptible under all that ink, but impossible to miss once you know it's there: that scar.

I am so lost in my thoughts that when I find him standing in front of me, I gasp in surprise.

He looks at me thoughtfully then asks, "What are thinking about, stranger?"

"Lots of things."

He gets so close that I can feel his breath on my face. "Tell me a few."

"I'm thinking about the philosophy test we have on Monday. About the work uniform I need to wash. And I'm thinking about you." I don't know where I got the courage to admit it, but he seems pleased.

"About me?" He strokes my cheek. "And tell me, what do you think about when you think about me?" I have to think a bit before convincing myself to speak, although the little voice in my head is screaming at me not to do it. As always, I don't listen to it.

"Thomas, can I..." I take a shallow breath. "Can I ask you a question?"

"You're going to do it anyway, aren't you, you little snoop?" He prods me, making me giggle.

"Well, I was wondering. The scar you have on your side... Is it from the accident you had with your motorcycle?"

The way his face immediately tightens, the way it takes on such a furious, chilling look makes me wish I could rewind this moment and go back thirty seconds to stop my mouth from running away with me.

"And what the fuck do you know about the accident?" he explodes, crimson with rage.

I swallow in fear. "N-nothing, I...Leila told me about it a while ago."

Thomas heaves a big sigh and closes his eyes. When he opens them again, he somehow manages to look even scarier. "I never want to hear you talk about that ever again, is that clear?"

"I didn't mean to..."

"Don't fucking push it!" he growls, attracting the attention of some people swimming near us. I'm speechless in front of him. I look around, embarrassed. I almost feel like crying.

"I wonder, is there anything I can talk to you about?" I turn to leave, but he grabs me by the arm.

"Where do you think you're going?"

"Away. I'm not going to argue with you for the third time in one day and this time in front of the whole university." I try to pull my arm out of his grip, but he won't let go of me.

"You're not going anywhere."

"Thomas, I want to leave," I tell him resolutely.

He takes a deep breath and whispers, "That accident was the end and the beginning of everything. A wound that will never heal." He pulls my wrist forward with an abrupt jerk and presses my hand to his side. "This scar reminds me every day of what I had, what I lost, and what I'll never get back. Never." The pain in his voice makes me crumble into thousands of pieces.

I touch his mouth with two fingers, dismayed. Whatever it is, I can see that it is destroying him, and that annihilates me. So, I don't push. "Please, don't say anything else. I'm sorry." I hug him, resting my mouth on the crook of his neck, and I can feel him relax into my arms. "I wasn't—wasn't trying to force you to remember. I just let my mouth run away with me like always," I whisper wryly, hoping to soothe a little bit of the tension I can feel creeping over him.

But Thomas doesn't laugh. He just holds me tighter, as if this pool were made for just the two of us, as though I might fly away from him at any moment. "There's too much darkness inside me for you to understand, but don't turn your back on me because of it," he pleads in a soft voice.

My heart breaks. I look at him and put my hands on his cheeks in a tender caress. "I won't," I murmur a few inches from his mouth. Right now I want nothing more than to kiss him. Kiss him until I take his breath away, until he forgets everything that hurts. But I don't think that's the right thing to do. "I'd like to get out of here," I confess.

Thomas nods, wraps his hands around my hips, and lifts me up to sit on the edge of the pool. "Let's go together."

"Okay," I reply, but it was clear from the tone of his voice that he wouldn't have accepted any other answer. As Thomas jumps out from the water and shakes his hair, smoothing it back with one hand, I search for Alex and Tiffany among the crowd of people in the pool. Once I spot Tiff, I mouth, "I'm leaving with Thomas," at her. She gives me a nod and a mischievous little smile.

I tell Thomas that I'm going back in to get dressed before we go. "I'll wait for you," he answers.

I pass the garden where some guys, decidedly tipsy, are playing soccer with a carved pumpkin and laughing loudly. I head for the pool house. There isn't a soul around because everyone is at the party. It takes just a few minutes to dress and get ready, then I leave again. When I walk back down the pathway to return to Thomas, someone with an iron grip seizes my wrist and pulls me into a dark corner, giving me a start.

"Couldn't you at least try not to rub him in my face?" The strong smell of alcohol makes me realize that Travis is not in full possession of his faculties. What is he still doing here? Tiffany said he was gone. Has he been spying on me all this time?

"Travis, let go of my wrist right now, you're hurting me." He doesn't let go. He keeps squeezing me angrily.

"You left me because I cheated on you. But you'll get with that guy? Who fucks one girl after another?"

"Let me go," I repeat in a stern voice.

He skewers me with a glare , but finally releases my wrist. I massage my skin, trying to soothe the pain. "I'm not with him. And you didn't just cheat, you did much worse. Also, am I to understand that you spent the evening spying on me?"

"I don't have to spy on you, seems like you're not trying to hide anything. So now you just spend your days getting fucked by that rat? I don't recognize you anymore. You're no longer the Nessy I fell in love with. She was a serious girl. She would never have done anything like this. I can hardly even look you in the face, knowing that he's touched it."

Oh, that's rich.

"If you had loved me even a little bit, you wouldn't have done what you did. For the first time in my life, I feel free to do whatever I want without any constraints. And you know what, Travis? If that means you can't look me in the face anymore, then don't. I'd rather be fucked by him than looked at by you any day," I confess, completely without shame and leaving him stunned.

"So this is how it's going to be from now on?"

I shrug. "Look away, if you don't like what you see."

He snorts in disbelief, ducking his head. "You said I was para-noid... But look what happened: I lost you because of him."

I goggle at him. "You did not lose me because of him. You lost me because of you!"

"Do you think I don't know that?" he says hotly, raising his voice. "I regret it, believe me! I hate myself for what I did to you. But I miss you. I miss you so much. I miss having lunch with you, sleeping with you. Picking you up and taking you to campus. I miss your voice, your touch, your smile… That's what I miss most of all. Seeing you every day and not being able to talk to you is killing me. I'm begging you, please forgive me. Give me another chance. Let me make up for my mistakes."

"You are crazy if you think I'd ever get back together with you." I give him a thoroughly disgusted look.

"I still love you."

"But I don't. I probably stopped even before I learned the truth. So I won't be getting back together with you, not now and not ever." I stare straight into his eyes.

"Nothing makes sense without you." And he sounds so desperate that it's hard to believe this is the same Travis with whom I spent two years of my life.

"I'm sorry you're suffering, but you should have thought about that before. Things aren't going to change."

He looks at me for a few moments before shouting, "Don't you think about how humiliating your attitude is for me? Every day I'm forced to deal with the piece of shit you fell in love with! Don't you ever think about how that makes me feel? Why, Vanessa? Just tell me why him of all people? I need to know." My heart skips a beat when he says "in love."

"I'm not going to talk about this with you." I try to push past him, but he doesn't move.

"I need to know why!"

"Travis, let me go!" I push him again, harder this time, but he resists.

"Tell me!" he yells in my face, making me wince.

"Do you really want to know why him? Because he's a breath of fresh air. Because he's showed me sides of myself that I didn't even know I had. Because he doesn't pretend to be someone he isn't. And because, from the first moment he looked at me, I felt…alive." Travis shakes his head, as if trying to fend off my words. "Is that what you wanted to hear? Now you know."

I pull away from him, and he finally lets me. He is staring blankly at nothing and, absurd as it is, it hurts me to see him like that. "I'm sorry, Travis, I really am sorry." The words bubble up from the bottom of my heart. They are true and they hurt. "But you and I...our chapter is closed now."

Before I can turn the corner and leave him behind, Travis grabs my arm violently. He slams me hard against the wall. Pain from the impact explodes inside me. He rams his mouth against mine, and I freeze for a moment before I'm finally able to react and push him away.

"Travis! What the hell is wrong with you!" I scrub my lips with the back of one hand, while gingerly touching my injured shoulder with the other.

Then, everything becomes a confusing whirl. I hear a dull thud. Unclear images cloud my mind. I am helpless, unable to move a single muscle. My ears are ringing. My body tingles. It burns. It shivers. One moment, Travis is in front of me, the next moment, he is lying on the ground. Thomas is on top of him, hitting him repeatedly in the face.

"Should've. Put. You. Down. Last. Time." There's a punch for each word, an angry punctuation. "But I'll be happy to do it today." Travis groans and writhes under Thomas's uncontrolled and unstoppable blows. He tries to wriggle free, but the blind fury of his opponent prevents him from doing so.

"Stop, Thomas! You'll kill him!" I scream as loud as I can.

My heart beats uncontrollably at the sight of blood spilling out onto the grass. Hands in my hair, I am begging for him to stop, but Thomas is consumed by feral rage. He doesn't even seem to hear my screams.

Alex and one of his classmates find us. They grab Thomas by the shoulders, and finally pull him off Travis. The latter, his face hugely swollen, tries to sit up. He looks at me, dazed from the many hits he's taken.

"Vanessa, please forgive me. I don't know what came over me. I didn't mean to hurt you. I-I lost control," he stammers in shock, as tears, mixed with blood, flow down his face.

Looking at him disgusts me. My body trembles. My temples throb. It feels as though my heart is going to explode, it's beating so rapidly. "Come near me again, and I'll go straight to the police."

I turn to Thomas, whose eyes are still on fire, his muscles tense, and his breathing irregular. Without a second thought, I take his face into my hands and force him to look into my eyes. "Thomas, you need to calm down. Please."

"Calm down?" Thomas takes my wrist, slowly, and touches the marks that Travis left on me. "He put his hands on you, and you ask me to calm down?"

"You did what to her?" Alex shouts, suddenly also beside himself.

"Alex, please, not now," I beg him because I know it's much easier to convince him to leave than Thomas. Then I return to Thomas. I try to gently take his hand, but he doesn't let me touch him and continues to stare hatefully at Travis. "Please, let's go." I grasp his face in my hands again. "I need to leave." If I want to get us both out of here without making anything worse, I don't think it's a good idea to tell him about the excruciating pain I feel in my back from where Travis shoved me against the wall. "I'm okay, but I need to leave." Only then, after lingering for a long time on both me and Travis, does Thomas allow me to drag him away.

Thirty-One

"FUCK YOU!" THOMAS KICKS THE front tire of his car, and I gasp in fright. He turns on his heel to face me and grabs my wrists, examining them for the third time. My eyes land on his swollen knuckles and I shiver. I take his hands and, when I touch the raw places, I notice a small grimace of pain cross his face.

"You have to stop losing control like this," I murmur, filled with fear.

"You should be grateful that prick is still breathing," he answers with a clenched jaw and short, heavy breaths. "Has this happened before?" His eyes are full of concern as he looks at me, lifting my chin with two fingers.

My eyes widen. "No. Absolutely not!" I cover my face with both hands and take a deep breath, trying to stem the tide of agitation. I'm shaken up; I want to leave this place as soon as possible. Hole up under the warm blankets of my soft bed and forget about everything. "Can we—can we get out of here, please?" I half-whisper in a trembling voice.

Thomas looks carefully at me, inspecting every inch of my body, lingering on my wrists and my shoulders. Then he nods. He guides me to the car, opens the door, and with a nod invites me to get in; we fasten our seat belts and go.

He remains silent for the entire ride, one hand on the steering wheel and the other on the gearshift. He busts all the speed limits and stares grimly at the road while I twist my fingers in my lap. I would like to talk to him. I would like him to reassure me. I would like to know that he is at least thinking about me. I need it, desperately. I need him, but Thomas is closed off in his own world, inaccessible to me. All I can do is curl up, resigned, with my back to him. I squeeze my hands between my crossed legs, in an attempt to stop the trembling in my body. Out of the corner of my eye, I see him reach an arm behind the seat to retrieve a black sweatshirt. He throws it over my legs without looking at me. I catch it and turn slightly toward him.

"Put it on. You're shaking," he orders impassively. I'd thank him, except that I can't figure out why he's so surly with me. I slip on the sweatshirt and am immediately overwhelmed by the unmistakable scent of vetiver and tobacco. I breathe it in automatically. Thomas looks at me furtively, with the expression of a person who has just caught someone in flagrante delicto. I feel my cheeks heat up. I immediately turn toward the window to keep him from seeing. I tug the sleeves of the sweatshirt over my fingertips and rest my forehead on the glass.

"You can keep it, if you want," he says.

"That's not necessary."

"I want you to have it."

A shy smile creeps onto my face. "Okay," I murmur.

Silence falls again between us, the reckless driving subsides a little, and I am finally able to relax a bit. I realize, though, that we are not going to my house; Thomas is headed to campus. I turn to him, confused, brush a strand of hair from my face and ask, "Aren't you taking me home?" He tilts his face slightly toward me and shakes his head no.

When we arrive, the campus is dark and deserted, illuminated only by a few streetlamps that give off a dim glow. As we're getting out of the car, the cold night air shocks me from my torpor. My teeth chatter, and I hug myself.

As soon as Thomas notices, he comes around the car to join me. "Can you explain to me how you are always so cold?"

I tilt my head to get a better look at him. "It's two o'clock in the morning, I'm wearing damp clothes, and my hair is still wet." Thomas wraps his arm around my shoulders and holds me against himself to warm me up, or maybe to comfort me, I can't tell. All I know is that I dig my nose into his chest and let myself be enveloped by his warmth.

The suite is empty and pleasantly warm. Thomas tells me that Larry is at a gamer party, so he won't be coming back anytime soon. Apparently, the only way to get him out of the dorm for the night is to engage him in a game of *Dungeons & Dragons*. I slip my bag off my shoulder and set it down on the table. This simple movement causes my mouth to twist in a grimace of pain.

"Does it hurt?" Thomas blurts out, watching me grimly. "And don't bullshit me."

"A little," I admit, as he moves closer to me, alert, and pushes back my shirt to check for bruises with his own eyes.

"It's swelling. You'll have a bruise tomorrow. Better get some ice on it," he explains coolly before backing off to reestablish a physical distance between us. I watch as he slips off his shoes, his sweatshirt, and his jeans, until he is wearing only his tight black boxers, which are still wet.

I remain motionless behind him before swallowing. "W-what are you doing?"

"Taking a shower," he answers carelessly. "Wanna join me?"

Another time, I would have taken it as a provocation. But the blank expression on his face leads me to believe he's not interested in joking right now either.

"Um, no, thanks. I prefer to shower alone. At my house," I reply, a little embarrassed.

"Whatever. There's beer in the fridge. Or, you know, water. Help yourself. Ice is in the freezer," he says, walking into the bathroom and closing the door behind him.

I sit on the couch and let out a deep breath. Propping my head up on the backrest and looking at the ceiling, the sound of running water lulls my confused mind. So much has happened; I feel like this has been the longest night of my life. In an instant, I went from resting in Thomas's arms to weathering Travis's outburst. I'd never seen him so upset before. When I think about just how much my life has changed in the space of a little more than a month, I don't recognize myself. All the familiar landmarks from my old life have collapsed, and now, on Thomas's couch, I also feel transformed. I sigh again and put my hair back in a ponytail. When I move my left arm, I feel another twinge in my shoulder. I decide to take Thomas's advice and put ice on it.

About ten minutes later, the bathroom door opens, and the living room is hit with a wave of steam. Thomas comes out with one white towel wrapped around his hips while using a smaller one to rub his hair. The prominent veins in his arms stand out even more with the motion. A few droplets of water run down his abs, before disappearing into the edge of the towel. His sculpted body makes me forget about everything else for a few interminable moments.

"Are you ever going to get used to it?" He smirks as he disappears into his room.

"G-get used to what?" I blink and shake my head, trying to banish that image from my mind. I put the bag of ice on the table. The pain has eased up a little.

"To my body."

I immediately turn red and am very thankful that he's in the other room. I close my eyes, grab a cushion from the sofa, and bury my face in it, cursing myself.

"You're so full of yourself, Thomas. I like your tattoos, that's all..." I stammer out, trying to sound believable.

"Yes, of course. I really like your eyes too," he answers mockingly from the other room.

I frown. "Are you trying to say that you don't really like them?" Should I be offended?

"I like your eyes." He returns to the living room wearing only a low-slung pair of sweatpants. His hair is still damp and tousled. "But I much prefer your ass. Your tits," he continues, looking me over greedily as he gets a beer from the fridge. "Your legs." He gestures to them with the bottle, advancing upon me with a sensual stare that lights me up from within. "Your cu—"

My eyes bulge. "Okay, stop! I get it," I interrupt him, face ablaze, as he laughs under his breath.

He sits down next to me, rests his beer on the low table in front of us and looks at me intently for a few seconds. "You've got my whole head fucked up, Ness. All of you."

My heart leaps in my chest. How can he say something like that so easily when I can barely hold his gaze? I smile at him, in my usual awkward and embarrassed way, sinking my teeth into my lip. He smiles back, but it is a weak, unhappy smile. The kind of smile that hides something. I have the feeling that he is not at peace with himself, like he feels some guilt toward me. I can see in his eyes that he wants to ask how I am and make sure I'm okay, but for some reason, he doesn't.

Instead, he grabs the remote control and turns on the TV in front of us. He settles deeper into the sofa, resting his crossed legs on the coffee table, folding one arm behind the back of his head and sipping his beer. I take off my shoes and cross my legs, putting a pillow on top of them. Thomas does some channel surfing, and we happen upon a rerun of *The Vampire Diaries*. My eyes light up instantly. With all the feeling of a little girl on her birthday, I beg him not to change the channel. Thomas rolls his eyes but agrees on the condition that I don't expect "cuddles or shit like that" from him while we watch. So I then repress the sudden, strong urge to curl up against him.

"This Stefan guy is a pain in the ass prig. He's pissing me off already," he announces impatiently after the first two minutes. I laugh out loud.

"Just think, he only gets worse as the seasons go on."

"Fuck, seriously?"

"Wait, are you telling me you've never seen this show?" I look at him in shock.

"What do you think?"

I squint at him. "Have you been living under a rock?"

"I've just been living."

Probably while I was tucked in bed dreaming about Damon Salvatore, he was busy banging some Katherine Pierce type. Throughout the episode, I notice that Thomas keeps giving me these little surreptitious looks. It makes me feel a little uncomfortable knowing that someone is studying my every move, but at the same time, I love that he is the one doing it, so I don't say anything about it.

We spend the rest of the time commenting on the episode, and Thomas seems gradually more interested. So much so that he almost doesn't protest when, at the end of the episode, another one begins immediately.

"Are you feeling better, Ness?" He looks at me, and I do likewise.

I smile shyly at him and nod, but he doesn't seem convinced.

He slides his right arm behind my back, grabs my waist, and, in one fluid motion, pulls me on top of him in a seated position. Instinctively, I put my palms on his bare chest to steady myself. Thomas covers my thighs with his hands, settling me astride his groin. My breathing immediately becomes more intense, and from the smirk on his face, I can tell he's noticed. Damn. I must seem pathetically predictable to him. My eyes dart this way and that as I desperately try to avoid eye contact with Thomas. Yes, sustaining that kind of fearless, penetrating stare is clearly a rather arduous task.

"You're still shaken up about what happened, aren't you?" he asks, stroking my jaw with his thumb as he watches me closely.

"No, I'm fine," I reassure him. And it's the truth: I am fine now that I'm here with him.

"I went overboard. I wouldn't blame you for being scared. The truth is, I'm constantly trying to tamp down all this anger that's just burning inside me, and when it explodes, it overpowers me and I end up losing control. But I want you to know that I would never do anything to hurt you. You are safe with me." I know I am. In fact, I've never felt more protected in my life.

I frown. "Do you think I am afraid of you? If that was the case, I wouldn't be here right now."

He lowers his eyes. " I saw the way you looked at me…"

"Thomas." I cup his face with my hands. "I'm not afraid of you. If anything, I'm afraid *for* you. I understand why you reacted the way you did and I'm grateful you did. But I don't want you to get in trouble because of me; I could never forgive myself."

"That won't stop me from beating his ass if he ever tries it again. In fact, I want to be very clear about one thing: if you think I'll just sit on my hands and watch the next time some asshole so much as lays a finger on you, you thought wrong." Arrogant. Possessive. Ruthless. As always.

I frown. I move my hands away from his face and lean back a little to get a better look at him. "You can't just attack anyone who hangs around me." I say this more sharply than I meant to, but I want to make sure he gets the message loud and clear.

"Wanna bet?" he answers insolently.

We stare, taking the measure of one another in silence for a few seconds. "You won't. I'm not your property. You have no claim on me," I say finally, confidently.

"I don't need a claim to let some dickhead know you're off-limits," he says boldly. I feel my blood begin to boil. What kind of caveman presumption is this? Off-limits? I stare at him with my mouth open, shocked by what he's said. I even consider making a thing about it, but then think better of it. I have no real desire to argue again; we've had more than enough arguments today. We'll deal with this topic another time because I am positive it will come up again.

I take a deep breath, suppressing the outrage I can feel growing in me. I shake my head and try to dissipate the tension. "Just promise me that the next time you feel like you're losing control, you'll count to ten instead."

"Ten's too much."

"Five?"

"Three. And that's me doing you a favor." He points a finger at me in a joking manner, but I am too tired to take it gracefully.

"Doing yourself a favor," I retort seriously.

"No, I'd be doing it for you, because I like to lose control. All that adrenaline pumping in my veins… You can't buy a feeling like that," he confesses contentedly.

I look at him, dumbfounded. "And how do you feel about spending the rest of your days in prison? Because that's where you're going to end up, sooner or later, if you don't chill out." He snorts, like I'm talking nonsense. I'm seriously starting to lose my patience with him. "Does that make you laugh? You really don't think something like that could happen to you?"

He rubs his forehead in an irritated fashion. "I think you're getting heated over nothing."

"Do you even listen to yourself when you talk?" I get up off his lap.

He sighs, rests his elbows on his knees and looks steadily into my eyes. "If you want to know the truth, I don't actually give a shit about the consequences, all right?" He leans back, spreading his arms across the back of the sofa.

My eyes widen. "No, that is not all right! Do you think your life is a game? Or the lives of the people around you? Don't you think about them? About the pain you would cause them if the worst happened?" I yell. One way or another, he always manages to turn me into a crazy person.

"This is why I don't want any ties. I don't want to be forced to do the right thing for the sake of someone else." In the face of my discomfited expression, he continues, "Don't act so surprised. This is me, Vanessa. Learn to accept it, because I'm not going to change, not even for you. You can take it or leave it."

"You are truly unbelievable, Thomas!" I dig my hands into my hair, exasperated, and turn my back to him.

"Please explain to me: Why are we fighting right now?" he asks, irritated.

I turn back to face him. "We are not fighting! I am fighting you!"

"And what are you doing that for?"

"I don't know!" I cross my arms and plant myself in front of him, looking sullen.

He looks at me in bewilderment for a few seconds before bursting into laughter as he shakes his head.

"What the hell are you laughing at?" I snap.

"You went on this whole long rant and you don't even know why?" He grabs me by the wrist and pulls me back to him. "Do you realize how completely insane you are?" he continues, with a smile on his lips that I struggle not to find attractive. I bend my right knee into the sofa, positioning it in between his legs.

"But I do know why. Because you're selfish. You take a sick pleasure in hurting the people around you. You don't care about anyone else, you just want to maintain control over everything," I tell him in my most condescending tone.

"Accurate description, Clark." Thomas unbends my crossed arms and takes my hands, intertwining his fingers with mine. "But isn't that what makes me irresistible?"

"No. It's what makes you sadistic."

He grabs my thighs, covered by my skirt, and pushes me back down on top of him. "So why are you wasting your time with a sadist like me?" The tone of his voice has changed, it sounds deeper. Rougher. It makes my head spin.

"Guess I'm a masochist," I murmur.

"Mhm." He rubs his nose against mine. "A sadist and a masochist: what a winning combination." He grins.

"Toxic, more like," I reply in a whisper.

"Tell me something, Ness." He uses one knuckle to push a strand of hair behind my shoulder, careful not to touch my sore spot. Then he slides his fingers through my hair and clasps a hank of it in his fist. With his other hand, he touches my lips. "When was the last time I kissed this mouth?"

We're so close that I can feel his breath on me. Beer and tobacco, it's a taste that sends all my senses into overdrive. A second ago, I was screaming at him, and now I find myself a heartbeat away from his lips, eager to take them for mine again.

"I don't know," I choke out, my breath becoming more and more irregular. Thomas moves his hands, rubbing my thighs in slow movements. He works his fingers under the tight fabric of my skirt. He wraps his hands around my buttocks and an electric shock sizzles in my lower abdomen. I lick my dry lips and bite down on them. "It's been a while…"

"Too long…" He brushes my mouth with his own until my lips open for him, until that slight contact becomes a gentle kiss with a slow, deep rhythm. Feeling his lips on mine once again, I feel a flush of heat spread through my abdomen and a thousand emotions completely obscure my reason. This proximity is kindling an overwhelming desire inside me. I throw my arms around his neck and, as I open my lips to welcome him, his tongue collides with mine, yearning, hot, impatient, as if this part of me has always belonged to him. Our kiss transforms into pure fire.

"You have the most inviting mouth I've ever seen." I feel a throbbing in my panties, and the heated feeling between my legs becomes even more intense. In an attempt to relieve it, I begin rubbing myself against his erection, which is steadily growing larger and larger under his sweatpants. Thomas bites my lip roughly and chases the movements of my hips with short, vigorous thrusts of his own. He's squeezing my ass so hard that it forces a moan of commingled pain and pleasure from me. I can feel him smiling against my lips, and I realize just how much he enjoys exerting this power over me. Feeling my body yield to him. Making me a slave to all his desires. What surprises me most, though, is that I like it too. This is a side of myself that I am only now discovering, and only with Thomas.

"You've been flaunting your ass in front of me for two days now, wrapped up in this skirt…" he says breathlessly. His muscular, tattooed chest is completely exposed. The unruly hair, the burning green eyes, the swollen lips… Beautiful. "And for two days, all I've thought about is how to get it off you…"

I press my body harder against his as he continues to suck my lower lip. "So what are you waiting for?"

Thomas pulls away from me, leaving me staggered for a few moments. I find myself giving a little moan at the separation. I want those full lips back on my mouth, I want his warmth again. He touches my cheek, resting his forehead on mine. "You're dangerous…"

"You're the dangerous one," I confess as my eyes and my fingers run along his broad shoulders. They slide over his defined biceps, his sides, his tense abdominal muscles leading down to the elastic of his sweatpants. I feel like I could spend hours upon hours exploring every part of his body with my hands and my mouth and never tire of it but, on the contrary, only crave more and more. Thomas urges me to grind my hips back and forth more rapidly. Shivers break out all over my body.

My breathing is labored with pleasure; I squeeze my eyes closed and tuck my forehead into the crook of his neck. I beg him to speed up, already feeling the heat burn its way through me. Suddenly, I feel the strongest urge to make him feel just as good as he is making me feel. I slip a hand under his sweatpants and am surprised to find that he isn't wearing underwear. When I look at him, he just gives me that crooked smile that drives me crazy. I lean over him and kiss him again because… well, because I can't help it. He responds with identical hunger, entwining his tongue with mine. I draw my hand over his erection; it is smooth and hot and, as I grip it, I can feel it getting larger and larger in my hand. Thomas lets out a hoarse groan and lifts his pelvis just a bit, just enough to lower his sweatpants and give me more freedom of movement. I move my hand over his entire length, and I feel him quivering under my fingers. A shy, triumphant smile creeps across my face as I realize he's just as aroused and completely lost as I am.

"Keep going," he grunts into my mouth. I wrap both hands around his erection, one at the base and the other around the tip, which is already leaking. I feel it stiffen as soon I begin to move my wrists up and down, coating it with liquid. The sight makes me wet too. Thomas pushes my panties aside and touches me, finally relieving some of the unbearable tension I've been feeling ever since he started rubbing himself against me. Then he pushes two fingers inside me and I am breathless. I toss my head back, gripping his hard-on even tighter.

"Fuck, you're hot." Thomas pulls his fingers out slowly, before forcefully filling me again almost immediately.

"Oh God…Thomas…" I gasp. "D-don't stop, please…"

"I won't stop," he replies against my lips. "I wanna make you come so hard. Until you pass out." He steals another greedy, passionate kiss, slipping a hand under my sweatshirt and squeezing my breast. We pleasure one other decadently, his fingers inside me, my hand on him. Moans, breathless and uncontrolled, spill from our mouths. "Christ, you're flooding my hand." He smiles smugly.

Oh, I am aware. And embarrassed. Yet, feeling him in my hands and watching him get off thanks to me, with his eyes half-closed, mouth slightly open, cheeks reddened…turns me on so much.

"And you're flooding mine," I answer, biting my lip. The gesture makes his member throb. Pleased with the reaction I've drawn out of him, I speed up my movements. I notice his abdomen tensing with each stroke.

"Fuck, yeah…like that…" His hoarse voice shakes me down to my bones. He uses his thumb to draw teasing circles around my most sensitive spot and thrusts his index and middle fingers in and out of me until I am delirious. Just a few strokes are enough to pull me over the edge. I contract around his fingers, trembling as I fall victim to an orgasm that Thomas tries to prolong as much as possible. Finally, he follows me with a deep grunt of passion. There is a hot, whitish gush from his tip, and it drips along his shaft and over the back of my hand. We are both hit by uncontrollable spasms. Eyes shut tight, we sink our hands into each other's bodies, tongues entwined, breath mingling. Then, Thomas pulls his fingers out of me; they are glistening with my pleasure.

He lifts up my sweater, peels aside the bikini top, and rubs my swollen breasts obscenely. He squeezes them firmly and runs his tongue along the curve of them. "I really want to fuck you now, Ness." He pounces on my mouth, thrusting his tongue inside in a way that feels like being touched with a burning brand. Everything he does, the way he speaks, how he moves, how he looks at me; it makes me feel something I have never felt before. I feel dirty, hungry. It's a brand-new feeling, but I like it.

He gets off the sofa, picking me up in his arms and walking us both to his room. He closes the door behind him with a kick. He grabs some tissues from his bedside drawer, and we use them to wipe ourselves clean. Then he puts me down on top of the desk, spreads my legs, and settles himself between them, pulling me tight against him. The room, previously silent, immediately fills with the sounds of heavy breathing and hoarse moans. In no time, Thomas has me out of my shirt and bikini top, throwing both of them to the floor. At the sight of my naked breasts, he emits a moan of appreciation. He stares at them before lowering his head and closing his hungry mouth over one nipple, sucking it and pulling it delicately with his teeth. I arch my back and push myself into him. He lavishes the same attention on the other breast, giving me shivers that make my whole body unsteady. He squeezes both my breasts in his cupped hands and goes back to kissing my mouth with the kind of passion that makes me tremble. His kisses are always possessive. The kind that make you a slave to his desires. The kind that impose his will on you.

"I want you naked and under me right now." His tone is imperious. He rips away my panties with an almost angry gesture, grabs me by the hips, and jerks me around, bending me over the desk. The press of my breasts against the wood gives me goosebumps.

He backs up a few steps and then returns. I turn my head to the side to get a better look at him and I see him tearing an aluminum packet with his teeth before pulling out a condom and slipping it on. "On second thought, I think I'll fuck you with the skirt on." The note of perversion in his words heats my skin. He rubs my shoulders, placing gentle kisses along my spine and on my injured shoulder. As soon as I try to get up, though, he holds me down with a hand pressed to the base of my spine.

Then he slips one leg between my thighs and spreads them, pushing his erection into the cleft of my butt. He grips my hair at the nape of my neck and, in a sensual voice, whispers, "Open those legs, Ness. Let me admire you."

"Thomas…" I moan, embarrassed. I offer some resistance, not because I don't want it but because I am not used to having sex like this, so shamelessly.

Seeing my hesitation, he tightens his grip on my hair and leans over me, rubbing his erection against me. He brings his mouth to my ear and licks it lasciviously, which only intensifies the sense of dizziness left by the orgasm. "You are everything a man could want to have in his hands, and between his legs." His tongue traces down my neck and I tremble. "Don't be embarrassed." He grips and positions himself against my opening, sliding slowly into my warm, moist folds. He penetrates me only with his tip again and again, taking his time without going further. Then he pulls right out and I find myself moaning through clenched teeth.

"Let go." His breath is hot and labored against my neck. Then comes another little thrust that leaves me breathless the moment he pulls back. Every fiber of my body longs to have him, to feel and possess him. I moan, squirming underneath him, and I push back against him with my butt. "Good job..." He lifts the hem of the skirt and slowly rubs my backside. "Give in to instinct." He slaps me on one cheek, making me purse my lips to hold back a moan and, exactly at that moment, he penetrates me with a sharp thrust that makes me arch my back, clench my fists, and scream his name. He is motionless inside me, his hands on my hips, giving me a moment to get used to his size. Then, he pulls out and pushes back in with more force, making me scream once again. His thrusts are so deep and wild that they tear screams of commingled pain and pleasure from me. Without letting go of his grip on my hair, he slides his other hand down my belly to my pubic mound. His fingers move rapidly over my clitoris as he continues to sink inside me so ferociously, dragging me closer and closer to the tipping point.

"Oh God, Thomas... What...what are you doing to me?" I have never experienced such intense, overwhelming pleasure in my entire life.

"I'm pleasuring you until you pass out." His sweat is mixing with my own, our bodies merging to a soundtrack of gasps and moans. I roll my eyes heavenward, overwhelmed by the devastating sensations. I can no longer control the chain of screams that are dragged from my lips.

I'm breathing erratically, shaking uncontrollably as the pace of his thrusting increases, becoming somehow even more brutal. My heart races, my knees are watery, my head is spinning…

"Don't come. Not yet." He pants out the order, as if I could actually control it.

"Thomas…I…I can't," I gasp, grinding eagerly against him.

He slows his thrusts until he finally stops altogether. With one movement, he skillfully flips me over, before picking me up and laying me down on the bed. "I want you to watch me make you come. You need to know that I'm the one who's making you lose control. Only me." He opens my lips with his tongue and sinks back into me forcefully, pushing the air from my lungs. Stunned, I watch him slide in and out of my body, I pant underneath him as I feel that wave of pleasure overwhelming me again. He stares at me with such intensity that takes my breath away.

He grabs my thigh with one hand and opens my legs up wider, as he continues to move relentlessly inside me. I am drenched in sweat, and all my nerve endings are tingling, overwhelmed with tension, pain, and insane pleasure. I clamp my knees around his hips, place my hands on his shoulders, sink my nails into his flesh, and explode with his name on my lips. He tenses the muscles in his arms and back, presses one hand into the mattress and thrusts himself into me with such unexpected force that I fear he might actually break me. I cry out, vibrating with extreme pleasure, chasing his movements with what little strength I have left, until I feel him stiffen. With his cheek pressed against mine, he gasps as his whole body quakes with his orgasm. My limbs are trembling like jelly, and Thomas, drenched and breathing heavily, collapses on my chest. We remain motionless for a long time, clutching each other, as our shared spasms slowly fade. When he does move, after having gotten his breath back, he does so to brush a few strands of hair from my temples. His face is pearly with sweat, his cheeks are flushed, and his hair falls over his forehead, softening his features. He stares at me confusedly, as if trying to tell me something with only his eyes. I try, but I just can't understand what he's thinking.

"Is…is everything okay?" I ask in a small whisper.

He nods half-heartedly, then presses his lips to mine and grins. "You're still wearing the skirt."

"Apparently it did its job well," I joke.

He studies me with wary eyes and pulls away from me to throw the condom into the trash can next to the bed. He looks back at me. "Did you put it on for me? To make me look?"

"I put it on because I felt like it. Or, maybe to attract someone's attention..." I bite my upper lip, uncertain whether to keep talking or preserve what little dignity I have left.

"Someone?" he presses, suddenly annoyed.

I nod and feel a stab of humiliation in my stomach as I admit this pathetic truth. I am compelled to cover my face with my hands to conceal my shame before saying: "You." I am motionless for a few seconds, saying nothing, while I imagine him with his usual irresistible asshole smile spread all over his face, ready to mock me mercilessly.

When he gently removes my hands from my face, his surprised look pierces me. "Did you want to get my attention?" he asks in a sweet whisper.

"I wasn't entirely aware of it," I babble, trying to underplay it.

"Did you think you had to dress sexy for me to look at you?" He traces the outline of my lips with a finger, and I can feel his renewed erection pressing against my crotch. That skin-to-skin contact makes me shiver. "Don't get me wrong, you succeeded. I have spent the last two days imagining myself sinking between your thighs, and fucking not only this"—he touches the still heated folds of my vagina with one hand—"but also this." His hand drifts mischievously to my butt and grasps it firmly, causing me to lift my pelvis slightly. "But you always have my attention. Even when you're wearing terrible teddy bear pajamas and questionable unicorn-shaped slippers." He laughs, pressing a kiss to the tip of my nose. It always amazes me the way he can utter the dirtiest stuff and accompany it with affectionate gestures like that.

"Hey, don't malign my pajamas and slippers, they're beautiful." I pat him tenderly on the chest, hoping I'm not blushing too hard. "I have to take a shower," I add quickly.

"Me too, let's go." He starts to get up, but I shake my head. Thomas must have sensed my embarrassment because, for once, he doesn't say anything. He leans over the crook of my neck and kisses it slowly. I shiver and close my eyes. I cannot get enough of his kisses, his touch. I wonder if it is normal, this addiction that I have to him? And will it only grow stronger and stronger?

"You'll let me fuck you but you don't want me to look at you…"

And there it is, the comeback I was hoping to avoid. He raises his head, waiting for an answer that won't come. I realize that this is silly. That, for the most part, people showering together is normal, especially if you've already shared the most intimate part of yourself with someone. But for me it's not like that. I shrug. "You know I don't feel comfortable with that idea."

He snorts. "How many more times do I have to tell you before you get it into your little head?" He bends down and kisses my breast; a shudder moves through my entire body. "You…" he murmurs, continuing to kiss down my belly as my back arches involuntarily. "Are…" He slips further down, spreads my legs, sticks his head between them and blows on my clit. "Perfect." His tongue caresses me slowly, and I find myself growing hot again, clawing at the sheets as if I hadn't just come twice and wasn't still weathering the excruciating and all-consuming sensations of climax. Can my body actually handle a third orgasm in a row? The answer seems to be "yes," especially when Thomas focuses all his attention on my most sensitive area, giving me a feeling of ecstasy that makes me bend my head back and bite my lip.

"Oh…God," I gasp.

The movements of his tongue send nearly unbearable shocks through me that quickly bring me to the edge. When my legs start shaking, Thomas grabs me by the thighs and holds me still, continuing to lick me even more intensely.

I writhe underneath him, threading my hands through his hair, pushing his head against my center. With my vision blurred and my heart in my throat, I half-sob, half-scream. I am overwhelmed by waves of sensation at once agonizing and satiating. Thomas keeps up this torture through my last pulse, drawing out this agony that sends me adrift for as long as possible.

While I am still spasming uncontrollably, he crawls on top of me and takes my mouth in a vise-like grip. He smiles, cheeky and yet tremendously sensual. "You have no idea how much I enjoy watching you come on me." He bites my lip and I rub the back of his neck with weak little movements. I struggle to reply, but I'm too exhausted. My body is still shaking wildly, and I don't have the strength to move, or to speak, or to think.

"You've destroyed me," is all I can manage, with the hint of a worn-out, yet satisfied smile on my face.

"I could keep fucking you all night. But you need to rest." He gets up and, with his erection still clearly visible, he pulls his sweatpants back on. "Come on, I'll take you to the shower." He lifts me up and I loop my arms around his neck, squeezing myself against him. In front of the tub, he gestures for me to get down and, for a moment, I feel so sapped of strength that I worry I'll just collapse to the ground. Thomas supports me with an arm around my waist. He helps me get my skirt off, leaving a trail of gentle kisses on both thighs and my pubic mound. After turning on the hot water, he presses his mouth to mine one last time and goes, leaving me with the calm that I need.

Thirty-Two

I GET OUT OF THE shower, wrap a towel around my breasts, and inhale the fresh scent of Thomas's soap all over me. My body is sore, and my lower abdomen is roiling. In front of the slightly fogged mirror, I flex my arm and touch my shoulder blade. The pain is still there, but it's much more bearable. The rest of my body, however, is covered with red marks left by my tattooed man.

My... No, that's probably not the right way to think about him. Still, he does feel a little bit more mine after tonight. And I always feel a little more his whenever he looks at me with those intense green eyes and I forget about the whole world, or when he touches me with that feverish passion of his. A passion that, tonight, he fully unleashed on me. Yet I did not miss the way he made every part of my body his own, except for my shoulder. He placed one soft kiss on it before diving into me with a thrust so powerful it bent my back. It felt like he was staking a claim on me. At the mere memory, I shudder and bring a hand to my belly, savoring those pain-and-pleasure twinges that only he can give me. I smile to myself, sinking my teeth into my lip, like a little girl with her first crush.

How stupid...

I shake myself out of these thoughts and in the absence of a brush, I detangle my wet hair with my fingers. Passing through the living room on my way to Thomas's room, I hear the sound of a key in the lock before the front door opens and Larry appears before me. Seeing me, he drops the books he was holding to the floor.

"H-hi," I mutter, caught off guard. I clutch the towel more tightly against my chest.

He stares at me with his mouth open, not saying anything, and I start to wonder why Thomas doesn't come out of his room and put a merciful end to this awkward encounter. At that exact moment, he walks through the front door with a bag in his hands.

"Went down to the gas station to get you a toothbrush," he says simply. He passes Larry as though he didn't even notice his presence, and hands me the toothbrush. I smile and thank him, surprised by the thoughtfulness of the gesture.

"You're not the girl who showed up here a few weeks ago in your slippers and pajamas, are you?" Larry asks, his eyes reduced to two slits, as if trying to focus on the memory.

Thomas gives me a crooked smile and whispers in my ear, "You came here in your pajamas?" He teases me, making my cheeks burn. I want to disappear. Now he and his enormous ego can have a good gloat.

I clear my throat and lean toward Larry. "Um, yeah. That's me." I extend a hand to introduce myself. "I'm Vanessa."

"Larry, pleasure," He takes my hand to shake and, as he does so, I realize his hand is completely coated in sweat. The moist feeling disgusts me, and I want to run back to the bathroom and wash myself all over again but I manage to restrain myself out of politeness. Thomas chuckles under his breath, as if he can clearly see my internal discomfort.

"Are you sleeping here tonight?" Larry asks, just a hint of annoyance in his voice as he loosens his grip. Then he bends down to pick up the books with awkward movements.

"Yes, she's staying," Thomas answers for me, sounding resolute. Does he want me to stay here with him? My heart does a somersault. I hadn't planned on staying, and I certainly didn't think he was going to request it.

"You know I sleep poorly when I know girls are here." Larry turns to Thomas as he places his books on a shelf in the kitchen.

"And you know that if you keep fucking with me, I'll make you sleep in the hallway," threatens the surly tattooed grump standing next to me.

Larry stands up straight and puffs out his chest, ready for a fight. "T-this is my apartment too; you can't just throw me out."

"Yes, and that," Thomas jerks his thumb at the door behind him, "is my room, and I'll let whoever I want in there." He ends the conversation and drags me back into said room. I barely manage to give Larry a wave goodbye before Thomas closes the door. I'm about to ask him why his roommate doesn't want girls around, but then I remember that he had already explained it to me. Larry doesn't want girls in the dorm because Thomas brought over so many that it started to bother him. And if I think about that too much, I'll be sick to my stomach.

"Everything okay?" he asks, seeing my troubled expression. "Don't pay him any mind. He's a weird dude, but it's all fine." He opens a dresser drawer and casually tosses me one of his shirts before lying down on the bed with his arms crossed behind his head.

I take off the towel without too much trepidation. The darkened room, lit only by the glow of the moon, makes me feel a little braver. I put on his shirt and, with only a little uncertainty, I lie down beside him, my hands in my lap. The sheets are still warm. I would like to hug him, to kiss him, and fall asleep tucked up close to him, but I am not at all sure Thomas would want that. After all, now that I think about it, he didn't even want me to snuggle up to him while we were watching television.

I roll away from him, somewhat reluctantly, but he wraps one arm around my waist and forces me to turn and look at him. My mouth is suddenly inches from his chest; his comforting scent invades my nose. He smells like tobacco and sex, the smell of our bodies joined together that still hovers in the room. He rests his chin on my head and hugs me.

"Did I hurt you?" he asks a few seconds later.

I frown and tilt my head back until I can lift my eyes to him. Although the darkness of the room prevents me from seeing him completely, I can feel his watchful gaze on me. I shake my head no.

"I was impulsive. I should have held back, at least for tonight."

"I'm fine. It felt good. Everything felt kind of...amplified, but I'm okay." And it's the truth. A truth that surprises me, too, but... that's how it is. I didn't mind being possessed by Thomas in that way. I found it exciting, at times painful, yes, but tremendously pleasurable. My body trusts him. And that's why I felt safe—because I was with him.

Sensing Thomas's distress, I caress his tense, rough jawline to reassure him, before moving on to his soft lips. I retrace the same path over and over again until I feel his muscles loosen, allowing me to continue my ministrations.

"How's your shoulder?"

"Better." I smile at his odd way of showing concern for me. The tone of his voice is cold and detached, but the way he holds me to him reveals something else entirely.

"You'd tell me, wouldn't you? If it weren't?" He frowns. I nod, but part of me isn't sure I'm telling him the truth. The fact is, he would probably beat himself up even more when there is nothing he can do to solve the problem. I think this is one of those cases where certain things are better kept to myself.

He squeezes me a little tighter while I move my fingers into his hair and begin to stroke it slowly. It's not long before I hear his breathing get heavier, and I realize that he has fallen asleep.

I, however, have no peace. Hours go by. Hours in which I should have been sleeping, but all I did was think. Thomas sleeps beside me, his back to me. I find myself staring at the window across the room, where the first rays of light from the sunrise are filtering in. The things he made me feel tonight overwhelm me like a hurricane. I don't regret it, but I can't stop thinking about how this will be all I ever get from him if I accept his proposal. Great sex, but nothing more. No walking hand in hand. No cuddling on the couch in front of a movie. No going out to the movies. No dinners out or unexpected gifts. No introductions to friends or relatives. Nothing at all. Above all else, he will continue to keep me in the dark about his past.

I want Thomas more than anything in the world. But not enough to become another Shana, waiting around for something he will never be able to give me. I would only wind up heartbroken in the end.

I reach down to the floor and check the time on my phone. It's six o'clock in the morning? Already? Dammit, I didn't get a wink of sleep all night. Fortunately, I don't have any classes today, and Thursday is my day off from the bar.

I slip out of bed and get dressed, careful not to wake Thomas. It's not nice to sneak away without saying anything, but I suppose that's also part of the "no strings attached" package. I'd rather leave of my own volition, saving him the inconvenience of trying to get rid of me without too much rigmarole.

I put on his sweatshirt, my skirt, and my shoes. I toss the bathing suit in my bag along with my sweater. Before leaving the room, I write a note and leave it on his bedside table, letting him know that I went back home. The first bus of the morning is due in exactly five minutes. If I hurry, I can still catch it.

When I arrive home, I see the Toyota parked in the driveway. I open the door cautiously, hoping not to find my mother awake, and the silence that blankets the house lets me know she's still sleeping. I sigh in relief.

I climb the stairs with soft steps and take refuge in my room. I take off my clothes and bury my nose in Thomas's sweatshirt to get a hint of that smell. Then I fold it carefully over my desk chair and put on my flannel pajamas. I close the curtains, silence my phone, and cover my eyes with my sleep mask before curling up under the covers, abandoning myself, finally, to a deep sleep.

Thirty-Three

A LOUD BANG RESOUNDS IN my ears. I whimper and stick my head under the pillow.

"Can I help you?"

"I'm looking for your daughter?"

"And who might you be?"

Maybe I'm dreaming, but I could swear I recognize that voice.

"A friend."

"I know all of my daughter's friends, and you definitely aren't one. Vanessa doesn't hang out with guys like...you. Go bother someone else."

What the...

"I'm not going anywhere." Wait a minute. That voice belongs to... Thomas! I sit up abruptly and tear the mask off my face in a panic.

"Get that hand off my door right now, you degenerate!"

I leap out of bed and rush downstairs. I take the steps two at a time while the vision of Thomas begins to resolve in front of me. He has one hand resting on the open door and, with the other, he holds a cigarette and a helmet. His jaw is tight and his nostrils are flared. I find my mother in a similar condition, facing him. Two banked fires ready to explode. As soon as they spot me at the foot of the stairs, they both stare furiously at me.

"Thomas, w-what are you doing here?" I stammer in shock as I join my mother in the doorway.

"Vanessa, who the hell is this?" my mother shouts indignantly, making me jump.

"Well...he's...a classmate of mine. And don't yell in my ear." I turn my attention from my mother to Thomas, giving him a *what did you come here for?* look. He glowers at me in return. So he's pissed off. Great.

"And can you explain to me why your classmate is showing up on our doorstep at this time of the morning with zero manners?"

Oh my God, all this early-morning melodrama is giving me a headache. I massage my temples, trying to calm some of my irritation. "I don't know, Mom. Don't you have anything else to do? I don't know, hanging out with Victor, for example?" I snap, glaring at her.

"Of course, but I'm not going to leave you alone with this...guy!" she spits out, giving Thomas a deeply offended look.

"Mom!" I shriek in shock. I gesture for Thomas to come in before turning back to my mother. "He and I are going upstairs now and you"—I stab a finger at her—"will stop acting crazy!"

"Vanessa! I will not be talked to like that in my own house," she seethes. "For all I know, he could be a serial killer and you're his next victim!" I shake my head and ignore her. I take Thomas by the sleeve of his jacket and walk him past her. Before entering the house, he pauses to toss his cigarette onto the wooden porch. When he passes my mother, insolent as ever, he blows the last lungful of smoke out just inches from her face. "I'm not sure, but I think I may have just stepped in some dog shit," he taunts her.

My eyes widen at his words, even though I realize he is lying. I tug Thomas by the arm, scolding him and telling him wipe that smirk off his face because he looks like a smug asshole. Then I turn to my mother, horrified.

"Mom, he's just joking. He didn't step in anything."

"Vanessa, we are going to deal with this when I get back. We are not done here." Her nostrils quiver as she focuses all her attention on the giant tattooed man with the rebellious expression and the terrible manners. "As for you, little boy, this is the first and last time I ever let you set foot in my house." My mother is angrier than I have ever seen her as she leaves, slamming the door behind her. I roll my eyes heartily before grabbing Thomas by the wrist and dragging him upstairs to my room. I close the door hastily before turning to glare at him.

"Did you really have to act like that?"

"No. In fact, I should have been much worse. I didn't even have time to open my mouth before she decided that she was looking at human garbage," he retorts irritably, putting his helmet down by the door. I run my hands over my face and take a deep breath.

"Yes, I know. I'm sorry. She's...particular."

"I don't give a shit about your mother. I want to know why you left."

I frown. "What?"

"I woke up and you weren't there. I did, however, find this." He pulls a small ball of paper from his jacket pocket and throws it roughly at me. My note. "What the fuck is wrong with you?"

The little voice in my head bursts into gales of laughter. Now you know what it feels like to wake up alone and find only a measly little note, eh, Collins?

I raise an eyebrow. "You came all the way out here for this?"

"Yes, Ness. Just for this." He brings his hands to his hips, pushing back the sides of his jacket. I can't help but admire him, statuesque in his looming pose. I sigh and pinch the bridge of my nose; I'm surrounded by lunatics, that's all there is to it.

I throw the note into the wastepaper basket and turn to him. "I don't see where the problem is. In fact, you should be thanking me. I saved you all that morning-after fuss you would have felt obligated to go through."

His eyebrows furrow in confusion. "What fuss are you talking about?"

"The kind where you remind me that it was just sex. Don't make it more than that because you and I are not together, blah, blah, blah... I mean, we've been through this before, remember?"

He rubs his face, taking a deep breath.

"I wouldn't have pulled any of that on you."

"Don't talk nonsense. You totally would have. But that's okay." I shrug my shoulders easily. "I wasn't expecting anything else."

He looks at me, perplexed. "I swear, I do not understand you."

"Frustrating, right?" I give him a poke and then walk away toward the bed. When I get there, I fish my little frog-shaped mask out of the blankets and put it on my forehead before lying down.

"What are you doing?"

"What I was doing before you showed up and my mother started freaking out: sleeping."

"Do you sleep with that thing on your head?" he asks mockingly.

"It's for my eyes. Don't make fun," I say. "And, just to be clear, 'that thing' has a name."

"I don't want to know."

"His name is Froggy."

"You're not well."

"And you are cordially invited to leave. Thanks."

"It's almost eight o'clock. Don't you have any extra nerd activities?"

"Not today." I roll over on my side, pull the comforter up to my chin and tug the mask down over my eyes. "Shut the door when you go."

Thomas doesn't answer me. I hear the hardwood floor squeaking under his feet, but instead of moving away he moves closer. The mattress dips down and I turn sharply, lifting my mask. I see him sitting there, intent on removing his jacket and shoes.

"What are you doing?"

"I'm staying here," he says resolutely, not even looking at me.

I snort. "No you're not."

He turns to me and slips under the covers. "You left without giving me any warning. So now you owe me a proper wake-up call. Cover your eyes with this ridiculous toad and go to sleep."

I scowl at him. "And in the meantime? What do you plan to do?"

"Momo, Sparky, and I will devise a plan to finish you off, like a serial killer in a true crime documentary," he answers, giving the stuffed animals at the end of the bed an intimidating stare. I shake my head, equal parts resigned and amused. I pull Froggy over my eyes and lie down with my back to him.

He leans close to my ear and whispers, "Your mother has a few screws loose, Ness. But you with this little mask surpass her by far." I burst out laughing and he does the same, resting his forehead in the juncture where my neck meets my shoulder. He kisses me behind the ear, wraps an arm around my waist and pulls me close to him. "Now sleep," he murmurs into my hair. And I do. I fall asleep with a smile on my lips and crazed butterflies darting around in my stomach.

Thirty-Four

THOMAS SURROUNDS ME COMPLETELY WITH the warmth of his body. My back is pressed against his chest and his arm encircles my waist. His face is buried in my hair. I can feel his slow, relaxed breathing against my neck. Finally feeling rested, I pull Froggy off my eyes and blink as I get used to the light dimly filtering through the curtains.

Unable to hold back my grin, I stare at Thomas's hand on my belly. I find myself tracing the veins that run down the back of it with my index finger. I touch the wounds on his knuckles and then the Old School–style letters that spell his sister's name.

I like his hands. They are large, rough, and enveloping. Under their touch, I feel protected from everything. But, more than anything else, I like waking up and finding him beside me. If I didn't know the way things really are between us, I would even allow myself the luxury of dreaming of awakening in such a way for the rest of my days. Instead, I force myself to drive this image out of my mind and try to come to terms with the reality. The same reality that drove me out of Thomas's apartment this morning and reminds me even now how wrong this all is. Yes, *wrong*. Because even though it is becoming increasingly harder to ignore the feelings that connect me to him, I still can't even pretend that the kind of situationship he's suggesting is okay by me.

Gently, I lift his arm off of me and sit up on the edge of the bed.

Only then do I remember to look at the alarm clock. I'm bewildered to see that it's already two o'clock in the afternoon. Have I really been sleeping all this time?

"So you've finally decided to open your eyes." His low, hoarse voice startles me; I thought he was still asleep.

He reaches out a hand across the mattress, brushing my fingers, but I pull back. It's not what I want to do, not even close. But I can't take the risk of falling back into bad habits again. I need to break these patterns for myself. I know that, if I let him get close to me, it will happen again. It always happens.

"You didn't have to stay here the whole time," I manage. When I pick up my phone from the bedside table, I have five missed calls. All from Logan.

My eyes bug.

Logan.

Suddenly, the big bubble I have sealed myself inside for these last two days pops, and I crash to the ground, forced to face reality. And my reality has me in a choke hold of guilt.

Thomas has managed to suck me into his orbit once again. He is like a tornado, picking me up and carrying me far away, cutting me off from the rest of the world. He's even made me forget entirely about Logan's presence in my life. I press the phone to my forehead, close my eyes, and let out a long, despairing sigh. Logan's not my boyfriend, and we haven't made any promises to each other, but I still feel that I've been unfair to him, insensitive to his feelings.

"What's wrong with you?" Thomas's low, exasperated voice rings out in the empty room.

"Logan called me," I tell him, not turning around.

"Ah, it was him," he mumbles.

"What do you mean?" I twist my torso slightly, giving him a sideways look.

I watch him bring his arms up behind his head and turn his gaze to the ceiling. "Your phone wouldn't stop vibrating." He tilts his head to look at me. "It was about to come to a bad end."

"Did you touch my phone again?"

"Do you think I did?" he snaps back.

"I'm asking you."

He's silent for a few seconds before answering. "No, I didn't touch it," he admits. "But the time has come to call it quits, don't you think?"

I frown. "With Logan? Why should I?" I certainly don't intend to keep dating Logan if the feelings I have for Thomas are so strong that I'm going to lose my mind whenever I'm with him. I would only end up making a fool out of both Logan and myself. But that's not a decision Thomas gets to make.

I can tell by the way he narrows his eyes into two slits that my answer took him by surprise. He lifts himself up on one elbow until our faces are aligned. "Why? Maybe because you spent the night getting dicked down mercilessly by yours truly," he spits contemptuously, leaving me speechless. *Dicked down mercilessly.* That's all it really comes down to in the end. Every emotion I felt, every form of intimacy I thought I shared with him, is annihilated and swept aside by his ruthless cynicism.

"My God, Thomas, what an asshole you are!" I turn my back on him again, on the verge of tears.

Out of the corner of my eye, I see him shake his head and immediately lean toward me. I jerk myself out of the bed and go to the window. I close my eyes, inhaling deeply, and let the wind caress my face as it tosses the dry leaves hither and yon outside. The grayness of the clouds suggests a big storm is on the way. Just what I need.

I hear the creaking of the mattress and Thomas's footsteps approaching. He takes the pack of Marlboros from his jacket pocket and leans against the windowsill beside me, looking up at the rain-heavy clouds moving swiftly across the sky. I'd like to tell him that there is no smoking allowed in here, but I know he wouldn't listen to me.

"You always have to push it too far, don't you?"

"You're the one who pisses me off."

"Just because I don't grant you decision-making power over my life? The understanding you proposed yesterday does not include that. It only includes what we did last night, or am I wrong?"

"It also states that there will be no potential assholes involved, Vanessa." He lights his cigarette with a nervous gesture, blowing out a big plume of smoke that is immediately lost in the wind. Then he turns to give me a ponderous look. "You thought about what I said?"

"Yeah," I answer, sucking in a deep breath. He remains silent, his brow furrowed, waiting for me to keep talking. I have to look away; his eyes have this power to make me bend to his will, every single time. "I stayed up all night thinking about it," I continue. "And I came to the conclusion that I can't do it. I cannot be in a relationship where I'm giving a hundred and you're giving fifty. I don't want to beg for attention nor wait in vain for the day when you'll finally open yourself up to me without reservations. Assuming such a day would ever actually come." I pause and bite the inside of my cheek. Then I turn my attention back to him. "You asked me for the sexual exclusivity of a relationship without the ties. But I can't do that because my body and my heart go hand in hand. They're a complete package. You can take it or leave it," I say, repeating his own words back to him.

I see the muscles in his shoulders tense. Thomas tilts his head to the side, angry, and replies only after a few long moments of tense silence. "Take it or leave it?" It is not a question, really, but a furious snarl that startles me. "Are you fucking with me?"

"Not at all," I answer, managing to sound confident despite the painful clenching I feel in my stomach.

"Help me understand, what is it exactly that you expect me to do? Put a fucking ring on your finger so you can make sense of our fucking and silence your stupid fucking prudery?"

"Stupid fucking prudery?" I repeat, bewildered. I turn away from the window and from him. "Forgive me for wanting something more from the person I'm sleeping with!"

He jolts and advances on me. Every muscle in his body is trembling with rage. "I told you I would never touch anyone else again. I told you it would be just you and me. What else do you want?"

"I don't know, Thomas, normal stuff, maybe! Going to the movies, holding hands, being able to hug you during a movie if I feel like it, for example." He lets out a derisive laugh.

"That's all bullshit," he says, staring at nothing in particular.

"For you." I point a finger at his chest vehemently. "It's all bullshit for you."

Thomas leans back on the desk and exhaustedly rubs his face. "I already told you yesterday." He looks me straight in the eye. "I can't give you what you're looking for. I can't now, and I won't ever be able to either."

I can feel my heart beating in my throat. With one sentence, Thomas has destroyed all my hopes. Those stupid, pathetic hopes, tucked deep down in the bottom of my heart. The ones that led me to believe that maybe, eventually, I would be able to break down the walls he uses to shut himself away from the world outside. Because while it is true that I was the one who told him that I couldn't accept such a relationship, there was perhaps a small part of me that hoped that, when pressed, he would choose to let me in.

My eyes fill with tears. I do my best to hold them back, but one escapes me. I wipe it away with an irritated swipe and shrug, trying not to let my despair show. "Well, in that case, I guess I can't do it either."

I feel exhausted. And there is an excruciating pain blossoming inside me: the realization that the feelings I have for him are not enough and never will be enough. Another tear rolls down my cheek. Enough, I cannot endure his presence for one more minute. I want to be alone and cry. Cry until I forget the source of all my pain.

"Go away," I say finally, my voice breaking.

I see a spark of sadness flare in his eyes, and I know it is capable of breaking what is left of my heart. "Fuck, Ness…"

He tries to move closer and reaches for my hands, but I step back.

"I'm serious, Thomas, I don't want to see you," I tell him coldly, staring out the window.

He just stands next to me. He looks at me for a handful of seconds, his breaths uneven and his fists clenched at his sides. Then, not needing to be asked twice, he puts on his shoes and jacket, picks his helmet up off the floor, and leaves my room, cursing.

I hear the front door slam and the wheels of his motorcycle skidding on the asphalt. I close the window, go back to my bed and lie down on my stomach. I bury my face in the sheets, which still smell of Thomas, and I burst into uncontrollable sobs.

Thirty-Five

AFTER DRAGGING MYSELF TO THE bathroom with all the vitality of a sloth and forcing myself to take a shower to make myself at least kind of presentable, I head down to the kitchen to assemble an impromptu lunch. I answer some concerned texts from Alex and reassure him after what happened last night. I should be more upset about Travis's anger and the violent way he expressed it, but the truth—a truth I am not yet willing to admit to Alex—is that it's Thomas's leaving that really hurts. To distract myself, I spend the afternoon in the campus library studying, trying to catch up on my notes for various classes. I would be a colossal liar if I said I wasn't hoping that Thomas might show up at any moment. I admit that part of me hopes I'll pass him in the hallways, the cafeteria, or the gym, if only so I would know exactly where he is. Because, if I'm being realistic, right now as I'm walking the halls of the university and watching the endless downpour out the window like a desperate, pathetic loser, he could very well already be in someone else's bed. A girl who's willing to give him what I couldn't. He's probably kissing her right now, the same way he kissed me. Touching her like he touched me. He'll be looking at her the same as he looked at me and he must be taking pleasure from her. With her. Owning her as he owned me. Oh, my God. The thought of it makes me sick to my stomach, and I crumple.

Suddenly, a shoulder slams forcefully into mine. I stagger and almost drop the coffee I was holding. I look up and see two blue eyes staring daggers at me: Shana.

"You little sewer rat, you oughta watch where you're walking."

"You're the one who ran into me. On purpose, I might add," I point out to her.

"Listen to her, 'it was on purpose!'" She turns to her two friends, who giggle. With one hand resting on her cocked hip, she draws closer, invading my personal space. "If I ran into you, it's only because you are constantly in my way." Then her voice drops in pitch, her expression becoming more threatening. "You are a plague." She points a finger into my chest. "A goddamn cockroach." Each word is dripping with disgust. The force of her finger pressing on my chest makes me arch my back slightly and tilt my head.

"You crawl all over campus thinking you can just take what doesn't belong to you. But maybe it's time you remember who you really are: a poor loser, so insignificant you bored the one guy desperate enough to pick you. So stupid you believed that someone like Thomas could actually be interested in you." She presses her finger even deeper into my chest, giving me a little push that makes me retreat a few inches further. Then she removes her hand and, with a self-satisfied expression, takes a step back to join her friends.

I straighten and adjust my shirt. I shouldn't feel so humiliated by her words. Yet, they went through me like blades. Without realizing it, Shana has given voice to my biggest fears.

"What did I ever do to you, Shana?" I ask, doing my best to appear impassive.

For a moment, she seems surprised by the question. But then, with a flip of her hand, she moves her long, fiery red hair behind her shoulder. In a bored drawl, already turning her attention elsewhere, she replies, "You exist." Then she takes her two friends by their arms and disappears with them down the corridor.

―――――――――

"I exist. Do you get that? Her problem is that I exist! I have never done her any wrong, yet she hates me that much! Can you believe that? My God, isn't college supposed to be a place where students can focus all their energy on securing a better future for themselves? Then someone please explain to me why I keep meeting the most arrogant, obnoxious people to walk the earth!" I'm yelling so loudly into the phone glued to my ear that I attract the attention of some people walking by. They turn around to glare at me, but I ignore them and continue straight home.

"Are you done?"

I close my eyes, take a series of deep breaths to calm down before answering: "Yes, Alex. I'm done."

"Nessy, I love you and you know I love you. But you should have guessed she was going to react like that. After all, you basically stole her favorite toy right out from under her nose. I don't know a lot about women, but I think she would consider that reason enough to make you suffer." What a bitch.

I snort. "I didn't steal that toy from anyone." I arrive in front of my driveway and roll my eyes when I see my mother's car parked there.

"Alex, I have to let you go now. I'm going into the house."

Alex advises me not to worry too much, and we say goodbye.

The moment I cross the threshold, the smell of garlic, tomato sauce, and freshly baked bread hits me. My mother is in the kitchen, intent on preparing dinner; I say a quick hello and, without lingering too much, start climbing the stairs to my room. "Vanessa, get back here. We need to talk."

I stop on the second step and curse under my breath, squeezing my eyes shut. Damn! I was really hoping to make good on my escape. I walk back to the kitchen and see her leaning on the sink, arms folded.

"Mom, I have a lot of stuff to study, I don't have much time—"

"Let's have a chat," she says coldly, interrupting me.

I sigh and enter the kitchen. "What's up?"

"What do you think? Do you think I've forgotten about that little scene from this morning?"

If only...

"Do we have to talk about this right now?" I gripe, resting my backpack on the floor.

"Yes, we do." She invites me to sit at the table, pointing at it with the sauce-covered ladle in her hand. "Who in the hell was that lowlife?"

I let out another weary sigh, running my hand over my face. "His name is Thomas, he attends OSU, and he plays for the Beavers. Is that enough for you?"

She raises her eyebrows in warning. "Are you kidding me?"

"No. You asked me who he is and I'm telling you."

She shakes her head, rests her ladle on the kitchen counter and brings a hand to her temple, as if trying to keep calm. "I knew that, sooner or later, this day would come."

"What day are you talking about?"

"The day when you would allow a guy like that to come into your life. You are my daughter, after all, you come by that recklessness honestly. But it's my fault. I've left you on your own for too long and now you've lost your way."

My God, why does she always have to be so melodramatic?

"Mom, the only person who has lost her way here is you. You're talking nonsense. You don't even know him," I blurt out. For the umpteenth time, I find myself defending Thomas even after he has ripped my heart to shreds. It's as though some part of me can't help but fight for him, like I can't quite rid myself of this stupid blind faith in a boy as cynical as he is tormented.

"He's rude, Vanessa, devoid of all good sense. No one has ever dared to speak to me like that before. He came into my house and disrespected me. How can you just accept that?" She sits across from me and stares me down.

I shrug nonchalantly. I know she's partially right.

"Well, if we're talking about disrespect, you did it too, Mom. You insulted him before you even knew his name. What did you expect him to do?"

"Are you justifying that kind of behavior, Vanessa?" she asks irritably. "My God, that boy is really changing you. Tell me, how long have you been seeing him?"

"That's none of your business. What else did you want to tell me?" I gesture for her to continue with a wave of my hand.

"Well, I just wanted to make it clear that he will never set foot in my house again. Never again. Do we understand each other?"

"Whatever you want." I can tell by the murderous look she gives me in response that she doesn't at all appreciate my blasé approach to this conversation. But this time, I don't care at all.

"One last thing," she adds, "I want your word that you will stop seeing him."

I laugh out loud and straighten up in my chair. "What?"

"I don't know how long this has been going on, but I know for a fact that you've changed recently. And I'm sure that he's responsible for it."

"And you say this on the basis of what?"

"On the basis of you being my daughter and my knowing you. I worry about you. I only want the best for you, always."

I snort. "You want the best for me?"

"Do you really think otherwise?" She presses her hand to her chest, as if I have stabbed her in the heart.

"I think that you love me but, most of the time, you just want me to be more like you."

She blinks at me, astonished. "Don't talk nonsense." She gets up out of her chair with a jerk and goes to the stove, where she stirs the sauce aggressively.

"Nonsense? After I told you about my breakup with Travis, you didn't talk to me for weeks. You defended him and condemned me. You blamed me for having the courage to end a relationship that was only hurting me, and do you know why? Because you never made the effort to look past the end of your own nose. If you had, you would have seen all the times he made me feel small and insignificant, when he shamed and humiliated me. As we speak, there's a bruise on my left shoulder that I could have gladly done without. Do you know who gave it to me? Your dear, precious, irreproachable Travis. He got drunk last night and lost it. And do you know who defended me? Thomas." I get up and join her at the stove. "Have you ever done that, Mom? Have you ever defended me?"

Disconcerted by my words, she is clearly surprised. "What do you mean, you have a bruise on your shoulder? Why didn't you tell me?" She grabs my arms and turns me around.

"Because it wouldn't have mattered. You would have found some way to justify it." I wrench myself out of her grip.

Her eyes grow wide. "How can you say such a thing? I'm your mother! If someone hurts you, I need to know!" she cries out.

"That's just the thing, Mom. Travis has hurt me many times, emotionally. Yet even after we broke up, I'm still the one in the wrong as far as you're concerned. Now, you want to warn me away from Thomas, thinking you know everything. But the truth is, you don't know anything!" I turn my back to her and stalk back to the chair where I had been sitting, picking up my bag and preparing to leave the kitchen. But she keeps talking.

"Maybe you're right and I don't know anything about him. But it only took me five seconds to see the kind of guy he is. So I'll tell you again: I don't want that person to be a part of your life," she orders.

"I'm almost twenty years old, Mom. I can do what I want."

"Not as long as you live under my roof," she spits out angrily. I look at her, reducing my eyes to two slits, trying to figure out if she's really implying what I think she's implying. "Remember that everything you have, you have because of me. And you know the sacrifices I've made for you. But I can take everything away, Vanessa. Do you really want to go that far, all for an insignificant little boy who will leave you the moment he finds something better?"

"Would you really do that?"

"If it would make you do that right thing, I would absolutely do it. Even if it made you hate me."

"Are you joking?" My blood boils.

"Not at all."

I shake my head in bewilderment. "You can't impose yourself on my life like this."

"I am your mother, Vanessa. I'll do what I think is best. This conversation is over. You can go." She dismisses me with a wave of her hand. She turns her back on me and focuses on the stove.

"I like him, Mom!" I cry. Only after the words come out of me do I realize what I've just said.

"Yes, Vanessa, I noticed that!" She turns away, her lips a thin, angry line. "And that is exactly why I find myself compelled to take drastic action. The feelings you have are clouding your judgment; they cause you to make bad choices. I will not allow that to happen. You are young. And guys like him always bring problems and sorrows. I understand that at your age it can be fascinating, but sooner or later, he's going to feel entitled to offload his troubles on you. And, by then, you'll be too much in love to stop him. Don't believe me? I've had a Thomas of my own before, and I guarantee you that the love you feel for him will push you to make so many mistakes. It will consume you, annihilate you, and take away every last good thing you have inside you. Until one fine day you will wake up and realize that you've spent the best years of your life chasing after someone who never, ever intended to stay. And at that point, it'll be just you with your broken dreams and your mistakes which you will have to live with for the rest of your life." There is a tremor in her voice. It's barely perceptible, but it leaves me completely confused.

As far as I have ever known, my mother had always been with thoroughly respectable men. I am surprised by all the regret and anguish I can hear in her voice.

"I-I don't understand what you're talking about. None of that is going to happen to me because I'm not in love with him," I explain to her in a softened tone.

"Yet, my just mentioning him was enough to make you fly into a rage. That says a lot about the feelings you pretend not to have."

My reaction has me confused as well. After what Thomas said to me, a smart person would just listen to my mother. Still, just the idea of not having him in my life anymore makes me feel like I can't breathe.

"It's not up to you to decide who I can or cannot date. It's unfair," I say in a near-whisper.

"I'm sorry, but as long as you live under my roof, I will be the one to decide. And I have decided that you won't see that boy again. Or you will suffer the consequences."

Thirty-Six

I RUN TO MY ROOM furious, ready to pack up my things and leave. Too bad I don't have anywhere else to go nor the money I would need to pay rent on some hypothetical apartment. As if that weren't enough, I hear Victor's voice from downstairs. He's always eating dinner here these days. But my mother can forget about playing happy family tonight. After what she told me, I flatly refuse to sit at the table with the two of them. I text Alex to ask him to come to my rescue with a takeout sandwich, and I see that Tiffany has also texted me. A simple, direct: coming to you, have updates.

A few minutes later, the doorbell downstairs rings at the same time I hear someone knocking on my window. Wow, Alex and Tiffany must have coordinated. As I open the window, I can hear Tiffany running up the stairs.

"Why are you climbing through our friend's window like a burglar?" Tiffany chuckles once they are both inside.

"And why are you entitled to front-door access? If I rang the doorbell at this time of night, Esther would have murdered me," Alex retorts.

"One of these days, you're going to break every bone in your body. You do know that, right?" I scold him jokingly, taking the bag with my dinner in it from his hand. It smells mouth-wateringly good.

"The one with the scribbled-on wrapper is yours, no lettuce, no cucumbers. Tiff, I didn't know you'd be here too," Alex says, a little awkward.

"Don't worry about it, I came unannounced."

"Did something happen?" I ask with some apprehension. I put their coats on the desk and invite them to sit on the bed with me.

"Um, yeah...I mean, nothing serious. The thing is, yesterday I was so scared, Vanessa. I have never seen Travis react like that before."

I swallow hard, a strange sense of anxiety settles in my stomach. "After you left with Thomas, I took Travis home and told our parents everything. I thought Travis was going to have another freak-out. I was afraid of that, in fact. But this morning he decided he's going to go into the Army."

I am astounded. "What?"

"Apparently he can't deal with all the horrible stuff he's done in this last year. He says he's hit rock-bottom, that he doesn't recognize himself anymore and he wants to redeem himself." Though she says it all in an impassive tone, I can sense a note of hurt in her voice.

"And he thinks he can do that by enlisting in the military? What happened to all his plans for the future? The economics degree? Basketball? Your dad?" Travis had always lived exclusively to impress his father. Basketball and college were just pretexts to get paternal approval. I can't believe he's throwing it all away.

Tiffany rolls her eyes. "Dad went ballistic. He'd already managed to get at least two sponsor contracts, so you can imagine how he reacted when he heard. But Travis was adamant about it this time."

So he's really leaving, then. I can't tell how this news makes me feel. On the one hand I feel sympathy for him, but Travis does need to get himself together, that's for sure.

"That's unbelievable..." I say, staring down at my comforter. "When does he leave?"

"In a few days. This all just happened; it was a very sudden decision. He's requested immediate transfer to basic training."

"And are you okay with that?" I ask her, knowing how close she is to him despite everything.

Tiffany shrugs and gives me a resigned look. "I just want to be able to look him in the eyes and see my brother again. If West Point is the solution to his problems, then so be it."

"I think so too, girls. Travis has been really lost this last year, and a change of scenery will be good for him," Alex interjects, a polite reassurance. "And Nessy, get it through your head that you have nothing to be sorry about. I don't want to hear you saying anything like that." I smile at him sweetly.

"Tiff, do you want to share this sandwich with me?" I ask her to break up some of the tension. The three of us get better settled on the bed and eat dinner while watching a horror movie on Netflix.

After the first hour we get bored by the plot and start talking about something else entirely. Tiffany and Alex are dying to know how everything went down with Thomas and me after seeing us so cozy in the pool. But, alas, I have no good news to report. Though I don't have much enthusiasm for the tale, I decide to tell them what happened this morning between Thomas and the woman downstairs. I tell them about how, last night, after the mess with Travis, we went to his house and I stayed there all night, leaving early this morning.

"I'd just fallen asleep and then, all of a sudden, I heard his voice. I went downstairs and found him standing in the doorway, can you imagine? My mother was furious, he was furious-er. They were glaring at each other like two lions about to throw down."

"And then what happened?" Alex's voice is interested.

"Nothing. I let him in, Mom freaked out, and he, shockingly, felt compelled to act like an idiot." This confuses Alex, and he gestures for me to be more specific, so I continue, "He told her he'd just stepped in dog poop. Right after blowing cigarette smoke in her face. It was a lie, obviously. He just wanted to provoke her." I roll my eyes and shake my head, still remembering my mother's gobsmacked expression.

Tiffany's eyes bug out, and she begins to laugh uproariously.

"What? My God, I can't believe I missed that!"

"Well, it's not really anything new. Esther White loses it because some dude got her carpet dirty. I'd say that's pretty common, actually." Alex laughs.

"Okay. I will admit that it was kind of funny to see her just quivering with rage and not knowing how to react. I've never seen anyone else succeed in shutting Esther White up, so I have to give him credit for that. But in hindsight, it was a stupid thing to do, given that I am now completely forbidden from having anything to do with him." I snort in frustration. "She still treats me like I'm a child. It's unreal."

"But you're almost twenty years old. You need to start standing up for yourself," Tiffany says. She pauses before continuing, "You can't let her boss you around like that anymore." Alex nods with conviction.

"Do you think I don't know that? Do you think I like any of this? It's gotten to the point where she's threatening me. She has lost her mind," I blurt out.

"What?" Tiffany sounds shocked as she sits up straighter.

I nod. "She told me very clearly that if I don't do as she says, she will take everything away from me." They both stare at me in disbelief for a few seconds.

"But you know what? It doesn't matter anymore."

"Why?" asks Alex frowning.

"After my mother left, guess what happened? Thomas and I had a fight. For the thousandth time since I've met him. I told him to leave, and he did. And he didn't contact me again all day. So, you know what that means." I bring my knees to my chest and rest my forehead against them. I feel so despondent.

"Come on, you don't think he…" Alex begins. But there's no need to finish the sentence, we all know what he's alluding to.

I nod. Because that's exactly what I think. I lift my head in his direction. "We're talking about Thomas here. The fact that he couldn't get what he wanted from me doesn't mean he won't go looking for it somewhere else. Plus he was pissed off. And, believe me, that never leads to anything good."

"What couldn't he get?" asks Alex.

"What?"

"You said he couldn't get what he wanted from you. What did he want?" I can hear Tiffany trying to hold back a giggle next to me; she'll have it all figured out by now. Dammit, why don't I ever pay attention to what I'm saying?

"Nothing, just forget about it. You wouldn't understand," I answer, averting my gaze and brushing some crumbs off the blankets.

Out of the corner of my eye, I catch the hurt expression on Alex's face. I wish I could tell him that the problem isn't talking to him about it. Rather, it is the incredible shame I would feel having to explain to my best friend about this absurd relationship that Thomas and I have developed.

"Try me," Alex urges me.

I stare at him for a few seconds, unsure what to do, before forcing myself to just spit it all out. "Okay. He...he wants to be with me, but he doesn't really want to be with me."

He frowns. "I'm not following."

"See? I told you you wouldn't understand." I sigh and try to find a way to say it more clearly. "He wants to be with me, but he doesn't want me to be his girlfriend because that would suggest an emotional involvement that he would not be able to reciprocate or sustain." I grimace unhappily. "Just the idea of having a relationship with me makes him laugh, Alex," I add, mortified.

"Laugh?" he echoes in disbelief. "I'm beginning to think this guy has even more problems than he appears to. So what is it that he actually wants? An open relationship where you're both free to date other people?"

I shake my head. "No, it would just be me and him."

The confusion in his eyes is increasing by the second.

"In my house, that is called a relationship."

"Yes, a twisted relationship, Alex. Basically, he says he doesn't want to be my boyfriend, but more often than not, that's what he acts like."

"I have a theory of my own," interjects Tiff who has been listening raptly this whole time.

"And what would that be?"

"I think he's scared," she suggests.

I stare at her in amazement for a few seconds before bursting into a fit of hysterical laughter. "Scared? Tiff, we are talking about the same person, aren't we?"

"He's offered a legit relationship to you but tried to disguise it as something it's not. Why would he do that except out of fear? Why else would a guy like him give up all the girls who will give him exactly what he wants whenever he wants it for you and impose the same limit on you? If you ask me, you're trying to break down an open door, my friend."

I freeze for a moment. "And, in your opinion, what's his reason? I mean, why would he be afraid of me? I'm a little lamb compared to him, and it's clear to everyone that, right now, he's the one holding the knife. I should be the one who's scared."

"Maybe that's it. Maybe, in his own way, he's trying to protect your feelings."

"I think Tiff is right," Alex interjects. "I mean, as a guy, I can understand it. I was a little afraid to really let myself fall for Stella, knowing that a long-distance relationship could wind up hurting me. Letting go like that requires courage."

"But that would imply that he has no feelings. And that I am not worth being brave for," I murmur. Saying it out loud hurts even more than thinking it.

Alex's face turns apprehensive. "I don't want to have to say what I'm going to say and I want to apologize in advance." He takes my hand and squeezes it with his own. "But you can't force someone to love you. And you can't blame them if it doesn't happen." Every word is like a stab to my heart.

"I don't...I don't blame him. It's not about that. It's just that, sometimes I get the feeling that he really cares about me but other times he treats me like I don't matter to him at all. But you're right. It's not his fault; he's always been clear about what he feels and what he wants. I'm the one to blame here. I should have backed away before anything even started."

"I don't think you should give up, though," says Tiff, leaning her head on my shoulder. "I've never seen you so into anyone before. I think you should give it a real try, 100 percent. You only live once," she concludes, as if to reassure me.

Part of me actually feels the same way Alex does. Yet, the mere idea of not having Thomas in my life anymore makes me feel like...like there's a knot in my throat keeping me from breathing. And that part of me wants to gamble everything, to go "100 percent." My God, this whole thing is crazy. I am crazy. Crazy about him.

Thirty-Seven

TALKING WITH MY TWO BEST friends has reassured me. I still feel like I'm caught in a whirlwind of emotions but I manage to get through the weekend without any casualties. On Saturday morning, Tiffany told me that Travis was leaving for sure, and I finally processed that news. I'm once again speaking to Mom exclusively in monosyllables; it has become our only form of communication. Alex updated me on his plan to visit Stella in Vancouver at the end of the month to celebrate Thanksgiving together. I'm just grateful that it's finally Sunday evening. For the last three days, I have had to constantly beat back thoughts of Thomas. His prolonged silence has only fueled my fear: he forgot about me right away and must be out having fun with God knows who. This suspicion burrows deep within my mind, making it hard for me to concentrate, even on studying. In fact, I've barely touched my books these last few days. Snuggled under the comforter, I am listening to music and trying not to think, when I get a message from an unknown number.

You awake?

Puzzled, I stare at the screen for a few seconds. Who's this?

Come out.

It's after midnight. No one in their right mind would ask me to go outside in the middle of the night, especially in this downpour. I come to the conclusion that whoever it is has simply gotten the wrong number or is trying to play some stupid prank on me. I don't reply and put the phone back on my bedside table. I lie back down and stare at the darkened shape of my ceiling. A few moments later, another message comes through:

I have something that belongs to you.

What the heck?

I pull the covers off and leap out of bed. I peel the curtain away from the window and scan the driveway and the front yard. Right at the corner of my house I catch a glimpse of something, but the poor lighting and the thick rain prevent me from really seeing it. I squint a bit and realize that it's a motorcycle. His motorcycle.

I spin around with my heart in my throat. I start pacing the room, nibbling my thumbnail, not sure what to do.

What is Thomas doing here? And how the hell did he get my number?

Oh God, if my mother finds out, she'll actually kick me out of the house.

Bad timing, Collins, really bad timing.

I'll give you five seconds, if you don't come down, I'll come up.

I goggle. No way.

I'm coming, I reply. I quickly slip on my boots and a gray chunky wool cardigan a few sizes too big for me. In front of the mirror I fix my fluffed-up, tousled hair, then I rush downstairs, trying not to make any noise.

Before opening the door, I close my eyes and take a breath deep. Be strong, Vanessa, and don't let your guard down for anything.

When I come out, I find him leaning against the wooden porch railing a few feet away from the door. His legs are crossed at the ankles in front of him, his arms crossed over his chest, his eyelashes are beaded with tiny drops of rain, and his damp hair is plastered to his face. His clothes are soaked. The black sweatshirt and dark, low-slung jeans give him that typical careless look that makes my stomach clench every time.

You like what you see, don't you, Vanessa? needles that stupid little voice in the back of my head. I shake my head slightly, trying to shut her up.

I close the door behind me and lean back against it.

"What are you doing here?" I ask determinedly.

Before answering, Thomas just stares at me for a few moments with a piercing gaze. The chills that run through me have nothing to do with the cold.

Come on, Vanessa. You can do this.

"I was riding." He nods his head toward the road behind him. "And I found myself here," he concludes, looking back at me.

"You were riding in this weather? That's not very wise of you," I answer, frowning.

Thomas levels a challenging stare at me. "Do I look like a wise person to you?"

I sit down on the small sofa next to the door. "Not even a little bit."

He shrugs. "I was already out when it started raining."

He was out late at night? Awesome. For my own sake, I decide not to investigate further.

"You should have gone back home," I say angrily, trying to look anywhere else.

"Didn't feel like it."

"I guess you were having too much fun."

"Not so much. I went to the Marsy for a few beers with the guys. You didn't work today," he says immediately.

"I swapped shifts with my coworker, Cassie."

"That's a rip-off. There's never shit to do on Sunday in this town."

"Yeah, well, it's not like I indulge myself on the other days." I push some of my hair, tousled by the wind, out of my face.

"That's because you're boring," he snickers.

I shoot daggers at him with my eyes. "Did you come here to insult me?"

"I didn't insult you," he answers seriously.

"If you tell someone they're boring, you're basically telling them that you think they're devoid of content. Empty. Useless. Inert," I hiss.

"If I tell someone they're boring, I mean only that they are boring. And you are. And you're also quite touchy." My blood is boiling in my veins. He's still just as arrogant as he ever was. I sigh resignedly.

"You said you have something that belongs to me, right?" I cut to the chase, crossing my arms over my chest.

"Oh, yeah...right," he answers, scratching the back of his head, suddenly distressed. He backs away for a moment, clearly hesitant. I arch a wary eyebrow. This change of mood bothers me. It is so rare to see him like this that it's almost funny. My lips turn up in an involuntary smile, which I immediately cover with my hand so he won't notice.

After a handful of seconds, he returns to the porch and kneels in front of me. I stare at him skeptically, having no idea what he's doing.

"I think I screwed up."

I furrow my brow at him. "What do you mean?"

"Like I said, I have something that belongs to you. But first you should know that when I left the house, it wasn't raining. It only started to rain later, but it was too late to turn back by then."

"I don't understand what you are talking about, Thomas," I say impatiently.

He ducks his head and then reaches for something he'd kept tucked behind his back, under his rain-soaked sweatshirt. A book. A book with a soggy, ruined cover. It seems familiar to me... I take a closer look and...my God, I don't believe it. I stare with my eyes wide before snatching it out of his hands. "But this is mine! And it's all...it's all wet! Destroyed! You destroyed my book! My favorite book!" I hiss, still in shock.

Thomas falls silent and does not take his eyes off the porch's floorboards. "I'm sorry."

"Do you realize how important that book was to me, you stupid asshole?" I moan. "It was a gift from Alex's mom."

"Fuck." He covers his face with one hand. "I'll buy you another one tomorrow, I promise."

"Buy me another one? You can't just buy me another one. It was a first edition, dammit!"

"So?"

"So you can't just find them lying around. And it was a gift!"

"So I'll buy you one that's not so hard to find," he replies simply.

"It's not the same, Thomas! And it wouldn't be my book anymore. It would just be a stupid reminder of you and the book you destroyed!"

"I'm really sorry," he repeats in a low voice.

"Oh, yeah, I really believe it," I snap irritably. "When did you even take it?"

"The night I came to your house, remember? You went on about this book, how much you like it and shit. I wanted to know what was so special about it, so before I left, I grabbed it." That's why it wasn't in my room that morning!

"Can I ask why you didn't tell me?"

"Because I didn't have time. We had a fight and then didn't speak to each other for a month."

"Well, you should have told me anyway; you can't just take other people's things without permission. Besides, you said you don't read."

"I wanted to challenge myself."

My eyebrows shoot up incredulously. "Did you really read *Pride and Prejudice*?" The mental image of it is almost enough to make me laugh in his face.

He stares down at the book I hold in my hands. Some locks of my hair have fallen over the cover, and he takes a strand, twisting it around his finger as he seems to consider something.

"It smells like you, you know?" He lifts his face and our eyes lock. "Sometimes, when I was reading it, it almost felt like you were there." I swallow and blink, staggered by the sweetness in his voice.

"Smelled like me," I correct him nastily, trying to hide the emotion in my voice. "Did...did you at least like it?" What I would actually like to ask him is why he was thinking about me when we weren't talking to each other.

"Fuck, not even a little." He chuckles.

"Why did you decide to give it back to me now?"

As I stare into his eyes, I realize that a part of me is desperately hoping that he did it because he felt an irrepressible urge to be near me.

"I don't know, I had nothing else to do." My throat burns and I, for the thousandth time, am left feeling like a prize idiot.

"You had nothing else to do?" I repeat with disappointment. He gives a surly nod. And I explode: "You know, I should really thank you for going to the trouble of bringing me back my favorite book—which now, thanks to you, will have to be thrown away—at one in the morning in a rainstorm. But the truth is, gratitude is the last thing you deserve from me." I stare ferociously at him before standing up and turning my back on him. Just as my fingers touch the handle of the door, Thomas grabs my wrist and stops me. "Let me go!" I warn him, wounded.

"Will you stop for a second?" He pulls me close to him and wraps his muscular arm around my waist, squeezing me like a vise.

"Why should I stop?" I press my palms to his chest in an attempt to create some distance between our bodies, but he won't let me. "The last time we spoke, you were awful, and now you show up here in the middle of the night just to insult me and return a ruined book!"

"I'm a fucking dick, I know that," he admits, looking into my eyes so intensely that I can't help but waver. "It's not true that I had nothing else to do. I wanted to see you and I thought the book could be a valid excuse for it." One corner of his mouth lifts in his usual crooked smile. And I find myself forced once again to summon all my willpower in order not to completely fold in the face of his incredible damned charm.

"And the urge to see me came upon you at one o'clock in the morning? Were you too busy before? And you also have my phone number, apparently. You could have called, texted…basically anything." I am no longer willing to be anyone's last resort.

"I spent the weekend in my dorm, catching up on my classes from last week. In the evening, the boys asked me to join them at the Marsy. I didn't really feel like it, but I was hoping I'd be able to catch you there. But you weren't there. On the bright side, I was able to get your number from Matt."

I sigh, trying to figure out whether he's telling the truth.

"I find it hard to believe you. With Travis, I was fooled for too long. I won't let it happen again."

"I'm not him!" he exclaims angrily, his jaw twitching.

"You keep saying that, but you're just as distant and domineering as Travis. Not to mention the fact that I never know what's going on in your head."

"What is unclear to you?" He scowls, letting my wrist go. I shrug and sit back down on the sofa. Thomas kneels down again to look me in the eye. A gust of wind brings his scent to me, fresh and intoxicating.

"Why are you so insistent on having me if you don't care about me? I mean, what you've asked me for...you could get it from anybody."

"But I want it from you," he breaks in.

"I don't get why. You said it yourself: you'll never be able to give me what I want, just like I'll never be able to give you what you want. We are an unmitigated disaster together, Thomas. For one thing, we never agree on anything. I am awkward, boring, and incapable of shutting up, which, by the way, pisses you off almost all the time. You, on the other hand, are handsome, popular, and confident. People respect you. So many girls are into you, girls way more confident and experienced than me. And what do you do? Waste your time with someone like me. Come on, look at me, and look at you. You can see for yourself that something isn't right, can't you?"

He cocks his head to one side and stares at me. "I could say the same thing to you."

I blink, confused. "Meaning?"

With one elbow resting on his knee, he fiddles with a tuft of my hair. "How is it possible that you don't know..." he says, lifting his face toward me. "You think I just want you for your body? Not at all. If I just wanted to fuck, I could pick up the phone right now." He pulls it out of the back pocket of his jeans. "Call the first number in my contacts." He swipes one finger across the phone and selects a name. "And spend the night with some random girl." He looks at me in silence for a few seconds while I stare uneasily back at him. He tosses the cell on the cushion next to me. "But that's not what I want. Because none of them are you." He takes my face between his hands and with a thumb he caresses my cheek, following the line of my cheekbone and pausing to look at me, specifically at my mouth. "The more time I spend with you, the more I want you. But I am also well aware of how wasted you are on me. I know it every time I look at you, every time you get close to me, every time I hear you talk or touch you. Every time I force you to deal with a heartless bastard like me. You could have so much more than this, you deserve more than this. And you know it. Yet, you keep trying to see something in me. Something good, but you've got it wrong. The person in front of you is just a fucking disappointment."

"Stop saying that. You are not a disappointment."

"Stop idealizing me."

The coldness in his voice cuts straight to my heart. Why is it so hard for him to see what I see? Sure, he's not a perfect guy, I realize that, but I know that there is good in him. I've seen it. I've felt it.

"Then I just don't understand what you want me to do. Basically, why did you come here? Why are you telling me all this? Are you asking me to accept you as you are or are you telling me to let you go?"

It takes him a while to answer, as if he were wrestling with himself. "You should leave me alone," he says with certainty, before adding, "although I hope you won't."

"Because you're selfish, right?" I murmur, aware and resigned.

He nods. "And I want you to be mine."

"Why?"

"Because I do."

"'Because I do' is not an answer."

"Because I feel good when you're near me."

I shake my head. "That's not enough for me."

He sighs and closes his eyes, bridling at the pressure I'm putting on him. "Ness."

"No, Thomas. You say you want me, but then you can't tell me why. I'm beginning to think you only see me as something to use for your own benefits. After all, you said it yourself, didn't you? You feel good when I'm with you. I am an object you use to feel at peace with yourself," I retort, getting angry.

He glares daggers at me. "Don't talk bullshit."

"Then you explain it to me. Why do you want me in your life if you think you don't deserve me?"

"Why are you being so difficult about this?"

"Because I'm tired of not being good enough." He stands up, upset and running a hand through his hair. I can tell by the tortured expression on his face that he would rather be anywhere else right now. But I don't give up. Not when he leans against the wooden railing, pulls his packet of cigarettes out and brings one to his mouth with a troubled air. And not when he takes a long drag in total silence, refusing to look at me. There is no sound but that of the rain falling on the asphalt and the roof above our heads. I hold his gaze, trying with all my might not to be intimidated and finally, after a few seconds that seem to last forever, he grants me one small admission: "You make me feel like no one else ever has before. Is that enough for you?"

"And how do I make you feel?" I ask in the faintest whisper, clutching the book in my hands in an effort to contain the explosion I can feel brewing inside me.

"What the fuck..." He grinds the heel of his hand into his forehead. "You make me feel good," he manages through gritted teeth. "But also like a complete asshole." He looks back at me. He reaches for me, getting onto his knees once more in front of me. Cigarette smoke envelops the both of us. It bothers me, and, as soon as he senses my discomfort, he wafts it away from me. "You're weird and awkward and sexy like no one else I've ever known. Just hearing you talk blows my mind. Or the way you twist your hair when you're nervous...and how you pull it over your eyes when you get embarrassed." He puts two fingers under my chin, forcing me to look at him. "When you look at me and, for some insane reason, your eyes shine. When you smile and wrinkle up your nose a little bit and push the tip of your tongue against your teeth... I swear, you drive me crazy."

He smiles. "I like waking up in the morning and knowing I'm

going to see you again. It makes my day better. I like walking into the classroom and seeing you sitting there in the front row, waiting for who knows how long for class to start. And I like your little pout when I do something or say something that pisses you off. I like you the way you are, even when you try to hide inside these giant clothes you wear. You are the only girl I fuck for pleasure, not just to get off. You're the only one that I have to watch come underneath me because when you do, you take my fucking breath away," he adds after a few seconds of silence. He takes one last puff from his cigarette before crushing the butt under his shoe. He put his hands on my hips, and only then do I realize that I have been holding my breath this whole time.

I look at him, incapable of answering. I am so confused and taken aback at the same time. My heart is pounding in my chest but I am insanely afraid that this momentary happiness will be shattered again.

"Are you...are you being honest?"

"With you? Always."

"Then why do you keep stopping me from being with you the way I want to be?" I ask, my voice cracking.

"Because what I told you the other day in your room is the truth. I will never be what you want. I like you. And I want you. But I won't make you promises I can't keep." I look into his eyes for a few seconds and that is long enough to make me give in.

I want him too. More than anything else in the world. And he's right here, in front of me, making me tremble all over with just a glance the way he always does. I don't want to think about anything right now except for him, except for us. So I wrap my arms around his neck and, the very next moment, my lips are pressed against his. I know this is wrong, that I'll probably regret it tomorrow and that I'm only further complicating a situation that already started off too complicated. But I can't help it. His mere proximity clouds my mind and makes me so vulnerable. I can't contain these feelings I have. While the storm rages in the background, I surrender to his passionate kiss.

Thirty-Eight

HIS MOUTH MOVES GREEDILY OVER mine. He is devouring me, and I'm losing track of my surroundings. I ignore the dark of the night that envelops us, the wind blowing above us, the fact that we are still on my front porch and the very real risk that my mother could come out at any moment and surprise us. I let myself be overwhelmed by the warmth of his tongue and feeling of his hands on me, sliding down my hips, down to my butt. He squeezes me enthusiastically and pulls me tight against him, making my chest press into his. I spread my legs slightly to better accommodate him, while his grip on my backside only gets tighter, dragging a moan out of me.

Thomas smiles against my lips, bites them and worries them between his teeth before slowly loosening his hold on me. "Do you even know what you're doing?"

"Not exactly," I gasp, my heart pounding. And it's the truth. I have no idea what I'm doing. Did I kiss him because I had on some unconscious level accepted his proposal of a "non-relationship"? Or was it just the heat of the moment? Hearing him confess all of this stunned me. He knocked me for a loop.

The only thing I'm sure about is what I feel when I'm with him: Rapture. Adoration. Connection. Desire.

Thomas leans his forehead against mine and looks raptly at me.

Those emerald-green eyes of his seem to pierce through me all the way to my soul. "And you're okay with that?"

I nod, trying to regulate my labored breathing. "I think so." We stand there just looking at one another for a few seconds in silence, letting our eyes do the talking for us. Then Thomas gets to his feet and I suddenly feel adrift. Like an invisible protection has been torn away from me, leaving me vulnerable to everything. I follow him with my gaze, and my instincts tell me that this will be the last time I see him today. My stomach is clenching. I hate it. I hate this feeling of torment mixed with disappointment that I get every time we separate. It makes me feel weak and dependent.

"Are you leaving?" I ask hesitantly, standing up as well.

"Already missing me, stranger?" He gives me an insolent grin as he pulls the motorcycle key from his pocket.

"Not at all." I sniff with my chin held high, pulling the sleeves of my cardigan over my fingers.

He chuckles. Relentlessly confident as he is, he doesn't buy it for a second. He reaches over and takes my chin between his fingers, planting a kiss on the cold tip of my nose. "It's late, and you need to rest."

"Are you worrying about me?" I tease him a little, quirking one corner of my mouth.

"I worry about your academic performance. If you don't sleep, you won't be focused for the test tomorrow. I could never forgive myself if you flunked for the first time because of me." A chill moves through me down to the bones, while my knees turn to jelly.

"T-the test?"

"Yeah, the philosophy test." He makes a dismissive gesture as if he couldn't possibly care less, while I'm feeling the earth shake under my feet. Slowly, I sit back down on the small sofa behind me with wide eyes, trying not to panic.

Tomorrow is the philosophy test, and I have completely forgotten about it. How the hell is that possible? I have never, ever forgotten about a test before.

"You okay?" he asks leaning toward me, looking worried.

I shake my head, unable to utter a word, and stare into the middle distance. He rests his palms on top of my thighs and looks at me seriously. "Hey, Ness, what's up?"

"I forgot," I breathe.

"What did you forget?"

"The test, Thomas. The test!"

He stares at me impassively for a few seconds until I see him struggling to hold back laughter.

I frown. "Does this seem like a good time for a chuckle?"

"Jesus," he snickers, "I thought you were having a heart attack. But you're just freaking out about a test. You're such a nerd." He starts full-on laughing, resting his forehead against my legs.

"Thomas, we have a test in a few hours, and I've barely started studying the material! And it's my favorite subject, to boot!" I wail in reply, upset by his amused demeanor.

"Come on, it's not the end of the world. As soon as I get back to the dorm, I'll email you some notes, they're simple concepts."

"I don't need your notes, I have my own. Also, sorry, but since when do you take notes? And since when do you prepare for things?" I ask, with wounded pride. I find it really hard to imagine him parked in front of an open book, studying intently.

"The notes aren't mine and, for your information, I am prepared for many things, young lady," he says smugly.

I cross my arms and give him a skeptical look. "That seems rather unlikely. You've never paid attention in class, I remember that clearly."

"We have different ways of digesting information." He gives me his shit-eating grin. He retrieves his phone from the sofa, turns around and walks to the bike. I get up and follow him, shielding myself from the now less intense rain with my cardigan.

"So, we...um, see you tomorrow," I say suddenly. Awkwardly.

"Yes, tomorrow." He takes his helmet from the handlebars and unclasps it. But before he slips it on, he grabs me by the edges of my sweater and pulls me into him. "I want you to remember what I told you tonight, really imprint it into your brain, because I won't say it again another time," he says hoarsely, giving me a gentle kiss on the lips. Then he pulls back, taps me on the nose with his index finger, and gets on the bike. He lowers his visor and starts the engine. I don't even have time to tell him to go slow before he speeds away like lightning.

I go back inside the house, close the door behind me, and lean heavily against it for a few seconds with the dumbest grin plastered on my face. My heart beats wildly, I touch my lips with my fingers. I almost can't believe what he said to me.

"You know, you should listen to your mother more." Victor's Canadian accent pulls me abruptly from my thoughts. I jump when I see him standing just a few feet away from me with a ceramic coffee cup in his hands.

I stand up straight and frown. "Excuse me?"

He gestures to the window with his cup. It overlooks the porch where Thomas and I had just been talking. And kissing. "Your mother told me what happened..."

I cross my arms over my chest and narrow my eyes. "What were you doing here? Spying on me?"

"No, Vanessa. I wouldn't dream of it. But I heard some noises coming from the porch and I was alarmed, so I came to check that everything was all right."

"There was no need for you to be alarmed. Corvallis is a quiet town. The only criminals we have here are kids who like to play ding dong ditch," I explain.

He shrugs and takes a sip from his cup. "An ounce of prevention is worth a pound of cure. In any case, don't you think it's pretty disrespectful the way you continue to defy your mother's authority?"

"I think that it's none of your business," I say defensively.

He looks down at the cup in his hands. "Yes, you're right." Then he brings his attention back to me. "But very soon it will become my business."

"What are you talking about?"

"You don't know?" he asks, surprised. Slowly, I shake my head no. A confused and apologetic expression crosses his face. "Oh, I thought she told you."

"Told me what?"

"In a few weeks, I'll be moving in."

I can almost feel my stomach tying itself into knots. "What?"

"Vanessa, I apologize." He moves as though he's going to approach me and lay a hand on my shoulder, but I stretch out an arm to stop him.

"I was sure your mother had already told you about it."

Now I'm wondering how long ago my mother made this decision without my knowledge, and when exactly she planned to tell me. Maybe the day before he moved in? Or maybe the day itself!

"You know, things have been going so well between us, and we talked about it—"

I interrupt him: "No."

"What did you say?"

"I said no. You are not going to live here. This is my house. My father's house. The house where he raised me. If your need to live together is so strong that you can't do without it, then go ahead and move in together but do it somewhere else." I push past him, glaring and leave him standing there astonished behind me.

How could my mother allow another man to come into our house and live there without even consulting me beforehand? I mean, does my opinion matter so little to her?

I take off my boots and leave them beside the door. I slip off the cardigan and lay it on the end of the bed. I sit down at my desk, turn on the lamp and take out my books and notes from philosophy. I intend to study as much as I can, although I'm finding it pretty difficult. My head is filled with all these conflicting emotions about everything that has happened tonight.

A few hours later, my eyes are burning from concentration and I have to throw in the towel. When I look at the alarm clock on the night-stand beside me, I realize that it is five o'clock in the morning. I open my eyes wide and rest my forehead on the desk, cursing myself under my breath. In less than four hours, I have to be on campus. Damn me for forgetting this stupid test! I turn off the light and curl up in my bed.

Thirty-Nine

THE ALARM CLOCK BLARES. I ignore it and continue sleeping. It goes off again and, grumbling, I press snooze again. I bury my head beneath the pillow, having zero desire to get out of this bed.

"Vanessa?" My mother's dull voice echoes in my ears. "Vanessa, you need to get up or you'll be late. It's already half past seven," she shouts, knocking on the door. Shit, she's right. Though it takes all the willpower I have, I open my eyes and get out of bed. I put on my bathrobe and drag myself to the door. When I open it, I find my mother leaning against the doorframe with a guilty look on her face.

"We need to talk." Victor must have told her about our little conversation last night. I can't think of any other reason for her full transformation into this helpless little lamb.

"Yes, we do." Yawn. "But not now. I have to leave now," I tell her in a voice both annoyed and sleepy.

"Vanessa, I was going to tell you, it's just that…" I brush past her, ignoring her completely, but she runs right after me as though nothing is wrong. "You seemed so busy lately, you know, with college, the breakup with Travis, the new job… I didn't want to give you something else to worry about."

I grin sardonically and turn back to her. "That's the official version, Mom. The unofficial version is that, as always, you made a decision without me because you think that any thought or feeling that doesn't come directly from you is superfluous. Yesterday, you threatened to take everything away from me, and then I immediately find out that Victor is moving in. You know what? I would rather live on the street than inside a house with two complete strangers. So if you want to kick me out, just know that you'll be doing me a favor." I lock myself in the bathroom after slamming the door behind me.

After taking a shower, I decide to put on jean overalls with a yellow sweater. I roll up the hems a bit and slip on my Converse shoes. I do my hair up in a long side braid and put just a touch of mascara on. When I go down to the kitchen to get breakfast, I find my mother intensely focused on squeezing orange juice and Victor standing at the stove as he pours the last drops of coffee into his cup. Great.

When he notices my presence—and probably the smoke coming out of my ears—he gasps in embarrassment.

"For your information, you are not the only person who likes to drink coffee first thing in the morning." I grab my bag, sling it over my shoulder, and leave the house without saying goodbye to anyone.

I head toward the bus stop, hunching over the tangled knot of my earphones; I am about to plug them into my phone when I hear the roar of an engine behind me. I don't have time to turn around before a black motorcycle pulls alongside me and slows to a stop.

"What's up with the Minion-chic?"

Dear, sweet, Thomas.

"There's nothing wrong with my overalls. And a Minions reference, really? Are you my grandma?" I taunt him.

He puts one foot on the ground and lifts his dark visor. His jeans cling to his muscular thighs. "My sister was obsessed with those movies when we were kids."

"Of course..." I chuckle. "What are you doing here?"

"I'm taking you to campus," he says seriously, handing me the second helmet he has hanging from his handlebars. "Hop on."

I adjust my bag to sit more comfortably on my right shoulder and bite my lip, unsure of what to do. "Uh...thank you, but I'd like to get to campus all in one piece."

"Come on, I promise I'll go slow," he insists with a cocky grin.

Against all common sense, I can't help but give in to those cunning eyes that pretend at innocence. "Okay."

Fortunately for me, he keeps his promise. The ride is slow and calm. My body is pressed against him, and every time he feels me tense up, he puts his hand on my knee and gives it a reassuring squeeze.

Our arrival at the college piques the interest of a few students, who give us curious looks. Thomas, heedless of everything as usual, slips on the Ray-Bans he had hanging from the collar of his sweatshirt. He puts his arm around my shoulders and plants a chaste kiss on my left temple. The awareness that multiple eyes are on me makes me stiffen. Uncomfortable, I pull away from the embrace and I distance myself a little.

"You ready?"

"I spent the night studying, so I'd say yeah," I answer vaguely, looking around.

"What's wrong with you?" he asks grumpily.

I frown and look up at him. "Nothing."

"Why'd you pull away?"

"Ah, no, that's nothing. It's just a little hot, isn't it?" I smile, trying not to show my discomfort.

He grabs me by the wrist and stops me. "Of all the bullshit excuses you could come up with, you picked the worst. It's November and you don't get hot. Ever."

Damn, he knows me better than I thought. "You know what the problem is. I feel uncomfortable with everyone looking at me."

He sighs, irritated. "Still?" He pulls me back until I'm beside him again and puts both arms around my shoulders, locking me in his embrace. "How long do you intend to let these dumbasses influence your life?"

"That's easy for you to say, Thomas. You're a man. You don't know what it's like. I'm sure whenever you turn a corner, the boys are there to high-five you and congratulate you on scoring once again. But it's different for me. You're not going to be the one who gets publicly humiliated in the hallway. Or labeled as just another girl who slithered into your bed."

"What are you talking about?"

I sigh rubbing my forehead. "Nothing, never mind." I could tell him about Shana's little jealous scene, but what would be the point? "I'm just saying that when a girl is seen to be with someone like you, she's inevitably thought of as easy."

"Someone like me?" He gives me a confused look.

"Yes, come on, you get it. You're not what one might call a chaste innocent, Thomas," I add, starting to get a little upset at his apparent willful misunderstanding.

"And how does this reflect on you?" he asks with surprising naivete.

"Well, because they'll think that I'm one of many—which, by the way I am—and that I'm exactly like you, which I am not. At all."

"You know what your problem is? You think too much. You care too much about the judgment of others. The people who love you know what kind of person you are. I know it too. That's all that matters. Everyone else...let 'em think whatever they want." He turns me toward him, so that we are facing each other, and wraps his arms around my shoulders. "You are not my slut." He emphasizes the word, alluding to that time a while ago when I had called myself that. "You are mine. Mine and that's it."

The look on his face is so reassuring that I almost believe him. Almost, because then I remember who I'm talking to and I come back down to earth. Thomas doesn't want girlfriends. He doesn't want relationships. He doesn't want ties. So, with a tiny smile to hide the bitterness, I remind him: "I'm not yours."

He gives me a mischievous smile and then kisses me, holding me close to him. One of his hands rests on my hip and the other glides greedily over my butt, giving it a shameless squeeze. Right in front of all the students who are passing by. I pull back and stare at him in disbelief. "You kissed me," I say a few inches from his mouth, my stomach clenched. He nods. "Why did you do that?" I ask, my heart hammering in my chest.

"Because I wanted to kiss you, and you needed to be kissed. Stop being paranoid." He gives me a decisive pat on the butt before bringing his arm back around my shoulders and walking us both into the liberal arts building. Once in the classroom, Thomas takes a seat next to me in the front row. While we wait for Professor Scott to arrive, we get lost in small talk. My ankle rests on his knee, his arm stretches along the back of my chair, and he plays idly with the loose strands of my hair. I tell him about spending all night studying, but I can't hide my agitation or the fear that I have not crammed enough. He laughs, amused by my nerves.

To my surprise, the test goes rather smoothly. I'm almost certain that I'm not going to fail. At the end of class, Thomas and I unfortunately have to part ways. We don't have any other shared classes today, and Thomas has practice in the evening, so who knows when we'll be able to see each other again. I admit that it weirds me out a little, no longer having someone asking me to follow him to the gym. I'm relieved, because it's terribly boring, but a very small part of me wishes Thomas would ask me to come. When Travis did it, it felt like an unbearable burden. But with Thomas, I kind of want to come, and the fact that he doesn't even ask me leaves a weird taste in my mouth.

After we part ways, I go by the cafeteria and catch a glimpse of Tiffany and Alex, sitting at the table next to each other, discussing something intently. I decide to join them.

"I'm telling you, I'm her favorite."

"Don't be stupid, I'm her favorite."

"You are delusional."

"Accept it, you can't compete."

"Hey, guys." I put my bag on an empty chair and sit down with them. "What are you talking about?"

"About you!" Alex exclaims.

"We were wondering, actually Alex was wondering, because I already know, which of us is more important to you?" says Tiffany, sitting right across from me.

My eyes widen in bewilderment. "What?"

"Yeah, who's your favorite?" Alex echoes with absolute firmness.

"I don't have one," I answer truthfully.

"Don't be ridiculous, there's always a favorite. I know that first-hand. My mother has spent the last twenty years saying she doesn't have a favorite, but that's bullshit. Her favorite is and always was Travis. I'm my dad's favorite, though."

"There's no need to argue about this. You both occupy special places in my heart. Equal places. I could never pick one of you over the other." I smile sweetly at both of them, hoping I've given them the answer they wanted and we could maybe get back to being the mature young adults we are supposed to be. But they are far from throwing in the towel.

"Who were you thinking of when you said 'one'?" Tiffany prompts me.

I frown. "Huh?"

"You said: I could never pick one of you over the other. So who's the one and the who's the other?" she continues.

I give her a puzzled look. "Tiff, I don't think…"

"She'll never admit it because she is too nice, and she would never hurt your feelings, but I'm her favorite. I've known her since she was six years old, you on the other hand have known her for how long? Two years?" Alex snorts and gives her a haughty smirk. I cannot believe this is actually happening.

"It's five years. Pretending not to know only makes you look dumb, Alex." Tiffany is starting to sound a bit irked. That usually means she's about one step away from flying off the handle.

"Whether it's two, three, or four, it'll still never be comparable."

"So you say. And yet, right before she got her diploma, it was my hand she wanted to hold for moral support, not yours."

"Yes, but who was the first person she thanked when she gave her speech? Oh yeah, it was me."

My God, this situation is rapidly becoming more ridiculous. Tiffany glares defiantly at Alex and I seem to have disappeared completely.

"Junior year of high school, Amanda Jones made fun of her in front of the whole class. I was the first person she told."

Alex lets out a mocking chuckle. "But I was the one who consoled her. I saw her with no teeth."

What the...?

"I saw her naked," retorts Tiffany with the air of someone playing a trump card.

"I stood by her through every failure," Alex says.

"I did that too, you idiot!"

"You two..." I try to make myself heard, but they don't give me even a sliver of their attention.

"I convinced her to dump my brother," Tiffany continues.

"Oh, please! You're also the one who convinced her to get with him in the first place. I still remember it, you know? My brother keeps asking me about you. You should give him a chance. Blah, blah, blah." He mimics her voice and gesticulations.

"What? That's not how it happened at all, you jerk!"

Tiffany throws her last two orange slices at him, he ducks to avoid them, and I find myself having to break up a loud citrus fruit fight, as though they were five-year-olds.

"Enough! What, did you two do crack before you came here? Stop it now!" I scold them. Both of them struggle to compose themselves, feigning indifference and refusing to give the other even a glance. "Now let's all take a breath and try to be adults. You can't seriously be arguing about this nonsense. You two are the other parts of me. I need you"—I look at Alex—"just as much as I need you." I look at Tiffany and grin, trying to wipe that pout off her face.

"He started it." She sniffs, looking away.

"All I did was tell the truth," Alex retorts huffily. I give him a dirty look.

"The truth." Tiff is immediately angry again.

I snap my fingers between the two of them. "Shall we start again?"

Alex rolls his eyes, sighs, and stands up. "I'm going to get a drink. Nessy, do you want anything?" I shake my head no. His eyes slide over to Tiffany, who has her back to him, and, after a few seconds of indecision, he asks her the same question. But she ignores him. He shakes his head and goes to the counter. As soon as we are alone, I take advantage of the moment to ask Tiff what's wrong. She seems way too upset for me to believe that it's all about that stupid fight.

"Hey." I take her hand. "What's up with you?"

"He was provoking me from the moment I sat down," she explains defensively.

"I'm not talking about you and Alex, I'm talking about you. Something's going on, tell me about it."

Tiffany sighs and slumps back against her chair. "This whole thing with my brother has me terrified. The situation at home isn't the greatest, and I keep thinking that maybe I could have done something to help him before everything got out of control…"

"Tiff, you have nothing to blame yourself for. He was in the wrong. And it's a lot to handle. But he finally did the right thing. I'm sure he'll get himself together. He has realized that he's lost his way, and that's already a big step." I give her a smile in the hopes of heartening her. And I make an effort to really believe my own words. Despite everything, I really do hope Travis rediscovers his best self.

When Alex returns, Tiffany seems to have calmed down and Alex has fortunately also laid down his arms. He sits down next to her and quietly hands her a small bottle of flavored water, the kind that Tiffany usually drinks during the day to keep herself hydrated. I smile at the cuteness of this gesture, even though they are like cats and dogs sometimes. "Truce?" he asks, smiling gently at her.

She looks sideways at him, trying to keep up an aloof air, but quickly gives in. "Truce." She takes the small bottle of water, suppressing a smile, and stuffs it into her bag. Alex envelops her in a warm hug and everything returns to the perfect balance we had before.

I spend the rest of the afternoon in the library with Tiffany. The intent was to study, but we mostly wind up finishing our conversation. At one point, she gets a call from her father asking her to come back home. Her house is in an uproar these days; the whole Travis thing has turned her family upside down. His imminent departure was just the coup de grâce for them.

It's almost eight o'clock, and because I'm starting to get a little hungry, I decide to head to the cafeteria to get something to eat before going home. I get in line and put what appears to be a Caesar salad on my tray, add a slice of toast to it, and pay for everything. Then I look around for a free table. I manage to spot one next to a small group of girls, and I step toward it. But as soon as they see me, they start muttering something to one another and laughing. For a moment, I'm afraid I have something in my hair or maybe a stain on my clothes, but when a girl with short curly hair gets up from the table to leave, I realize that Shana has been sitting across from her. She looks at me as though she's trying to make me disappear with the power of her mind. I roll my eyes and turn around. The girl is stalking me.

Fortunately, I find another open table at the back of the cafeteria, away from those harpies. I'm about to snag it when someone behind me puts their hands over my eyes and presses their lips against my ear. For a moment, my whole body stiffens under that foreign touch.

"Did you miss me?" someone whispers in my ear. And a faint sound, barely audible, yet it makes me shiver. Whether it's from pleasure or fear, I can't really decide. An arm wraps around my waist and a wet mouth rests on my neck.

Oh my God. Logan is back.

And he's kissing me.

Forty

WITH MY HEART BEATING WILDLY, I spin around, sending my entire dinner sliding disastrously off my tray.

"Dammit!" I curse under my breath. I crouch down and pick up pieces of chicken and lettuce that are scattered all around.

"Sorry," Logan say, crestfallen. "I didn't mean to scare you." He crouches down to help me pick up the rest of the food remnants. Fingers trembling with anxiety, I pull my hair out from behind my ears and, coward that I am, I use it to hide from his gaze.

"N-no, don't worry, you didn't. I just wasn't expecting to see you here," I blurt out in one breath, continuing to pick food up from the ground.

"I wanted to surprise you, but apparently that was a bad idea," he answers, embarrassed.

"What are you talking about? I'm glad you're back..." Only now do I notice that he's holding a bouquet of red roses. I swallow the lump in my throat, overwhelmed with guilt. Because, since the moment he left, I've done nothing but ignore him. Because, since the moment he left, while he was thinking about me, I was thinking about Thomas. Because he left thinking he had me and returned unaware that he had lost me. And now he is here, with a bouquet of roses, eager to spend time with me, but I can't even look him in the face because I'm too ashamed. "A-are those roses for me?" I ask in a trembling voice.

"Who else would they be for?" he answers, handing them to me with a big smile.

He takes the tray with one hand and helps me up with the other. When I get back on my feet, with the roses in my hands, it seems completely natural to plunge my nose into them and sniff deeply. A sweet scent overwhelms me and I close my eyes.

"These are beautiful, Logan, really," I murmur, observing the red petals underneath my nose. "Thank you."

"Don't thank me, I was happy to do it," he says touching my cheek. "Each rose represents a moment when I thought of you." He moves closer, clearly intending to kiss me, but I can't let that happen. It's not fair to him. But what am I supposed to tell him? *I'm sorry, Logan, you can't kiss me because, while you were away, I got involved in a strange quasi-relationship with Thomas, and if he were to see us here together you'd end up in the hospital and he would, in all likelihood, end up in jail?* I've always believed that honesty is the best policy and I intend to end things with him honestly, but not like this, not in a cafeteria, surrounded by gossipy people. And just a few minutes after he got back to boot! Logan deserves to know what I did with Thomas; I need to show him the same respect he showed me during our entire acquaintance.

When he is just inches from my lips, I react instinctively; I drop the bouquet on the ground and, with a snap, I duck out of his way to pick them up. Logan is stunned.

"God, I am such a klutz. All the coffees I had today are taking their toll," I explain myself with a nervous chuckle as he watches me warily, rubbing the back of his head.

"Okay, maybe it'd be better if we went and sat somewhere?" he ask, his face twisting with confusion.

"Yes," I say with my head still hanging down, "maybe that's for the best." He puts an arm around my waist and guides me to a nearby table. We are facing each other, so at least the table will keep us at a distance. "So, how are you?" I ask, trying to conceal my discomfort. "Did the trip go well?"

"Yeah, very chill, I like driving." He takes off his jacket and drapes it over the back of the chair.

"How far is Medford from here?" I arrange the roses on the empty part of the table next to me.

"On the PCH, it's about three and a half hours."

"For some reason, I thought it was farther away." I stop to think for a moment and involuntarily, I begin peeling the cuticle from my thumb. "Did everything go well with your family? Did you celebrate?"

"Everything's fine," he answers vaguely. "But I don't really want to talk about that right now." He takes my hand and clasps it between his own. "I haven't seen or heard from you for a week—I want to know about you, how you are, what you've been up to, how long the chocolates I bought lasted you…" He says it jokingly, but I can't help fidgeting in my chair.

If only he knew that those chocolates never touched my mouth, but were instead gobbled up by Thomas, he wouldn't look at me with that adoring expression on his face anymore. My palms are sweating and I can feel my throat getting dry. I slip my hand from his grasp and, with both hands, I rearrange the few strands of hair sticking out of my braid. Looking him in the eye, I gather all my courage and start talking. "Um, I'm fine, studying is fine and the chocolates were…good," I say around the lump in my throat. "But there is something I'd like to talk to you about…"

"I'm not sure," he interrupts me, looking at something behind me with a furrowed brow, "but I think Shana Kennest is coming over here."

A cold shiver runs down my spine. "What?" With a nod, he invites me to turn around, but I don't have time to do it before Shana materializes right in front of us. With her long crimson hair, her very long eyelashes coated in mascara and that thin line of eyeliner that brings out the glacial blue of her eyes. Suddenly, I'm completely on edge.

Standing in front of our table, she crosses her arms over her chest and fixes us with a smug stare. "God, Clark, you don't let any of 'em get away…" She gives me a malicious look, then turns her attention to Logan and, for a moment, I seem to detect a kind of mutual repressed hatred in their intense gazes. I am almost positive they are giving off some intensely negative vibes. I can practically feel it on my skin.

"Do you need something?" I ask her, annoyed. I already have my own issues to resolve with Logan; I don't need her presence making everything worse.

She reluctantly tears her eyes off Logan and focuses back on me. "Actually, yes."

I raise my eyebrows, waiting for her to expand on this.

"You know"—she lightly shakes the plastic cup she has in her hand, agitating the liquid inside—"I was wondering... Do you like coconut?"

"Coconut?"

"Yeah, coconut," she repeats. "Magda, the chef, always sets aside a smoothie for me, but apparently today was coconut day, and alas, it's not my favorite of the fruits. I'd hate to have to throw it out, so I thought maybe you'd like it."

I'm stupid, sure, but not that stupid. This sudden courtesy is surely cloaking some sort of meanness. I'd not be surprised to discover that the drink had some sort of laxative or poison in it.

"And why did you think of me?"

"Well, I know your tastes run to the"—she throws another sharp sideways glance at Logan—"second rate." I notice that he has that same tense frown on his face again.

"Sorry, coconut makes me...vomit," I say, trying for a little zinger.

Shana curls her lip and exclaims, "Too bad. Guess I'll just have to throw it out now," she says, considering the cup.

"Don't mention it. So, I don't want to keep you a minute longer..." I gesture for her to walk over to the garbage and recycling bins at the entrance to the cafeteria.

But instead of leaving, she just stands there, completely immobile. "No, I don't have to go that far. Luckily for me, there's a true garbage dumpster right in front of me," she says with a sinister grin.

In a flash, she pours the whitish liquid into my lap, leaving me petrified with shock.

"Oops. What a disaster." She grins wickedly, holding the glass upside down over me with one hand while, with the other, she covers her mouth. Beneath her fingers, perfectly manicured and painted red, I can see her haughty smirk.

My heart is in my throat. I blink several times, unable to react while the cold juice drips between my legs, through the fabric of my jeans. I look at my stained clothes. I look at the students around us, giggling under their breath, trying not to be obvious. I look at Logan, visibly incensed. He remains motionless, though, as if something is preventing him from speaking, from defending me. I am humiliated.

"I'll give you a little tip." I am transfixed by Shana's sharp voice. "The hand soap in the bathroom works wonders. If I were you, I'd go and clean myself up right away," she says with a snobbish air. Then she backs away a few steps before letting the plastic cup fall to the ground and smiles coolly at me. Finally, she turns away, crosses to the cafeteria exit and disappears into the hallway.

I look down again at my now-soaked jeans, which give off the sweet smell of coconut.

"Vanessa, why..." Logan rests his forearms on the table and leans toward me. "Why did she do that?"

"Don't...don't say a single word." I take a big breath and force myself to look up at Logan. "I'm going to the bathroom to clean these stains. When I come back, we're going to pretend this never happened," I pronounce implacably, with the blood still boiling in my veins. I don't get why he didn't say a single word in my defense. I get up slowly and leave, saying nothing else.

I don't want to cry in front of everyone, but dammit, I really need to cry right now. All I want at this moment is to burrow under my comforter and hug one of my stuffed animals to my chest. Instead, I'm here in this bathroom rubbing soap into my overalls while tears blur my vision.

Why does everything go so wrong? Why do I have to pay such a steep price to get what I want?

I hear the clicking of a pair of heels on the floor and then the bathroom door opens.

"You know, I knew I'd find you in here, whining like some pathetic little girl," says a sharp voice that I know all too well.

Standing in front of the rectangular mirror above the long row of sinks is Shana, in all her unbearable haughtiness.

"I assume there is something about me being so pathetic that just absolutely fascinates you, Shana. I have no other way to explain it."

"What is it that you can't explain?" she asks irritably, taking a tube of scarlet lipstick from the clutch she carries. It matches her hair.

I move closer to her until I'm standing right beside her. "Your obsession with me."

She looks at me blankly in the mirror for a few seconds before she bursts out laughing. "Sweetie, I am not obsessed with you."

"Then why do you keep tormenting me like this?"

"Because it's fun." She opens the lipstick and applies it to her mouth. "You're perfect entertainment for these moments of down-time." She presses her lips together and lightly rubs them. "And, to be honest, I needed to find a way to talk to you." She pauses and turns to look directly at me. "In private."

"And to do that, you just had to pour a smoothie on me, in front of everyone?"

"Well, I had to get you in here without asking you directly. Besides, let's face it, I also wanted to have some fun."

"Yeah, because you're a bitch," I spit, full of vitriol. She brings a hand to her heart and makes an exaggerated pout, pretending to be hurt.

"You really got me there," she sneers.

My eyes narrow to two slits and, nerves completely shot, I snap at her, "Would you just tell me what your problem is? I mean, do you really think that bullying me will make him come back to you? Has it ever crossed your mind that maybe, just maybe, it's not actually my fault that he doesn't want you? That it probably would have happened just the same without me? That maybe having great legs and a tight ass sometimes isn't enough, if all you have in your skull is sawdust?"

A sort of derisive, devilish laugh escapes her. I wonder whether it's even possible to hurt this girl.

"You are truly delusional. How long do you think it'll be before he comes back to me? Hmm? I've known Thomas since the day he set foot in this town. Sometimes he wanders, it's true, but in the end, he always comes back to these 'great legs.' Because I give him something he can't find anywhere else. And I'm not talking about sex, but about so much more."

It's as if my whole body has just been charged with an electric shock. My knees are shaking, my head is spinning endlessly.

"Quiet, Clark. It's quiet that he needs," she continues, in the face of my clear astonishment.

One word. Five letters. And I crumble like a leaf dry in autumn. Because I get it. I understand what she is saying. Thomas wants "quiet." A quiet that I am unable to give him because I...I am constant noise.

My questions are noise.

My insecurities are noise.

My fears are noise.

Even my curiosity is noise.

And Thomas doesn't like noise.

Thomas likes quiet.

"So enjoy it while you can, for as long as he lets you, because sooner or later, he will come back to me. He always comes back," Shana concludes, without a hint of doubt.

It's a hard admission to swallow, an admission that hurts. One that scares me. Should I be expecting her words to come true? Should I expect to have to watch him go back to her when things get bad? When he realizes he's made a mistake? When whatever physical attraction he feels for me is gone? When he starts to see me as a burden, when he gets tired of me... Because, sooner or later, everyone gets tired of me. Will that be the moment... Will he go back to her? I swallow with some difficulty because there's a knot clogging my throat. "So is that what you wanted to tell me?"

"No," she says. Just for a moment, it seems like her eyes lose that little spark of hatred they usually always have when she looks at me.

"Then talk. I don't have time to waste," I snap impatiently.

"First, I want to make one thing clear: do not make the mistake of thinking that, just because I'm telling you this, things between you and me are going to be any different from now on. I detest you and will continue to do so."

"I can assure you that the same is true for me."

"Good. Having established that, I just want to tell you to open up your eyes and pay closer attention to the people around you."

"Could you give me a little more clarity on that?"

"No. All I can do is tell you something my grandmother used to say a lot. And she was right." She turns back to the mirror and talks to my reflection. "She used to say that, in this world, there are predators and there are prey. Predators are smart, perceptive, good at disguising their intentions and their emotions. But, beneath the mask, there's something vile and ruthless. Prey, on the contrary, are docile creatures, defenseless, innocent. So innocent that they believe there's good in the soul of the predator and let him get close. But the moment the prey finds herself in the predator's clutches... Well, the prey is doomed, isn't she?"

I frown at her, even more confused than before.

"I don't understand what…"

Her cold, unforgiving voice overpowers mine. "I'll give it to you straight: you are prey, Clark. And, if you're not careful, you're gonna end up in the hands of a predator and, at that point…you'll be done for."

She picks up her clutch from where it was resting on the sink shelf, turns her back on me and walks out. Leaving me bewildered and struggling in vain to make sense of her words.

As soon as I go back into the cafeteria, I feel a chill run through me from my head to my feet. It's strange, because I'm not cold and the cafeteria is actually the warmest place in the entire university. I ignore my body's unusual reaction and pluck up my courage before heading over to Logan.

He is still sitting at our table, wringing his hands with his shoulders tense and his head bowed.

When I'm a few steps away from him, he snaps to attention,

standing up and putting his hands on my shoulders. "Oh my God, you're back! I was starting to get worried. I thought you'd left." He stares at me with wide eyes and I notice that he's flushed.

"No, I just had a…visitor," I say.

At this, Logan stiffens. "In the bathroom? What kind of visitor?" I look at him puzzled, and only then does he try to pull himself together. He smiles at me and sits back down. I do the same.

"Would you believe it if I told you Shana wanted to talk to me? As if humiliating me in front of everyone wasn't enough for her. No, she had to sink the knife all the way in," I tell him, thinking back to the one sentence that keeps echoing in my head with the force of a jackhammer: He always comes back.

"What did she want?" he asks with a strange hint of nervousness.

I am about to tell him about the ridiculous little story about "prey and the predator," when, all of a sudden, the little voice in my head slams on the brakes. Whatever Shana was trying to say to me, she clearly didn't want anyone else to hear. Though I can't explain why, I decide to keep quiet, to abide by her wishes and not tell Logan anything.

"Nothing, she just wanted to spit more cruelty at me," I lie.

"She didn't tell you anything else?" he presses, shaking his leg under the table.

"What else was she supposed to tell me? Is there something I don't know?" I ask.

"No, of course not. I'm just sorry that she treats you that way." He smiles at me and continues. "But maybe we should stop talking about her. Let's not give her importance that she doesn't deserve. So, what did you want to tell me?" I give him a dubious look. "Before Shana came, it seemed like you were about to tell me something," he explains.

Damn, my speech. I clear my throat and begin picking at the cuticles on my hands again, looking, from time to time, over at the paper wrapped roses to my right. I am here at the moment of truth, and though I hate the idea of doing it here with all my heart, I cannot wait any longer.

I let out a long sigh. "Logan, listen…I need to tell you something."

The gentleness of his face only makes it harder.

"Tell me."

"Well, I'm not...I'm not very good at this sort of thing, so I don't really know where to start..."

I am interrupted again, this time by his phone ringing. And, suddenly, I can breathe again. Logan pulls the phone out of his pants pocket. He looks at the display, then frowns. He seems annoyed.

"Sorry, but I have to take this," he tells me.

"Sure, go ahead," I say. Will I be able to talk to him by the end of the day?

"Mike, I'm busy, what is it? Yes... Are you kidding? Can't you call your brother? Oh, come on." He rubs his forehead, irritated. "All right, all right. Yeah, I know. I'm coming. Give me a minute to get there, I'm leaving campus now. Bye." He ends the conversation and, with his eyes still on the phone, shakes his head slightly.

"Everything all right?" I ask.

"Not really. A friend's car broke down just outside of the city, and he wants me to pick him up." He puts his phone back in his pocket and gets up from his chair. "That's okay with you, right?"

I instinctively get up along with him. "Sure, of course it is."

"Okay, we can save this conversation to another time. Would you like to have dinner together tonight?"

I lower my eyes to the tray that had, until recently, held my dinner and then look back at Logan. Tackling this conversation privately would actually make my conscience feel more at ease. So I nod, because I really just want to put an end to this thing as soon as possible.

"I'll make a reservation at the restaurant, pick you up in an hour?"

Restaurant? Absolutely not. Terrible place to dump someone. Although, to be fair, Logan and I are not technically together.

"Um, honestly, I'd actually prefer somewhere more private. If that's okay with you. Besides, it's already after eight o'clock. I don't want to be out too late." I shrug.

"Okay," he says, still not entirely convinced, and slips on his jacket. "Let's order a pizza at my place, then?"

This suggestion seems even more inappropriate than the last, but I don't see any alternative.

"Okay," I reply in a small voice. "I'll wait for you right here."

"Good. I'll see you in a bit." He grabs the roses from the table, walks over and puts them back in my hands. Then he lifts my chin with two fingers and, staring intently into my eyes, says, "I'm going to hold you to that—don't run away." He kisses me on the cheek, lingering a bit more than necessary.

And I get the strangest feeling in my stomach. Almost nauseating, as if every inch of my body is suddenly rejecting this small contact.

"I'm not running away," I answer with a tiny smile.

Logan winks at me and leaves the cafeteria. I watch him walk away and only then do I realize that Thomas is here. He's standing at the back of the cafeteria, with his arms folded, leaning back against the wall. He's surrounded by a few guys from the team, but he's staring at me, and the look he gives me makes my blood run cold. The full body shivers I had felt earlier are back and even more intense.

Oh, God. Thomas.

How long has he been standing there?

Forty-One

I REMAIN RIVETED BY THE sheer force of his stare. Thomas's face tilts slightly. His eyes move from my eyes to the roses I hold in my hands. From the roses to my cheek, which, until a few moments ago, had Logan's lips attached to it. And finally he comes back to my eyes.

Was he already there when Logan kissed me? Was he there when Shana poured her juice all over me? I want to believe he wasn't. I feel like he definitely would have done something if he had been there. He would have defended me, right? But would he have? Even if it meant going against the girl that "he always comes back to." Yes, he would have defended me. I know it. I can feel it.

A few quick strides and Thomas is standing before me in all his glory. I don't need to hear him speak to know that he is beside himself with rage. "What the fuck were you doing with him?" He demands through clenched teeth.

"Thomas…" I say his name weakly, in a pathetic attempt to calm him down.

"What were you doing with him?" he repeats, enunciating each word carefully.

I look around uneasily. "Can we talk about this somewhere else?" He stares into my eyes for a few seconds without uttering a word, then he contemptuously snatches the bouquet of roses from my hands and heads for the exit. I hurry after him. I realize what he's planning to do too late because, by the time I reach him, the roses are already in the garbage. Part of me would like to scold him, but the other part knows perfectly well that if I did, we would just end up fighting. And that's not what I want.

I follow him down the hallway, begging him to stop. He doesn't pay me the slightest bit of attention. At the end of the hall, he takes a right, and I follow him. We go down a flight of stairs until we find ourselves in a small classroom, usually used by students to work on group projects. There are no windows in here, the whole room is lit by one dim overhead light. To my right is a small vending machine and a water cooler; there's a round table in the center of the room and a little bookcase against the back wall.

Thomas fills a cup from the water cooler but does not drink. He sets it down on the table instead. Then he slumps in his chair while I remain standing on threshold, psychologically preparing myself for what awaits me. He takes a pack of cigarettes out from the pocket of his jeans, pulls one out and brings it to his lips.

"You can't smoke in here," I point out to him wearily.

"I smoke wherever I want," he pronounces with an autocratic air.

"You'll impregnate the room with cigarette smoke and might give someone an asthma attack. If you have to smoke, you can do it outside," I snap, irritated by his shameless attitude.

"You're wet," he says, lighting his cigarette while staring at me challengingly.

I blink in confusion. "What?"

His gaze drops to the damp patch on my jeans. "You're wet," he repeats with an eerie calm. "And it's cold outside."

I lower my head and stare at the wet fabric. "Oh yeah. That." Awkwardly, I rub the tip of my nose with my index finger. "It's a long story."

"I'm curious to hear it." He billows out cigarette smoke. Cold eyes. Voice low and intimidating.

"I don't feel like talking about it." The bitter smile that twists his lips hides a certain disappointment. But I don't have the courage to tell him about everything that happened with Shana; it was too humiliating and I would feel pathetic all over again recounting it. Especially because I just let her do that to me, without even trying to defend myself.

Thomas takes another drag on his cigarette and, shrugging his shoulders, says "Then tell me why you were in the cafeteria with Fallon and not at the Marsy serving customers."

Here we go.

Sighing, I close the door behind me and sit in the chair across from him. "Two hours ago Derek called me and changed my shift tonight to a double on Saturday," I explain.

"And you didn't think to tell me?"

"I didn't think I needed to tell you about that kind of thing. Besides, you were at practice, and I didn't want to bother you."

Thomas doesn't respond. He keeps his eyes fixed on his right hand, clenched into a fist on the table. His knee is bouncing nervously. "How long had you been standing there?" I ask finally, hesitantly.

"For a while," he says shortly.

"What did you see?"

"Enough."

"Define 'enough.'"

He knocks the ash off his cigarette into the small paper cup in the middle of the table and rubs the back of his neck, looking at me. "The other night you asked me to count to ten. I told you that was too much but that, for you, I would make the effort to get to three. For you. Only for you." I can hear the frustration in his voice, and my heart aches. "Wanna know how far I've gotten?"

"Thomas, I..."

"I started counting after practice was over, when I heard that you were in the cafeteria with him and that he had kissed you." He continues, not allowing me to get a word in edgewise. "I kept counting in the locker room. On the stairs. In the hallway, until I got to the cafeteria and I saw him sitting at the table, with his gelled hair and that fucking golf sweater of his. I was about to go over to him, but I saw that you weren't there. So I thought that it was all just a misunderstanding and I stopped…for you. Because if it was up to me, I would have at least had a little fun with him." His mouth curls up into a skin-crawling smirk and his eyes shine with wickedness. "But then, a little later, I saw you come in. I saw you go to him, I saw you look at him and smile at him. I saw you let him touch you and kiss you."

I close my eyes, disheartened. He misunderstood everything, but I can't blame him, I probably would have done the same thing in his place. I bow my head, dismayed.

"It wasn't what you think, I…" I look back up at him. "I didn't know he was coming back today. He showed up here out of nowhere and I panicked." I stretch my hands out on the table and entwine them with his, hoping that this will draw his focus back to me, but Thomas is just staring at the table, lost in who knows what spiraling thoughts. "Thomas, listen to me…"

"Did you tell him?" he interrupts, darting his eyes up at me.

For a moment I feel my heart pounding in my throat. I look away from him and shake my head. "No, not yet," I admit.

Suddenly ashen, Thomas leans forward and pulls his hands away from mine. "And what the fuck were you doing the whole time? What, were you exchanging makeup tips?"

I cock an eyebrow. "Did you really think I was just going to tell him everything in the middle of the cafeteria, in front of all those people?"

He gives me a casual shrug. "I don't see the problem."

"The problem is that he deserves basic respect, Thomas, which I haven't been showing him." I let myself collapse against the back of the chair, exhausted.

"Let's hear it then: When do you plan to tell him?"

"Tonight."

"Tonight?" I can feel his anger all the way down to my bones. I nod. "When exactly?"

"In a little while. In his room." As the words come out of my mouth and I watch the expression on Thomas's face grow increasingly grim, I realize that perhaps going to Logan's room alone wasn't the best idea…

"The answer is no," he says after a few moments of silence. An extremely tense silence.

I frown. "Excuse me?"

"You will not go to his room," he pronounces.

"I'm only going there to talk."

"I don't give a fuck what you go there to do." He snuffs out his cigarette in the cup of water and, in one sharp movement, gets to his feet. "Don't be alone with him." Furiously, he throws the phone on the table and points at it. "Call him and tell him. Now." I blanch, looking from him to the phone in shock.

"No," I say resolutely.

"No?" He stares incredulously at me.

"Maybe you are used to acting this way, but I have no intention of breaking up with him over the phone," I inform him resentfully. "Also, I must have missed the part where I asked you for your permission. You have no right to tell me what to do or what not to do. You are not my boyfriend, Thomas," I say defiantly.

He narrows his eyes to two slits, his whole body tenses. He shakes his head and rests his palms on the table, bends forward to lock his eyes on mine. "I don't want you to go see him."

I lean forward as well and retort with the same audacity, "And I don't want you to control my life like that. Whether you like it or not, I'm going to see Logan, and I don't want to discuss it anymore."

"Jesus Christ!" He pounds the table so hard the cup of water wobbles and I cringe in my seat. "Why the fuck do you have to make everything so difficult?"

I press a hand to my chest, shocked. "I make everything difficult? Do you realize that you're the one making a huge deal out of nothing here?"

"Because I'm worried about you!"

"You have no reason to do that!"

Thomas hangs his head and breathes deeply. After a moment of silence, he begins speaking, this time in a calmer tone, as though he's trying to soothe both of our tempers. He looks me steadily in the eye. "I don't trust him, Ness."

"But I do."

He huffs. "You trust everyone." He says it like it's a damning condemnation, as if this is reason enough for him to look at me with pity in his eyes.

I frown. "That's not true."

"Right, you're right. Apparently, the only person you don't trust is me, or am I wrong?"

It's true that when he took me to the tree house, I told him that I didn't trust him. But how can he believe that's still how I feel after everything that's happened between us? I wouldn't have done any of the things I did with him if a part of me didn't already trust him.

"So is this how things are going to be between us from now on? You're going to decide where I can go, what I can do, who I can meet... all because you think I'm this naive waif incapable of taking care of myself. Am I right?"

"Don't talk nonsense. You're free to do whatever you want."

"Except see Logan."

"Exactly."

I snort, frustrated by this surreal situation. "I'm sorry, Thomas. But regardless of what you think, Logan has always treated me well. Can you say the same?" I realize too late that I have said this more contemptuously than I wanted to.

"Are you serious?" he asks resentfully. For a moment, it hurts me to see such bitterness on his face. But I can't just forget how many times he's managed to break my heart in the last two months.

"Yes, I am serious." As I say it, his face twists in anger. His nostrils flare and his eyes blaze with fury.

"You know what?" he says, looking me straight in the eyes. "There's a party tonight at Matt's. I wasn't going to go because I had other plans, plans with you. But, in the end, you're not really that important to me." He offers an indifferent shrug and keeps talking, "So who knows? Maybe I'll go and maybe I'll lock myself in a room alone with some girl." He stares at me with a sinister glint in his eyes. "But just to talk, of course." I am frozen stiff.

I bite the inside of my cheeks until they bleed, trying not to cry in front of him. It takes me a while before I find the strength to reply in a steady voice. "You don't need to resort to these cheap threats, Thomas. If you want to fuck someone else, just do it," I spit with all the contempt I can manage. I rise slowly from my chair, making an incredible effort to keep holding the most bewitching and deadliest gaze in the world, all while he sits motionless. "And, for the record: you do hurt me. You are hurting me." I feel like I can't breathe, like all the oxygen has been sucked from the room. I turn and walk shakily to the door But, just as I open it, Thomas pounces from behind me and slams his palm into the door to shut it again.

"You're not leaving." The low, commanding voice stuns me just as much as the wave of vetiver and tobacco.

"You're going to keep me here by force?" I say, the warning in my tone undermined by the trembling of my voice.

"If I have to, yes."

I shake my head, disappointed but also indignant.

"You are crazy, and I must be even crazier because I'm chasing after you. You just told me you wanted to spend the night with someone else. What the hell do you want from me?!"

"I want you to listen to me!" he yells in my ear. He slaps the door so hard that I jerk in fright. When he realizes he's gone too far, he leans his forehead on the back of my head and rests his hands on my shoulders, exhaustedly. He takes deep breaths, until he regains his composure. "Listen, I don't want... I don't want to fight. I don't want to be like this with you."

"And yet, this is what always happens," I murmur with tears in my eyes.

"I'm not good at dealing with emotions, especially when it's about you. I wish I knew how to do it. I wish I wasn't always so..." He leaves the sentence hanging, as if struggling to find the right words.

"So?" I swallow with difficulty, staring at the dark grain of the wooden door.

"Angry," he whispers against my ear, "constantly angry."

"Why?" I ask softly, almost a whisper.

"About too many things, Ness." His hands slide down, traveling the curve of my hips, before coming back up to my waist. His arms surround me and squeeze me tightly. "Sometimes, you calm that anger. Other times, you set it off like nothing else. And you know the weird thing? When I first saw you, I made the mistake of thinking you were just a spineless little brat. Instead, you are this indomitable, stubborn little brat who drives me out of my mind."

"I-I'm sorry," I babble, as the caress of his fingers on my hips and the delicious sensation of his lips so close to my skin cloud my thinking.

"For what?" Still behind me, Thomas strokes my back before grabbing my chin and tilting my head to one side, exposing the curve of my neck. My heart thumps wildly.

"For failing to live up to your expectations," I murmur breathily. Thomas traces the pulsing vein in my neck with his lips. I can feel them curving into a smile. He laps at my skin with his tongue, sending shivers all through my body, when all of a sudden, my phone starts ringing.

I grimace. I pull it out of my pocket and see that it is Logan: he must have come back. "I have to go now," I say trying to move away from Thomas. He won't let me; he tightens his grip on my side, grinding his pelvis against me.

"Thomas, don't do this…" I beg him, almost in a trance.

He bites my neck, making me moan softly. "Don't do what?"

"L-Logan is waiting for me," I tell him. I can feel his tongue on my neck and desire swamps me like high tide.

"Let him wait." He begins to nibble on my neck, his tongue moving slow and firm, sucking ardently on my skin.

I can't hold back my moans, which escape in strangled gasps from my parted lips. Involuntarily, I tilt my head back to rest against his shoulder. Thomas wraps a hand around the back of my neck, kissing my skin with increasing passion. He's lingering on one spot; my throat is on fire and tendrils of flame reach down to my stomach. But then something happens… With my one last glimmer of clarity, I realize what he is doing.

I turn away, outraged, and push him off my neck, sending him staggering backward just a little. "You gave me a hickey?" I accuse, bringing a hand to my damp skin, surely already turning purple.

He gives me a smug half smile and answers, "What do you think?"

I widen my eyes and my mouth drops open. "You...you deliberately gave me a hickey right when I'm on my way to meet Logan!" The evil grin that lights up his whole face makes me realize that this was his plan from the beginning. He wanted to brand me as if I were his property!

"See it as encouragement to end this whole thing quickly," he says, shameless as ever.

"God. You are truly impossible, Thomas!"

But none of my outrage seems to faze him. He grabs my jaw with one hand and plants a searing kiss on my mouth. "You're right, I am impossible. But you are mine. And you had better remember that while you're dumping his ass."

"Go to hell! I mean it, Thomas, you can go to hell!" I turn away, dazed and angry, and stomp out of the classroom, slamming the door hard behind me. Immediately, my phone vibrates in my pocket again. It's a text from Logan telling me to meet him in the student union. As I turn the corner and walk up the stairs, I rapidly undo my braid and nervously try to hide the hickey with my hair.

Forty-Two

WHEN I ARRIVE IN THE student union, I find Logan chatting intently with a boy I recognize from Tiffany's criminology course. Even with his back to me, I can still see the two pizza boxes he's holding in his hands. I was very hungry before he showed up. Now my stomach is so tight that it will be a miracle to get water into it.

"Hey, I'm here." Logan gives me a radiant smile, his eyes lighting up when he sees me. As though I don't already feel guilty enough.

"You came!" he exclaims enthusiastically. "Vanessa, this is Mike, Mike, this is Vanessa," Logan says, looking between me and his friend.

I extend my hand toward Mike to introduce myself and he does the same. He apologizes to me for needing Logan to leave, but I tell him it was no problem.

"Hey, what happened to the roses?" Logan asks, catching me unprepared.

"Y-your roses?" I echo. "Well, I-I wasn't sure how long you would be and I didn't want them to wilt, so I asked a friend to take them to her room and put them in a vase."

"Oh." He seems pretty confused. "Okay. Well, as you can see, it didn't take me long. We can go pick them up if you want?"

"No! S-she's not there right now, she's out, she'll give them to me tomorrow." I want to slap myself for telling so many dumb lies. Luckily, Mike interrupts us, asking Logan something about his car and all talk of roses fades into the background. After a little more back-and-forth, Mike says goodbye and leaves us alone. Logan and I head for his room, which by some strange twist of fate is also located on the fourth floor, on the opposite side of the hallway from Thomas's.

Inside, the two rooms are also furnished in the same way. Yet somehow it lacks the warm and cozy vibe I felt in Thomas's room. Although the room is heated by radiators, I still feel cold somehow. Everything feels foreign here. And for some reason that I can't quite name, I have the oddest feeling that I'm in the wrong place. With the wrong person. What is going on with me? I'm losing it.

I shake my head in an attempt to banish these thoughts. I'm not going to let Thomas's ridiculous insinuations influence me.

"I didn't know what toppings you liked, so I got two Margheritas," he says, taking off his shoes and putting the pizza boxes down on the table.

"That's fine, don't worry about it." I follow him in and smile. Logan goes to the kitchenette and takes some cutlery from the drawer. He returns to the table and cuts the pizzas into slices. I linger in the kitchenette, not really knowing what to do.

"Do you want to watch some TV?"

When I say yes, he takes the remote control and turns on the plasma TV. He grabs his pizza box and sits down on the carpet in front of the TV, where he invites me to join him. Sitting next to him at a safe distance, we watch a rerun of *America's Got Talent* and eat our pizzas. Or rather, he eats, while I stare blankly at the TV, trying not to think about Thomas at that damn party, locked in a room with some girl. Or, even worse, with Shana herself. He always comes back.

"Aren't you eating?" Logan asks after a while, giving me a concerned look.

"Oh, um." I tuck a lock of hair behind my ear, being very careful not to reveal Thomas's hickey. "To tell you the truth, I'm not very hungry right now."

"Do you not like it?"

"No, the pizza is fine, it's just that...I don't think I'm feeling very good."

He frowns. "Are you sick? I can give you something." He tries to stand up but I grab his hand and pull him back down.

"Don't worry, that's not necessary." I don't think there is a medication that treats this kind of sickness.

"Okay, do you want to tell me what's going on with you? You've been weird since I got back. Have I screwed something up and not noticed it?" he asks, upset.

"What? No, absolutely not. You...you haven't done anything wrong." I use my fork to poke at the pizza crust.

"So what's going on?"

"Logan..." I put my fork on the pizza box and turn to face him. "Some things happened while you were away."

"Meaning?" he asks frowning.

I lower my eyes and bite my lip. I open my mouth to speak, but nothing comes out. I gulp, cover my face with my hands and then finally spit it out: "Before you left, you said that when you returned you would want an answer from me, remember?"

"Is that what this is all about? Did you get scared?" He touches my hand but the moment he tries to interlace our fingers, I pull away.

"No, I didn't get scared." I sigh and try to ignore the clenching in my stomach. "Believe me, the last thing I want to do is hurt you. You deserve honesty, though. You deserve it because I would want it if I were in your place and because you've always been good to me. Being honest is the least I can do."

"Okay..."

"I can't be with you, Logan. I can't because...I don't feel the same way about you that you feel about me." He sits silently, just staring at me, as if he is trying to process what I've just told him.

"You're ending it?"

I nod softly. It's the only thing I can do right now.

"Wow...jeez." He pauses, and for a moment he looks incredulous. Then he gives me a serious look before saying, "Maybe I should have expected this. After all, you didn't contact me while I was gone and never answered my calls."

"I really am sorry."

He seems to be thinking something over. "But it's not just that, is it?"

"What do you mean?"

"Are you ending things with me because you don't have feelings for me or because you have feelings for someone else?"

I let the silence stretch out for a long time before I answer. Be honest, Vanessa.

"I have feelings for someone else."

Logan lets out a bitter laugh. "Thomas," he says resignedly.

I nod again as I try to puzzle out his face. I can see acknowledgment, sadness, and anger in it. So much anger.

"Are you with him?"

"No," I answer quickly.

"No?"

"Or rather, yes." Sigh. "Actually, it's complicated."

"Are you his girlfriend, yes or no?" he asks, clearly needled.

"No."

"Good."

I blink in confusion. "Good?"

"Vanessa, I like you. I want to be with you. And if to do that, I have to wait for you to realize just how wrong Thomas is for you, then that is what I'll do." He gently touches my cheek, but I shake him off.

"Sorry, did you not hear what I just said?"

"Yes, I heard. But in all honesty, I don't care. You can't control your feelings, and the ones I have for you are so strong that they won't allow me to give up."

"Maybe you should," I retort, getting irritated.

"Is that what you want me to do?"

"I don't want problems. If you don't back off, I assure you there will be problems."

"So you're asking me to back off because you're afraid for me, not because that's what you really want?" It's a question with a healthy dose of presumption in it. Afraid for him? Well, yes, of course. I am partially worried about him, but he can't seriously think that's the main reason I'm making this decision?

"Do you think I'm afraid of Thomas?" I ask softly, getting more annoyed.

"Don't think that I don't know how sketchy and out of his mind that dude is, and I don't blame you for feeling intimidated. You are just one more poor victim who has fallen into his trap. I see he was careful not to define your relationship. What a disgusting coward. He convinced you to be his but he didn't actually make you his girlfriend. With me, there would be none of that. You could be happy, you could have everything that—"

I interrupt him, because I have heard more than enough.

"You've got it wrong, Logan. Completely. I'm not telling you this out of fear. I'm telling you this because I don't need to be his girlfriend to know that what I feel for him is stronger than anything else I've ever felt. I don't need to be his girlfriend to know that he is the person I want by my side. Him, and no one else. I'm sorry if I hurt you and I'm sorry I acted the way I did, but don't ever talk about him like that again, because you don't know him." I dart a quick look at him before I get up off the floor, grabbing the bag I left beside the table. I slip on my shoes and head for the door.

"Vanessa, wait." Logan stands up and joins me. "I'm sorry if what I said upset you, that wasn't my intention. I'm just confused and angry right now. I need a moment, okay? I think I'm entitled to that, right? I mean, I just found out you spent these last few days with him. But please, please don't go. Stay with me, at least for dinner. No hard feelings."

"It's late, Logan, and I said what I needed to say to you. It doesn't make sense for me to stay any longer." I'm about to grab the doorknob, but he stands in front of me.

"I can take you home at any time, that's no problem. But don't leave me alone. Please, I don't like feeling abandoned." He stares desperately at me.

"Logan..." I say uncertainly. I can't deny that seeing him like this makes me sad, but I don't want to give him false hope by staying here.

"Please," he begs me again.

I sigh but finally decide to humor him. If what he needs now is a little company, I can give him that. "Okay, but only for a little while. And I don't want to talk about Thomas anymore."

He nods fervently. "Whatever you want."

I put my bag back on the floor and I head for one of the two armchairs in front of the TV. I sit in it, while Logan takes the one next to it. We pass the time with a little more TV, and once we get past that initial awkward silence, the situation becomes less and less tense. To melt a little of the ice that has inevitably formed, Logan offers to make me some hot ginger tea. He tells me about his family, how he spent his days at home. I learn that his mother is a very successful lawyer and that his father is a judge. He doesn't have any brothers or sisters and so he often goes home to help his parents. Time passes slowly and, before I know it, I am overwhelmed by an inexplicable drowsiness, so I begin to doze.

Slowly, I slip into a kind of strange, confused half-sleep. I could not tell exactly when I fell asleep nor how long I'd been that way before I started hearing muffled knocks, as if someone were pounding ferociously on a door.

I can hear my name being called over and over again. I can hear the tension and fear in the voice that is saying my name, like a cry of alarm. I want to answer, but for some reason I can't. I feel stiff and weak. The voice, which is gradually becoming more and more familiar, keeps calling tirelessly for me. I begin to realize who it is.

Thomas...

"Ness, open this door!" I open my eyes with difficulty, but I see only nothingness. I blink over and over again, trying to pick out something, anything, but the darkness envelops me completely. "Where am I? Why does Thomas keep calling me and why am I lying on a bed that isn't mine?"

I've fallen asleep. How? When? My throat tightens. I jump to my feet and rush out of the room.

Sitting in the armchair in the living room, watching TV unperturbed, I find Logan. Why did he let me sleep? Why didn't he drive me home like he said he would?

"Logan." At the sound of my voice I see him jolt. "What am I doing here? Why did I wake up in your bed?"

"You fell asleep in the armchair but you looked uncomfortable, so I took you to the bedroom," he answers calmly.

The knocking on the door continues unabated, as does Thomas's voice ordering me to come out. I wasn't dreaming, Thomas is really out there! When I realize the gravity of the situation, my eyes widen and I turn my outrage on Logan. "What were you thinking, letting me sleep here? And can't you hear that Thomas is outside? Why the hell didn't you open the door?"

I pull my phone out of my overalls pocket and, in addition to realizing that it's two in the morning, I also see an endless series of missed calls from Thomas. And now he's right out here, more enraged than ever. And he has every reason to be. I move quickly to the door. I hear the squeak of the armchair and realize that Logan is following me.

"Wait." As soon as I put my hand on the doorknob, he grabs my wrist.

I look down at his hand and then back up at him, giving him a sideways look. "Let me go now."

More knocks rattle the door. "I swear if you don't open this fucking door in three fucking seconds, I'm gonna break it down," Thomas bellows. Logan looks at me blankly for a moment and something in his stare disturbs me. Then, as if he has just come to his senses after a bout of amnesia, he quickly lets go of my hand and recoils as though stunned.

What the hell is going on in his head? I open the door, and Thomas barrels in. He grabs Logan by the neck and slams him against the wall. The crashing sound makes my hands fly up to cover my mouth.

"What the fuck did you do to her?" he yells, inches from Logan's face.

"I-I didn't do anything to her." Logan is struggling to speak, but Thomas's fingers are tight around his throat and prevent him from doing so.

"Thomas, stop! He didn't do anything to me!" I pull on his arm, hitting him several times on the bicep. But it's no use because Thomas cocks back his right arm and sends a punch flying right into Logan's face. He slumps to the ground immediately, his nose bleeding.

"If I find out you laid a finger on her, you're dead." He punches Logan again in the stomach, before grabbing him by the hair and forcing him to tilt his face up. "Dead," he repeats. Then he turns to look at me, his face aflame, and for one moment, I am afraid of what he might do. He grabs me by the arm and drags me out of the room. In the hallway, I see some students peering out their doors, trying to see what's going on.

"Thomas, slow down, you're hurting my arm." I try to pull free from his grip, but he ignores my protests. When we get to his room, he shoves me in forcefully and, after closing the door, he slams his fist into the wall.

"Tell me, Vanessa, what the fuck is wrong with your brain?" he yells, venting all his rage.

I dig my hands into my hair, unable to believe what's happened any more than he can. "Thomas, listen to me, you have every right to be—"

"I have every right to be what? Mad? Pissed off? Furious? I am so much more than that, I'm out of my fucking mind! I've been calling you for hours!" The veins in his thick neck seem ready to burst.

"Because I didn't hear the calls, I-I fell asleep and I didn't—"

He interrupts me, skewering me with his gaze. "You what?"

I swallow. "I-I fell asleep," I stammer, continuously pulling my hair behind and in front of my ears in little nervous movements. "I-I have no idea how it happened. I was very, very tired. I remember curling up in the armchair and then that was it, I collapsed."

He stares at me in shock. He stabs a finger at me and warns, "This is the last time you see him. That you talk to him. That you so much as say hi. That you do anything you can think of with him. The last time."

"Thomas, you have to believe me, he didn't do anything to me, honestly."

"I don't give a fuck what you think. If you had listened to me before, we could have avoided all this shit!" Thomas is right. I was wrong. I was wrong to go see Logan; I was wrong to stay there. "I know, I...I'm sorry."

"I'm taking you home," he declares harshly.

I stare at him in bewilderment. "What? No!"

"It wasn't a question," he snaps.

I shake my head firmly. "I-I don't want to go home." I want to stay here with him. Calm him down, reassure him, clear up this whole this thing, fall asleep with him, clasped in his arms, surrounded by his smell and his warmth.

"I don't want you here." The cold, authoritative way in which he says it makes me shiver. My heart starts pounding in my chest, as I feel that familiar burning sensation in my eyes.

"Thomas." I say his name desperately.

"Move." He grabs a set of keys from the counter and walks out the door without giving me a chance to say anything.

On the back of his motorcycle, I cling to him despite feeling how detached he is. As we race along the asphalt, ignoring the speed limits, the wind whips my tears away. We stop in front of my driveway, with the engine still running. Thomas rests one foot on the ground to help me off the bike. I unbuckle my helmet and hand it to him. He hangs it on the windshield, lowers his visor, and, without giving me even one more glance, he hits the gas and disappears into the night.

"I'm sorry," I whisper to myself, alone and hurting in the middle of a deserted street. I feel my tears flooding uncontrollably. The wind picks up, some damp leaves flutter around me, and the first raindrops streak down my face, merging with my tears. My stomach is tight, in a painful clench.

And he's gone...

PLAYLIST

ACKNOWLEDGMENTS

And here we are at the end of this first part, which has only laid the foundations for another chapter in this story. Know this: up until this point, we have been having a good time, laughing and dealing with a few minor emotional problems, but things are about to change drastically, and poor old Travis is about to become the least of our worries.

Before I say goodbye, I would like to offer some thank-yous. The first goes to my family, for the patience they have shown me all those times when I took refuge in the darkest corner of our home and stayed there until I lost track of time.

Thanks to the Salani publishing house for choosing me and wanting me and for giving me the chance to take a big step like this. I'd especially like to thank Marco and Francesca for always being there for me. But most of all, I thank my editor Chiara Casaburi, who dedicated body and soul to Better at any hour of the day or night. You have been invaluable. I would also like to give a special thanks to all my friends and fellow writers, without whom my journey would not have been the same. You have been an essential part of this for me.

Now, though, the most important thank-you is missing.

And that's the one addressed to you, my beloved readers.

Let me tell you how incredible and completely unexpected it has been, getting here. If someone would have told me two and a half years ago that the little project I was starting for fun and without any expectations would have led here, I would not have believed them. Not for all the money in the world. Better was born on a gloomy afternoon in late October; the rain has been my muse from the beginning and it has continued to be so all the way to the end of the writing process.

But what really pushed me to continue this story was the enthusiasm, support, and unconditional love that only you readers were able to show me day after day, with your messages, shares, videos, pictures, and freak-outs. Especially the freak-outs. I will be eternally grateful for all of it. Thank you for believing in me and in this story. For understanding Thomas and Vanessa and accepting them with all of their flaws, their mistakes, and their impulsivity. You have taken them by the hand and given them the chance to take flight. The opportunity to enter your homes and lives.

I told you long ago, and I tell you again now: I do not know where we will go nor how far we will go. The only certainty I have and will always have is you, who have never abandoned me. You have stayed by my side through it all. You have trusted and relied on me all this time just as I have done with you with the publication of this book, which is meant to be my way to simply say, "Thank you." Thank you for making all this possible.

See you soon, strangers.

ABOUT THE AUTHOR

Carrie Leighton is the pen name of a young Italian writer who prefers to remain anonymous. An avid reader of romance fiction, she debuted on the Wattpad platform, gaining great popularity in a very large community. When not writing, she enjoys watching TV series. She's author of the Better trilogy: *Collisione* (*Collision*, 2022; Better #1); *Dannazione* (*Damnation*, 2023; Better #2); and *Ossessione* (*Obsession*, 2023; Better #3).

Instagram: @carrie_leighton_
TikTok: @carrie_leighton